FENNA EDGEWOOD

STARWATER PRESS

THE GARDNER GIRLS SERIES, Copyright (C) 2021, Fenna Edgewood

Thank you for buying an authorized edition of this book and for complying with copyright laws by not reproducing, scanning, or distributing any part of it in any form without prior written permission by the author(s), except where permitted by law.

All rights reserved. The use of any part of this publication reproduced, transmitted in any form or by any means, electronic, mechanical, photocopying, recording, or otherwise, or stored in a retrieval system, without the prior written consent of the publisher is an infringement of the copyright law.

This is a work of fiction. Names, places, characters, and incidents are either the product of the author's imagination or are used fictitiously, and any resemblance to any actual persons, living or dead, organizations, events or locales is entirely coincidental.

Warning: The unauthorized reproduction or distribution of this copyrighted work is illegal. Criminal copyright infringement, including infringement without monetary gain, is investigated by the FBI and is punishable by up to five years in prison and a fine of $250,000.

For more information, email: info@fennaedgewood.com

Cover Design by Josephine Blake, Covers & Cupcakes

Flourish Art by Gordon Johnson (GDJ) & Emmie Norfolk

Special Thanks to: Made Me Blush Books & Cara Maxwell, Author

http://www.fennaedgewood.com

Fenna's Newsletter

Sign-up for my newsletter at www.fennaedgewood.com to receive the latest book updates, opportunities for ARCs (advance reader copies), giveaways, special promotions, sneak peeks, and other bookish treats, including a FREE special extended epilogue for the Gardner Girls series coming in late 2021, exclusively for subscribers.

Dedicated to my sister.

My truest friend and the very best aunt two little boys could ever possibly ask for.

Contents

Chapter 1

London

The fallen angel staggered towards the bridge.

His Grace, Angelus Dante Beaumont, Duke of Englefield—commonly known as "Angel" to his friends—had been told more times than he could count that he resembled a golden angel from heaven. Mostly whilst in bed.

But surely in heaven the liquor would never leave such a pain in one's head.

Therefore, he must have come straight from hell.

Or a tavern, which was close enough.

He had a vague recollection of a long evening stretching into the night, full of boisterous laughter, ribald song, and the consumption of many tankards of metheglin.

The mead had been Hugh's idea. He had expressed a wish to imitate the Vikings of old and after six or seven rounds of the heady, overly sweet stuff, had even endeavored to stand up on a table and recite a skaldic poem.

He had fallen off the table a few stanzas in.

Angel had left him where he fell—passed out on the sawdust floor snoring peacefully. The owner of the Red Hart was well-acquainted with the pair, tolerating their antics for the sake of the business the duke's patronage brought, and had promised to see him conveyed to a bed. As there was clearly no waking Hugh, Angel decided that would have to suffice.

He vaguely wondered why he had not called a hackney, then remembered it was a fine night and he had decided a stroll home would clear his head.

So far, it had not, but it was a good idea in theory.

It was a worse one in reality. It was past two in the morning. The streets were dark and the silence deafening.

A wiser, less intoxicated man might have been more concerned for the safety of his personage.

But it was too late to turn back now. He was almost home. A few blocks past the bridge, then inside, to bed, rest, a tonic. Brown would have a tonic, good chap. Excellent valet. Would also make an excellent nursemaid.

He crossed the bridge, managing to walk in a mostly straight line.

Peering ahead he could see two figures towards the end of the bridge, their faces hidden under the hoods of the cloaks they wore.

He tripped on a cobblestone and nearly fell forward, catching himself on the bridge rail just in time. If the two strangers had seen, he must look a right fool.

A fair assessment.

Not that he was too concerned about the judgement of two strangers, but they were hooded which was a little odd on a warm summer night. Angel was lightly dressed, cravat loosened around his neck and tailcoat unbuttoned for optimal coolness.

The hoods were somewhat mysterious. Suspicious even.

Might get ugly. Could be footpads. Waiting for a drunk rich sod to come by. Might think he was an easy mark if they'd seen him trip. Be surprised then. Hopefully wouldn't come to that.

Probably just a lovers' tryst. Hoods up to protect identities.

He was nearing them now, and could see that one of the figures was quite slight. A woman.

A tryst then, definitely a tryst. He had had his share of midnight rendezvous. A lady might not want a home visit from a lover. What would the neighbors think? What would the husband think?

He heard the woman's low voice, then the man's deeper tone as he replied.

Deuced awkward to be interrupting a lovebirds' moment. He made sure to stay on the opposite side as he walked.

Couldn't help a curious glance though. Only human. Might even be someone he knew. Not that he'd ever breathe a word. Not that kind of a man.

He spotted a glint of shining metal.

It was in the woman's small, outstretched hand. She didn't know how to hold a knife whatsoever. Grip was all wrong, couldn't do much harm that way.

He had been walking quietly if not steadily, unnoticed or at least ignored until now.

He could keep walking. Ignore them.

Perhaps she was a lady footpad. Who worked alone.

Though one would think she'd be better with a knife.

Or perhaps something else entirely. A doxy, trying to get a client to pay up.

That made the most sense.

Still, didn't want to see bloodshed. Must uphold the king's peace and all that.

Not that there was a chance of much blood, the way she was holding that knife.

Still, gentleman and all. Must do what's honorable. Assist damsels and so on.

He crossed over.

The woman was saying something in a breathless voice. Didn't sound happy, that much was obvious.

He cleared his throat and was a little delighted when they both jumped.

"Holding that knife all wrong, you know," he began conversationally, his attention on the woman. He pointed to her blade. "Won't do much good like that. Easy to disarm. Probably don't want to stab someone tonight anyhow, really. Witnesses and all that."

The lady's mouth had formed a pretty round circle as she stared at him. Everything about her was pretty from what he could see. Which admittedly wasn't much. Her hood was up and her cloak fastened around her. A few strands of fair hair fell over her face. She had large blue eyes and they were opened very wide right now.

He looked at her and found he could not look away. Deuced strange. Rather hypnotic. Must be the mead. Head a jumble.

In the meantime, Angel realized, the man being accosted was staring at him rather intensely.

Well, Angel was rescuing him, wasn't he? Made sense the fellow would wish to keep the image of his rescuer in mind. Struck with overwhelming gratitude probably.

"Be on your way," the man spoke up. Rather coldly, in fact. Not a hint of gratitude, in fact.

Angel raised his eyebrows.

The man's tone became even more commanding.

"I must insist you go about your business. This is no concern of yours. I have the matter well in hand."

"Don't see that you do, really."

"I beg your pardon?"

The man's hood overshadowed his face. It was disconcerting speaking to a voice with no face.

Overall, Angel found he did not particularly care for the victim of this plight.

An angry, threatening voice. Must not have been a very pleasant client for the doxy. Thus, the knife.

The man's hood shifted slightly and Angel caught a glimpse of striking grey eyes. If he wasn't so foxed, they might even have been familiar, Angel thought hazily.

He shook his head a little. Wouldn't do to pass out like Hugh had at this juncture. He'd made it this far. 'Sides, might end up thrown in the Thames with the way these two were going.

"She's holding a knife. Seems to be interested in poking you with it. Might not know how to use it. Either way, wouldn't say things are at hand. In hand. The knife is in her hand, yes. But not in your hand."

The man eyed him disdainfully. "You are drunk."

"Correct. And you, sir, are standing on a bridge in the middle of the night with a knife to your throat."

Angel looked at the knife. "Not really at your throat," he conceded.

He stepped towards the lady. She backed up against the rail. He gently touched her hand. "May I?"

He corrected the knife's position. "Much better this way. Can thrust upwards now. Or slash across the throat. Very effective. You see?"

Trembling, she nodded.

"What the devil do you mean by giving her tips for cutting my throat..." The other man said hotly.

Angel cut him off. The gentleman was unmannerly. No reason not to interrupt.

"I suggest you pay your ladybird and go on your way, sir." He chose a gentler term than the commonly used one.

The lady let out a little gasp. Surprised a knight had come to her rescue, he supposed.

"*Pay* her?" The man curled his lip into a cruel smirk.

"Pay her what's owed. No argument. Pay up." Angel turned back to the woman. "I'll see that it's done. Won't leave you alone here. No need for that knife now. May as well put it away."

He spoke gently, reassuringly, as he would to a timid horse. Wouldn't do to scare her. She seemed scared enough as it was.

Slowly the woman lowered her shaking arm.

"Damn your eyes," the man snarled. "Get off the bloody bridge and be on your way. This is the last time I'll tell you."

"Or what?"

The other man sneered. "Or what?"

"Or what will happen?" Angel looked him up and down. "Military training, see? Noble, yes. Soft, no. Served my country. Lots of spare time in the army. Lots of waiting. Nothing to do but hit each other. Decent boxer. Fair right hook. Not afraid to use it."

"Are you threatening me, sir?"

"Don't look surprised. Not like it's the first time tonight, is it? Besides you started it. Don't have a knife. Rather be punched then stabbed, wouldn't you?"

The man gnashed his teeth. "You, sir, are an utter idiot."

"Not the first time someone's said so," Angel said cheerfully. "Might be true, sometimes am. Not always the brightest in the room. Not always the dimmest either. Might be surprised."

He looked reflectively at the other man. "Not sure you're in any position to judge intelligence, come to think of it. About to be stabbed by a doxy. Think you had better go. Lady?" He looked at her.

She nodded slowly.

"Lady thinks you should go, too." He remembered. "Pay her first, mind you."

"Devil take you! You and your bloody penchant for interference. If I were not in a mind for subtlety this evening, I would..."

"Yes, what would you?" Angel was rather eager now, his blood hot both from the residual effects of the mead and the anticipation of knocking some teeth out.

The man ignored him, turning to the woman. "This is not over, you understand. You have merely been granted a little more time."

"The devil is a gentleman. If thou hast no name to be known by, let us call thee devil." Angel grinned.

Might have mixed up his Shakespeare. Two different plays. Still, same meaning. Went well together. Even drunk, he remembered his lessons. Always liked a good soliloquy.

"What the devil are you going on about now, you ass."

"Yes, devil. Devil indeed. Has no name, but looks a devil. Well, Angel's here now. Best be off with you, devil. No rest for the wicked they say. Might not sleep well. Not my concern. Better leave now, devil. 'Tis what the lady wants. Am I right, mi'lady?"

He could hear himself babbling. He looked at the woman. She opened her mouth then closed it again. Not a Shakespeare admirer? Pity.

"You bloody bedlamite. You really have no idea of who you're dealing with, do you?"

Angel looked at the hooded figure. The words seemed like nonsense.

"Should I? You do sound like a villain in a bad play. Can't say which one though." He scratched his head. "You still haven't paid her, you know. If you won't pay up, you'd best leave. I'll see to the lady. Sound satisfactory to you, lady?"

"It does." She finally spoke. A low, quiet voice. Sounded more like a lady than a doxy, but doxies could be ladies he supposed.

Anyone could learn to speak more eloquently. Elegantly. Elocution. Anyone could learn elocution. Or unlearn it. He should know. Case in point.

The hooded man opened his mouth. Closed it. Angel could fairly hear the gnashing of teeth. Quite biblical really. Teeth must be wearing down from all the gnashing though. Was probably a common thing with this fellow. Would need false ones soon. Maybe had them already.

With a whirl of his dark cloak, the man spun on his heels and strode away from them back across the bridge.

Very dramatic. Shakespearean even.

Angel looked at the lady. She looked at him.

"Thank you."

"Ah, finally a thanks. Would have thought the other fellow might have done the thanking. No gratitude. What is the world coming to? Etcetera."

The woman looked confused. That was all right. Fairly baffled himself.

"I would like you to know... I am not a...doxy," she said quietly, eyes cast downwards.

Angel stared. She was a very pretty girl. Woman. Maybe in between. Younger than himself. Older than a girl. Mid-twenties maybe. Lovely face, really.

Might easily be called an angel as well. Golden hair, blue eyes.

Deucedly lovely in fact.

Too much so.

He had thought his appraisal merely aesthetic but apparently parts of him believed otherwise. He shifted on his feet awkwardly in the hopes of loosening his suddenly uncomfortably tight trousers. Last thing the poor lady needed. Wished he had a cloak.

"A thousand pardons for my error, milady." He managed to execute a graceful bow, which, with an erection was no small feat. He also didn't tip over, which was rather a miracle. "Hope to restore amends. Be friends. Hope you won't mind me saying, seems like you need a friend."

He smiled encouragingly. She did not return it. He would have liked to see her smile. Probably a very pretty smile.

Who was she if she wasn't a doxy? Easy way to find out.

"Shall I escort you home?" He held out an arm.

"No, thank you. I have a carriage waiting." She took a deep breath. "Truly though, I do thank you. You did not have to step in."

She looked in the direction the man had gone. "I don't think I would have stabbed him."

"Would have liked to though?"

"Yes. Very much." Even then she did not smile. Not a smiling matter then.

"Bad situation, I see," he said quietly. "Wish I could help."

She looked a little surprised.

"No one can help. It's a mess of my own making." She glanced away. "Well, thank you..." She gave a little laugh. "I've said that already, haven't I? Well, good night."

He watched her walk away. He told himself it was simply to see her safely across. No other reason.

Didn't want to follow in case that made her more afraid.

When she reached the end of the bridge, a conveyance slowly rolled up and she stepped in.

Perhaps she really wasn't a doxy then. Ladybird may have been accurate. Spat with her patron.

He gave a great yawn. Adventurous evening. He turned towards home.

Letter 1

MISS GWENDOLEN GARDNER TO Mr. Robert Wyndham

May 1, 1811

London

My Dear, Dearest, Most Dear Wyndham,

How those words do not suffice! Not when you have signed your last letter with such great tenderness and revealed your heart so thoroughly and completely.

I shall reply in turn then and say, my Beloved. For that you are.

How my heart trembles to think of how easily we may not have met! If I had not attended the ball at Lady Hampton's, if you had not been so bold as to approach me when I was alone for a moment, if you had not received permission to ask me to waltz... Would some other girl be your love now? No, never! Say it could never be so—your loyal heart could belong to no other. We are destined, you and I, for one another and I cannot wait for our life as one to begin.

And now my beloved, my soldier, my brave one—will you kiss me once more? I shall see you tonight as you request so desperately, outside the servants' entrance. Be as silent as you can. Will we ride for Gretna Green tonight? Or tomorrow? Has your commanding officer granted you leave? Oh, make it soon, Wyndham, make it soon.

Longing for you, with all affection,

Your Gwen

Chapter 2

THE BORED FEMALE VOICE drawled on.

"...when Lady Danforth last hosted a house party, two duels nearly took place, Lord Melbourne was caught by his wife in bed with a lady's maid, and that prim little Miss Sarah Norbert was shipped off to an aunt in Edinburgh only a week into her first season. I shall leave it to you as to guess why. A diverting weekend, all in all, I suppose, compared to some. I find diversion so necessary during the season, don't you? The activities become quite dull, so repetitive. The same old faces, the same old places... Do you not agree, Your Grace?"

There was a long pause.

"Your Grace?" The young woman's voice was irritated now.

"Hmm?" Angel's eyes popped back open just in time to avoid tripping over a tree branch on the path.

"Am I boring you, Your Grace?"

His attention returned to the woman next to him who was targeting him with an icy stare.

Raven-haired with brilliant green eyes and a full pouting mouth, Lady Julia Pembroke was not difficult to look at. Voluptuous curves filled a dark blue dress covered with yards of the ruffles and lace that were so in style. Some had been very well-placed, so as to draw the eye directly to Lady Julia's full, high bosom which threatened to overflow its constraints most enticingly.

Many men would have fought to be by Julia's side even for something as mundane as a stroll through Hyde Park on a Sunday afternoon.

Angel would not dispute that she was beautiful.

But was she boring? Oh, most definitely—though he had no plans to admit this to her face. Not to mention cruel, callous, and cold—as Angel had quickly discovered within their first fifteen minutes together.

Yet Lady Julia was widely considered a belle of the ton—this in spite of the fact that it was her fourth season.

He was sure it was not for a lack of offers. She seemed determined to hold out for... well, he supposed for a man of greater title and wealth than what she already possessed as the spoiled only daughter of a marquess.

In other words, someone like Angel.

This was Aunt Eliza's idea of a joke.

She had asked him to walk out with the daughter of a friend and his head had been splitting so badly at the time that he had mumbled his agreement without much comprehension.

If he had been less foxed, he might have noticed the mischievous glint of pure evil in her eyes when she waved him out of the house, down the steps, and into the arms of Lady Machiavelli.

But he had not noticed, and now Aunt Eliza was doubtlessly laughing at him as she sipped her madeira and smoked cheroot in the library with a thick book in her hand and her great hulking brute of a dog at her feet.

Surely, she did not expect him to return home in anything but a worse mood than when he left.

Surely, she did not expect him to actually consider the company of a debutante of the ton like Lady Julia as anything but a torment.

If she had, he and Aunt Eliza would not have got on as swimmingly as they normally did.

No, this was revenge. Pure and simple.

But for what?

It was not as if there was a single item on the list.

More a series of failures and catastrophes which Aunt Eliza generally overlooked... or cackled over.

But now Angel belatedly recalled the destruction he had wreaked on Aunt Eliza's new curricle the week before.

Rather unfair, really, as it was Hugh who was truly to blame. If he had not insisted on trying to race on such a narrow street...

Well, it was no use thinking of. He would simply have to muster a much better apology.

Either that or seek his own revenge.

But as Aunt Eliza was a much more proficient schemer and had far more years of experience, going up against her was unwise.

It would be much more expedient to simply buy her a new curricle. Something scarlet and black. With gold trim. She would enjoy that.

"Your Grace!" Lady Julia's tone was turning shrill. Angel nearly clapped his hands over his ears.

He noted her narrowed eyes. Something flickered behind them and he suspected it was disdain. She did not like him either.

So why the pretense?

Simply another young woman determined to marry a duke, he supposed.

An uncatchable one at that.

To land Angel would be no small feat. So far, he had spent nearly twenty-nine years avoiding girls exactly like Julia.

"My apologies, Lady Julia. I find I have the most splitting headache this morning." He struck a tone both bored and lofty, aiming to match her own.

He had no doubt she would understand what the pain in his head was from.

Indeed, she sounded unusually worldly-wise for a young woman on the marriage mart. But then, this was her fourth season. Not to mention the Pembrokes did not exactly have a reputation for naïveté or virtue.

She forced a tight-lipped smile.

"It is of no consequence, Your Grace. Shall we speak of something else? Your interests, perhaps. I have heard you described as an excellent boxer. I should love to see you in a match, Your Grace"

"Call me Angel," he said, almost automatically, tiring of the saccharine sweetness of her constant address, then wished just as immediately that he hadn't. It was a familiarity he generally reserved for those whose company he genuinely enjoyed. "Yes, well, not much opportunity for that. Not supposed to fight in the ring generally. Must protect the line and all that. Do enjoy backing a few bruisers now and then."

"Yes, I have heard you take lessons with Gentleman Jackson. How impressive."

She had done her homework. Sadly, it would not pay off.

"Yes, good exercise. Nothing better for working up a sweat."

Ah, even a jade like Lady Julia could color once in a while!

Angel smiled at her discomfort. He could not easily see Lady Julia working up any kind of a sweat.

Under any circumstances.

Whoever she wound up catching in her sticky web would not be in for any great nights of passion, he suspected. All flounce and no substance.

He sighed a little, knowing she would perceive his faux-pas as bad breeding and disdain him even more. Gossip to her friends about what the dukedom was coming to. There were so many rules amongst the young ladies of the ton, a fellow didn't know what to say half the time.

Especially with her harpy of a maid trailing behind. Not that she was needed as Angel had no intention of doing anything to risk either of their reputations.

He could ask her about her needlework, he supposed. Or if she enjoyed watercolors. Not that he was interested in the answers.

She did appear to enjoy a nasty scandal. As well as taking delight in the misfortunes of others. Unfortunately for her, Angel was not interested in cruel gossip.

He wondered at her eagerness to be seen with him. The Duke of Englefield had cultivated a reputation for dissolution, hedonism, and utter lack of regard for society standards when he had returned from military service abroad. Stepping foot onto English soil, he had quickly been reminded of how worthless the peerage he and so many better men had fought and died for was.

In spite of his title, looks, and impressive record of service, the mamas of the ton with more discretion were not keen to have their progeny associated with His Grace with the Angel Face.

Or Lord Englefiend, as the broadsheets enjoyed calling him.

There were more but that was the one that had really stuck. Confounded Hugh had made sure of that. He openly chortled each time he saw the nickname he had given used in print.

"Angelus." What a deucedly unfortunate name for a man.

He would never stick something like it on one of his offspring. Simple, plain names for them. If there ever were any.

"Shall we walk on this way?" He gestured broadly, trying to avoid the fluttering. "Mrs. Price's is not far. A syllabub, perhaps?"

The beloved Cheesecake House of the eponymous Mrs. Price stood on the north side of the Serpentine and was a popular spot with strolling park-goers.

Angel's hangover from the previous night was finally fading and he was ravenously hungry. Syllabubs and cheesecakes were not the most fortifying, but they would have to do. His stomach rumbled at the prospect.

"If that is to your liking, Your Grace. I acquiesce utterly and completely to your desires."

Was he imagining the fluttering of eyelashes?

He cleared his throat. Now it was his turn to force a smile.

The idea of Lady Julia *acquiescing* to him was not as appealing as she likely believed it to be.

As they rounded a bend in the path, Julia drew in her breath sharply as she looked straight ahead. Angel followed her gaze with curiosity.

He saw nothing untoward. Merely a lady and a little boy coming towards them, hand in hand. The little boy had a kite slung over one arm.

The lady was quite young, perhaps not much older than Julia herself.

He could hear the bubble of sweet, throaty laughter as she swung the child's hand back and forth. A smiling maid followed behind, carrying a wicker picnic basket.

As the young mother glanced down fondly at her little boy, they made a perfect picture together, passing over the sun-speckled path beneath an overhang of greenery. Angel was struck with a peculiar pang of envy towards the man to whom this little family pair belonged.

The two parties approached one another. The lady looked up, her gaze colliding with Angel's.

She was a lovely woman, perhaps a few years Julia's senior, with curling golden hair, and flushed lips arched in a half-smile. She was clad in an elegant leaf-green dress that drew Angel's eyes almost against his will to its low neckline where full breasts peeked over a chiffon trim and complimented a sweetly curving figure. The pretty sprigged gown was dotted with flowers and spoke of burgeoning spring, new life, and beautiful growth.

Of course, Angel was used to the appeal of a fair head of hair—he had the gilded curls of a cherub, after all. He used to curse his bad luck when the boys at Eton would chant "Angel Face" at him. A few bloody noses and most shut up after that.

But this woman was more than angelic-looking, and there was nothing cherubic about her. She had the features of a golden goddess, a Venus perhaps. Or a Persephone. Her smiling upturned mouth was a rosy flower, lips parted to let a merry laugh ring forth. Her eyes were a rich sparkling blue.

As his gaze lingered a little too long, Angel realized the lady was looking back at him bemusedly.

Beginning to color like a schoolboy, he was surprised to see her eyes suddenly widen and a look of recognition appear.

Was it for him?

For Lady Julia, more like, he guessed as he glanced at his walking companion. Clearly Julia knew this woman. She was holding herself rigid, straight as an arrow. If she lifted her chin any higher, she would soon be tripping over her feet, unable to see the path.

But it was unavoidable. The encounter was going to happen whether she liked it or not.

"Why, Julia!" the other woman exclaimed with a warm smile. "It has been ages."

It was only when she spoke that Angel recognized her.

Put a cloak over her shoulders and draw the hood over her gleaming hair and you had the pretty doxy from the other night on the bridge.

Not a doxy, he corrected. Now that he saw her in the light of day, he felt he had been a fool to assume so. Intending no offense towards doxies in general, of course.

The moment of truth, Angel thought, as he watched the two women. The fair-haired woman was looking perplexed as Lady Julia stubbornly refused to meet her eye.

She also seemed equally determined not to meet Angel's.

In fact, Julia appeared to have been stricken deaf, dumb, and blind and as the seconds passed and she continued walking, head held high, Angel realized she was going to cut the other woman completely and walk right by.

He had never seen the cut direct given so... well, directly.

This would not do. Not when he was so thoroughly intrigued.

And yet, what could he do? Demand an introduction? It was tempting, except Julia was marching on past the woman and child, past the maid holding the basket, towards a curve in the path ahead, looking nothing so much as a soldier on drill.

Angel lagged behind. He tried once more to catch the lady's attention but she seemed just as determined not to give it.

It was only when the little boy let out a yelp that Angel's wish was granted.

Encouraged by the wind picking up, the little boy had unfurled his kite string while the adults had been busy awkwardly avoiding interacting. Now the kite had been blown off course and out of his control, into the branches of a nearby tree. The boughs were low by Angel's standards.

He ran over to the kite and easily disentangled it, then walked back and kneeling, presented it to the little lad like Sir Lancelot bending before King Arthur.

The boy was a short but sturdy chap. He could not have been more than four or five. His chubby cheeks reflected the last vestiges of baby fat, giving a soft sweetness to his features. He smiled bashfully revealing dimples which Angel suspected would win over even the hardest hearted of women—well, perhaps not Julia—and grabbed the kite back eagerly, whispering a shy "thank you."

His mother, on the other hand, seemed determined not to meet Angel's eye a second time and was looking at her son, then her feet, then the maid, the tree, the path—anywhere but at the man who had been the rescuer of her son's precious toy.

Angel might have been annoyed at this, but it was easy to see how uncomfortable she was—her face had flushed a rosy shade. He decided he could not press her. If pretending not to recognize one another was so important to her, he would maintain the pretense.

He turned to continue back down the footpath towards Julia, but the walk was narrow, and as he stepped politely around the pair, the little boy shifted and jostled his mother, causing her to brush up against Angel.

The spicy scent of vanilla and sandalwood, the warmth of her body through the thin fabric of her light spring dress, the touch of her hip as it slid against his—the sensations were intoxicating. Lightheaded, with a strange emotion he knew was desire, Angel felt even more awkward and knew the blood was rushing to his face.

"It is a lovely day!" he blurted out. He cringed inside as he heard the banal remark come out of his mouth. All he knew was that he wanted to spend as much time as he possibly could in the presence of this captivating woman.

Finding out why she had been on that bridge—well, that was certainly another motivation.

She turned back to him, a small smile escaping which he found encouraging.

She met his gaze—this was progress. Her mouth opened. He leaned forward, intent on catching whatever words rang forth.

Whatever she was going to say was drowned out by a strident female voice calling from further down the path.

"Your Grace, you are straying from the path. Are you quite all right?"

With a roll of his eyes heavenward, Angel looked to see Julia standing down the path with her arms crossed. She might as well have been tapping her foot, too.

He turned back to the golden lady but she was already walking away, her son's hand firmly back in her own.

With a muttered oath, he picked up his pace and caught up with his petulant companion.

"Sweet little fellow, wasn't he?" He spoke casually, when they had gone a few steps. When he looked over, she was staring intently straight ahead, lips pursed as if she had recently tasted something sour.

He had a feeling she looked like that often.

"How did you know the lady?" It was clear that she did, so why beat around the bush?

Her steps faltered.

"The Countess of Leicester," she finally said. "Her husband was a friend of my father's."

"Was?" Angel asked innocently.

"He passed away more than a year ago."

Ah, a widow then. Angel had known his fair share of merry widows. Generally, he did not prefer those with small children. But perhaps an exception could be made.

"Was there a reason you cut the countess?"

Not that Lady Julia's choice of friends or enemies was of much interest to him, as he had no plans of continuing to keep company with her after this tortuous interlude. But Angel was still interested in the answer. Knowing Julia, even as little as he did, he felt sure it would be informative.

There was a calculating look in her eyes.

"They say she has had countless lovers," she said eventually. "Before, during, and after her marriage. My mother says Gwendolen is shameless and that it is a sin for her to show her face in polite society." She shrugged. "Yet here she is, prancing through the park as if she were innocent as a maiden."

Angel considered her coldly. If she was expecting him to share her condemnation, she was in for a disappointment. If there was one thing that could have lowered her in his estimation even more, it was a malicious attack on another of her sex.

What was more, he could see right through it.

Her mother had said no such thing.

It was a fiction of Julia's own creation. And had taken her mere seconds to think up, thanks to a mind evidently made for manipulations and malice.

"Indeed," he said shortly, keeping his gaze fixed and steady.

The staring contest continued until finally Julia looked away with a blush.

Angel decided he'd had enough.

This was no way to spend a beautiful afternoon.

Especially when the sight of that flaxen-haired goddess had served to remind him of much more pleasant female company he could be enjoying.

"You know," he said slowly, putting a hand to his temple. "I do believe I should do something about this dreadful headache. You must pardon me, but I shall have to pass on those delectable cheesecakes."

He gestured vaguely in the direction of the street. "I would offer you a ride, but I have only the highflyer and Arabella is awfully skittish…" He looked at her doubtfully. "Wouldn't do to sit a lady behind her."

"Arabella is the horse, you see," he explained, as Julia looked at him with narrowed eyes.

"Yes, I understand that perfectly well." She sniffed. "Do you mean to say you are going to leave me here, alone in the middle of Hyde Park?"

"Of course not. That wouldn't do at all, would it?"

He smiled at her with a hint of condescension.

"No," Angel went on. "If it meant leaving you alone, I would never leave you. 'Pon my honor."

Lady Julia appeared slightly mollified.

"But, thank Heavens, you won't be alone." He gestured to her maid who followed a discreet distance behind out of earshot, before mercilessly donning his cheekiest and most charming smile.

"What a dashed relief for me to know I'm not leaving you to the wiles of footpads and the like. Wouldn't want to risk your maidenly innocence now, would we?"

He gave a sly wink and then, before she could finish opening her mouth to answer, turned on his heel and walked quickly down the path in the direction of the street.

If he moved quickly, he could be completely away before she even considered attempting to catch up, and then Lady Julia would never have to know that he had in fact arrived in a covered carriage with a driver.

That wouldn't do at all.

Letter 2

MRS. CAROLINE GARDNER TO the Right Hon. Earl of Leicester

July 5, 1793
Orchard Hill

My Lord,

I know you have no reason to desire to hear from me nor to receive this letter with any benevolence of feeling. Nevertheless, I must count upon your graciousness and sense of justice in having taken this letter in hand and read so far.

Perhaps you are shocked to hear from your runaway bride. Indeed, it was a shock to me to become one in the first place. As it is my great shame to have caused you embarrassment or pain when I left you that evening at the ball held the day before we were to wed.

I am sure you know that I am now wed to Henry Gardner, the young man to whom I was betrothed for the larger part of our lives. Only the breach between our two families severed our engagement.

For a time, I believed myself to be better off with it broken, having been falsely informed by those closest to me that my former fiancé had not kept faith. Therefore, when my parents encouraged a new match, between you and I, My Lord, I acquiesced to their wishes with only a little reluctance and was determined to fulfill my duty.

You were a kind and patient suitor, My Lord. Never failingly courteous and always inclined to consider my feelings. You could not have known that at that time, my feelings were a thing no one besides yourself bothered to spare much consideration—not even myself.

My senses were deadened within me. While I went through the motions of life, I could feel nothing but detached—as if I were living the life of someone else entirely and not my own.

It was only on the night of our wedding ball that I felt them come alive again.

If my reawakening to life and to happiness could have come while sparing you pain or embarrassment, I would have chosen that path. Even now I reproach myself for the way in which I abandoned you in the ballroom without a word of explanation or farewell.

I fully admit, I acted very badly towards you. My conduct was shameful and abhorrent.

And yet... It was also the bravest moment of my life. Can you imagine that?

Remaining there beside you and taking vows the next morning seemed like it was the path sure to cause us both great pain.

My Lord, I must speak frankly. If I had believed your depth of feeling towards me to be strong, I may have acted otherwise. But our match was one between two families, wishing to unite us for their own goals and purposes. Neither of us were disinclined to the arrangement and I have no doubt you would have endeavored to be an adequate husband in every way.

But I do not believe you loved me, My Lord. Nor did I feel I had given you any reason to believe I cared deeply for you.

I fear, therefore, not that I wounded your heart, but rather your pride, your honor, and your reputation. None of which are any less valuable to a man, I know.

Thus, when I received the news quite recently that you had wed and that your wife had born a child, my heart felt a weight had been lifted and only then did I understand how the dread of your unhappiness had rested heavily upon me.

While I appeared to act without feeling or remorse, please believe I am not without feeling towards you. You have been on my mind frequently, and now having received news of your changed situation, my husband and I wish you every congratulation and pray for your happiness and the health of your wife and child.

I pray that for my sake and for the sake of your lady-wife, you will allow me to beseech you to forgive my husband as well as myself.

I hope you will agree that some good has come of it all.

I wish you again the greatest happiness on the birth of your child. Having recently born a daughter, I well know the joy a child brings and hope you and your wife will find every joy in your increasing family.

I remain your humble and obedient servant,

Mrs. Henry Gardner

Chapter 3

GWENDOLEN WAS BACK ON the bridge.

In the dead of night.

Alone.

Her hands were cold and numb. She was lonely, nervous, and not a little frightened.

But most of all, she was angry. Angry that for the second night in less than two weeks, she was standing in the dark, an unaccompanied woman, on Blackwater Bridge, waiting for a man she loathed to show up. And for what? So that he could threaten to take away what she held most dear.

She still had not decided what she would do when he arrived.

Their first meeting had ended abruptly and not the way she had expected.

She did not anticipate being saved so precipitously a second time.

She had brought the knife again.

Silly though it was, she had even practiced holding it before leaving the house. The man who had interrupted them on the bridge that night had corrected her positioning. She had spent an hour trying to remember exactly how he had arranged it.

She had been rather distracted at the time. Not only had Redmond been standing there, glowering and trying to look as menacing as possible, but the other man had been rather distracting in his own right.

He had called himself an angel.

He had surely looked like one. A young Alexander the Great, in flesh instead of marble, with that chiseled jaw, Greek nose, and golden curling hair which framed his face and added a softness to all of his other features.

Moreover, he had been strong and tall and broad and welcomingly imposing. A stalwart masculine body placing itself between herself and Redmond.

Then, in the park yesterday afternoon, he had appeared again. This time for a much more minor rescue of her son Henry's kite. Her father, the late Henry Gardner, had loved flying kites with his four daughters. His namesake, little Henry, took after him in that way already, though he was still mastering the skill.

It would have been the perfect opportunity to thank the stranger. But how could she without also offering some word of explanation for why she had been there in the first place? He might be overly curious. He might wish to know too much. Moreover, Julia Pembroke had been with him and her behavior had been decidedly odd. Almost as if she had not recognized Gwendolen at all.

She sighed. She remained a mystery to the angel, and he a mystery to her. If she were honest, it bothered her—probably more than it did him—to not know his name, to have not had the chance to learn it.

But pursuing strange, attractive men was not at the top of her list of priorities of late.

She was on her own now and she had to learn how to manage this dilemma as it unfolded.

If she still had such a faithful protector, perhaps she would not be in this mess. Her late husband, the Earl of Leicester, John Gibson, had been a shield between her and danger. But he was gone, and had been for more than a year.

She was alone. Standing on this dark bridge in the dark and listening for the sound of the footsteps of a man she had quickly come to fear and loathe.

"Spare a sovereign, missus?"

Gwendolen whirled around.

A strange man stood a few feet away. His tread had been so light she had not heard him approach. He was grinning through a mouth of missing teeth. Week-old stubble coated his face.

Other than that, his clothing was shabby and patched but relatively clean. Perhaps just a fellow down on his luck who had not been able to find work that day.

Gwendolen tried to breathe calmly. Perhaps this was merely his attempt at an encouraging smile and he meant to put her at ease.

Then he drew his hand out of his pocket and she saw the flash of metal.

It was ridiculous. Having a knife pulled on her when she had one in her very own pocket for the same purpose.

She hoped he was not more adept with his than she was with hers.

She smiled widely at the man before she could think twice.

"What's so funny?" The man narrowed his eyes.

She waved a hand and gave a little hiccup, half fear, half laughter.

Perhaps the large tumbler of madeira she had gulped down hastily before she had slipped out of the house was finally taking effect, or perhaps she was merely becoming hysterical. Who could say?

"This. All of this. You. Me. Us together on this bridge." She let out a sound that was a snort mixed with a giggle.

"Are you a thief, sir?" She stared at him interestedly. "Have you come to slit my throat?"

The man's eyes bugged out.

"Pardon me, I see that I've made you uncomfortable. Has no one ever asked you that before?"

"Asked? If I was going to slit ther' throat?" He cleared his throat. "No, mi'lady, yer the first."

"How odd. Is this the first time you have done this sort of thing then...?"

"What sort 'o thing? Askin' for a sovereign?"

She laughed out loud. "Oh, yes. Well, if it is a sovereign you want." She rummaged around in her reticule and pulled one out. "Here. You are quite welcome to it. From one lonely soul in the dark to another."

She held it out, her palm open.

"Aren't you going to take it?"

He coughed. "Well, it's only that..."

"There's sure to be more where that came from? Of course. I take it that is where the knife would come in? What do you usually do at this point?"

She truly was curious now. "Should I be screaming perhaps? Or trying to run away? Perhaps I should step closer towards you so that you can grab me? Or do you usually step towards them?"

The man shifted on his feet uneasily.

"No words of instruction? This is my first time. You might be a gentleman about it and give me a hint." She raised her eyebrows.

"She's crazy" she thought she heard the man mutter under his breath.

"I do apologize. I am making you ill at ease again. Let me try once more. I feel certain I can do better."

She cleared her throat and spoke up clearly and loudly. "You are frightening me, sir. I pray, please, put that knife away and let me p-p-pass..."

She burst into giggles.

"Say! What's going on here?"

She clapped a hand over her mouth.

The voice changed to surprise with a hint of cheerfulness. "Oh! It's you again."

A second man had approached and stood a meter or so behind the thief, catching the man with the knife as unaware as Gwendolen had been only a moment ago.

She peered through the dark to see who was joining their motley crew of fools.

It was her angel.

She put her hands together in delight. Her life had shifted once more from drama to farce, it seemed.

Her body felt warm all over. Was it the madeira or the excitement of being threatened? Or the suspense of waiting for Redmond, only to be so strangely and unexpectedly visited once again?

She beamed at the angel and he grinned back. Not toothlessly. His teeth were white and quite lovely.

"I do believe the lady is sauced," he drawled.

"Sauced?" She looked at him doubtfully.

"Foxed. Bosky. Jug-bitten. With malt above water. In your cups. A trifle disguised."

She stared at him blankly.

"He means yer drunk," the thief explained, speaking up and reminding Gwendolen he was still very much there.

"Ah! Yes, I see. Are there truly so many words for it?" She looked at the angel with interest.

"Oh, loads. Bit of a hobby of mine, actually."

"Are there more?" she asked curiously.

He nodded and began counting on his fingers. "Let's see... Castaway. You've eaten Hull cheese. You're tap-hackled. Properly shot in the neck."

"Yuv forgotten top-heavy," the thief supplied.

"Ah, yes! So I have. Thank you."

"Shot in the neck? That is a rather gruesome one, isn't it?" Gwendolen wrinkled her nose. "I wonder where that one comes from."

"Must've been a chap shot himself in the neck while sauced, I s'pose." The thief looked thoughtful.

"Indeed. Or shot another fellow," the angel said with another roguish grin.

"Maybe a lot of fellows. Mayhaps they all shot each other. Must've been a sight to see. I say, yer a sharp one..." The thief was interested now. He started to turn around to see who this brilliantly witted man might be.

As he did so, the angel moved smoothly to his side and before she could say "shot in the neck," the thief had both arms pinned neatly behind his back and the knife had clattered to the cobblestones.

The angel bent over and quickly scooped it up, still holding the man's wrists firmly with his other hand.

"Now why'd you do that for? I wasn't hurtin' her none," the thief grumbled. "Thought we was havin' pleasant conversation."

"Oh, we were. I was quite enjoying it. Nevertheless, can't have you waving this around in the lady's face."

The angel let go of the man. The thief backed away, rubbing his wrists gingerly.

"Was gonna offer ta buy you a pint," said the man, glaring at the angel.

"Very sporting of you. I must decline this evening, I'm afraid, but I certainly appreciate the thought."

"Would you have used my sovereigns?" Gwendolen wondered. "He had not offered to buy me a pint," she explained, in the angel's direction. The thief glared at her crossly as if she had tattled, then turned back to look at the knife the angel held and pointed.

"Tool 'o the trade. Means o' my livelihood."

The angel looked amused. He looked to Gwendolen. "What say you lady?"

"Me?" Gwendolen took up her part in the play again. "A tool of the trade, you say? And what might that trade be, good sir? Threatening helpless women and robbing them at knifepoint?"

"Not s'helpless," the thief muttered, looking down at his feet. "Got him, don'tcha?"

"I do, don't I? He does seem to pop up rather frequently." She met the angel's eye and he looked back at her with that easy smile. A warm jolt went through her from the top of her head to the tip of her toes. This time she was quite sure it was not from the madeira.

"Yes, well. Most women will not have a guardian angel to save them. Therefore, I must insist that you find a new tool." She looked at the thief consideringly. "Perhaps even a new trade."

The thief was hanging his head. "Dunna know what the missus is gunna say to this. Bringing nothin' back for the whelps."

"You support a family with your thievery then?" The angel rejoined the discussion with interest.

The thief shrugged. "Make a decent livin' most nights. Not tonight. Shaken up proper, I am."

"A cup of tea will be just the thing," Gwendolen said soothingly. "Have your wife put the kettle on as soon as you get home."

She looked at him sympathetically. "Do you have many children, mister...?"

"Baggins."

"Mister Baggins. Do you have a large family, Mister Baggins?"

"Not so big," he answered, seeming thoughtful. "Only eight of 'em isn't there."

"Eight children! Gracious! No wonder you have pursued this desperate avenue." She rummaged in her coin purse again and filled her hand. "I insist you take this. If not for yourself, for the children."

"Right generous of you, missus," the man muttered sheepishly as he emptied her outstretched palm of its baggage.

"Truly, the lady is the real angel this evening." The angel declared, winking at Gwendolen. "Awfully decent of her, all things considered."

"I thank yee, mi'lady. God bless." The thief doffed his hat and turned to go.

"Now see you call it a night after this," the angel admonished. "I don't want to see you on this bridge again. At least, not after sundown."

The thief nodded as he walked off.

"Well, that's that then. Shall we get on with it?"

"Get on with it? I certainly hope you are not mistaking me for a doxy again, sir."

The angel stepped a little nearer, just as the moon peeked out from behind a cloud, a sheepish grin on his face.

"It seems we have a habit of unexpected meetings, countess. I recognized you in the park earlier this afternoon but you did not seem keen on an introduction."

Gwendolen colored. "It was not polite of me, I know."

"Of course, the lady who accompanied me might have given an introduction, but she seemed oddly put out by the sight of you."

"Lady Julia Pembroke, you mean? That was rather strange," Gwendolen agreed. "My late husband was quite a close friend of her father and we used to get on very well."

The angel looked as if he were about to say something but thought better of it.

"Well, I am in your debt yet again, sir," she went on. "Will you enlighten me as to your identity or shall I simply go on thinking of you as a superhuman specter who appears mysteriously in the night?"

His grin was truly something magnificent. There was a charismatic power to it that made one immediately smile back.

"I rather like the idea. Perhaps I shall bring a mask next time and look for more people in need of rescue. As it stands, this was quite accidental...again." He cleared his throat. "As it so happens... Regarding names, I mean..."

He was looking sheepish again. Gwendolen saw his face redden a little. It made him appear quite boyish.

"Duke of Englefield, if you must know. But please—call me Angel. No bowing or scraping, after all we've been through. All we've shared." He winked again.

In the daytime and with a belly full of food and not spirits, Gwendolen might have been provoked by his familiarity. But at the moment she could only find it wildly amusing that here she was standing on the bridge with a duke who had just saved her from a pickpocket. A footpad. A criminal.

One she had just handsomely rewarded and shooed home to his family.

"Yes, you've acted as my angel once again, as I already mentioned..." Was he fishing for another compliment or did he have a larger ego than it appeared?

"No, no. You don't understand." The duke colored. "Angel. My name. First name is Angelus." The poor man looked quite uncomfortable. "Horrid name for a boy," he muttered, kicking the cobblestone.

"Was your mother Italian?" Gwendolen was fascinated. "It is quite an uncommon name for an Englishman."

"No, she was as English as you or I. Merely fanciful. Which was part of her charm. Though I wished she hadn't pinned it on me." He shook his head.

"It is rather lovely," she said consolingly. "And very fitting. It suits you, I think."

He looked down at her from beautiful wide eyes with long lashes, his bashfulness only making him more becoming.

Gwendolen felt a current of fire pass over her once again. She shivered a little and wrapped her arms around herself.

Angel was already starting to shrug out of his coat. "Are you cold? What was I thinking! After the fright you've had—of course you are. Here. Take this—" He held it out, opened, so that he could place it around her shoulders.

Gwendolen was wearing a light velvet pelisse with a hood and had expected it to suffice. But she had not anticipated standing outside quite this long and there was a chill breeze coming off the river.

"I was not frightened," she objected, a little crossly. "I was holding my own."

But she let him slip it around her shoulders without protest. It was warm and smelled... heavenly. A warm musky masculine scent mixed with a spicy smell that must have been a specially blended fragrance. Whatever it was, it was rushing straight to her head as intoxicatingly as the madeira.

She closed her eyes to steady herself. When she opened them again, he had stepped nearer, looking concerned. Putting his hands on her shoulders he rubbed them vigorously.

With him, the familiarity did not seem improper. On the contrary, his touch made her feel quite safe.

"We can't have you passing out. Do you feel faint?"

She shook her head. "No, nothing like that. I'm merely... fatigued."

He looked bemused. "Yes, it is rather late. But then, you seem to enjoy your midnight strolls."

She stared at him in confusion.

For a few blessed minutes she had forgotten all about the reason she was on the bridge in the first place.

"What time is it?" she exclaimed.

Angel raised his brows but pulled out a watch.

"Half past two. Why?"

Redmond was to have met her at one. She had waited perhaps an hour, then, before the thief arrived and set this dramatic scene in motion.

"It's nothing. I was to meet a friend," she murmured distractedly.

Redmond was not coming, that was clear.

Had she gotten the time wrong?

Perhaps he had missed the meeting on purpose, wishing to keep her on tenterhooks, heightening her fear even more. If so, it was working.

"Here now. A friend you say? I find it hard to believe a friend would make you look like that." Angel was staring at her hard. "What kind of a friend asks you to meet in the dark of night on a bridge in the first place? Not a friend who cares much about your safety, if you ask me."

"Yes, well. You may have a point there." She stared off at the river water. The dread was slowly seeping back. The young man's presence had pushed it away for a little while, but even his proximity was not enough to distract her from the knowledge that if her tormentor had his way, she might stand to lose her son.

"Worse and worse," said Angel softly, his brow furrowing as he watched her expression deepen.

"Come now, it cannot be that bad. We have already established you are not a doxy. I believe I have successfully argued that you are not awaiting a friend. If you are waiting once again for that dastardly looking fellow from the other night... Well. I find it difficult to believe he is your lover, however..." He pressed his lips together and looked at her appraisingly.

"He is not," she exclaimed hotly. She grimaced as the horrid memory of Redmond's last touch flitted to mind.

"And yet he has something on you. Something hanging over you. What is it? What is he threatening you with?"

Gwendolen stayed silent.

"All right, we're back to this game again. I shall have to guess." He put a finger to his lip. "A murder? No one saw the crime committed but him and now he is threatening to expose you to the world. Although you could hardly hold a knife the other night. I have trouble believing you could murder with premeditation."

"I could not! I am not a murderess." At least, not yet.

"Very well. Not a lover, a doxy, or a murderess. Probably not a thief, although you were very sympathetic to one just now. No honor amongst thieves though. If you were a thief, the chances are you wouldn't have shown such commiseration—probably quite the opposite."

He assessed her carefully. "You're a spy for the French."

"A spy?" She looked at him doubtfully. "My French is hardly passable. Languages are not my forte."

"Ah, but you would say that, wouldn't you? You wouldn't want to reveal just how proficient you are. Yes, I'd say a spy is a definite possibility."

Gwendolen tilted her head. "It would be exciting. However, you forget I have a young child. Would a spy bring her son along?"

"Fair point. Although he would add excellent cover."

Now that Gwendolen had thought of Henry, she could not put him from her mind. She bit her lip and turned back towards the water with a doleful expression.

"Not a matter to make light of, I know," Angel said quietly, coming to stand beside her. "We have met three times now, countess. How does the expression go? Third time's a charm? Won't you tell me what this is all about? Perhaps I can help. I am a duke, after all."

She looked at him wryly. "All involved are members of the peerage, so I certainly do not expect that to help me."

"Although you do outrank him," she added without thinking.

Could it be true? Might this man have some greater influence? Something to sway Redmond?

But to do so he would need to know details. Secrets she had kept buried for years.

Chapter 4

THE GIRL on the bridge was in trouble. That was plain to see.

Not a girl, Angel reminded himself. A woman. A widow. A mother.

A countess. Lady Leicester.

Odd how motherhood conferred immediate maturity on a girl though, for appearance-wise she was still pure maiden. She could not be more than a few years past twenty.

The countess looked out over the water. She had pushed back her hood. Moonlight illuminated her hair, making it shine like true gold.

She seemed very much alone.

"Do you have brothers, Lady Leicester?"

She looked towards him. "Brothers? No, I do not."

"Is your father living?"

"He passed away some years ago. My son, Henry, is named after him. Besides Henry, I have only my mother and my three sisters."

"All women," he said quietly. "I see."

No male relatives. No husband. No man to turn to for protection. Not that women were incapable—quite the contrary; Aunt Eliza was living proof of that. But in some situations, the threat of male... well, brute violence... could be a most powerful sway.

He remembered the knife. Absolutely amateurish but a sign of her desperation.

"Does your family know about...?" He waved a hand in the air.

She shook her head. "I do not wish to trouble them. If they knew..." She bit her lip again. "Well, they could not help. To know would merely make them miserable. What use would that serve?"

So, it was something which might bring her family shame or dishonor. A painful secret.

Not murder. Not espionage. Not that he had ever seriously thought either one.

Lady Julia had suggested the countess was a fallen woman with many lovers. Angel would not begrudge a woman her pleasures. Aunt Eliza had had her fair share, not that he cared to know the details of her romantic life. But no, somehow, he knew this was not a matter of a torrid love affair.

A manipulative man, a peer, blackmailing a lady with a small child.

The seeds of an idea were taking root in Angel's mind.

A preposterous idea.

An idea so outrageous it might almost be mistaken for a prank.

But a quite permanent prank. And one which would be pulled on all the world, for that matter.

Yet at the root of it was a watertight fact—he would be aiding a woman in desperate need.

Angel considered his motives as dispassionately and as quickly as possible. What would he stand to gain? What would he stand to lose?

Were his motives pure?

He might be a scoundrel, but he had also been a soldier. He had the scars to prove it.

For four years, he had lived the life of a warrior. A hard life at times. Poor food, poor conditions. The cold, the wet, the godawful everlasting dampness in one's boots.

He had not been a duke back then. His parents had not wished for him to purchase a commission. As their only child, the sole heir, their position had been understandable.

But he had been a spoiled son. They had refused him nothing, loved him totally. Eventually he had won out.

He had been in Portugal when news of their deaths came to him. Eventually, there was nothing he could do except return home when he could put off duty no longer.

But despite appearances to the contrary the military discipline he had learned had not simply faded away, even after some years of soft living and lax behavior.

Nor had his code of honor.

Back to the problem at hand. The countess remained quiet, staring out over the water, her hands clasping the front of his coat to keep it tight around her.

There was something about the image of soft femininity she presented which moved him greatly. He thought of the little boy who had been with her in the park.

"How old is Henry?" he asked softly.

She looked at him with a little surprise. "He is five years of age, Your Grace."

"Five years old." Such a little lad. "This dark business you are involved in..."

She blanched and he hurried to add, "Do not misunderstand. I do not ask you to tell me what it is about. What I am merely asking is... Does it concern your son? His... safety?"

Her lower lip quivered.

Angel clenched his fists instinctively. He had a very strong urge to hit something. Hard. Preferably the face of the man who was making this woman so terribly unhappy and afraid.

She nodded briefly.

"I see." He came to stand beside her. He leaned his elbows on the side of the bridge, feeling the coldness of the stone through the thin fabric of his shirt.

"He looked like a fine little chap. When I saw him in the park, I mean."

Their arms were only inches apart. He sensed her relax a little.

"He is the sweetest little boy in all of Christendom," she said softly. "My pride and my joy."

Angel felt a pang somewhere in the vicinity of his heart. Hearing her speak of her love for her child, he could not help but be reminded of his own mother and his own happy childhood. His mother's cool hand on his forehead when he was sick. The swirls she would gently make on his back with her hand to soothe him. The feeling of her arms around him when he would sit on her lap, until he grew too big.

He took a deep breath.

"This man, who threatens you and your child. He preys upon you because you have no protector, because you are now widowed? I take it he did not bother you while your husband, the earl, was alive?"

She shook her head slowly.

"Well, then it seems to me that another male might prove to be a similar deterrent. No?"

She furrowed her brow. Clearly, she had no idea what he was getting at.

God, he was botching things. He moved to pull his flask out of his coat pocket, then remembered he was no longer wearing it.

Gesturing to the coat, he asked "May I?"

He fished around in the left pocket, located the flask, and pulled it out.

He was so close to her he could feel her breath on his face. The sweetness of the madeira which she had probably drunk for courage.

Her proximity unnerved him.

Perhaps more liquid courage was what they both needed.

He took a deep swig and held out the flask. She seemed about to shake her head, then thought better of it and took it.

She coughed and sputtered a second later.

"Oh, yes. It's whisky. Quite a strong vintage, in fact. I do apologize."

She handed back the flask. "It is utterly disgusting. How do men take pleasure in the stuff? Have you no tastebuds?"

Angel was amused. "Perhaps the cheroot burns them out." He took another swig, feeling the whisky course through him warmly.

He could do this. It made sense the more he thought of it. And the more he drank.

He took another long swallow, nearly draining the flask.

She was watching, a skeptical look on her face.

"It is an acquired taste," he said with a grin.

"You certainly have a strong stomach." She took a breath. "Well, I believe it is time for me to go..."

He touched her arm. "Wait." He took his hand away quickly.

"Stay a moment." He cleared his throat. "I have a proposition for you."

She raised her eyebrows.

"Here. Have another go." He passed her the flask. When she took a sip, he spoke.

"We should get married."

She choked and sputtered, a hand to her mouth. "What did you just say?" she asked between gasps.

"I said we should marry." He raised a hand. "Hear me out. I propose a transactional marriage—" Seeing her eyes narrow, he tried to explain, "A marriage in name only, if you wish. I offer my protection, to you and your son, on my honor as a gentleman."

A thought came to him. "Wait—your son. Is he to inherit...?"

She shook her head. "He is... He was my husband's second son. Now, I truly must go. I thank you for your offer, but—" She looked pointedly at the flask. "—I do not think you know what you are asking. It has been a long night. We should both go home to our respective beds."

Beds. The mention of beds stirred his blood as he appraised the countess, head to toe. She was a well-proportioned woman. Even the bulk of his coat could not hide that.

She pushed a tendril of hair off her face. The breeze off the river was increasing. He looked at the strand of golden hair and the delicate hand touching it.

He wondered what it would be like to take this lady to bed. Had her husband satisfied her?

The thought of her in bed with another man, even her husband, did not sit right with Angel. He frowned.

"I assure you, I am not yet sauced, if that is what you are implying. Perhaps in five minutes, yes. Right now, no. The idea came to me before I had taken a single sip. I am completely serious, I assure you. When you think about it, you will see how sensible it is. Now, I do not mean to suggest you must share my bed, if that is your concern. I am quite content to..." He tried to phrase it delicately and failed.

"Seek your pleasures elsewhere?" she supplied wryly.

"Yes, precisely." She was looking at him from under a furrowed brow. He sighed and ran a hand through his hair. "See here. I am not the most reputable of men. I do not claim to be. I live my life in a way some might describe as..."

"Hedonistic? Scandalous? Utterly disregardful of moral standards?"

"I was going to say carefree, but that will do. I resent the last though. I do have morals. If I did not, I would not be making such a proposal."

It was her turn to raise a hand. "Angel." His name on her lips stopped him in his tracks.

"Angel," she repeated. "It is a kind offer. Please do not think I do not appreciate what you have done for me tonight. Or the previous night. But to take on a woman and child is a responsibility you do not seem ready for. We would be burdensome to you. Within a very short while I have no doubt you would regret your decision and feel quite trapped. No, I cannot do that to you. Nor to Henry."

She smiled sadly. "Believe me, it is more tempting than I can say. But no. Now goodnight, Your Grace."

She turned and walked away. Even though the whisky was starting to take effect, Angel knew better than to follow.

Even though she was wrong.

He would tell her so the next morning, when he came to retrieve his coat.

Letter 3

THE RIGHT. HON. John Gibson, Earl of Leicester to Mrs. Henry Gardner

July 27, 1793

London

My Dear Madam,

I beg you, please put your mind at rest. I harbor no rancor against you nor your husband.

How does the saying go? All is well that ends well.

Believe me, I know a little about risking much for the one you love.

While I recall with pleasure our conversations and companionship, you are correct to surmise my heart was not, in fact, unsalvageable after your departure. A little wounded pride, perhaps (it would be unmanly for me to admit otherwise).

However, life goes on and these days I find I am quite content when it comes to the domestic sphere. Maria, Lady Leicester, is an excellent companion and wonderful mother. Our Cecil is thriving. His nursemaid complains he has a never-ending thirst.

As you may remember from some of our conversations, brief as they were, I am frequently abroad. I must have mentioned my unquenchable love of ancient history, particularly anything to do with the kingdom of Egypt. My search for antiquities and artifacts with which to broaden my collection often has me journeying to distant locales in their pursuit. I do take my dear friend and secretary, Matthew Stevens, along on such ventures. But they are not the sort of trips on which one can take a wife and small child.

I fear my countess may at times feel quite neglected, you see.

Therefore, if I may ask one favor of you, my dear Mrs. Gardner, let it be this: The next time you visit London, will you stop in and see her?

Lady Leicester is a stalwart sort, a very plucky girl. She would not complain, of course. But her health has been rather poorly and she has been confined to the house a great deal this year.

I fear I will be rather a negligent husband when it comes to regular companionship for Stevens and I plan to make a pilgrimage of sorts back to Cairo in the summer and it is certain to be some months until my return. I have told her of you (only good things, of course) and your newborn daughter. I know she would be pleased to meet you and to have another woman and mother with whom to commiserate.

Faithfully yours,

Leicester

Chapter 5

"THE TERMS OF THE will are quite clear in this regard..."

Gwendolen gripped the arms of the hard wooden chair she sat in. For such a beautifully carved piece of furniture, it was dreadfully uncomfortable. Her husband had been in his sixties when they married. His home had already been furnished to his liking. His study, full of antique books and artifacts, which he collected, was gloomier than she would have liked with dark red damask curtains and heavy mahogany pieces.

Such as the imposingly large desk across from which she sat right now, as John's son Cecil Gibson, the new Earl of Leicester, droned on. She tried to focus.

"My father was conscientious about most things. However, the will had not been updated in some years. I expect he did not anticipate..." He cleared his throat. "His unexpected passing. However, the terms of the will are quite clear."

"Yes, you've said that," Gwendolen interrupted, meeting his eye.

She did not like this man. She did not like the way he was pretending to care about her welfare while scarcely bothering to hide his excitement at being the sole benefactor of his father's wealth. She did not like the way he looked at her—the way he had always looked at her—with a considering glint in his eyes that made her cringe.

John had never noticed it. Cecil could do no wrong in his eyes. Nor could Henry, to be fair. He was a doting though mostly absent and distracted father, constantly traveling around the globe to seek out artifacts and antiquities to add to his collection.

Had he loved her? Perhaps as a kind of third child. Never as a true wife.

She knew he had been fond of her.

Though apparently not fond enough to have made a clear provision on where she and Henry would reside upon an untimely passing. Perhaps he had such confidence in Cecil's generous spirit that he believed his eldest son would divide things up fairly and ensure his younger brother and stepmother would be well-provided for.

John had not known his son's true nature at all.

Now they were to be homeless.

Cecil narrowed his eyes. "I beg your pardon. I simply thought I should remind you of what the document states. I believe I have been more than patient. Although my father left this house to me, I have permitted you and your son to remain here throughout the year of mourning. However, at this point in time, I believe the sale of the property is necessary and other arrangements will have to be made."

"Of course, I am open to being more...generous," he added, scrutinizing her closely. "Were you to be congenial to an arrangement which provided incentive for both parties.... Well, then, I believe we might both come away satisfied."

Helpless rage swept over her. "And what might these incentives you speak of be, Cecil?"

He smiled smoothly. "To speak plainly? You are not without your own, let us say, assets, Gwendolen. I am sure you are aware of how greatly I have admired you from the moment we met."

Admired? Lusted after would be a more honest adjective. With no sense of decency or propriety, with no respect for his own father.

He walked around the desk and came over to her. Cecil was a large, fleshy man. Shorter than his father and thicker in build. She supposed he must take after his mother, for he looked nothing like John. He had a florid complexion, which became even redder when he was agitated.

"You are a most alluring woman, Gwendolen. My father never truly appreciated the prize that was in front of him. You have had me quite under your spell these past six years. Will you not finally end my torment?"

He reached out to lift her chin. She flinched and twisted her head away.

End his torment? She would increase it if she could. Cecil gave no consideration to the torment he was causing her. Or that he would cause her son by evicting him from the only home he had ever known.

She met his gaze directly. "I find I have very little interest in doing that, Cecil. You know your interest has never been returned. To speak of it even now shows the greatest disrespect for your own father."

His face beginning to color, he leaned back on the desk and looked at her.

"You would rather be out on the streets with your son than swallow your pride and consider me as—"

"As your what?" Gwendolen interrupted. "Your mistress? Your wife? You have not made that precisely clear."

Cecil pursed his lips. "You cannot truly expect me to marry my father's widow. The impropriety..."

"Yet you can suggest your father's widow become your mistress? Or worse!" Gwendolen cried. "You see no impropriety in that?"

She gave a bitter laugh.

"I see a means for you and your son to continue to retain your home, your manner of living," Cecil replied tightly. "The arrangement does not have to be so distasteful as you make it seem, Gwendolen. In time perhaps you would even grow accustomed to, nay, enjoy my companionship."

Gwendolen stared with bafflement. "No, I assure you I would not. Your proposition disgusts me, Cecil. Can you not understand that? Moreover, your father would be sickened by the way you are treating Henry and I. Do you truly not see that? I suppose you do, but you simply do not care."

His jaw clenched. "Be careful, Gwendolen. My generous offer may be withdrawn as quickly as it was made. Do not provoke me."

As he lecherously eyed her from head to toe, as if she were a hat to be purchased from a milliner's, she decided this had gone far enough. She rose to leave.

"Then withdraw it, Cecil. Withdraw your lewd proposal," she said, disdainfully. "I will never acquiesce to what you are asking. Never in a thousand years. I am not so desperate as to stoop..."

But as she spoke, he moved towards her. Gripping her upper arms tightly he pushed her back into her seat. Hard enough to knock the wind out of her.

As she struggled to catch her breath, he leaned down, moving his mouth towards hers. She twisted her head as far away as she could, feeling his lips graze the skin of her neck. His hands dug into the soft flesh of her arms and she let out a cry of pain.

"You've always thought you were better than me, Gwendolen," he hissed. "Do you really think that now that you've lost everything?"

There was a knock at the door and Cecil quickly stepped back.

"Be gone!" Cecil called, commandingly. "We are not to be disturbed!"

But at the same time Gwendolen managed to shakily cry, "Please do come in."

The door opened a few inches and the butler's face appeared.

"Pardon me, my lady. There is a caller here to see you..."

"Send them away," Cecil snarled. "Lady Leicester is occupied."

The butler looked less put-off than he might have. The household staff were familiar with Cecil and his frequently boorish demeanor. The man cleared his throat. "I did suggest that, My Lord, but they are most persistent."

Someone pushed the door open from behind. "Most persistent indeed."

"Pardon me, Your Grace," the butler mumbled, moving so the caller could pass.

The Duke of Englefield stepped into the room. He scanned the room quickly, and finding Gwendolen, met her eye and smiled broadly.

Gwendolen put a hand to her face. Her cheeks were wet. Tears of fear and humiliation. Even in what should be her own home, she could not be safe from brutish men.

She felt repulsed by Cecil's continued nearness. Her skin felt dirty where he had touched her, and she rubbed a hand over her neck. She was furious with herself for being discovered by the duke once again in such a helpless and mortifying position.

Angel's smile flickered as he took in the scene.

He crossed the room and reaching her chair, crouched beside her.

"My Lady, you do not look at all well," he murmured, as he reached out a warm and reassuring hand to touch her own.

He lifted it away again quickly, as was proper.

But his touch had not repulsed her as had Cecil's. The duke was a different type of man entirely, though she was not yet sure what sort.

An angelic enigma.

She looked up at his calm and handsome face. He was an extremely tall man, broad and powerfully-built where Cecil was sloping and soft. His brawniness sharply contrasted with his more delicate facial features. Wide brown eyes with almost girlishly long lashes. High but solid cheekbones. A strong jaw that was imperceptibly clenched right now as he looked at Cecil.

"She is fine," Cecil snapped. "The only thing that is wrong is your unwelcome presence. Who the devil are you and what gives you the right to barge in on a private conversation?"

Angel stared at Cecil in silence a moment, before turning back to Gwendolen.

"Will you do me the honor of introducing me to your friend, Countess?" he asked softly.

Gwendolen nodded. "Cecil, this is His Grace, the Duke of Englefield. Your Grace, Lord Leicester."

"Ah! Your stepson," Angel smiled, showing his teeth. "How delightful to see the family connections being maintained."

"Indeed," Cecil returned stiffly. "However, we are in the midst of a pressing conversation concerning the countess's living situation. Your visit is most inopportune."

"Your Grace." Angel continued to smile but the sight of his strong, gleaming white teeth reminded Gwendolen of a lion baring its teeth to its prey.

"Pardon me. Your Grace." Cecil and Angel looked at one another in silence for a moment.

It was evident neither liked what they saw.

"I really must insist, Your Grace, that you return at another time," Cecil said once more.

"Ah, but the countess's welfare is very much my concern. Not to mention, my love—" Angel turned to Gwendolen whose eyes immediately widened at the endearment. "—It was my understanding that we were to drive out this morning. Have I mixed up the time? Dash it all, have I confused morning with afternoon? I'll give that secretary of mine a scolding when I return."

Angel carried a dark blue driving coat over one arm. He had made haste from the foyer then. Had their voices carried? How much of their conversation had he—and the butler—overheard?

The sight of his coat reminded her of the other which he had put around her shoulders last night. She had gotten all the way to her room before she had realized she was still wearing it, and had hastily shoved it into the back of a wardrobe before her maid could see it that morning and wonder.

Gwendolen also noted the duke's well-fitted white leather breeches and top boots with spurs. There was a riding crop in his hand, along with white leather gloves and his hat.

He was not the kind of young man she was used to being around. He was certainly nothing like the one she had married. One might even call Angel the rakish sort, she supposed. He had already hinted at a wild reputation, and he seemed quite accustomed to late nights and liquor.

Cecil was glaring so furiously at the duke that Gwendolen decided it would be more enjoyable to be amused than to protest whatever was unfolding. She sat back in the chair and anticipated Cecil's discomfort.

After all, she had ample reason to believe Angel would once more prove a skilled actor.

"What did you just call her?" Cecil snapped.

"The form of address is 'Your Grace,' Lord Leicester," Angel replied lazily. "I am beginning to wonder if you may have a speech impediment. Or perhaps you were merely untutored in your youth. Education is in a sad state of affairs these days. I am an Eton man myself. But, *repetitio est mater studiorum* and all that, I suppose." He waved a hand magnanimously.

Cecil gritted his teeth. "I do beg your pardon. Your Grace."

"All is forgiven, old chap," Angel said smoothly. "Shall we, my dear one?" He moved to take her hand.

"Stop!" Cecil snapped. "What is the meaning of this nonsense? Why are you addressing her in such an improper manner? I demand an explanation."

Angel stopped, raised his eyebrows, and waited.

"Your Grace," Cecil muttered.

"Improper?" Angel scoffed. "I don't see anything improper in addressing my betrothed with deep affection."

Angel slipped an arm through Gwendolen's as she stood up. Cecil was becoming a beet-like shade, she noticed.

She looked up at the duke. She was not sure what exactly was happening. But he was male. He was tall, strong, and impressively imposing.

All things combined, the feeling of him there by her side was remarkably comforting.

As were his words, which were clearly driving Cecil mad with frustration.

"Your betrothed?" Cecil exploded. "What hogwash is this! Gwendolen is not betrothed."

"To the contrary, I assure you, she is. We have plighted our troth. We are engaged. Affianced, as the French say. We have pledged ourselves. Made promises, as it were. I should even go so far as to say we are espoused."

Gwendolen's lips twitched. She was fully prepared for Angel to begin ticking off his list with his fingers.

Meanwhile, Cecil's pupils had enlarged so widely she wondered if they might possibly pop out of his head altogether. One could hope.

"Now, if that is out of the way, will you not wish your stepmother congratulations?"

"This is ridiculous. Gwendolen is not marrying anyone. She is in mourning." Cecil put his hands on the desk and leaned forward towards the duke. Perhaps it was meant to be intimidating, but all Gwendolen saw was a pathetic man fighting a losing battle against a craftier opponent.

Angel was eying Gwendolen, not in a leering fashion. Merely considering. She resisted the urge to follow his gaze and look down.

How must she appear to him?

She was dressed simply in a rose-colored day dress of the lightest Bengal muslin. White leaves were embroidered along the border of the bodice. Her hair was curled and twisted up in a white lace turban. Small pearl earrings hung from her ears. She reached a gloved hand to touch one, a little uncertainly.

"Is she?" Angel folded his arms and frowned. "Am I missing something, Lord Leicester? I see no mourning clothes. More than a year has passed since the late Lord Leicester's demise. I am sorry to make mention of it, my sweet," he said in a lower voice. To Cecil, "Are you suggesting there is some impediment to our being wed? I assure you—" He straightened his back and gave the impression of taking up even more space in the room. "—I shall overcome *every* obstacle for my beloved."

Gwendolen bit her lip to keep from smiling. It was absurd for him to call her so. Yet reassuring.

She had no doubt he meant what he said about overcoming obstacles. He was clearly incorrigibly stubborn.

Well, he would soon find she was equally so.

"You cannot have known each other more than a few days!" Cecil was nearly shouting now, doggedly pursuing what was clearly a lost cause.

Angel arched a brow. "Does the countess generally keep you abreast of all of her comings and goings? Do you keep a list of her friends and acquaintances? If you do, it must be a poorly kept one for you not to already know that she and I have known one another since childhood."

"What!"

"Yes, what?" Gwendolen almost added. She kept silent. She did not know how to play this game as well as Angel did.

He was doing a marvelous job all on his own.

"Ah, yes, we have known one another since we were in nappies, haven't we, my precious sugar lump?"

Gwendolen put a hand to her mouth to suppress a snicker.

"Yet sadly," Angel went on, "years passed us by. The cruel sands of time trickled on. Until a few days ago. Oh, what a splendiferous day that was. Heaven was truly smiling upon us."

Cecil appeared eager to disagree with that statement, but Angel had pulled out his watch.

"In any case, Lord Leicester, if you are quite finished with this bizarre interrogation, I should like to depart. Dearest, shall we? You know how the park becomes quite crowded in the late afternoon."

"Of course," Gwendolen murmured, avoiding Cecil's eyes.

"I am sure we shall meet again. Not at the wedding, of course. That will be a small affair. Close family and friends only. I'm sure you understand. You will try to remember the proprieties next time, will you not?"

And then with a devilish wink at Lord Leicester, he swept her out the door.

Letter 4

THE RIGHT HON. John Gibson, Earl of Leicester to Mrs. Henry Gardner

November 3, 1801

London

My Dear Madam,

Thank you for your kindly written letter of condolence.

I apologize for the lateness of this response. Stevens and I have only returned to England this past week. It took us over a month to find safe passage home from Abyssinia. The wretchedness of the voyage was an apt precursor to our bleak arrival.

So strange to return and finally know with certainty that my wife is really gone. Maria has been buried these past three months.

I fear young Cecil will not soon forgive my lengthy absence. My son was very close to his mother and her loss has left him utterly bereft. I will be sending him to my brother and his wife in Cornwall for a time. They have a large family. Perhaps they will be of benefit to him, help to bridge the time until he enters Eton.

Heaven knows I am an inadequate parent. Caring for a child came quite naturally to my wife. She was ever tender-hearted and patient.

To tell the truth, my dear Mrs. Gardner, although we spent much time apart, I find I feel Maria's loss more than I anticipated.

We were companions for only a few short years, and yet there was a comfort and familiarity to knowing she would be here each time Stevens and I returned.

Stevens has just said to me, in fact, that he can see the absence of Lady Leicester's touch in the household already. The alterations in menus, the dust on the mirrors... He notices such details more than I do.

I do not know where I would be without him most days, Mrs. Gardner.

Like Hadrian and his Antinous. Well, you know my love for ancient history. (Although you did not know it quite so well when you selected our attire the night of that masquerade ball so many years ago, hmm? Really though, your choice of Hephaestus and Athena amused me. Stevens thought it was apropos and I saw no harm in it. He had come as Patroclus, you remember. Certainly, most of the ton missed the references altogether despite most having had the benefits of a classical education.)

How long ago that night feels now, as I write this with Stevens sitting across from me. Maria's portrait hangs on the wall nearby. A calm and steadying presence. Which reminds me, I must have a miniature ordered for Cecil to take with him when he departs.

But pardon me, my dear, you must have other things to fill your day than reading these dull digressions. I pray your family remains well.

If ever I may be of service to you or your loved ones, I trust you know that I remain,

Your faithful servant,

Leicester

Chapter 6

ANGEL WAS PRACTICALLY CHORTLING as they reached the bottom of the steps.

Gwendolen looked at him with amusement. "Enjoying yourself?"

He cleared his throat. "Well, I..."

"A small wedding? Close family only? Your 'sugar lump' am I? You appear to have ironed out quite a few details on your own since I last refused your proposal, Your Grace. I would not have taken wedding planning as one of your interests, I must admit."

Angel choked. "Wedding planning?"

"Next I suppose you will tell me you have my trousseau all picked out. Are we to have an elaborate wedding breakfast or will it be a small affair?"

"Wedding breakfast..." Angel repeated, nervously.

"Will we wed at St. George's or would you prefer your family's parish for the service?" she went on.

"Well, I had not thought that far…" He tugged at his cravat as if it were too tight.

Gwendolen put her hands on her hips. "If the prospect of marriage is so terrifying, Your Grace, why on earth are you torturing yourself with this pretense? You do realize that Cecil is not the most discreet of men and will surely make inquires. It will not take long for him to learn that we are not, in fact, engaged."

"Or that we are only recently so," Angel countered, getting back into the spirit of things.

Gwendolen threw up her hands. "Look at you! You are trembling in panic at the thought of a wedding breakfast. What is the purpose of this charade? You do not seem particularly keen on the settled, domestic life!"

Angel looked thoughtful. "I would have thought the purpose was obvious—to get you out of the room and away from that cretin. What was he doing to you, anyways, when I came in?"

"Doing?" Gwendolen faltered.

"I realize it is none of my business. But I must say, I am rather curious as to what exactly that little scene was all about."

He crossed his arms over his chest and waited.

As if he had any right to an answer in the first place!

She looked away, biting her lip in a manner some men might find incredibly provocative but which Angel had already come to understand meant she was indecisive about how to respond and how much to reveal.

He did not wish to push her, but part of him—a rather feral, savage part—was extremely keen to know if her stepson was the man from the bridge.

"You mentioned that the man who has been bothering you is a peer..."

"It is not Cecil," she interrupted.

He studied her a moment. "Why were you crying?"

"What?"

"When I entered the room, you were crying. Why?"

She looked up at him from under long silky lashes, her cheeks flushing a delicate shade of pink. His fingers twitched as he resisted the urge to touch one smooth cheek. He already knew it would feel as soft as satin.

"Tell me, Gwendolen," he said, gently. "I realize you hardly know me, but I hope my behavior to you has at least shown that I would never take advantage of a woman."

She set her lips stubbornly.

"Do you have another soul in this city you can turn to with this problem? If you do, say the word, and I will leave and never bother you again."

She parted her lips then closed them again.

He decided to change tactics. "It is a lovely day—" Perhaps an overstatement as it was cloudy and cool, but at least it was not yet raining. "Shall we walk? Or drive?" He gestured to the gleaming red phaeton he had waiting a few steps away.

"I prepared for multiple eventualities." He flashed her another grin. "Shocking though it may be, I can be quite sensible at times. I was not sure if you would prefer to stroll or to drive, and I was determined to get you out of the house one way or another."

"Why?" She said with puzzlement, looking at him intently. "Why come here at all? Why not go on with your life? Last night on the bridge... I did not respond favorably to your proposition. Why press the matter?" She narrowed her eyes. "Do you not have places to be? Hedonistic activities to partake in? Debauchery to enjoy?"

"I managed to get all of my debauching done last night. So, you see, my schedule is quite free." He smiled cheekily. When she did not return it, he sobered.

Her questions were fair. But it was rather simple.

"Why, you ask? I simply wish to help." He gave a rueful smile. "Gwendolen, I am a relatively young, single man with more wealth than I know what to do with. As you so cleverly deduced, I spend my days and my nights drinking, gambling, carousing. Whatever pleasure I desire, I indulge in. I am not a cruel or a callous man, but I also have no real attachments."

He sighed. "Then I come across you one night, trying to stab a fellow—very, very badly. And again in the park the next afternoon. Accompanied by a sweet-looking little chap who appeared very attached to you. I go for another stroll the very next night, and what do I find? Why it's you—in distress a second time in as many nights."

"I should not say I was quite 'in distress,'" Gwendolen countered, crossly. "I was doing rather well, I thought."

"You hadn't been stabbed yet, at least," Angel agreed. "All right, all right. Not in distress then. Merely conversing with a rogue threatening your purse and perhaps your life. I am sure your verbal barbs would have bowled him over eventually. Or he would have left you with considerably lighter pockets." His eyed her mischievously. "But then he did, didn't he?"

"For the good of his family," Gwendolen stressed.

"Yes, his eight whelps." Angel quirked his mouth. "Do you suppose they exist?"

"Are you saying you think they do not? He may have been a thief, but would a man really lie about having children to feed?" She glared at him. "From one mother to another, I could not let him return to his wife and children, empty-handed. It is not as if I could not afford to pay him."

"Indeed. It was a kind gesture. I am not saying otherwise," Angel said, hastily.

He brightened. "Now please accept mine."

"Are you comparing me to the thief, his wife, or their empty-bellied children?"

"None of those, of course." Merely the thief of his attention. For truly, he had not been able to think of much else since she walked away last night.

That was because she was a woman in peril and had a child to boot, he told himself. For no other reason. Certainly not because her hair was as yellow as honey with a face equally sweet to match. Or because she possessed an entertainingly sharp tongue and an impressively quick wit.

She was diverting. He enjoyed her company.

He did not immediately despise her as he did society girls like Lady Julia.

Being married to Gwendolen would not be so great a sacrifice and it had to be done sometime, as Aunt Eliza was wont to remind him. So why not now and why not kill two birds with one stone, as it were, and help a lady out in the process?

A lady in real need—not merely a sycophantic debutante who simply desired him because of his title and his fortune.

No, this was a woman in dire straits and in need of something Angel was confident he could offer in abundance—his strength and protection. Indeed, he was only too eager to take on whoever had been threatening her. He had not felt this heightened sense of anticipation since... well, since the battlefield.

Of course, it was a mad scheme.

But he had already saved her twice. He was involved now, whether he liked it or not.

There was no one else.

It was not as if he had anything better to do, did he? As the countess had already said, his days were a blur of drinking, carousing, gambling.

With a decent amount of fornicating thrown into the mix. If fornicating could ever be described as "decent." He decided he would not pose the question.

Well, all those could continue. Nothing in his life had to change, really. He was proposing a chaste marriage. That was what he had told her. He certainly did not wish to force her into an arrangement that was quid pro quo.

For once in his blasted life, could he not save a woman with no strings attached? With no failures?

In Portugal, he had tried to do so.

And failed, miserably. The lady in question had lost everything, including her life.

He would not fail a second time.

He gestured again to the carriage. "May we talk as we walk? Or drive? Or whatever means of transport you prefer. Or would you prefer to stand here and wait for Leicester to come out?"

She glared, but started towards the conveyance.

When they reached it, she paused to turn and look up at the stone façade of the house.

"This was my home," she said quietly.

"Is it not still?" But he was beginning to understand. "Did your late husband make no provision for you? For your son?"

She shook her head slowly. "I suppose he never expected to pass so suddenly. A fever of some sort, is all we were told. He was overseas at the time. Alone save for his secretary and companion, who died alongside him. His will had not been updated in years. His barrister had urged him to..." She trailed off, as she met his eyes. There was true puzzlement there. "I know he cared for us. For Henry."

"He simply did not expect to die," Angel said softly.

He wondered if she had loved him very much. His impression was that the earl had been an older man, but perhaps he was not so frail as all that. He had been virile enough to sire a son. Two sons, he reminded himself.

"Yet he left us nothing," she said, more with bewilderment than bitterness. She shook her head. "Perhaps he thought he could count on Cecil to do right by us."

"I take it that he is failing to do just that?"

She let out a deep breath. "We are being evicted."

Angel held out an arm. "In that case, I strongly suggest we drive on. For if he comes out of that door, I cannot make any promises as to his safety."

She smiled slightly and gave him her hand.

He almost pushed his suit again then. But he told himself to wait, to be certain.

Not that Angel's was a changeable temperament. On the contrary, he could be stubborn to a fault. Now that he had set himself to this course of action, he did not see himself turning back. Though God only knew what Aunt Eliza was going to say.

Not to mention the rest of society.

He thought of Lady Julia's face when she heard the duke she sought was about to marry a widow with a child and brightened.

"How old are you?" the countess asked, as he climbed into the carriage. She eyed him curiously.

"Twenty-eight. Why? How old are you?"

"I am twenty-four."

Twenty-four. Married and widowed and left to raise a child alone. What a different life women led.

Before Angel could help himself, his eyes darted over her figure, beautifully rounded in every way. Every way that he could see.

"Why not think of this as an act of brotherly kindness?" He blurted out the words before he could stop himself.

Good Lord, where had that come from?

"Brotherly?" The countess raised her eyebrows. "How would it be brotherly?"

"Christianly. Christian brotherhood. I mean—" He was doing this badly. Why on earth had he used the word "brother" when he had certainly just been appraising her in no way a true brother ever would? "—I mean, in the sense of... Christian charity, of course. Being Christ-like." Oh, shut-up, Angel. He wanted to hit himself in the head. Instead, he sat down beside her and took up the reins.

"Are you now comparing yourself to Christ? Has your name quite gone to your head?" Her lips quirked upwards.

"Oh, never mind," he grumbled. "Shall I drive you back to the bridge and drop you off now for your next assignation? Clearly you have no wish to avoid another."

She was silent. He glanced over. Her eyes were fixed back upon the house. She was looking up at the second floor.

"What is it?" He spoke more gently.

"Henry. He is up there with his nurse," she said quietly. "He has... no idea..." She looked away.

"You love your son very much." It was a statement, not a question.

She nodded. Her hands met and clenched in her lap. Dash it all, he was about to make her cry again, wasn't he?

Without thinking, he reached over and placed his hand briefly atop her smaller ones.

"It will be all right." He took his hand away hurriedly.

There was silence for a few minutes as they drove along the street. He focused on the road. Wouldn't want a repeat of the other night with the overturned curricle. His valet had still not managed to get the smell of ripened vegetables out of those clothes.

"Do you not wish to marry for love, Angel?"

He glanced over.

"Or for a better reason than simply—" She searched for words. "—well, a better reason than self-sacrifice. If that is what this truly is. Do you not wish to have an heir?" She stumbled over her words. "Or, perhaps I misunderstood..."

"No, no," he said hastily. "You did not. It would be a marriage of convenience in every way. I would not... trouble you...in that manner. I would never trouble a woman like that if they did not wish it." A little ironic coming from the man who seemed to be following trouble as if it were his birthright. "Look—I have no true need of an heir. The line is in no danger of dying with me. I have a cousin—decent sort of a fellow. Has five sons. Five! So, believe me, there are ample Beaumonts standing ready to take up the dukely mantle."

He was lying, of course.

He was the last of his line.

There was no reason for her to know this. Things would work themselves out one way or another. Ensuring the succession had never been one of his top priorities, anyway.

He tried not to imagine the look on Aunt Eliza's face as he explained he had committed himself to chastity...within wedlock.

She would either strangle him or split her sides laughing.

He shrugged. "Besides, I have never seen myself as the fatherly sort. As you say, my life is a bit on the wild side. I have a... reputation, I suppose."

She tilted her head, her mouth turning up at the corners again. "You suppose?"

"Very well. I'm a proud bearer of the noble title of rogue. Scoundrel. Hellion, even. You may even have seen my name in the—" He cleared his throat and named a daily paper that made its reputation on scandal and gossip writing. "Not that they can ever get anything close to a decent likeness." He rolled his eyes.

"Oh!" She clapped a hand to her mouth. "Were you in the one with the..." She waggled her hand impatiently. "The one last week! With the curricle? Henry showed it to me. He enjoys coloring over the pictures."

"Lord Englefiend and the Great Wall of Cabbages? Yes, I believe Aunt Eliza has that one still on her desk. She says she plans to make copies for her friends."

Gwendolen looked as if she were about to issue a smart remark, but then abruptly looked around before gripping the seat tightly with both hands.

"Oh, for pity's sake," he exclaimed, as he realized her concern. "I can drive perfectly well when..." When I am sober, he had been about to say. Would she find that reassuring?

"When you have not drunk many drams of whisky?" she provided.

"Yes, exactly. You are quite safe."

She gave him a cold look. "You do realize, Your Grace, that I come with baggage. A child, I mean."

"Of course! I am not quite the dunce you seem to believe. In fact, you may have mentioned his name once or twice. George was it not?"

He felt her eyes bore into him.

"Henry," he said, hastily. "It is Henry. Of course, I know that. He is named after your father. See? I remember. Of course, I know you come with a child. It's very convenient really. My aunt has been nagging me to marry and have a family. Well, here is one ready-made. All we need are the papers."

"You make it sound as if you were purchasing a horse, Your Grace."

"I hope it's a fast one. Is Henry a good runner?"

"He is only five years old, and I would prefer that he not perish in a carriage accident any time in the near future."

"You may have your own carriage for yourself and Henry. A pony cart. As many ponies as he likes. He need never ride with me, if that is what concerns you. Not that I wouldn't be happy to teach him horsemanship," he added. In fact, it might be somewhat pleasant to show such a small fellow what was what.

"That is very generous of you, Your Grace. I shall certainly give great consideration to the offer."

"I suspect you don't truly mean that. Not very civil of you, must say. I do have my good qualities, I'll have you know."

She blushed. "I do know."

There was a pause.

Then her hand darted out and she clasped his forearm briefly.

"You have been very kind to me, Angel," she said, hurriedly. "Please do not think I don't realize that. You have done more than you ought, more than I had any right to expect. And now, today... Your bold entrance. The look on Cecil's face after he had been...Well, it was rather heroic of you," she finished in a rush.

Angel hardly took in her words.

His arm felt like a hot coal had singed it.

Her hand had hardly touched him, and only through the wool of his coat at that.

But he could still feel it there, her small hand pressing down on the muscle of his arm, as if holding on for safety.

It was a strange feeling. One which was making him quite dizzy.

His hands went slack on the reins and the phaeton veered sharply to the left causing Gwendolen to let out a sharp cry.

"Oh, confound it all." Angel pulled himself and the horse together and straightened out.

When no accident was forthcoming, Gwendolen settled back in her seat.

They drove quietly for a few minutes, Angel still thinking about that touch. He was not sure what she was thinking about. Probably how daft she had been to step foot in a carriage with such a reckless rogue.

"Very well," she said, abruptly. "Let us proceed."

Angel nearly dropped the reins.

"Please," she added, "do not bring us to our deaths before we can be wed. That will leave Henry in an even worse position than he is in now."

Angel looked over and grinned at her. "You won't regret this."

He saw her open her mouth to speak, then her eyes widened as she looked ahead of them.

He whipped his gaze back to the street and pulled sharply on the reins, swerving around an elderly man pushing a wheelbarrow of potatoes just in the nick of time.

"I very much hope not," Gwendolen muttered. "Now, shall we discuss the wedding breakfast?"

Letter 5

MISS GWENDOLYN GARDNER TO Mr. Robert Wyndham

June 23, 1811

Orchard Hill

Wyndham,

Why have you not responded to my letters? What am I to imagine by your silence? Every day I expect to hear from you and to see you. I begin to fear I wait in vain.

When last we met, you were so altered, so rough, Wyndham. I know you spoke of love, but you left me in an awful plight. Ignored my tears, my protests, my pain. I cannot see how that was loving.

And now—can you truly be so cruel as to delay? Even on such a grave matter? I cannot suppose it possible. Yet if my last missive failed to stir you, I know not what I may say that will do so.

You will see from the postscript that I have returned home to Orchard Hill. My mother wishes to write to your commanding officer. I have begged her not to. I was certain you would respond with haste.

But now, days turn into weeks. You must understand it is a matter of great urgency for me. Yet still, nothing. There is a dreadful coldness in my heart and a voice in my ear that says I have misjudged you greatly, trusted you terribly. I pass night after wretched night grieving and tormenting myself with your absence.

As for that other guarantee, which we made to one another with open hearts, if only in private. Did the words mean nothing to you, I now wonder? Am I truly forsaken?

I wish to acquit you, to defend you—to myself if no one else. I beg you, Wyndham, write to me. Save me from this dreadful torment. This is unbearable in all ways.

Your faithful wife, if only between us two, before the eyes of God,

Gwen

Letter 6

COL. GEORGE LUCAS TO Mrs. Henry Gardner

June 30, 1811

London

Dear Madam,

The soldier of whom you inquire, Robert Wyndham, left my regiment only last week. He was redeployed to a cavalry regiment at his own request. To my understanding, Wyndham recently came into an inheritance which permitted him to purchase a commission as an officer in a dragoon regiment, the 12th I believe. He left with great haste and was to join up with his new unit near Lisbon.

I have taken the liberty of forwarding your inquiry to him there. I hope you receive a favorable and swift response.

Sincerely,

George Lucas, Col.

---- Militia

P.S. Madam, if I were you, I should keep my daughters away from such a man. He is an incorrigible scoundrel, and I mean that in the worst way.

Chapter 7

ANGEL THREW HIMSELF ONTO a sofa and looked over at his aunt. She was engrossed in what she was reading and had not yet glanced up.

Her mastiff, Hercules, lay curled up at her feet. How they could bear the weight of such a giant he would never know.

He suspected Hercules slept on her bed, but he was too much a gentleman to ever sneak in and check.

Aunt Eliza picked up the cheroot that lay smoking on the table and took a little puff.

When her first husband had died—a kind man she had been very fond of—Aunt Eliza had liberated herself from convention and committed herself to living life as freely as any man.

Those had been her words, not his, and she was still prone to spouting them from time to time as if they were her motto.

Angel had no issue with how his aunt chose to live her life. His mother and father had always had a relationship closer to that of equals rather than the strange hierarchy that he supposed many marriages entailed.

Why should a man, particularly a privileged one, lead a life of total freedom while a woman sat at home making doilies and lace caps? Or whatever ladies were supposed to make.

Aunt Eliza was not the fancywork type.

She was more of an Amazonian.

He could easily see her leading troops into battle.

If women such as Eliza had been allowed to enlist, he felt certain things with Napoleon would never have reached the state they had.

Instead, his aunt had to settle for simpler pleasures. Smoking, drinking—those were rather discreet ones. Lovers, on the other hand... Well, Angel was not in any position to judge.

He looked at the face of the woman who had been his only family for the past six years. By his count, she was roughly fifty, though did not look a day over forty.

Certainly, Eliza had no trouble finding willing paramours. She grew a little bit stouter each year and he could see the laugh lines deepening around her eyes, but she was a pleasant-featured woman and what was more, she had a sharp wit and could keep a roomful of people laughing uproariously for hours.

She smoked and she drank but she did so with much more restraint than Angel. Her dark brown hair had streaks of silver, but was styled becomingly with soft ringlets around her face. Which made quite a contrast to the cheroot she held in her hand. She shared her late brother's dark features. Angel's fair looks had come from his mother.

Angel gave up waiting to be noticed.

"I'm getting married, Aunt Eliza."

There. He had done it.

Her expression did not change. She turned a page. "Mmhmm?"

"I said, I'm getting married." He raised his voice a little. "To a woman."

"I am not deaf, nephew. There is no need to shout. A woman? What else would you be marrying? An elephant?" She kept reading.

He sat up and swung his legs down.

"Yes, a woman. Would you like to meet her?"

"Why? Have you brought her home with you?" Another page turned.

"No, I.. She..." She was toying with him, that's what she was doing. "You are really not taking this in the way I expected."

"How did you expect me to take it?"

"Seriously?" he said, hopefully.

Her lips twitched. "Angel, the word does not suit you in the slightest. It could not be further from your domain. What is more, I thought you were quite proud of that fact. Has something changed?"

She looked up at him finally and narrowed her eyes. "You haven't visited that opium den again, have you?"

Angel shuddered. "Good Lord, no. Learned my lesson the first time. Wretched stuff. Though Hugh insists he had incredible dreams that night."

The second son of an earl, Hugh Cavendish was ostensibly Angel's private secretary. But as Angel already had a man of business, an estate steward, a barrister, and a bevy of solicitors, the position involved serving as more of an epicurean companion and fellow carouser.

"No, I am right in the head, I assure you. As right in the head as I ever am," he amended. "The truth of the matter is that I have met a lovely lady, very amiable woman. Things have moved rather quickly, and, happily, she has just today accepted my proposal."

"Do you know how one goes about getting one of those special licenses thingamajigs?" he added, realizing that, although the afternoon with Gwendolen had passed without any mention of her predicament (something he thought she had rather made sure of) time might be of the essence to her.

Especially if it meant getting her out of the clutches of her lascivious stepson. Despite her hesitance to elaborate, Angel felt certain more had been going on than a mere message of eviction.

"The *truth* of the matter?" his aunt repeated, stressing the word. "I should think not. Now begin again and tell me what really happened." She eyed him suspiciously. "Are you being blackmailed? I've always thought you were too intelligent to fall for that sort of thing, but has this woman convinced you she is—" She coughed here delicately. "—increasing."

Angel gaped. "No, nothing like that. By Jove, I should be a poor sort to leave a lady in such a situation if it were the case, but no, that is not it at all."

"We Beaumonts have always cared for our by-blows," Aunt Eliza acknowledged magnanimously. Angel smiled slightly at the way she spoke as if she might have sired a few. "I assume you would take steps to care for any offspring."

"Of course. But I have no by-blows." He thought for a moment. "That I know of."

A fellow never knew for certain, of course. One of those mysteries of life dissolute young noblemen rarely gave much thought to. Yet another thing women were left to deal with.

"Very well. Who is she and why the great haste? I hope you do not mean to try to convince me you have fallen in love." She snorted derisively.

Although he knew exactly what she meant, Angel's back went up. "What's that supposed to mean?"

"Only that you are not that type. You are like me—much too pragmatic for that sort of thing. We take our pleasures where we can find them. In fact, I am still finding it near impossible to believe you are serious about this marriage business at all."

"I believe my parents loved one another," he replied, a little stiffly.

Aunt Eliza's expression softened. "They did."

"Why is it impossible to believe I might marry for the same reason?"

"Are you? Do you love this lady?"

The question made him color like a fool. "Of course not," he stammered. He crossed his arms. "Nevertheless, I am going to marry her."

"Shall I continue to inquire as to why or is there no hope of an honest answer?"

He met her eye. "She is in trouble."

"Aha!" She clapped her hands together. "If there was one thing which might entice my scoundrel of a nephew to wed, it would be a damsel in distress. I should have made that my next guess."

Angel slouched. "Am I that predictable?"

Aunt Eliza studied him a moment. "You have always been a very sweet-natured boy, Angel. The nickname suits you more than your dimwitted friends, not to mention the general public, realize." She sighed. "But surely this lady—she is a lady?" He nodded. "Surely there is some way to help her that does not require wedlock. Perhaps she would even prefer an alternative to a state so... permanent?"

Angel shook his head stubbornly. "No."

He thought for a second after he answered. Was there any truth to what she said?

The countess was beset by at least two rogues, one of whom had no qualms about attacking her in her own home—which should have been her one safe haven. Her child was at stake in some way, although he had no idea how, nor did he have any confidence she would ever tell him.

But Angel was determined to find out. What was more, when he did find out exactly what she was being threatened with, he wished to have the legal and the moral right in the eyes of the world to bring the blackguards to their knees begging for her forgiveness.

It was a pretty picture. He could even imagine Gwendolen reclining on a gilded throne. She made a lovely queen in his mind's eye. Her long golden hair unpinned and flowing around her shoulders. Her eyes full of wit and mischief, but also maternal wisdom. A beautiful Athena.

Well, he would be proud to have her on his arm, unconsummated marriage or not. She would make a fine duchess. He suspected she had not even thought of the title she would gain, nor did she care. It was probably the furthest thing from her mind.

Second only to their wedding breakfast, of course.

Aunt Eliza was looking at him strangely. "Who is she?"

"She is the Countess of Leicester—for a few more days. Gwendolen Gibson."

His aunt turned the name over in her mouth. "I cannot say I know her. Oh! Leicester, you say?" She tilted her head. "That cannot be right. John Gibson, the antiquarian? Leicester died in the Far East, didn't he? I have met his secretary, Matthew Stevens. Third son of Lord Biltshire, I believe. He had a row with his family and they cut him off. It was very strange. He was an interesting fellow. Well, they both were. They both passed away overseas, did they not? It must be going on a year or more now. Leicester did have a young wife. I recall her now. A pretty thing. I saw her at a ball once. She glowed like a star. She would be a little younger than you. But that Lady Leicester has a child. And she is a widow."

"The very same."

She was quite star-like, Angel agreed silently. So even Eliza had noticed her.

His aunt took another puff and looked thoughtful. "You are marrying a widow? One with a child?"

"A son. Henry is his name. He is five years old." Angel felt proud of himself for remembering. Not that he knew much else about the boy. Besides him liking kites. Well, that could be remedied. He would make an effort to be approachable. It might be fun to have a child in the house.

He pictured himself playing on the floor with Gwendolen's son and remembered his set of blocks. He had played with them for hours when he was Henry's age, constructing all sorts of fabulous structures. Then knocked them all down in a most satisfying smash, of course.

"Very well." Eliza re-opened her book.

"Very well? Nothing more?"

"No, I believe my questions have been answered," she said, absently. "Perhaps this will be good for you."

Her head snapped up abruptly. "Heaven knows you need someone to temper your rampages. Do not think for an instant young man, that I have forgiven or forgotten the state of my poor curricle. I weep for its untimely passing. Even that wonderful caricature of you splattered with tomatoes does not suffice to comfort me. That cherry red phaeton you were driving today should make up for its loss nicely, however."

Angel opened his mouth and closed it again. Fair was fair, he supposed. He had planned to buy her one like it, but she may as well have his.

He sighed and stood to go.

"I shall have the clipping framed for you. As a wedding present," she called, as he left the room. "It is a wondrous likeness."

Gwendolen was exhausted when she returned to the house. A quick word to the butler, Carson, who was in fact a kind sort of man and seemed to dislike the idea of Cecil being his new master as much as she did, confirmed that Lord Leicester had departed shortly after she and Angel had left. That was a relief.

She untied her bonnet and dropped it on a table in the hall.

Somehow, she had come through the day unscathed.

With all her secrets still intact, too.

She put a hand to her forehead and closed her eyes. So many secrets, so many lies. Or, if not lies, then omissions of truth.

If the duke knew all of them, would he care?

It was too late to worry about that. Perhaps Angel was a fool for making his proposal, but he was to be her fool now. She had given her word to enter this unholy venture and she would not withdraw it.

Besides, like it or not, he was her best hope.

No, she corrected herself, he was Henry's best hope. And Henry was all that mattered.

She heard the sound of footsteps and saw Carson emerging from one of the servants' passages.

He wore a nervous expression.

Gwendolen's face fell. "Do not tell me that his lordship has returned …"

Carson startled. "No, no, nothing like that. It is merely—" He cleared his throat. "—in the upset of the day and your arrival, I realize I forgot to mention…"

"Yes?" she encouraged.

"You have another visitor." He added hastily, "A more pleasant one. If you will permit me to say so, My Lady."

The sound of giggling could be heard as Gwendolen went towards the nursery. Presumably hearing her footsteps, the giggles quieted and changed to excited whispers.

"Hello? Henry?" She was smiling as she peeked around the corner and into the room her son used as playroom and schoolroom.

A large blanket was laid out on the floor. There were bulky shapes quivering beneath it.

Gwendolen bit her lip to keep from laughing.

"Hello? Is anyone there? Henry?"

Loud whispers.

"Now?"

"Now!"

The blanket sprang to life and two figures emerged shrieking.

"Were you very frightened?" Henry asked with delight, running into his mother's arms.

"Terribly," she assured him. "I had no idea we had ghosts in the nursery. And in the daytime, no less!"

She looked up at the other, larger figure.

Her younger sister, Rosalind, stood there beaming, her curly yellow hair tousled around her shoulders from where it had come unpinned while playing with Henry. Rosalind was a petite girl with a buxom figure too rounded to be considered fashionable. But her vivacity meant she would always stand out in a crowd. Even amidst the ton of London, Gwendolen had no doubt.

Rosalind was not *the* youngest, for there were four girls in the family altogether. Gwendolen was the eldest, at twenty-four. Claire was the second at eighteen. Rosalind was a year younger, while Gracie was a mere seven years of age. Her sisters lived with Gwendolen's mother, Caroline, at Orchard Hill, near the small village of Beauford.

"Are you surprised?" Rosalind asked, with an exuberant smile. Her eyes sparkled with excitement. "I came on the coach. I had to beg mother to let me go alone."

"I could have sent a carriage for you if you had but written! The coach is not a safe means of travel for a young girl." Gwendolen narrowed her eyes. "Mother said yes?"

Rosalind colored. "Well, she *will* say yes... when she reads the note I left."

Gwendolen rolled her eyes. "She will not have much choice at that point, will she?" She sighed. "Well, come along then. Shall we ring for tea and biscuits?"

She had heard her son's stomach growling. She picked him up, groaning at his heaviness.

Five-year-olds grew so very quickly.

In just a few years, her baby had disappeared to be replaced by a toddling little boy. Now there was hardly a trace of the baby in Henry at all, except for his sweet rounded cheeks with their lovely dimples. She kissed one soft cheek and sighed again. Time could run so quickly and so slowly. The beautiful moments passed too soon, while the dreadful ones dragged out like an eternity.

Life was strange.

The thought of dreadful moments reminded Gwendolen of how she had spent her day...and the previous nights.

Rosalind's arrival might be a challenging complication.

Her sister was young, but incredibly precocious. Nosy, you might even say. She was clever and astute and, now that she was older,

Rosalind had a nerve-wracking tendency to ferret out secrets from unexpected places.

Gwendolen had not spent six years guarding hers only to have them come to light now.

There was only one other person privy to the lesser-known aspects of her life. Her most trusted advisor and beloved counselor. Her mother. And she would prefer it stay that way.

"Henry tells me you may be moving house," Rosalind said in a low voice as she walked beside her sister down the hall to the stairs which led to the morning room. Henry had run on ahead, unwilling to keep such a sedate pace.

Gwendolen turned her head quickly. "How did he... Well, it is no matter. Yes, we shall be moving house."

She suddenly realized she was engaged to a duke yet had absolutely no idea where she and her son were to live once her marriage actually took place. It was idiocy. Idiocy she had agreed to. She must be a bedlamite.

She gave Rosalind a tight-lipped smile. "Come, let's talk downstairs." She took her sister's arm.

They entered the room Gwendolen used as part library, part sitting room, and part second nursery. Some toys of Henry's were strewn on the floor by one of the large bow windows. It was a pretty room—airy and light, decorated in pale blues and golds. It reflected Gwendolen's style more than the rest of the house.

Henry immediately ran over to the toy pile and began to build with some wooden blocks. He beseeched his aunt to come and build beside him, but Rosalind put him off and came to sit beside Gwendolen.

"You look different somehow. I can't put my finger on it."

The interrogation had begun so quickly. Gwendolen tried to hold Rosalind's gaze but had to look away. She felt her cheeks reddening and had to suppress the wild urge to laugh hysterically.

"What on earth is it?" Rosalind asked curiously. "Is it something to do with your move? I had always thought you to be quite happy in this house. But are there too many memories? With John gone?"

Rosalind and her mother had always been fond of Gwendolen's late husband.

He had been a friend of their parents since before Gwendolen was born, though she still did not know their exact connection. Certainly, the earl had been a faithful friend to the Gardners—more than Gwendolen's sisters knew or appreciated. Indeed, her sister Claire believed John to have been a negligent husband and did not share Rosalind's fondness. To Claire, it was unthinkable that the man Gwendolen had married had chosen to journey thousands of miles to dig up ancient relics in an Egyptian desert rather than staying by her sister's side when she was in her confinement. Especially so soon after they had been married.

Claire had not been impressed with the earl's frequent trips which meant that Gwendolen was, more often than not, living alone most of the year.

But truth be told, Gwendolen had not minded her husband's absences. He was a benevolent husband but an absent-minded one. More comfortable with his friend and secretary, Stevens, who traveled with him at all times as his companion, than he ever seemed to be with his young bride. Gwendolen would never have complained about her husband's decisions to spend more time with his friend than with her. At the time, all she could do was feel grateful to have found such a kind and accepting man at all—though Claire thought she had gone soft in the head to have lowered her standards for a husband so much.

Gwendolen smiled weakly. "No, it is not that." She hesitated, unsure of how much to say regarding Cecil. Rosalind had only met him once or twice.

Perhaps she had best come to the point straightaway.

She took a deep breath.

"Don't tell me! Let me guess," Rosalind suddenly commanded. She looked her sister over carefully from head to toe.

"You're in love."

The hysterical laughter Gwendolen had been doing her best to hold in burst out and she gave an unladylike snort. "No, it is most certainly not that."

She looked at Rosalind's perplexed expression and choked out the words.

"Although, I am to be congratulated, for you see, I am to be married. Very soon, in fact. This week, most likely."

And then she sank back against the sofa and let the laughter come.

Rosalind peered at her.

"I wish I could share in your merriment," she said slowly. "But I am not quite sure you are serious. Though it is a strange joke, I must say. You are not in love. Yet you are to be married? And soon?"

"Yes-s-s," Gwendolen gasped. "Very soon. With all haste."

"Why?"

Gwendolen quieted and gazed back at her sister. "Why?"

"Why with all haste? It seems a bit strange to be rushing in head first, especially if you are *not* in love."

Gwendolen stared. She had not thought of an adequate explanation. Of course, she could not give the real one.

Her meetings with Angel had been welcome diversions from the fear she had felt leading up to her meeting with Redmond, both the first time interrupted and the second time when he failed to appear.

Days spent pacing and nail-biting and shedding soundless tears. All the while trying to appear cheerful and normal for Henry's sake— as well as the household staff. One of whom must have already let it slip to Henry that they were to move. She would have to discuss that with Carson later.

"I was joking," Gwendolen said very slowly, her mind racing. "Not —" she added, seeing Rosalind about to speak. "—about the marriage part."

She gulped.

"About the being in love."

Rosalind squealed in delight. "You were? Truly?"

Gwendolen nodded weakly. "Truly."

Her sister gave another loud shriek that caused Henry to look up in surprise from his playthings. Seeing no cause for alarm, he still came over to wrap his arms around his mother, then his aunt, before cramming a biscuit into his mouth and returning to his architecture.

The sisters looked after him.

"Such a loving little boy," Rosalind murmured. "I remember hoping you would have a girl. But Henry is as sweet as a girl, isn't he? You know what I mean, of course."

Gwendolen smiled. "He is. I do."

Henry reminded her of Angel, in fact. They gave their affection and loyalty so fiercely and so completely.

Not that the duke had any actual *affection* for her, of course. But he had certainly committed himself to her cause.

"Well, who is he? Will I meet him soon?" Rosalind took a sip of her tea. "Mmmm. Is this a blend John brought back?"

"From Ceylon, I believe, yes," Gwendolen said distractedly, trying to think of a compelling fiction. "He is... a duke."

"A duke! First an earl, now a duke. Aren't you the lucky one?" Rosalind's eyes danced with mischief. "Not that you've ever really cared about such things. Nor have any of us. We know better than to see a man's value in his title—Mama taught us that much. But still, a duke. Rather impressive. Where did you meet? I did not think you went out much these days. You have always been too reluctant to mingle in London society. I have never understood why."

Gwendolen grimaced. She had never desired to be a social butterfly like Rosalind. After John's death she had become even more reclusive, seeing only her family and a few friends.

Redmond's reappearance had made her even more committed to a private life.

"We met... while out walking in the park."

"And?"

"And... he was very friendly." That was true. "And... well, very handsome." Also true, as Rosalind would soon see to her utter delight, Gwendolen had no doubt, so no point in downplaying it.

"He...is very fond of children," she finished lamely. Then she remembered Angel had not formally met Henry. Well, he would soon. And she had no doubt they would be friends. Angel had a charming way about him that would put Henry at ease.

"Well, it is not easy to explain..." She bit her lip.

Rosalind patted her knee. "Of course. Who can explain how these things happen? Falling in love is inexplicable. At least, that is what I have read. I cannot wait for it to be my turn." She looked dreamy. "Although I believe I will follow in John's footsteps first."

"John's footsteps? Whatever do you mean?"

"Seeing the world, of course. I have always envied him his adventures. Whenever he would visit, I would sit at his feet and listen to him and Stevens tell their stories of far-off places, new people and ways of life. I quite envied that you got to live with him and hear his stories all of the time."

Gwendolen looked at her sister affectionately. She would not dissuade Rosalind of her impressions of the earl.

She suspected Rosalind had heard far more of John's stories than she ever had. Even when he was home, most days they rarely spoke more than a few words to one another—not because of any upset or anger, but simply because that was how her husband was. Kind but reticent. Fully engaged in his own separate, private life and sphere. One she had never been able to enter.

Now she was about to marry another man out of convenience rather than love. Would it mean a life of even greater loneliness?

Well, she was used to it. She would not complain about her own lot if it meant securing Henry's safety. She took a breath and determined to give her sister a story as compelling as the ones John had told.

The story of how she fell in love with an Angel.

She already knew the Angel in question would not mind.

He was an excellent actor after all. He had already made her believe he cared enough about her to marry her, had he not?

Gwendolen smoothed out her skirt and started to speak, "Let me tell you about when I first saw him..."

When Gwendolen retired to her room later that evening there was a letter waiting on her bed.

For a long moment, she merely looked at it—resting there so unobtrusively against her pillow, as if it could be any sort of missive at all. An invitation. A letter from a friend.

But it was nothing so benign and she knew it.

She picked it up with surprisingly steady hands and broke the seal.

The contents read exactly as she had expected them to. The same threats, the same demands.

Along with vitriolic accusations that she had not come alone to the last meeting.

Redmond had been there then, watching from afar. Perhaps he had even laughed at her expense at first as he saw her accosted by the robber, only to have that laughter turn into gnashing of teeth as he saw her rescued a second time by the same white knight.

She wondered if he had stayed long enough to see that part of things or had simply left her to the wiles of the footpad without waiting for the outcome.

Finally, the letter listed the time and place of a new assignation.

One she had no intention of attending.

She planned to be married by then. When she was, Henry would be safe behind a moat of dukely protection.

She would not let herself wonder if it would be enough. It had to be enough. She had nothing else in her pitiful arsenal.

Her marriage to the earl had seemed to keep Redmond at bay for six years. The threat of a new male protector—a younger, even more privileged one—had to be a similar deterrent.

Had to.

Her hands began to tremble as she ripped the note into tiny pieces. Not because of the letter itself, but because of what its placement meant.

Either Redmond had broken into her bedroom, or there was a spy in her house.

Letter 7

MRS. HENRY GARDNER TO the Right Hon. Earl of Leicester

July 2, 1811

Orchard Hill

My Dear Lord Leicester,

I write to you only after having availed myself of every other avenue. You have been a friend to our family these many years and with Henry's passing you have graciously offered your service to us on more than one occasion. I have never had a reason to require it until now. Your friendship and visits have been generous enough.

However, I come to you now out of desperation regarding a matter of the utmost delicacy.

For you see, My Lord—my daughter, our Gwendolen, is with child.

I must wipe away the tears as I write those words and pray the ink is still legible enough for you to read. Truly, she has been a foolish girl and her judgement most unwise. Her father's death last year left us all adrift. I blame myself for not seeing just how lost Gwendolen had really become until it was far too late.

Be that as it may, the error was not hers alone. I know she is my daughter and I see through not unbiased eyes, but John, I must have you know—she was preyed upon by a man who, I am wretched to admit, fooled us one and all only to ravish and abandon her.

Before you ask it, there is no hope of his return—regardless of your influence and regardless of what kind of a husband such a man would surely be. He has left England for the Continent. The timing of his departure was precipitous for it would appear it came as soon as he learned Gwendolen was increasing.

I do not believe even you could move heaven and earth in order for his return to come in time, even if he were willing—and I do not believe he would be.

So, I must come to the question I have been dreading asking.

It has been over a decade since you became a widower. I well know now the loneliness that comes with such a grievous loss. Until now, I comforted myself with the knowledge that just as you have always had Stevens' faithful companionship, I have that of my girls.

But now I must ask if there might be room within your heart, or at least within your home, for the presence of a wife. If you have, if ever you had considered such a thing or if considering it now is not too distasteful a prospect, I beseech you to think of my Gwendolen.

Regardless of what you decide, I beg of you, John—come to us with all haste here at Orchard Hill.

I have grievous need of your wise counsel, my dear friend.

I remain your faithful servant,

Caroline Gardner

Chapter 8

"HOW DO I LOOK?" Angel straightened his cravat and shifted restlessly.

"Sweaty. Pale. Terrified. How do you feel?"

"Terrified."

"Try not to swoon, would you? You weigh at least fourteen stone. I'm not sure I could catch you before your head hit the floor." Hugh eyed Angel skeptically. "It's not too late to bolt, you know. I have a fast horse."

"I am not going to bolt," Angel hissed in indignation. "The lady is moments away. I have given my word."

"Besides," he added, a moment later. "It is not as if I was forced into this."

"No, you enter into bondage quite freely. Though I am not sure you are in your right mind. I hope that is not one of the conditions for marriage."

"It is not." Angel glared at his friend. So-called. "Remind me of why I invited you again?"

"Moral support." Hugh grinned. "Do you have a ring?"

"Of course, I have a ring." He reached into the pocket of his tail-flap instinctively and touched the metal. It was not an elaborate piece of jewelry. But it had been his mother's wedding ring. The band was gold. In its center rested a small diamond surrounded by a border of small pearls which formed a daisy pattern. It was pretty, rather than ostentatious. Angel had always liked it. He could remember touching the flower as a little boy sitting on his mother's lap. He could picture the way it had looked on her finger even now, and the feel of her soft warm hand curved around his own small one.

He had been tempted to have it engraved.

But then he had not been able to think of anything appropriate.

What did a man put on the ring he was giving to a woman he had only met four times, talked to three times, and who was marrying him only to save herself from a fate she deemed more dreadful than tying herself to a near-stranger?

So, he had left it as it was.

Aunt Eliza had looked surprised when he had asked its whereabouts, but had not argued—merely shown him to the location where it rested in one of his mother's jewelry boxes.

Now his aunt sat in a pew on one side of the church, and Hugh was beside him. Other than that, it was empty save for the minister who was presumably lurking somewhere close by.

Shadows darkened the nave. The two men turned their heads to see three figures standing in the open doorway.

One was Gwendolen, holding her son by the hand.

The third was her sister, Rosalind Gardner, a petite plump girl with ringlets the same golden shade as the countess's own.

"Who is the girl?" Hugh whispered.

"Her sister," Angel hissed back. His eyes passed over Rosalind and Henry, and came back to rest on his bride.

Gwendolen glowed so brightly that he could hardly look away as the trio approached. She wore a pale green silk dress that hugged her softly curving figure. Her fair hair was braided and circled her head like a crown. He had never seen the style on a woman before. There was something sweet and rustic about it that made her look even younger than usual.

Only the little boy hanging on her arm reminded him she was a mother, and a widow besides.

He shook off a twinge of jealousy at the thought of the countess's first husband. He had been an older man. That did not mean he had been an inadequate lover. Angel had only grown in experience over the years. He wondered how much of her husband's experience the countess had picked up.

It was utterly irrelevant as the marriage would never be consummated. After all, he had assured her.

"You certainly picked a stunner," Hugh said admiringly. "Still absolutely certain this will be merely a marriage of convenience?" He shot Angel a sardonic look.

"Of course," Angel replied, a little stiffly.

Hugh had been enlightened as to the reasons behind the hasty marriage. He was a close friend. What was more, Angel was confident he would have dug the truth out eventually. Anyhow, it was not as if Hugh would treat Gwendolen with anything less than the respect owing to Lord Englefield's bride and duchess. He might be a mocking knave, but he also had three sisters and knew how to treat a lady.

The trio approached. Rosalind kissed Gwendolen on the cheek before taking Henry by the hand and leading him to an empty pew. Was it Angel's imagination or had Gwendolen's sister winked at him?

The minister had appeared, as if by magic, and was now clearing his throat, obviously ready to begin.

Angel looked into Gwendolen's eyes as she came to stand before him. He saw something there he had seen before: fear. Her lips were pressed tightly together, and she seemed reluctant to meet his gaze.

He looked down to where her hands were clasped together and reached out his own to gently tug them apart. When he had her cool, smaller hands in his own larger, warm ones, he leaned forward to speak into her ear.

"It is not too late for second thoughts. You may yet change your mind." He squeezed her hands a little as he spoke, for encouragement —though for himself or for her, he was not sure.

His words hung in the air for a moment.

Then he felt the pressure returned. She shook her head carefully and forced a small smile to her lips.

"As long as you are sure," he whispered, stepping back a little but not letting go.

He nodded to the minister and the service began. It was a ritual of words they had all heard before.

He glanced over to where Hugh sat beside Aunt Eliza and saw his friend raise his eyebrows and then look pointedly at their joined hands.

He decided to strangle Hugh later, perhaps on the church steps. But before the wedding breakfast. Definitely before.

The minister was droning on. His voice was not made for public speaking, being more the soporific sort than the charismatic.

Nevertheless, Angel found some of the familiar words permeating his mind.

"...not by any to be enterprised, nor taken in hand, unadvisedly, lightly, or wantonly, to satisfy men's carnal lusts and appetites..."

He gulped.

Looking downwards to avoid meeting his bride's eye, he found himself staring at her ample bosom which had the least wanted effect. Lush swelling curves with that most tantalizing of valleys dipped down into her bodice, leaving it to Angel's vivid imagination to picture the soft skin that lay beneath, to think of how it would feel to cup those breasts, bare, in his palm...

He jerked his gaze away and looked resolutely at the minister instead, which had the desired effect. The man was short, stout, and had a sheen of sweat on his red forehead.

"...but reverently, discreetly, advisedly, soberly..."

Awful lot of adverbs. One couldn't help wondering who had written the service in the first place. Mentioning "carnal lust" seemed in very bad form on a man's wedding day. Angel thought of all of the hundreds and thousands of men, probably most of them young idiots much like himself, who must have stood uncomfortably through the same recitation, struggling not to fill their minds with exactly the kinds of fantasies as the minister was decrying.

"...ordained for the mutual society, help, and comfort, that the one ought to have of the other..."

Well, that was all right then. Help and comfort. The very things he had in mind. His goals were noble ones. Sacred even, you might say.

He stood a little straighter and even let his eyes roam away from the minister's shiny forehead and back to his intended. Her face, mind you—only her face.

"...why they may not lawfully be joined together, let him now speak, or else hereafter for ever hold his peace..."

If he had not turned back, he would not have seen the countess stiffen at these words or notice the change in tenseness of her hands.

Angel thought he knew what she must be afraid of and he glanced around the church. There was no one there but themselves and their guests. No menacing figure lurked in the shadows.

He applied a little pressure to Gwendolen's hands and when she met his eyes, smiled reassuringly.

She seemed about to return the smile, but as the minister's voice shifted to a sterner tone her face fell.

"...if either of you know any impediment, why ye may not be lawfully joined together in Matrimony, ye do now confess it. For be ye well assured, that so many as are coupled together otherwise than God's Word doth allow are not joined together by God; neither is their Matrimony lawful..."

The countess had lowered her eyes and turned pale. Angel felt her hands begin to tug away, but stubbornly he gripped them tighter, giving his own little tug in return until she looked up again.

He shook his head at her slightly. None of that now, he tried to say with only his expression to convey it.

He had no idea what she had been reminded of. Nothing good, clearly.

But whatever it was, whatever fear or secret sin she fretted over, he determined, he did not care.

He simply did not care. What was it someone had said in the Bible? Let he who was without sin cast the first stone?

Well, he—the Duke of Englefield to some, Englefiend to others— was certainly not one of those. There would be no stone throwing. Not today, not ever.

The color was returning slowly to his bride's face as the service continued.

Angel decided he did not like this minister. His pious tone, the extra emphasis he had placed upon certain passages. This was his family's parish but the minister had changed recently and Angel had not attended regularly enough to notice much difference.

The former vicar had been hearty and warm, even jolly you might say. If he were performing the service, Angel felt sure Gwendolen would not be as uncomfortable.

Finally, the service drew to a close.

The ring slid over Gwendolen's finger, fitting like a glove.

The vows were recited, quickly and quietly.

And then their hands dropped apart and they turned to face their audience.

They were now man and wife.

And yet Angel felt oddly hollow, as if he had lost something when he had let go of his bride's hand.

As if they had returned to being strangers once more.

The deed was done.

The wedding party had returned to Sweetbriar Hall, the Englefields' London residence.

The house was formerly known as Englefield Hall, Angel had explained. When his mother married his father, she had decided it was a dull-sounding name and had renamed it, more in jest at first, Sweetbriar for the wild roses which grew in the back gardens. Angel's father had liked the name, taken it up, and it had stuck ever since.

A little brass plaque next to the door displayed the name proudly. Gwendolen touched it with a finger as she passed through the doorway. Her new home. It still felt too strange to be real.

She had been, if not happy, then content at Leicester House. It had been familiar and comfortable. Mere blocks from Hyde Park, she had enjoyed taking Henry there most days in the summer. The location was convenient for shopping and paying visits.

By contrast, Sweetbriar bordered Green Park and was far less house than it was mansion.

Or small palace.

It was a beautiful but imposing home. The layout was Palladian style with a *corps de logis* flanked by two service wings, with a neoclassical exterior facade of Bath stone with a high six-column portico. Elaborate cast iron railings led around the front of the house.

Approaching it for the first time, Gwendolen could not help but wonder what Angel would think of little Orchard Hill. Did he realize he had married a woman of genteel but modest origins, with scant family fortune? And after growing up in a place like this, she could easily understand why such mundane matters as money were irrelevant to a duke.

Entering the hall, they quickly went through the customary greeting of the new duchess by the staff. Gwendolen made note of names and spoke warmly to each individual, but had previously made it clear that she would defer to Angel's aunt on household matters.

She already felt like a usurper by coming into an established household. Not to mention the disruption of bringing a child. She did not wish to butt heads over anything so trivial as a dinner menu.

A brief introduction to Angel's aunt had also given her the instant impression that Eliza was a woman with strong opinions who was likely set in her ways of doing things. Fortunately, Gwendolen was used to living with someone exactly like this. The earl had an already established system when they had married and she had done very little to disrupt it.

Aunt Eliza had lived at Sweetbriar House since the death of Angel's parents. She had come to London to make arrangements in the event of their death, for—as Angel had explained—he had refused to leave his regiment and return home, despite having the title thrust upon him unexpectedly. She had not asked again. Merely handled matters herself and remained in London until he returned.

Shortly after that, the Battle of Salamanca had begun. It was nearly a year before he had finally shipped back to England. After that, Angel and his aunt had gotten on so well together he had not thought of her leaving.

Gwendolen understood. It must have been awful enough to know his parents would never walk the halls of Sweetbriar again. At least Eliza had been a familiar presence.

Two hours later, a delectable wedding breakfast had been enjoyed by the small party in the dining room. Heartier fare was included, as well as biscuits, puddings, chocolate rolls and, of course, a wedding cake—proudly produced by the household's cook and delivered on a silver tray by two footmen.

Henry had noted the elaborately decorated fruit cake with great interest and ate two large slices.

When Hugh announced they must save a piece of the cake to be eaten at their first child's christening in a year or two, Gwendolen blushed wildly. Perhaps Angel had not enlightened his best friend as to all aspects of their nuptial agreement.

If Angel was shooting arrows from his eyes at Hugh, Gwendolen was doing the same with Rosalind.

Her sister had met the duke only once before the wedding and briefly at that. Yet today she was behaving as if she had known him much longer, casting knowing looks in his direction with a twinkle in her eye. Gwendolen had even seen her give Angel a friendly poke with her elbow when she seemed to think he had been staring at his bride too long.

This had gone on all throughout the wedding breakfast, where Rosalind had been seated across from Angel next to Henry, until Gwendolen, sitting next to Angel, finally delivered a sharp kick to her ankle beneath the table. She smiled sweetly when Rosalind squeaked and glared back.

"What the blazes is your sister doing?" Angel whispered from beside her. He had been busily polishing off a plate full of ham, eggs, hot buttered-rolls, and an exceedingly large mound of bacon and so had not been the most active conversationalist.

Gwendolen realized there was no way around it.

"She thinks we're in love."

Angel looked more amused than annoyed. "What?"

"I couldn't tell her I was marrying you because...you know!" She hissed. "I had to make this sound...well, real."

"You don't know Rosalind," she added miserably, pushing her chair back from the table. The others were standing and making their way through the adjoining door into the drawing room. "She has a nose like a bloodhound when it comes to sniffing things out."

"Secrets, you mean? Secrets one might not even share—" he paused dramatically. "—-with one's own husband?"

Gwendolen glared.

"Come, let's have none of that, my sweet..." he paused.

"You were going to say angel, weren't you?" She rolled her eyes.

"...cherub. My dear, darling cherub."

"Cherubs are short, fat, and generally children. Male ones. Not the finest compliment I've received."

"What's this sentimental claptrap I hear you spouting, nephew?" Angel's Aunt Eliza had wandered over unobserved and now appeared diverted. "Singing praises to our new bride, are we?"

She took a swig from the glass of brown liquid she was carrying. Gwendolen picked up a familiar aroma. This must be where Angel had picked up his penchant for whisky.

Angel was looking a tad uncomfortable at having his faux romantic jests overheard.

"What's the matter, my darling sugar lump?" Gwendolen asked, touching his arm lightly, unable to resist the urge to tease him. "Surely you are not embarrassed by our love?"

"Oh-ho! Love is it?" Angel's friend Hugh joined the group, which only left Rosalind who was on the other side of the room watching with unconcealed interest.

"Englefield finally in love," Hugh was musing. "To think I'd live to see the day."

"You make it sound as if you were Methuselah," Angel said, a little crossly.

"Undoubtedly as wise, if not in years," Hugh answered promptly. "But come now, do not let us intrude on what was surely an intimate moment of whispered sweet nothings."

"Angel was just calling his lovely bride his 'cherub,'" Eliza offered.

"Oh yes, it is his favorite endearment for me," Gwendolen explained brightly, deciding there was nothing for it but to join in the fun. She tucked her arm into Angel's. It was a very solidly built arm, she noticed. She had to resist the sudden urge to run her hand along it. "Second only to sweet dumpling."

"So, so touching," Hugh murmured, looking at his friend with a glint in his eye. "But then, he's always been rather soft."

"Soft, am I?" Angel looked down at Gwendolen accusingly. She put on what she hoped was an angelic smile. "Soft, you say? Well, then, I suggest you both vacate the vicinity and let this soppy, doting bridegroom have a moment of peace with his..."

"Cherub?" Hugh supplied helpfully. "Oh, please, have no qualms on our account. It's a beautiful sight to behold, is it not, Eliza?"

"Excessively heartwarming." Aunt Eliza took another sip.

"You have not even kissed your bride, Lord Englefield," a bell-like voice belonging to a female devil chirped from across the room. It appeared Rosalind had the ears of a bloodhound, too.

A dangerous spark appeared in Angel's eyes. Gwendolen gulped. Perhaps she had taken things too far.

"I have not, have I?" he said thoughtfully.

"Not even a little one! Not even on the cheek like Mummy kisses me," Henry's little voice added loudly.

Good Lord, they were conspiring against her.

She tried to untuck her arm from Angel's so she might step away. Or step out the door entirely. She was experiencing a longing for a nice quiet nap.

"Not even a little one," Angel repeated.

He grinned, widely and wickedly, the expression transforming his handsome face into something beyond handsome, beyond charming, far beyond what a man had any right to be.

With a quick pull and a twirl, she was in his arms.

His lips were on hers before she could duck away or even turn her head as she had done with Cecil.

But this was no Cecil.

Cecil was a pitiful excuse of a man compared to this Adonis who held her now, gently but firmly applying his lips to hers.

She might even have swooned, if she were the swooning type, and if Angel's hands were not wrapped so stubbornly yet pleasantly around her waist.

She had never been kissed this way. Even when she had thought herself in love with Wyndham, his kisses had been of a different sort. She did not care to recall them. The earl had never kissed her on the lips. A peck on the cheek from time to time, like a kind father might.

Not like a husband.

This was most certainly a husband's kiss. She felt as if she were being claimed, body and soul, before all these witnesses.

Why, if kisses could be like this, then what need of marriage services were there? When a simple kiss could speak such volumes and be so much more pleasurable besides.

But through the haze, a voice inside of her said this was not that kind of kiss at all. These were mere byproducts, unintendedly produced emotions.

Angel was kissing her for spectacle, for show, to prove a point. Nothing more.

And so, she did not kiss him back.

After a moment longer he released her and dropped his arms.

Hugh was whooping, Aunt Eliza was clapping, Rosalind was beaming, and Henry was looking rather shocked.

"That is not how Mummy kisses me," he announced, and the room filled with laughter.

Gwendolen stole a glance at Angel. He was smiling but as he looked back at her she saw something else there besides mirth. Whatever it was, it was unfathomable. She did not know him well enough to identify it.

She looked away.

She had not kissed him back.

Angel felt ashamed. In the spirit of the moment, he had swept her into his arms as if she were a serving girl. Or worse.

He had stolen the kiss, thinking only of silencing Hugh and startling his aunt enough that she dropped her whisky (she had not).

He had not considered how unwanted the gesture might be to his new duchess.

Nor how much he would enjoy doing it.

Her lips had been soft as rose petals, opening up to him instinctively. He had planned for it to be only the briefest of kisses, but when his lips met hers, the sensation had been intoxicating, like sipping sweet ambrosia.

What trite swill was this? Angel gave himself a shake.

She had not kissed him back.

He would apologize as soon as they found a moment alone.

Which, he decided, must be quite soon based on the subtle but bawdy jokes Hugh was now making about seeing the newlyweds to their bedchamber. Rosalind was laughing as he spoke. Her happiness had brought a pretty color to her cheeks and Angel could now more easily see her resemblance to her older sister.

She was not half so pretty though. Not in his view.

He looked for Gwendolen. She had scooped Henry up and now stood by a window, holding him and talking softly. Blithely ignoring Hugh, which was just as well.

He crossed over to them.

The little lad has his cheek pressed against his mother's shoulder. He looked at Angel with halfhearted interest through drowsy eyes.

"This little one needs a nap, I believe," Gwendolen said ruefully. "A certain aunt kept a certain boy up far too late last night playing with blocks and telling stories."

"Not to mention all of the rum-soaked wedding cake he devoured," Angel said, smiling at the lad.

"I'm n-n-not sleepy," Henry protested, trying to stifle a yawn.

"Would you like me to carry him upstairs?" Angel asked quietly.

"Oh, would you?" She looked relieved. Not angry then. The kiss had probably been as insignificant to her as she thought it had been to him. "He's become so much heavier the past few months; it is a bit of a struggle. Though I could ring for a footman…"

Angel was already shaking his head and reaching for Henry. He lifted the little boy gently from his mother's arms, trying not to let her nearness distract him. She smelled like roses. Not overly cloying like that scent could be on other women he had known, but soft and sweet mixed with a hint of something that was all her own and which was going straight to his addlepated brain.

Henry squirmed, trying to get back to his mother. Then he gave up, too sleepy to struggle, and put his head against Angel's chest.

Gwendolen whispered to her sister before following Angel out of the room as he walked towards one of the two huge winding mahogany staircases in the main hall which led up to the east wing.

They walked in silence a moment before Angel got the words out.

"I'm sorry."

She looked perplexed.

"For...you know. Back there." He inclined his head. "Hugh goaded me but I should not have let his goading to cause me to act so discourteously."

He snuck a look. She was staring straight ahead as she walked.

He heard her sigh.

"I suppose most would say there is nothing discourteous about a man kissing his own wife," she said.

"No, but you and I are not everyone and knowing what kind of arrangement we agreed on, I should not have taken the liberty."

"Yes, well..." She gave him a tight-lipped smile. "All is well. There is no harm done."

They were nearly at the door to Henry's bedchamber. Gwendolen pushed down the handle quietly, then crossed to draw the heavy curtain, then pull back the coverlet. Entering the dim, shadowy room, Angel placed the boy gently on the bed, then stood back as his mother tucked the blanket around him and kissed his cheek softly.

It was the sweetest of scenes, as far as Angel was concerned.

From curricle races and bordellos, he had somehow strayed so far that he saw real beauty in this simple moment. In a mother loving her child.

His throat felt constricted as he remembered his own mother's tender touch. Looking at Gwendolen and Henry made him wonder what his own children would have been like.

He had claimed not to want any. Well, he had given his word on that.

He supposed he could always keep a mistress, have children in that way—he had promised Gwendolen he would never trouble her, that he would live as he had been living, debauched and carefree, had he not?

Only, now it was not as appealing a prospect.

A celibate life for him, then, at least for a while. For the idea of bedding another woman was not as attractive as it had been only a week ago.

He watched Gwendolen smooth back Henry's hair with her newly ringed hand. In profile, her face was as beautiful as a marble sculpture —only the few loose golden tendrils that had come out of her braided crown revealed she was a mortal woman of flesh and blood.

Now that he had spent more time with her, he could acknowledge (though not understand) that not all might find her so exceptional. She was not the tallest of women, nor the shortest. Not the most slender and willowy, nor the most voluptuous. Her hips had seen childbearing, he knew, and it would not have left her unscathed.

But...she was perfect.

And then he knew.

The plague was finally upon him.

He stepped back out into the hallway quietly and leaned against a wall to gather his thoughts.

Letter 8

THE RIGHt Hon. Earl of Leicester to Mrs. Henry Gardner

July 7, 1811

London

My Dear, Dear Friend,

Stevens and I shall leave London for Beauford the day after tomorrow. I send this letter now, by private messenger, to put your mind at rest as quickly as I can.

Of course, Caroline. Of course, I shall help your daughter. I have known Gwendolen since she was a girl. She is a fine young woman. A single mistake does not change that. Our society's standards for women are preposterous, as I'm sure you will agree. We prize their virtue more than their minds.

I do ask that you prepare her, however.

I am sure I am not the man she hoped she would someday marry and she must grieve that loss.

Furthermore, I am not an ideal husband, as you already know. Maria and I shared an understanding. She was a patient woman. My travels take me from England a greater part of the year.

Gwendolen will want for nothing and will be treated with the utmost care and respect, but I will not be an attentive husband—you must see that and understand.

For Stevens and I, the quest is the spice of life. I was not made to sit in a stuffy club or to attend fancy balls or house parties in the country. However, if Gwendolen wishes that sort of a life and attends as Lady Leicester, that is another matter. She shall have her freedom in every way, as far as I am concerned.

Stevens and I send our best wishes for her health.

We shall say no more of the matter which has led to this arrangement, Caroline. Let her find what happiness she can as we each must do. I shall do everything in my power to see that she is content.

As always, I remain your humble servant,

Leicester

P.S. Regardless of what you say, I shall make inquiries into the young man in question. I ask that you provide his name when we arrive. If only a good thrashing were possible. I am not as young as I once was, but I am sure if Stevens held him up, I could knock him down. I am sure your hands itch to do the same. A blackguard if there ever was one to do this to a girl. I promise you on my honor, he will never have opportunity to harm her again while I live.

P.P.S. Stevens has just remarked that it will be a pleasure to have a youngster in the house again and I must second his enthusiasm. It has been quiet for too long. The golden years when Cecil was a little lad passed by all too quickly. To think that now we hardly see one another.

Adieu

Letter 9

THE RIGHT HON. EARL of Leicester to Lord Cecil Gibson

July 10, 1811

London

My Dear Boy,

I hope this letter finds you well and that your travels are bringing you satisfaction. Certainly, the list of expenditures my man of business has been receiving would suggest you are going along in a splendid fashion akin to an ancient emperor on his royal progress.

But I do not write to chide you.

My boy, I shall get to the meat of the matter. By the time this letter reaches you, I shall be wed. "To whom?" I hear you ask. To the daughter of a dear friend. You may recall the family—the Gardners who live near Beauford. The eldest girl, Gwendolen, is to become my wife in two days' time.

I hope you will welcome her upon your return, whenever that may be.

Your loving father

Chapter 9

"ANGEL AND I ARE taking Henry for a walk to the park. Would you care to come along?" Rosalind panted breathlessly, leaning in at the doorway of Gwendolen's new sitting room. Angel had insisted Rosalind use his first name as well, and she had been only too happy to oblige.

Gwendolen's sister's pretty round face was flushed and her hair was a tumble, loosened from its pins—probably thanks to a boisterous little boy who she had spent the morning playing with in the nursery. Rosalind was such an impetuous, warm-hearted young woman. Gwendolen wondered how she would fare when it came her turn to seek a husband.

"You and Angel?"

"Yes, your husband. He lives here, you know," she said, sounding not a little sarcastic. "I sought him out and invited him. Shockingly, he was not averse to the idea of spending time with his new stepson or sister-in-law. And Henry is very eager to have his new Papa along. He has already begun to call Angel that. Have you noticed? I suppose he can hardly remember his own father now, which I know is sad, but perhaps in the long run it will be better for them both." Rosalind paused her gushing and contemplated her sister with narrowing eyes. "You know, for newlyweds supposedly in love, you do not spend an awful lot of time with your husband. One might almost think..." She broke off.

"Think what?" Gwendolen closed the book she had been reading more firmly than she had intended. The idea of her sister going on a walk with her husband and son without her was grating. Rosalind was truly presumptuous.

Of course, part of her knew exactly what her sister was trying to do. A smaller part of her even appreciated it.

Rosalind blushed. "Well, it is none of my business, but..."

"No, it is not," Gwendolen snapped. "How long did you say you would be visiting us?"

Rosalind's face fell. Gwendolen immediately regretted her words.

Rising she went over to the door and put her arms around her sister. "I'm sorry. It's only that... this is all new to me, too. A new house. New people. You are much more comfortable here already with them than I am."

Rosalind sighed. "But Gwendolen, that is exactly what you must change. You cannot simply sit in here day in and day out avoiding him—or Eliza. Dinner is the only time you seem to speak to anyone but myself or Henry."

"I talk to the servants," Gwendolen mumbled.

"You know what I mean." Rosalind crossed her arms. "One might almost think you were...afraid of your husband."

"Or if not afraid," she continued hastily as Gwendolen opened her mouth. "Then...intimidated? Shy as a schoolgirl? Completely cowed by his ridiculously perfect—" She coughed meaningfully. "—face?"

Gwendolen blushed.

"Aha!" Rosalind said triumphantly. "You are! But shy? Really?"

The truth was more complicated. Ever since the kiss, something had changed. She and Angel shared adjoining rooms, but the door between them had never once been opened.

He had been a perfect gentleman in every way, as he had promised. The kiss had been the only slip.

Gwendolen found herself wishing on a regular basis that he would slip again.

But he had not.

Why would he? The kiss had simply been for the sake of a joke.

Now his part in their farce of a marriage was complete. He could go on with his life, knowing that she was safe behind these moated walls. (Truly, moated—a moat ran around Sweetbriar, the original building having been constructed over a century and a half ago and designed to withstand siege.)

What did that life entail for him exactly? Gwendolen only had a vague idea pieced together from their all-too-brief encounters, sardonic comments from his Aunt Eliza, and caricatures she had seen in the papers.

All in all, she had formed a mental collage of liquor and gaming hells, bawds and brothels.

She had to try not to imagine it too closely.

But clearly, the Duke of Englefield had been a wild-living hellion before his marriage.

Not to mention one of the most sought-after bachelors in London, possessing the holy trinity of desirable male qualities, being young, handsome, and rich.

What did it matter if scandal was his middle name? He was a duke. For many matchmaking mamas of the ton, that was enough.

True, Angel was no longer a bachelor, but that did not mean he did not still possess all three.

Which meant he would remain an attractive prospect for many women. Those who saw marriage vows as elastic rather than binding.

After all, what were the bonds of marriage to a man like Angel?

Evidently, he did not take them very seriously, or he would never have married Gwendolen.

She knew that was not fair, not charitable. He had married her for a highly noble—and even romantic—reason: To protect her.

How was she to know she would find herself wanting him to do much more than that?

Rosalind was still waiting for a reply.

She must tread carefully or soon her younger sister would be asking questions along even more indelicate lines—such as her wedding night, and nights thereafter.

After the falsehood she had told Rosalind, it would be humiliating to disclose that there had been no wedding night. Merely a long night of tossing and turning in a strange new bed.

"I will come," she said abruptly. "Is Henry ready? Let me get dressed. I will be down in ten minutes."

It was not a great deal of time, but small boys could not stand still for longer than five minutes and so it was double the amount that was wise.

Fortunately, her maid, Nancy, had deft hands. She also had a small son of her own that she kept in a boarding house somewhere in London. She well understood the haste with which Gwendolen needed to ready herself some days. Regarding Nancy's child, Gwendolen asked no unwanted questions and never would. She had simply refused to dismiss her when John's housekeeper had encouraged her to after it became clear the girl was unwed and increasing.

Some months later, Nancy had returned to service and they had gone on as before—closer than before, even.

Having a secret in common could have that effect, Gwendolen had found.

And if she gave Nancy some pocket money now and then, ostensibly so she could buy treats for her son, no one had to be the wiser for it.

Seven and a half minutes later, Gwendolen walked quickly down the stairs to the main hall.

She had dressed quickly, but composed the outfit with care, and had the pleasure of seeing Angel's eyes widen appreciatively as she came down the steps.

The promenade dress she wore was perfectly suited to the warm spring day. It was also extremely becoming—an ivory muslin that clung to her womanly curves (even more womanly after having Henry, but not unattractively so, she suspected...not that anyone had ever told her), with a square neckline that was not immodestly low but certainly aided the imagination along. An emerald green and gold velvet sash hugged her waist while an Indian shawl composed of rich greens, reds, and yellows hung loosely from her arms. Her hair hung in loose curls around her face—more the result of a lack of time than style, but she felt fairly confident it was flattering in a girlish way.

Rosalind shot her a wink which left Gwendolen in no doubt.

"Are we ready?" she asked brightly. Angel stepped forward with his arm and a smile.

Rosalind conveniently gained a lead as she walked ahead with Henry.

Angel appreciated his sister-in-law's quick pace, for it meant he was finally able to have a moment alone with his bride

"I believe you have been avoiding me, my lady-wife," he drawled, trying to sound casual while stealing a closer look at his companion.

Gwendolen's bonnet covered her crown of gold hair, but a few stray curls peeped out. She put up a hand to tuck one away and he saw the flash of the gold ring on her finger.

His ring.

His heart quickened a little. Knowing she wore his ring did something to him.

Something in the vicinity of his heart and if he was being honest, at times in the vicinity of his trousers. Perhaps the idea of possessing a woman was more of a primal instinct than he had realized.

Though he did *not* possess her, had not possessed her. Not in the way his body wished he had.

Under the law he knew he actually owned her. But he would never think of any woman that way, as a piece of property—Aunt Eliza would kick him most unpleasantly if he ever dared.

Yes, his pretty new duchess was his. But in name only.

He could easily imagine possessing her in other ways. For an instant he allowed himself to imagine lying her down naked with only that glorious bright shawl beneath, stripping off his clothes and covering her with... He swallowed hard and averted his eyes.

"The house is large, I know, and easy to get lost in," he continued. "But you would think we would encounter one another more often than we have this past week. Have I done something to disturb you? Please say the word if so. I assure you; I am not easily offended. Or perhaps it is the running of the house itself? The cook served fish when you would have preferred beef. The footmen are not handsome or young enough. Our butler is not as crochety as your last..."

"No, no. Nothing like that." He heard the smile in her voice with relief. "Your butler is perfectly cranky enough, thank you. And besides, I have not been avoiding you."

A pause. "I mean, I have. But you have done nothing wrong."

He raised his eyebrows. "Nothing wrong, but also nothing right? Are you so unhappy already?"

Angel had spent more of his week at home than he had in years. He had ignored invitations from friends to join them at the club... and other less proper places. Instead, he spent hours in the library with books, brandy, and cheroot.

He had also taken to loitering rather embarrassingly outside the nursery, hoping to catch Gwendolen visiting her son, but his timing never seemed to coincide with hers, and as a result he had simply wound up spending many hours playing building blocks and reading fairy stories to a demanding little chap with boundless energy and endless questions about every element of existence.

A little boy who had also asked if he might call Angel "Papa."

That would be a conversation for another day, he decided.

"No, not at all!" Gwendolen was exclaiming. "Truly, I assure you, Your Gr—" She caught herself. "Angel. I assure you, there is nothing wrong. I am as happy as I can be." She gave a little smile.

"As happy as you can be..." He rolled the words over his tongue slowly. Well, that was simply not good enough. He began to open his mouth to tell her so and to demand what he might do to improve her level of happiness when two figures coming towards them caught his attention.

"I say, is that...?" he began.

"Cecil," Gwendolen said, sounding dismayed.

Rosalind and Henry had already crossed over to the park-side of the street and were entering a grove of trees. There would be no buffer there.

"And Lady Julia Pembroke," Angel murmured, recognizing the young woman walking beside Lord Leicester.

He felt Gwendolen's hand tighten instinctively on his arm, and equally instinctively placed his other hand on top of it, giving a gentle squeeze.

"Stick with me, I'll see you through," he assured her quietly.

"Why, Lord Leicester! Lady Julia. How delightful to see you both. Are you not just the picture of perfection together. Truly, a perfectly matched pair. Do you not agree, my dear?"

Lord Leicester could not have been much older than himself, Angel realized, looking at the man more closely this second time. Perhaps even younger. He was not especially handsome, though neither was he repulsive. He was dark-haired like Julia, and a little shorter than Angel—which Angel took pleasure in noting. The most striking thing about Cecil was the arrogant expression he seemed to constantly wear.

In that way, he was Julia's perfect match for she was the picture of ton haughtiness, her beautiful eyes already honed in on Gwendolen, as if knowing her for her rival.

"Why, you must be cousins!" Angel was continuing, getting into the swing of things. "Or brother and sister! There is such a strong resemblance between you. Do you not agree, my love?"

"We are not related, you id—" Cecil began, only to be cut-off in a wordless grunt as Julia give him a sharp jab to the stomach with her elbow. He glared at her.

"Your Graces," Julia said, much more calmly, with an attempt at a radiant smile. "What dear Cecil means to say is that we are, in fact, affianced."

"Lud!" Angel grinned like a fool, not entirely sure why he was deciding to play the role. On second thought, that was not quite true. Something about Cecil brought out the devil in him and playing the part of the dimwitted knave who his stepmother had chosen as a new husband seemed to irk the man beyond belief. "You're telling me a Banbury Tale! She's your sister, tell the truth now."

Taking a page from Julia, Angel gave Cecil a hearty jab of faux camaraderie, feeling satisfied when he felt his elbow meet an unexpectedly soft exterior. "Well, don't I feel like a chucklehead. Your children will be alike as peas in a pod, I dare say."

Cecil seemed exceedingly willing to agree with his former point. His mouth opened with a sneer, but Lady Julia's hand remained firmly pressed on his arm, so reluctantly he closed it again.

Angel bowed gracefully, without letting go of Gwendolen's arm, which was no small feat.

"May I offer my sincere congratulations to you both."

"Thank you, Your Grace," Lady Julia replied, batting her eyelashes and rewarding him with a pretty smile. One had to admire her—she was persistent in her fawning.

In fact, she had yet to take her eyes off him and acknowledge his new bride, he realized.

Recalling how Lady Julia had cut his duchess ruthlessly the last time they met, Angel decided he was going to enjoy this next part.

"Lady Julia, Lord Leicester—allow me to present to you my new bride, the Duchess of Englefield." He turned proudly to Gwendolen, which was no pretense—she was looking extremely lovely this afternoon. Though he could not help but notice she had drawn her shawl more closely around her upon Cecil's approach. "Of course, I am sure that your fiancée has already enlightened you as to his stepmother's newfound joy."

Lady Julia merely appeared perplexed. Genuinely so. Her eyes had widened and, if Angel hadn't known better, he would almost have believed he'd seen a tremor in her lower lip.

Was she pretending to be shocked? To care? Or had Cecil truly not informed her?

It was possible. It was also more than possible that Lord Leicester had not informed his fiancée of the way Angel had caught him accosting his stepmother.

Now that she was engaged to the worm, Angel felt something very like pity for her. Of course, finding out her fiancé had tried to maul his wife would most likely only add to her enmity towards Gwendolen.

He wondered how and why that enmity had begun in the first place. For such a beautiful young woman, Julia was certainly not a happy-seeming one.

"I wish you both marital felicity equal to what I have found with my bride." He finished, smiling cherubically at Julia and awaiting her reply.

But unexpectedly, she was silent a moment, staring first at Angel then at Gwendolen, with something inexplicable in her expression.

Finally, she quietly said, "You must be joking."

"I assure you, I am not," he replied politely. "The announcement was in the Times at least two days past. We were married a week ago." Gwendolen said nothing. He squeezed her hand gently and after a moment felt a slight return of pressure.

"Why, less than two weeks ago, we were..." Lady Julia began, before evidently thinking better of it.

"Two weeks ago, you and I were sharing a delightful stroll through Hyde Park when we encountered Lady Leicester and her son. Yes, indeed. My interest was piqued that very day thanks to the special notice you gave her." He winked impishly, deciding to maintain his presentation of the fool in love. "I proceeded to hunt down the mystery lady and—voila! Here we are today. Man and wife. Newlyweds. In heavenly bliss."

"How exceedingly odd," Lady Julia mused, tapping a finger to her lip. Ah, now this was more like the Julia he had seen in the park.

"Is it? How so?" He kept smiling.

"You say you are married, but…" She waved a hand dismissively. "Oh, it is no matter."

"Do go on, we are all ears. Are we not, my dear?"

"Well, it is just that, my cousin Redmond—"

"Your cousin!" Gwendolen exclaimed. Angel felt her arm quiver under his hand.

Lady Julia blinked innocently. "Why yes, the Earl of Redmond is my mother's sister's son. He mentioned that he and Lady Leicester were…" She waved her hand again. "Well, it is no matter. I must have misheard."

"You must have indeed, Julia," Gwendolen said softly, speaking for the first time. "Shall we, Angel?"

Lady Julia's lips pursed sourly. In a few more years, they would be permanently positioned that way, Angel decided. Julia seemed set on a course to unhappiness—or at least a life of bitterness. Marrying Cecil would certainly not improve her outlook.

With a last congratulatory word to the other couple, Angel led his wife away, fully expecting to be struck down by lighting at any moment for telling such falsehoods regarding their hoped for happiness.

"Their children will be tiny serpents, rather than babes," he said quietly as they walked.

He heard Gwendolen make a sound. It might have been the start of a laugh or the start of a sob.

He looked over to see which it was. Perhaps a mix of both. It was difficult to say.

"I could not help but notice that you and the esteemed Lady Julia have some history together."

"My husband was close friends with her father. Before we wed, John used to visit their home often." She hesitated. "She has never been particularly...warm towards me."

That was a charitable understatement.

"My husband was a widower for many years before we married. Julia was just a girl, but she adored John, looked up to him immensely. Perhaps it is silly, but I believe she had some hopes of..."

"...Retaining her title and place in the peerage by wedding her father's friend?" Angel finished. "Yes, I see."

An older, manageable widower no less. One with considerable wealth—he had had his man check into the earl's state of affairs.

When the late Lord Leicester passed, he was in no way insolvent. Yet he had left his young wife and son unprovided for. Angel could still not wrap his mind around that. Gwendolen did not mention him often, but nothing she said suggested he had been an unkind man.

Cecil had fallen far from the tree.

He hesitated a second, then dove in. "Have you met this Earl of Redmond fellow before?"

A pause. She nodded.

"And...?" When there was only silence, he went on. "The name evidently means something to you. Not something very pleasant by the look of it. Won't you..."

"Will you take me back to the house?" she said abruptly, as if she had thought of something. "I wish to return immediately. If you would like to continue on and find Rosalind and Henry in the park, I can easily make my own way back."

They had only walked two blocks. Sweetbriar was not more than five minutes away. He had no doubt she was capable of returning unescorted. But he was not about to allow her to walk alone.

"I will escort you back," he said, trying not to let his frustration show. "But..."

"Then will you send a footman for Rosalind and Henry? Just as soon as we return, please. I wish for... I wish for Henry to return home." There was a beseeching look in her eyes.

He nodded.

They turned back to the house. Angel was still not sure what had gone wrong. All he knew was that somehow everything had.

Angel trudged upstairs, loosening his cravat and unbuttoning his tail coat as he went.

He was tired and ready for bed.

Gwendolen had not come down to dinner.

He had made pleasant conversation with Aunt Eliza and Rosalind, and hoped they had not seen how forced his smiles had been.

After, he had retired to his study where he had slouched in a chair, where he smoked and drank more madeira than he'd intended, while staring vacantly out the window into the London night wondering what the devil haunted his new bride.

It was like a Gothic novel. Melodramatic tripe with a maddening plot. Secrets were at the heart of it. If this were a novel, surely the secrets would soon be revealed. He was not as confident of that in his own story.

Obviously, this Redmond fellow Lady Julia had mentioned had something to do with it all.

He was an earl, Lady Julia had said.

He also seemed to inspire instant unease in Gwendolen.

As well as fear for her child's safety.

Which meant he was most likely the man from the bridge.

If he was, Angel would soon tell him where he could go and what he might do with his damned threats and malice. While dangling him over the deep end of the Thames... did the Thames have an end deeper than the other? Well, regardless, he would hang the man off the bridge over the water until he had felt a particle of the fear he had made Gwendolen feel.

And it would feel good to do so, Angel knew. He had had a taste of bloodshed. The animal rush of adrenaline. Satisfying and terrible. The horrific violence between men that left an indelible print on one's soul, yet left some men thirsting for more.

Angel was not such a man. He preferred a fair fight with his fists, any day.

But this was not a fair fight. Someone was playing entirely by his own rules.

He passed by his duchess's bedchamber door and opened his own. His poor valet, Brown, had gone to bed long ago. Thank goodness men's clothing was much easier to get out of than women's.

He had just begun untucking his shirt when he heard Gwendolen scream.

It was an abbreviated scream—as if she had tried to stifle it midway.

Or as if someone had.

And at that thought, Angel's heart leapt into his mouth. He barged through the door that linked their two rooms without another thought.

She was alone.

There was no masked intruder with a hand over her mouth.

It was her own hand, and it still rested there as she stood staring towards the bed.

He took in the scene, looking first to his wife. She appeared unharmed. She was in her nightclothes. A white cotton rail that made her look child-like at first. It was not as high necked as the ones Aunt Eliza sometimes wore under her dressing gown some mornings, nor did she have on one of those infernal white caps. Her hair was loosely braided and hung down her back, nearly to her... Well, her hair was much longer than he had realized until now. A beautiful golden cord.

The cap sleeves left her arms bare and he could see the skin puckered with goosebumps.

His eyes shifted to the bed and he saw the white folded square on her pillow, sealed with red wax.

Before she could stop him, he strode over and ripped it open.

She let out a wordless cry of protest, but it was too late. He scanned quickly.

"Gwen,

You will not keep him from me. I shall have him in the end.

You merely delay the inevitable.

R."

Letter 10

THE Right Hon. Countess of Leicester to Mrs. Henry Gardner

September 7, 1811

London

Dear Mother,

Thank you for the package of books. It was a comfort to see those familiar covers revealed beneath the brown wrapping paper. John (it still feels strange to call him that after addressing him as Lord Leicester for my whole childhood, but he insists) has given me a very pretty morning room to do with as I like, and of course, one full wall of shelves is already full of books. The earl has a wide collection in the library already, but this will be my own. As many novels as I may please to purchase will soon fill them. I have special ordered extra copies of some recent favorites to send to you and the girls. I remember how precious a good book can be during a long country winter.

You asked if I am well. I am, thank you. My stomach has finally settled, it seems. John's physician says I am in good health and that all is as it should be.

I look forward to your visit next month and wish it were even sooner.

My husband will soon depart England again, with Stevens, of course, and I will be quite alone. They have had the expedition planned for some time and John saw no reason to put it off.

I quite understand and know it is nothing to complain over. He leaves me with every comfort. He is kind, considerate, and thoughtful. But... it is a large house, especially compared to homey Orchard Hill. And I know he will not return for some months, perhaps not until next summer. It will be strange to spend the winter months alone and without all of you.

Until then, I am not so alone. Stevens has helped me to feel more at home and visits me some mornings to share coffee and regale me with travel tales.

Speaking of Stevens, there is a matter of delicacy I wish to broach. Perhaps it would be better to speak of in person but I find it cannot wait. I have put it off for weeks already.

My husband has yet to visit my bedchamber.

There. It is said.

Not once since we married. Now I must admit that the waiting is becoming intolerable. I begin to think he may never come. Have I done something wrong? Something to displease him? He does not act as if I have. But I cannot help but wonder. He knows my past and I did not think it...repulsed him.

But who can say.

It is not as if I mind sleeping alone. I cannot say I wish for nightly visits.

But... is this what it is to be like? I know that you have known John for many years, Mother. I know you might say more if you chose.

I hope you will choose to when you visit. Please, help to put my mind at rest. I do wish to be as good a wife as I can, under the circumstances.

I miss you, and my sisters. It is too quiet here.

Kiss the girls for me and Gracie twice.

Love,

Your Gwen

Chapter 10

"WHAT THE BLOODY HELL!" Angel's face hardened as he took in the facts. Someone in his own household must have placed the note there, on his wife's pillow. Perhaps only mere moments ago when she had stepped behind the privacy screen.

He turned around, intending to speak more sternly and insistently than he had that afternoon, to demand to know who "R" was, among other things, only to hear Gwendolen stifle a sob.

Both of her hands covered her mouth.

Unable to scream, unable to cry. Unable to share her secrets.

In an instant he had her enfolded in his arms, shushing her gently like a child.

"Hush now. It will be all right," he murmured.

"Who could have done this?" she whispered, keeping her head pressed tight against him.

Angel set his mouth in a hard line. "I don't know, but I assure you I will find out. Then I'll throw them in the Thames. In a potato sack. Tied tightly. Not even the fishes will be able to reach them to nibble their bones." He hoped to provoke a smile, but she simply burrowed her head against his shoulder, her body trembling like a leaf.

It was utterly endearing.

He tightened his embrace, running a hand gently over her back. The wrapper she wore was thin and he could feel the heat of her body beneath it.

He closed his eyes. She felt incredibly good to hold. Her hair sweet smelling, her body soft and pliant against his chest.

He wished only to provide her with comfort and reassurance, but his body had a will of its own. He opened his eyes again, aware that he was becoming uncomfortably aroused.

His mouth twitched as he contemplated the irony of being embarrassed to be stirred by his own wife.

He sighed and shifted, loosening his arms around her, and stepping back a little.

She tried to cling to him as he did.

Looking down, her eyes were filled with unshed tears.

"Don't go. Don't leave me alone." Her lower lip trembled precariously and in an instant Angel was reminded of another girl, in another place, at another time, who had looked up at him in much the same way.

He hesitated a moment and saw her flinch in disappointment. "No, no, you misunderstand," he said softly, cupping her cheek with one hand. "Wait here, only a moment."

He stepped out into the hall, leaving the door carefully ajar behind him, and flagged down a passing footman. With some relief he saw it was Albert, a Yorkshire lad who had been with them since he was a boy. He was seventeen now and carried out his duties as a footman with the seriousness of a chaplain. There was no way he would have done this thing.

A moment later and the lad was running to the nursery to check on Henry.

Angel stood in the hall, tapping his foot.

Albert reported back quickly: the little boy was asleep, with Miss Rosalind resting beside him. She must have come to tuck him into bed and fallen asleep as well. Henry was safe.

Angel considered rousing his aunt, a formidable ally in any situation, but decided it could wait till morning. He conveyed a few additional instructions to Albert, whose chest puffed up as he strode off, filled with the import of his message. He would relay it to only a few trusted servants, sturdy men one and all.

Tomorrow Angel and his aunt would find the traitor in their house, and then...

But Gwendolen awaited.

He opened the bedchamber door and stepped back in. She was still standing in the middle of the room, looking at the door. She had been standing perfectly still, waiting for him to return. Her fists were clenched at her sides, her body stiff.

Facing him, he could see the night rail she wore was of a gossamer material.

He could see a great deal more than that, in fact.

He quickly averted his eyes, trying not to let himself steal a second look at the lovely full breasts and puckered nipples that begged for his attention. Or the curving hips and rounded thighs, with the ever-so-slightly-dark triangle between.

He would not think on them. He would not.

He raised his eyes nobly to his wife's face.

"Henry is safe. I have a footman stationed at the nursery door. Another man will replace him in a few hours. I trust these men, completely. In the morning, we will find out who did this, I swear to you." He stopped.

"You... wished me to stay?" he asked haltingly. Oh, if only she knew what a wretched beast of a man he was to be thinking of her so lewdly as she stood there frightened.

She nodded slowly. "Angel..." He saw her bite her lip. To stop from asking for what she wanted? What she needed?

Then he understood.

He crossed over, lifted her effortlessly, and carried her to her bed. The coverlet was already drawn back—the note had been tucked beneath on a pillow, waiting for her to turn down the bed to notice it.

His blood boiled as he thought of the gall of the one who had planned such a thing, of the servant who had crept through his house at night, and left such poison in his wife's bed.

Taking a deep breath to calm himself, he lay her down carefully, then went around to the other side. Gallantly, he spread himself out on top of the coverlet beside her, leaving at least a foot of space between them.

"Shall I stay until you fall asleep?" he murmured.

She had immediately curled up and turned to face him, her blue eyes fixed upon him intently.

"Please."

He wavered, then reached out a hand to brush his knuckles gently over her face. "Go to sleep, my—" He stopped just in time.

He had almost said "my darling." Hurriedly, he removed his hand.

"—Go to sleep, Gwendolen. Rest easy. I am here. Henry is safe."

He yawned, then added, "And your ferocious wildling of a sister is in with him."

Gwendolen's lips turned up a little. "Though she be little, she be fierce."

"I have no doubt of that," Angel agreed.

He pitied anyone who went up against Rosalind Gardner.

Combined with the footmen who would be just outside the door, he felt confident Henry was safe until morning.

Gwendolen's eyes closed. He watched as her body relaxed and sleep stole over her.

She looked peaceful. But he knew she was not, not truly.

She would be soon.

He closed his eyes and promised himself that she would be soon.

In the morning, Angel woke first and experienced a moment of disorientation.

A soft female body was curled in his arms. He could feel her warm breath through the thin fabric of his shirt.

It took a moment to recall where he was. Who she was.

It was not as if it were the first time he had woken with an unfamiliar lady beside him. A nameless beauty he had tumbled for a night. Often through a drunken haze, if he were to be honest.

But it was the first time he had awoken holding a woman he felt this strongly about.

It was terrifying. Feeling so invested in her well-being. Her happiness. Her safety.

Not to mention a small child's.

Was this how his parents had felt about one another? About him?

He could not imagine how much more strongly Gwendolen must feel about her child, her own flesh and blood. The enormous weight of responsibility for a small person.

A small person a ruthless man wished to steal away from her.

He sighed. Secrets to be revealed at another time. Unless he could discover them unaided. Today, he would try.

He loosened his arms, resisting the urge to pull her tighter against him, to lower his mouth to hers and kiss her until she awoke, then slide her nightdress down her shoulders and...

With a groan, he untangled himself and slipped out of the bed. Gwendolen had not stirred.

The gray light of a cloudy dawn was seeping through the curtains. Aunt Eliza had slept long enough.

When Gwendolen opened her eyes, he was gone.

It was as if she had dreamed him.

Seeing the ruffled state of the other side of the bed, she felt relieved. Angel had been there.

All night?

She remembered waking in the dark and finding she had moved much closer towards him in her sleep. He was snoring softly with his arms wrapped around her. She considered shifting and moving away, but that would risk waking him.

Well, that was not the only reason.

She felt safe in his arms.

He had kept on his shirt, but snuggling in closer, she could breathe in the scent of him. With a finger, she lightly traced a line down the linen shirt, watching his face to see if he stirred. A few curling hairs peeked out from above the open neck. In the daylight, she knew they would be golden. How far down did they go? She moved her finger lower until she reached the top of his trousers.

What lay below that boundary was mostly a mystery to her.

What would Angel think if he knew the truth? That her husband had never once held her this way. Had never visited her bedchamber at all in the span of their marriage.

She had never even slept beside a man until now.

It was not as if she had not longed for the earl's nighttime company. Quite the contrary. Although she had been prepared to do her duty, of course.

In fact, once she had finally realized the earl would never visit her bedchamber, she was able to relax and feel much more comfortable around him. And even more grateful than she had been before—for John asked nothing back in exchange for what he had generously given: Safety and the protection of his name. Acceptance of Henry.

Never once did he inquire into her son's parentage. He treated her with respect and with kindness. In spite of her mother's gentle assurances, she could not help but feel it was more than she deserved.

She had thought that was all she would ever receive from a husband.

Even when the earl had died, she did not expect to remarry.

For a few months, she had wondered if she would have more freedom and control over her own life as a widow than before.

But it had been a foolish thought that was not to be.

She did not want to think about that now. She looked at Angel's face instead. Calm and peaceful in his sleep. Boyish with his blonde locks, which fell across his forehead. She touched one gently. It was as soft as it looked. His hair was a little longer than was in style. But she found she liked it. Like Michelangelo's David. Not that she had ever seen the sculpture before. She had never traveled further than London. But the earl had a wide collection of paintings—many of ancient nude men, which had been most enlightening.

She brushed a finger over Angel's lips and he shifted a little, scaring her from her explorations. When after a few minutes he did not move again, she inched closer.

This was very silly, she scolded herself. But she knew she was not going to stop.

She took a deep breath, then brushed her lips lightly against his.

It was the second time their mouths had met.

Kissing a sleeping man was not nearly as pleasurable as one awake. But a part of her had simply yearned to have that touch again.

She lay back with a sigh. It had not been the same. It had merely left her hungry for another taste.

For a true kiss.

What would that be like?

There was a time when she had thought she knew what love and passion were, what a kiss should be.

But then her love had stolen much more than a kiss, and left her alone, raw, and sobbing.

A horrid memory.

The very idea of such a man touching Henry, raising her boy. It could never be.

She would stab him, shoot him—do anything she had to do to stop it. Far better for Henry to have a mother go to the gallows and to live with his grandmother and aunts than to be raised by such a wolf of a man.

Oh, he could be very charming when he chose—she knew that. How cruel a trick to play on a young girl dreaming of love. Not for the first time, she wondered how many other girls' hearts he had stolen only to leave them living a nightmare.

She could never see a man like Angel doing such a thing to a woman.

He might be a scoundrel—he had called himself one—but he was not a fiend. Not a cruel man. Not a rapist.

She wondered what it must be like to be a man, as free as Angel must be. To have such power, vast fortune. Looks and youth besides. To have any woman he chose, whenever he chose.

How-ever he chose.

She knew there were more ways than one, and even in the dark she blushed a little imagining some of the positions she had seen in one of the earl's illustrated folios. Pictures from a far-off place of men and women engaged in acts of pleasure she could never have imagined.

Some very creative indeed.

She wondered if Angel had tried them all.

She wondered if he would still do so.

Well, of course he would. He was a man, wasn't he? He could not be expected to remain a monk.

After all, he had not married her out of desire, merely a misplaced sense of honor. He would need to seek his desires elsewhere. She was sure he would never think of turning to her to satisfy them. Had he not made that clear? That he would never expect it?

He might as well have spoken more plainly and told the truth— that he did not desire it. That he did not want her in such a way. That he saw her as merely a mother, with only a brotherly kind of affection. Had he not said just that in the phaeton the other day?

Christian brotherly love. So noble. So chaste.

Part of her wanted to move out of his arms after that. But she considered when she would next have an opportunity to lie in them again.

Perhaps never.

She stayed.

Eventually, she slept.

Aunt Eliza's face was grim when she entered the breakfast room later that morning. She nodded to Gwendolen, Rosalind, and Henry, then gestured for Angel to follow her out into the hall. Hercules sat on his haunches beside her, panting quietly.

"Who was it?" he asked bluntly. "Tell me quickly so I can throttle the man."

"It was not a man, but a girl. The newest kitchen maid, Sarah. A man approached her when she went to throw out some rubbish and offered her a guinea to deliver a letter." She pursed her lips. "He claimed to be your bride's lover, simply wishing to deliver a *billet-doux*."

Angel clenched his jaw. "Of course, he was not. You know this."

"I shall believe whatever you tell me, Angel," she said matter-of-factly. "I do not know Gwendolen well enough to know one way or another. I trust that you do."

"I do," he assured her firmly. "Where is the girl?"

Aunt Eliza looked uncomfortable. "She is still in the kitchen. It was a single error in judgement, Angel. If we dismissed her, she would be out on the streets, without a reference, without a..."

"It's all right," he cut her off. His aunt was far more tender-hearted than she wished anyone to know. "I understand." He ran a hand over his face. "I wish to speak to the girl, to ask her what the man looked like."

"You may try, but I have already asked. All she could recall was that he was about your height, dressed all in black, with a hooded cloak pulled up over his head, and grey eyes."

"That is not exactly enough for a Bow Street Runner to go on," Angel acknowledged, with disappointment.

"If this man is as dangerous as you seem to believe, then he will be back, will he not?"

Angel nodded. "Aunt Eliza..." He paused, debating a moment. It would be foolish not to trust her. "I believe it is Henry the man is primarily after. Not Gwendolen."

"That little boy?" His aunt looked shocked. She had already become quite fond of the lad. Hercules enjoyed having a new inhabitant in the house who had boundless energy for running and playing as well. "But why?"

He shook his head. "I still do not know."

"She will not tell me," he amended. "But... I have hope that she will. Soon."

His aunt surveyed him, then spoke carefully. "There is a ball tonight, at the Monteiths'. It is late, but I shall respond and let them know that the Duke of Englefield and his new duchess shall be attending." She looked at him pointedly. "If you truly wish for Gwendolen to be accepted as your wife, the new Duchess of Englefield—with all that the role entails, you must make an effort to present yourself as her husband."

Angel opened his mouth to object, then closed it again, as he saw the look in her eyes. Dash it all if his aunt wasn't too confoundedly perceptive for her own good.

"Very well. I will speak to the duchess," he said, taking his cue from his aunt. It was the first time he had referred to Gwendolen that way.

Aunt Eliza seemed amused. "Yes, you do that." She went back into the morning room, Hercules trotting behind her like a miniature pony.

A ball... Angel could not remember the last time he had attended one. Somehow, he doubted balls were something Gwendolen was much accustomed to either.

He suspected she would protest leaving Henry and decided to talk to the head footman about bringing on a few extra reliable and well-known men. Perhaps have them come up from Englefield Abbey, in fact. Then their trustworthiness would be unquestionable. He felt better having thought of this idea. With a regular Swiss Guard surrounding the house, his bride would, hopefully, feel safe enough to leave her son for a few hours.

He imagined stepping into a ballroom with her by his side and ran both hands through his untidy locks. Brown would have his work cut out for him.

Gwendolen slipped into the library. She knew Angel was in here somewhere for she had asked a housemaid.

It was her first time entering the library at Sweetbriar and she found it was vaster than she had imagined. Which was saying something, for the earl had valued his library above all rooms in his house and had accumulated an incredibly wide collection.

Sweetbriar's might have put it to shame, however.

The room was spacious and beautiful, with high vaulted ceilings covered with plaster moldings shaped in Grecian motifs of palmettes and scrolls. Alcoves of books lining tall mahogany shelves stretched far ahead of her, ending in a huge half-circle seating area with floor to ceiling bow windows. Skylights overhead let in light along the aisles and without which the huge room would have been gloomy indeed.

She walked slowly, treading upon a long, soft Turkish carpet that ran through the center aisle of the library, looking left and right for signs of occupancy, passing little nooks with comfortable leather chairs and broad library tables covered with maps and folios.

She was peering into a shadowy alcove to take a closer look at a globe on a gilded stand when a deep voice spoke directly into her ear.

"Looking for something?"

She let out a most indecorous squeak and jumped what felt like ten feet in the air.

"You startled me," she said accusingly, spinning around and nearly knocking her nose against Angel's coat.

He was closer than she had expected. She swallowed, remembering how close they had been last night. In her bed.

She peered up at him.

"You scared me," she said, with a little more poise. "I was looking for you."

"And now you have found me," he said with a beautiful smile. He gestured to where he had been sitting—a larger alcove with a grand fireplace, unlit now, flanked by dark red leather armchairs. Gilt lacquer circular bookcases stood on each side of the chairs, decorated with exotic scenes and filled with book sets.

Gwendolen sank into one of them and gave one of the pretty bookcases a little twirl.

"I do apologize for the fright though," Angel added, sitting down across from her, and displaying a more serious expression. "After the night you've had…"

"Yes, that is why I've come." She was about to continue as she had intended, but then thought of something. "Have you learned anything? Was there an…intruder?" She was not sure which would be more frightening—a spy in the house or the idea that Redmond had broken in himself.

Angel shifted awkwardly. "It was not an intruder. It was the new kitchen maid. Bribed by a man who claimed he wished her only to deliver—" Angel cleared his throat. "—love letters."

Gwendolen threw up her hands and gave a brittle laugh. "Ah, yes. I so enjoy receiving surprise *billet-doux* from my lover." She shook her head. "If only that was the case."

"I mean," she said hastily, "That is not to say..."

"It's all right. I know you do not have a lover," Angel said with amusement. "I mean, I do not *think* you have a lover." He eyed her mischievously. "*Do* you have a lover?" he asked playfully.

"I do not! I have never..." She stopped.

"Never?"

He waited. "Never is an awfully long time," he said softly, with an inscrutable expression.

Gwendolen suddenly wondered if he had been more aware than she had realized last night. What if he had felt her kiss him? She colored.

But he was blushing, too, she realized. What did he have to blush over?

Had he kissed her in her sleep as well?

Her blush deepened at the idea. If he had, she would not have minded.

But they were getting off track.

"Angel, I..." She bit her lip.

"Ah, the biting of the lower lip. Which means you're trying to decide whether or not to do something which may or may not be awful, awkward, amazing, or perhaps all of the above." Angel grinned. "I know you already, you see. Am I not an attentive husband?"

Gwendolen could not help smiling a little. "You are an excellent husband, Your Grace. Angel."

"Thank you, Your Grace. Gwendolen," he returned, trying to look humble. "We do our best."

They would never make progress at this rate and soon she would lose all her courage.

"I wish to tell you what this is all about," she blurted.

She watched his eyebrows raise in surprise.

"I had only expected to receive that information on my deathbed. Or perhaps your deathbed. Whoever's deathbed happened to come first, I suppose..."

"Oh, will you shush a moment?" She sighed. "Please."

He folded his hands in his lap.

"Thank you."

"Of course, Mistress Beaumont. Only, do not tell Mother I was not paying attention to my lessons."

Her glare silenced him.

"Very well. Serious face. I am ready. Pray, continue, milady."

When she hesitated, he leaned forward encouragingly. "I must admit I am longing to know more. At least for the express purpose of bloodshed. I find I itch to commit the most shocking acts of violence towards the man who left the note. The man who plagues you. Very primitive of me, I know."

"The idea is not entirely displeasing." She took a breath. "But you should know that he is the Earl of Redmond."

"Related to the Pembrokes, I believe? Never met the fellow."

"Please, let me finish. Let me speak," she said rather desperately. "If you do not, I will not be able to go on at all, Angel."

He was out of his chair in a flash and crouched beside her. He took her hands in his.

"I am sorry," he said softly. "The truth is... I am a little nervous."

"Nervous? Whatever for?" She stared.

"Well—" He hesitated. "You are about to trust me with something I know you do not truly wish to share. I feel... honored... to be trusted thusly, I suppose. I admit, I am also... afraid."

"Afraid?"

"Afraid to hear the story. For it cannot be a happy one, can it?" He looked up at her with an almost stricken expression that made her soften.

"Oh, Angel." She sighed. "It is not a happy one. It began that way, but it did not end well." He opened his mouth and she put a finger to his lips. "It is a common enough story. Tiresomely so. Boy meets girl."

She pulled her hands away and drew back from him a little. "Boy convinces girl he loves her. Girl falls for lovely words and promises."

She looked up at the ceiling, willing herself to finish. "Boy..."

"...turns out to be a hideous monster of a man who abandons beautiful girl?"

"Quite."

He had called her beautiful.

"Abandons said girl... when she is..." Angel paused. She would not look at his face. "With child?"

"Quite."

"I see."

"Perhaps I should have told you from the start." She bit her lip, hard this time, before continuing, as if in penance. "Perhaps you had every right to know this before you married me. To know that I was —" She swallowed. "—unchaste. Wanton. Soiled."

"You sound as if you are describing a handkerchief and not a person," he said incredulously. "Stop it at once. Did I ever say I expected us to disclose every indiscretion in our lives before we wed? Did I share any of mine with you?"

"Well, only the ones which were already public knowledge, such as the encounter with the vegetable cart..."

"Yes, thank you for that pleasant reminder. That suit had to the discarded, I'll have you know. The tomato stench would not come out. I have not been able to enjoy one since."

"Such a pity," she clucked her tongue.

"You are mocking me, woman."

"Am I?" Gwendolen could not help smiling. She felt unexpectedly free. Filled with relief. She had not shared everything, but it was a start.

Already he had turned it all around, made it... better somehow. Lifted some of the weight. It was amazing. He was amazing, her Angel.

"Thank you," she said abruptly.

"Do not thank me for being a decent man. I know you have little experience with them, but I assure you, I am low in the ranks of decency. Indeed, you might have found a much more decent fellow to marry than myself. Perhaps you will soon find yourself wishing you had held out for one."

"I doubt that," she said quietly, and enjoyed watching him blush a little.

"Let us sum up then. A vile seducer and abandoner of young women has come back into your life. He is an earl."

"He was not one then. But yes. Correct so far."

"And he is Henry's father."

"He is," she said miserably. "Oh, my poor Henry."

"From what I have seen, Henry appears to be completely a Gardner —and I mean that as a compliment. But what consequence is it? He left you. I take it you married your husband soon after?"

She nodded. "John...saved me. He was a friend of my parents. His first wife had died years before. I do not think he had ever planned to re-marry, but... he did. I was spared humiliation thanks to a deception."

Angel waved a hand dismissively. "Why should women *not* be spared the humiliation. Why should one sex get away with flagrant dalliances while the other must literally wear the evidence of it like a scarlet flag?"

"I believe you mean a scarlet letter. But yes, I suppose I must be thankful we are not Puritans."

Angel was not listening. "Henry was born after your marriage to Lord Leicester—the honorable Lord Leicester, not the leering, sniveling one I hope to have an opportunity to bruise one day. Therefore, he was legally your husband's child. Now you have remarried, and Henry is legally our child. My child? The laws regarding children and women as property are utterly bizarre and I must admit I'm murky on this part."

"Actually," Gwendolen put in, "I consulted with John's barrister before we wed."

Angel raised his eyebrows. "Before you and I wed?"

She nodded. "You are legally not responsible for Henry. You are not even considered his guardian. At least, not yet. You must apply for that status. To Chancery Court."

"I shall certainly do so as soon as possible if it will put your mind to rest."

"Thank you."

"But this does not mean your earl—oh, we cannot call him that. This does not mean the *evil* earl—yes, that's much better. This does not mean the Evil Earl has any legal claim to Henry." He looked reflective again. "And for that matter, why on earth does he want Henry in the first place? Why doesn't he go and beget some new children? On a woman he treats more civilly, preferably."

"Apparently," she took a deep breath. "He cannot."

"Cannot?"

"Is not able to beget...children. Physically, I mean."

"Good God. How on earth did that happen, I wonder?" Angel instinctively shifted as if to reassure himself all was in order down below.

"I believe it was a war injury of some kind."

"He was a soldier?" Angel asked with interest. "Must not have been a very good one if he lost his bollocks. Serves him right for what he did to you." He shuddered. "Awful thing for a man. Almost makes me sorry for him. Almost."

"I believe he is still able to..." She coughed.

"Oh! Well, that is all right then." He eyed her strangely. "But how would you know?"

She shivered unpleasantly. "He...assured me of it. When we last met."

"When you last met..." As understanding dawned, he leapt to his feet. "You mean he threatened to harm you. To ravish you? The bloody bastard. The blackguard. Damn his eyes! I'll thrash him. I swear I will."

Gwendolen felt an odd surge of pride, happiness, and excitement all together. It was awful, perhaps, to be so filled with joy at the idea of Redmond being thrashed—or was it? Could not women desire revenge as much as men? And she could not enact her own revenge properly—or at least, had been ineffective in doing so thus far. The idea of a brawny, bold man like Angel doing so was a stirring one.

"Yes, would you, please?" She murmured, half-to herself. Angel was not listening anyhow.

"What does he expect?" Angel continued, furiously. "For you to hand over your child to him? The child he chose to abandon? Not that you would have wanted him for a husband or father, of course, considering how he turned out. He expects you to pass Henry over like a parcel? And if you do not, he shall what? Break into your bedchamber? Into this house? Do you injury? Take Henry by force? I'll shoot him if he tries."

He stopped to catch his breath. "Perhaps I should simply go to him and call him out. Where is his estate? Where does he live? Is in London?"

"Call him out? As in, a duel?" Gwendolen was horrified. Thrashing was one thing but having Angel exposed to Redmond's bullet was another. Besides, she could not see Redmond fighting fair. She shook her head, somewhat relieved. "The Redmonds' seat is in Derbyshire, I believe. He must be staying somewhere in London, but I do not know where."

She decided not to tell Angel further details. Such as how Redmond had threatened to take the matter before the courts, demand guardianship of Henry, expose Henry's illegitimacy—to hell with Gwendolen's reputation, the reputation of her family. Whether Redmond won or not, she would be ruined. Not that traipsing about in polite society was particularly high on her list of favorite things to do, but being on the fringes by choice and a desire for solitude was a very different thing to being shamed and ostracized.

Furthermore, there was always the chance that he might win.

"Perhaps my aunt will know," Angel mused. "She has oodles of information at her fingertips. One might think she ran her own fleet of Bow Street Runners. Or chimney sweep spies. That's not half a bad idea, actually. Should we ever go into espionage, please remind me of it."

He rubbed a hand over his handsome face and Gwendolen watched. In Angel's presence, she found herself constantly shifting between her default state of misery to one of hope.

It was temporary, of course. The horror was not over. But she had someone to share it with now. A man of consequence, of honor, and of courage.

Her heart swelled again uncontrollably.

This would not do. She would have to learn to control it. She could not go around feeling such uncontrollable swells of feeling for her husband. Especially not when such feelings stirred up desires and when desires became deeds. Deeds like secretly kissing her husband in bed while he was sleeping.

She thought of all of the many couples for whom this would not be a problem. Couples in which the husband and wife had perhaps even fallen in love and slept in the same bed on a regular basis. In one another's arms even. And kissed frequently. And enjoyably. By choice.

One could not have everything.

Angel was her protector, and he was becoming her friend. That must be enough.

"Oh! I almost forgot." Angel's eyes were wide upon her. "Or perhaps Aunt Eliza already mentioned it to you?" he asked, hopefully.

"Mentioned...what exactly?"

"The ball tonight? At the Monteiths'?"

"A ball!" Her heart thumped mutinously.

"Do you have to sound quite so horrified? I am told many people actually choose to attend these functions—" He dropped his voice to a whisper. "—for enjoyment."

She rolled her eyes. "Yes, but I had no idea you counted yourself one of them."

"Touché. Nor did I. However, Aunt Eliza seems to feel that I should present my new duchess to the world. And by the world, I believe she primarily means the ton. How else but in a very public setting before hundreds of strangers we hardly know who will happily gossip behind their hands as we waltz?"

"Waltz!"

"Yes, it is a foreign custom, I believe, but has become very popular in England. You see, a man and a woman step onto a dance floor. The man places his hand upon..."

"I know what a waltz is!"

"Do you?" He put a hand to his chin and endeavored to look sufficiently skeptical. "I thought you had lived in seclusion these long years and then spent the last one in mourning. I would not have expected you to have had much opportunity for waltzing."

She glared.

In fact, she had never waltzed in her life. Except with her sisters—for they had not had a true dancing instructor. Merely a lady from the village who taught them country dances.

What was more, she had not attended a ball since the one she had met Wyndham at. John had avoided such large events like the plague, and she had always been too shy to attend alone. Musicales, yes. Morning visits, fundraisers, the theater from time to time—yes. But not balls.

"I do not have anything to wear..." she said slowly, grasping at straws. "I cannot possibly..."

"Yes, well, Aunt Eliza said something about having a gown for you." He frowned. "Not sure how she knew one would be needed already. But she has exquisite taste, you may trust me on that."

He looked at her and cleared his throat. "She has already accepted the invitation on our behalf. But if you like, I will tell her you are indisposed—" He moved as if to walk away.

Gwendolen thought quickly. It was a kind gesture and she did not wish to reject it solely due to timidity. Furthermore, the prospect of waltzing with Angel—ideally while wearing a splendid gown— was not precisely off-putting in spite of her lack of dancing experience.

"No!"

Angel paused.

She lowered her voice. "I mean, I should... like to go. It is just that. Well, what of Henry? Is it responsible to leave him alone?" She shook her head. "I would never forgive myself if something happened to him while I was gone."

He put his hands on her shoulders. "He will not be alone. First, a duo of fearsome warrior women will be by his side. Sides. Secondly, a demon mastiff from hell with drool as plentiful as the River Styx. If an intruder comes in, he will surely drown in the drool while Rosalind and my aunt thwack him to death with toys and teapots. However," he continued, seeing she had not been completely reassured by his imagery, "If that should not suffice, I have also called up some very burly and reliable men to stand about the house, inside and out, doing nothing but keeping a lookout for trouble. I promise you, Henry will be as safe as a... princess in a tower."

She looked doubtful. "The princess almost always gets out of the tower somehow."

"Very well, as safe as the crown jewels in the Tower of London. Aha! Now that is an analogy you will find no fault with," he said smugly.

"Although I know he is much more precious," he added. "The little chap is quite growing on me. Why just yesterday he said to me that I might keep his wooden rabbit, if I would be so good as to sneak him extra chocolate biscuits from the kitchen. I know not when I received an offer half so generous." He patted himself down until he had found the object and pulled the rabbit from his pocket.

"Well, there was the offer of a pint from the footpad on the bridge," Gwendolen recalled. She looked at the toy. "That is Henry's favorite. I am surprised he made the offer."

"Well, it was a very large plate of biscuits. And, if I am being honest, he did not say I could keep it. I believe that offer was withdrawn after he had eaten half the plate and revised to merely a twenty-four-hour loan."

Gwendolen smiled. "That is more believable. You had best make sure to return it before nightfall," she cautioned. "I am surprised he could fall asleep without it at all. But then, I suppose that explains why Rosalind fell asleep with him. He was probably crying for it but she did not want to trouble you."

Angel looked troubled. "I say, I had no idea. I'll go and take it up now before it slips my mind." He started to walk away, then stopped and looked back at her. "I will see you this evening then, my duchess." He winked.

Gwendolen surprised herself by winking back. "I look forward to it, my duke."

And she did.

The dress was made of shimmering scarlet silk and fit her like a glove.

Tighter than a glove, in fact. She was not sure she had ever worn a dress so snug—nor so revealing. Diaphanous material covered the tops of her breasts which threatened to spill out beyond the confines of her bodice. The tips of her nipples sat just below the top seam, and while the translucent fabric was apparently meant to provide a modest covering, all it seemed to do was draw the eye even more directly to the naked flesh beneath.

She was not sure whether Angel's aunt was a genius or a lunatic.

Angel had said she had excellent taste, so she supposed she would just have to trust that the gown was appropriate for the event and would not result in her being labeled a fallen woman and shunned from polite society.

Rosalind lay on the bed watching admiringly.

"Everyone will be looking at you tonight if you go out in that. Especially the men. They'll be undressing you with your eyes."

"Rosalind!" Gwendolen narrowed her eyes. "A sixteen-year-old girl should not say such things."

"Even if they are true?" Her sister smiled prettily. "And the women —well, they'll want to rip it off you for quite a different reason."

"Yes, well, let us hope I return with it in one piece. But perhaps a pelisse? Or a shawl? It is a warm night."

"Not a shawl," Rosalind countered. "You'll only be tugging it over your bosom constantly and spoiling the effect. A pelisse and make sure you leave it at the door, mind you."

"Yes, Mother," Gwendolen retorted. "You are quite the bossy little miss, aren't you?"

"I simply have excellent instincts when it comes to style, much like Angel's aunt. When it is my turn, I will happily wear gowns such as that."

"Oh, you won't have a chance! This is not a gown for an unmarried girl." Gwendolen studied her reflection. "I am not sure who this gown is for. I am not myself in it."

"No, you're not. You are a sophisticated duchess whose husband's jaw is going to drop to the floor when he sees you," Rosalind said happily.

Gwendolen bit her lip. On that, she hoped Rosalind would prove correct.

Letter 11

MR. B. M. Watson to the Right Hon. Earl of Leicester

August 24, 1815

London

My Lord,

I know you are fond of brevity, so I shall come directly to the point of my missive. I am sure you are busy with preparations for your upcoming expedition. I have been reading about it with great interest in the newspapers.

It has now been three years since your second marriage to Lady Leicester. We have spoken before on the subject of renewing your will, particularly for the purpose of making a settlement upon your wife and second son.

As I understand you will be departing imminently on another lengthy voyage, with all the risks that any journey involves, I would like to take the opportunity of once again strongly urging you do to so before you depart. If something were to befall you, My Lord, your lady would be left in what could be a very difficult situation. By law, as your present will states, all will go to your eldest son, Cecil Gibson, other than the amount you have settled on Matthew Stevens.

I strongly encourage you to similarly put provisions for Lady Leicester on paper. Perhaps the London house, at the very least, for it is not entailed with the rest of the estate.

Lastly, I must speak plainly and remind you that the financial conditions of the estate which Cecil stands to inherit are not the best. Settling certain money and securities upon the countess and your second son could only stand to benefit them, separating what they will receive from the main part of the inheritance—if that is what you desire. Of course, not all of the lands and properties are entailed. You have great freedom, if you so wish, to redistribute things as you choose, my lord.

I beseech you to consider these matters before you leave England.

Your most obedient humble servant,

Benjamin Meyers Watson

Letter 12

THE RIGHT HON. EARL of Leicester to Mr. B. M. Watson

August 26, 1815

London

My dear fellow,

Of course, I do not begrudge you your cautionary words! And, of course, you are very correct. I have put off doing what you suggest for far too long. My dear friend, Matthew Stevens, who you have met on more than one occasion, is sitting here echoing your reprimand even more sternly, I'm sure you will be glad to know.

Yes, of course, I wish to provide for Lady Leicester and little Henry. However, I will remind you and Stevens both that I am not of ancient years just yet and so while I will certainly handle this matter soon, I do not foresee its imminent necessity. We are in the midst of preparations for our autumn expedition and I am caught up in a whirlwind of tasks to be completed. I shall add this one to the list, I promise you, and do my very best to call at your offices before we depart.

Yours sincerely,

Leicester

Chapter 11

ANGEL'S JAW DID NOT drop all the way to the floor, but he did have to covertly wipe away a small drop of drool from the corner of his mouth. Dashedly embarrassing, but he was fairly sure Gwendolen had not noticed.

She had floated down the stairs with a nervous look on her face. He had no idea why. She was devastatingly beautiful and must have some idea of that fact. Mustn't she?

He wondered if the earl had ever told her how beautiful she was. The more she spoke of him, the more he sounded as if he had not known quite what to do with his lovely and very young wife.

He had not taken her to any balls, that much was clear. What a terrible waste.

Why, if he had a wife as beautiful as Gwendolen—and now he did, he reminded himself—he would show her off like... well, like a diamond. A diamond one wore frequently.

He swallowed thinking of wearing his wife—having her spread over him in that dress. That dress that just teased to be pulled down below the bustline, letting its rich contents spill out completely— preferably into his waiting warm hands.

"You look very handsome," Gwendolen said as she approached.

"My valet has done himself proud, I suppose," Angel acknowledged.

"And I do not smell a whiff of tomatoes," she noted.

They looked at one another and laughed.

"As for you—" Angel paused to admire. "You look simply stunning. My aunt has truly outdone herself." He wondered if this was his aunt's sly idea of a wedding present. And if so, was it meant for his wife or for himself? "Shall we, my lady?"

She took his arm shyly and he led her to the door.

At nearly eleven o'clock that evening, the carriage pulled away from Sweetbriar Hall. It was a pleasant summer night and the top was left down. Gwendolen cast one last look up at the second floor of the house. Henry had been asleep for hours. Rosalind had promised to check on him frequently.

Angel had reassured her that the men he had hired were stationed around the estate. Two would patrol the hall outside Henry's room at regular intervals.

Henry was almost excessively secure. So why did she still feel worried?

Because she was a mother. Once a baby was born, a mother's worry never stopped. It only lessened, from time to time. She could still recall the countless times she had woken in the night the first year Henry was born, to make sure the infant was still breathing. Her heart would catch in her mouth as she'd wake abruptly, filled with overwhelming terror, and put a hand out to feel her babe's chest, only calming once she had felt the slow breathing, in and out.

That terror of the first year had receded gradually as Henry grew older, stronger, larger.

But Redmond's reappearance had caused it to return with a vengeance.

She inhaled deeply, clasping her clammy hands in her lap, then quickly moved them to either side of her on the seat for fear of getting sweat on the silk.

Angel sat across from her watching.

"Are you all right?"

What could she do but nod?

He smiled a little but did not appear convinced.

As the carriage took a corner quickly, Gwendolen slid to one side with a gasp.

Before she could reposition herself, Angel was beside her.

"You seem ill at ease," he said quietly, his thigh resting against hers. She could feel his warmth through the thin silk. It was both comforting and provocative.

She was becoming accustomed to Angel inspiring both of those states in her.

"Shall I ask the driver to turn back?"

"No!" Gwendolen said, more sharply than she had intended. "I mean, no, thank you. I...am fine." She tried to smile. "It is only a mother's nerves."

Angel's kind eyes stared back. "It is nothing to be embarrassed about. Most mothers do not have to worry about their children being snatched from their homes." His eyes widened as he seemed to realize that may not have been the wisest choice of words. "I apologize. I truly believe Henry is safe, but if you are anxious, let us return. I will not think less of you for wishing to do so. It will not inconvenience me in the least."

Gwendolen nearly bit her lip, then remembered Angel's comment about her habit of doing so and stopped herself. She clenched her hands together instead.

"No, thank you," she said again. She could hear herself—stiff and polite, as if she were talking to a stranger. But wasn't he one?

Why was she doing this to herself? Why not take up his offer, go back home? Write off this silly and probably ill-fated attempt at a social evening together. That was probably what Angel was wishing right now—to return home. Perhaps he would even go out once he had seen her settled, to his own pursuits.

Even to another woman.

Gwendolen set her lips stubbornly.

"I see you will not budge." He seemed amused. "Perhaps something to calm our nerves then? We cannot be fretting over Henry all evening, can we?" She appreciated his including himself in the comment, though she was sure it was an overstatement.

He pulled something from his pocket and held it out.

When she looked at it suspiciously, he laughed. "It is not whisky. Try it."

"Do you carry this everywhere? Even to church?" she asked, taking it from him.

"Do you mean, did I have it when we said our vows?" he replied with a grin. "I may have imbibed outside the church. Dutch courage, you know. Women being so much braver than men, I assume you did not require the same to fortify you."

She was not sure whether to be flattered or put-off by the idea that her bridegroom had required liquid courage. But then, if she had not had Henry and Rosalind with her, perhaps she might have done the same.

She took a small sip from the silver flask. Warmth flooded through her but she did not choke. Spicy with a hint of sweet fruitiness.

"Cherry brandy," he explained. "I thought you might prefer it.

"Very thoughtful," she said, and she meant it. So, he had anticipated sharing liquor with her this evening, had he?

She took another tentative sip which became an unexpectedly larger one as the carriage lurched. Angel put his hand over hers to hold the flask steady before it could spill onto her gown.

"Thank you," she said, trying to suppress a cough.

Angel was looking around. "I believe we've arrived."

The carriage was rolling to a halt before a stately house. Like Sweetbriar, it was not a typical London townhouse, wedged tightly between other homes. The Monteith's manor was closer to country estate though it lay within London's boundaries. The Monteiths' must be rich indeed to afford such a large property.

Angel had stepped out and was offering her hand. As she took it, she looked up at him and nearly slipped off the carriage step.

She had always known the Duke of Englefield was an extremely handsome man.

This evening he fairly shone.

Well over six feet tall, with a broad chest and wide shoulders, he perfectly filled out his elegant clothing—a well-tailored black coat and fitted buff trousers. Very well-fitted.

His cravat was a brilliant white, tied in an elaborate knot. His valet's work, she presumed.

His single-breasted waistcoat was the one flash of color in his ensemble—a dark red satin which complemented the shade of her gown. Had Aunt Eliza tipped off the valet?

Above it all glowed Angel's halo of sun-streaked hair, and the lovely golden skin of his face with its strong jaw and regal nose.

And never mind those full, beautiful lips. She would not even think about the lips.

Let alone how they felt.

How had she not noticed before? Was it the brandy—already warming her blood? She felt flushed from head to toe. She could not go in like this. Not beside him. He was far too perfect, too... well, too angelic. Perhaps even godlike. Adonis had been too meager a comparison; he was more like Apollo. She could not stand beside him and be announced as his wife. What would everyone think of her? A little country girl, a plain widow, who had hardly mingled in society before now.

Everyone would laugh and wonder how she had managed to land such a man.

She would be wondering the same.

Her heart sank. The liquid courage melted away, and she felt faint and cold. She staggered a little coming down off the step. Angel caught her by the arms, her hands pressing up against his chest.

"Too much brandy?" he murmured with a puckish grin. Then he looked down at her more closely, not letting go, and his smile disappeared to be replaced by something more enigmatic. She heard a sharp intake of breath. "You are beautiful, Gwendolen. That dress..."

He let go and stepped back a little. "Well, let's just say it suits you very well. Shall we?"

An imperial staircase led into the ballroom, allowing guests below to look up as each new arrival was announced. Gwendolen held tight to Angel's arm as their names rang out across the expanse of people.

"Their Graces, the Duke and Duchess of Englefield..."

Was it her imagination or did the hum subside for a moment as many eyes turned towards them?

She tried to look above the crowd, rather than at any one face in particular.

John had been such an absent husband and disinterested noble that she had never had the unwelcome opportunity of being observed so minutely as if through a magnifying glass by the ton. It was not a particularly comfortable experience.

"Steady," Angel whispered, his hand over hers. "I have more brandy."

She nearly opened her mouth to retort that she would not require any more Dutch courage, thank you very much, but then saw that he was teasing.

She smiled tightly and he swept her down the stairs and into the magnificent throng.

Two hours later, Gwendolen's feet ached and she had still not waltzed with her own husband.

Instead, she had been introduced by Angel, in a courteous but bored voice, to many, many people whose names she had desperately tried to remember.

She had exchanged small talk with a constantly changing group, mostly bright-faced women eager to congratulate the duke and his new duchess on their nuptials. But beneath the brittle smiles, Gwendolen thought she sometimes caught hints of darker sentiments such as jealousy, malice, and disdain.

Were they wondering why on earth he had chosen her?

It was a fair question.

Only when Hugh had appeared, surrounded by his sisters and two of their husbands, did Gwendolen feel herself genuinely smile. Hugh's sisters were as light-hearted and kind as he was, and they worked to put Gwendolen at ease. Their husbands had danced with her through three different sets, interspersed with other less pleasant partners who Gwendolen had done her best to adequately converse with.

On the other hand, Angel had taken up his role splendidly. There was constantly an elegantly dressed woman to either side of him. He was never unpartnered for a dance set—simply never with her. His laugh rang out across the room all evening as he charmed those around him with jokes and stories.

Gwendolen was watching her husband dance with a stately red-haired woman, perhaps past forty but still a beauty, when Hugh approached bearing two glasses.

"Ratafia?" he offered.

"Detest the stuff."

"Excellent. Perhaps you'll enjoy this madeira." He beamed.

She accepted the glass, and took a sip, unable to keep from smiling back. Hugh seemed to have that effect upon others.

"He's rather neglecting you this evening, isn't he?" Hugh murmured, coming to stand a little closer.

Gwendolen shrugged uncomfortably. "I suppose he knows a great many important people and they all wish for a small amount of his attention."

Hugh shot her an appraising look. "Indeed. Next thing you know he'll be taking up his seat in Parliament, and then the crowd will really be something to see."

He took a sip. "Nevertheless, it wouldn't do to have all of those great many important people speculating on why the duke is not dancing with his beautiful new bride. I shall have to have a talk with him."

"Please, don't," Gwendolen said quietly. "I am fine, really." She took a breath. "I am simply out of my element. My late husband and I did not have much of a social calendar, you see. He was more likely to be found in a musty ruin thousands of miles from here than at a ball. Truthfully, I did not mind."

"A secret wallflower?" Hugh teased.

"Can one be a wallflower when a wife? And for that matter, it is not much of a secret." She finished her glass and put it on a passing tray.

"Angel is not usually inconsiderate," Hugh mused, looking towards where his friend danced. "Especially to you. He seems very fond of you."

Gwendolen laughed. "How can you tell? We have not known one another long. That is no secret at least."

Hugh shot her another glance. "That's why the fondness is so impressive. Not to mention the proposal. Despite the silly reason he claimed for making it."

She blushed.

"I suspect Angel is rather out of his element himself, you know," Hugh said softly. "He has avoided these sorts of outings like the plague for years."

"Preferring higher class establishments, I suppose?" she quipped.

Hugh grinned. "A public house to a ballroom, yes." His face turned serious. "Which is why his bringing you here tonight says a great deal."

He touched her arm lightly, gently, and stepped away.

She looked after him, wondering about the comment. But as the night went on, she shrank more and more within herself, feeling unnoticed and out of place. Hugh seemed as popular as Angel and while he at least sent encouraging looks her way, he was not the man she had arrived with. That man was very busy indeed with other people.

When the last set she had been dancing finally ended, she thanked her partner and then, instead of returning to where she had been standing with their group, snatched a glass from a passing tray held by a footman, and slipped out a door to the terrace and gardens.

Closing it firmly behind her, she crossed quickly to the rail and placing the glass on the cold stone ledge, leaned over, resting on her elbows.

It was quiet. Blessedly quiet.

No one asking her how she had met the duke or where they had wed or who had designed her gown or where they would spend the next season, fall, winter, spring.

Simply silence and the calm darkness of a summer night with the mellow, rich scents of earth and foliage radiating from the gardens below.

She closed her eyes for a moment, then picked up the glass and drank—cautiously at first, then more deeply as she tasted familiar madeira.

She wondered how long she could hide out here. Perhaps hours. It might be ages until Angel realized she was gone. If he ever did.

He was probably waltzing with a young, beautiful, single lady right now, one much more eligible than Gwendolen, and regretting his hasty decision to throw away his future, not to mention his lineage, in a foolish act of nobility.

She tucked a loose strand of hair behind one ear. She had only herself to blame if she was suffering from a case of jealousy.

She had let herself become too attached, too quickly. At first, she had thought herself immune to Angel's charm. On the bridge those two nights, she had been much too distracted to give much thought to her rescuer's appearance. Or to truly appreciate his charming demeanor.

After their third encounter, her mind had been on Cecil and the loss of her home. Angel had been there—steady and friendly. It had seemed like a wise decision, to marry for practicality once more rather than love. Or passion.

Oh, why, oh, why had he had to go and kiss her?

It had thrown her completely off. It had changed everything.

Like a taste of forbidden fruit.

Now, childishly, she longed for more of it. Yet had to exist knowing there was no way to satiate her craving, though the fruit dangled there before her just out of reach.

She heard the terrace door open and close behind her and her heart gave a silly hopeful leap.

She twirled around, already thinking of what to say...

But it was not Angel.

Lord Leicester stepped towards her. Cecil. The second last man in the world she would wish to be confined with—second only to Redmond.

"Lord Leicester," Gwendolen said, icily. "I was just about to go back inside."

"Oh, please, don't leave on my account. I'm sure the terrace is large enough to accommodate us both. The room was so hot that I thought a bit of air would be a pleasant change. I see you had the same idea."

Cecil did appear rather florid. But then, that was not unusual. He had always been prone to drinking too much. Now she could smell the liquor wafting off him.

He walked closer. There was plenty of room on either side. Gwendolen stood, poised tightly, trying to decide whether to dart around him.

In the end, she stayed, frozen, feeling rather nastily like a prey animal on some desert savannah.

But this was not even Redmond—merely a wormy inferior. She could deal with Cecil, couldn't she?

She pulled herself up straighter and prepared to walk inside.

"Good night, Lord Leicester. Enjoy the air."

She had underestimated his speed. In a flash his arm shot out and gasped her wrist—so tightly she let out a hiss of pain.

"Stay a moment. And since when have you become so formal with me, Gwendolen? Call me Cecil. We have known each other too long for titles." He tugged her closer and she gripped the stone railing with her other arm, digging her fingers in, trying to hold her place.

He tugged harder. "Stop. Being. Foolish. Gwendolen, let go. Can we not speak face to face, like adults?"

"I am not the one who is tugging like a spoiled child," Gwendolen said breathlessly, not letting go of the rail. "Now let me go. My husband is just inside. I shall scream."

Cecil smirked.

He was not a lion of the savannah, she decided. More like a vulture. Or a warthog.

Dangerous, disgusting, stupid.

As was she—stupid—for not realizing he was in attendance, for letting her guard down, for venturing out alone.

All of a sudden, she felt exhausted. Why should she not step out alone for a moment? Why must her guard be constantly up?

Because wicked men like Redmond and Cecil existed in the world and acted as if everything in it were theirs for the taking, a small voice said, and she knew it was right.

"Go right ahead," he said calmly. "Call for your husband. The orchestra music is quite deafening. I am not sure he will hear you. Not to mention what he will think if he does."

"What do you mean by that?" she shot back.

"I mean that he may find you enjoying yourself far too much than is decent."

He stepped towards her and grabbed her other wrist from its place on the stone rail. He was stronger than she was, by quite a lot. It was frightening to realize.

She leaned back against the rail as he stood gripping her hard by both of her wrists. The hard stone pressed into her back through the thin material of her dress. A dress she had hardly appreciated that evening, despite feeling beautiful in it before she left the house.

Right now, she wished she were wearing a dress that came up to her neck, preferably one made out of thick wool. Certainly not a ballroom gown with a plunging neckline which made her breasts thrust upwards as she leaned backwards to get as far away as she could from Cecil.

"Look at you—on display for all the world to see," Cecil said, looking appreciatively at her chest. She was revolted by the sight of his large red tongue rolling over his thick lips.

Then that tongue plunged towards her breasts and she screamed.

"Shut up, you slut," he hissed. "Don't pretend it's anything you haven't done before. Don't pretend it's anything you haven't thought of a thousand times before."

"You forget that I am not, in fact, you, Cecil. Thank God," she hissed back. "Now stop this instant before you utterly disgrace yourself."

"I'll take my chances," he said with a smirk, letting go of one of her wrists so that he could cup one of her breasts through the gown instead. He gave a hard squeeze and she cried out in pain.

"What the bloody hell is going on out here?" A man's voice barked.

Gwendolen choked back a sob of relief.

"Get your filthy hands off her." Angel strode towards them, his face a mask of righteous fury.

Cecil held on a moment longer, then let go.

Winding up her arm, she slapped him in the face, hard, and had the satisfaction of hearing him cry out.

"You little bi—" The word was cut off.

Angel grasped the shorter man by the collar and pulled him away as if Cecil were a small boy caught stealing sweets.

"I beg your pardon. What did you say?" Angel asked calmly and carefully, still holding Cecil by the scruff. He looked at Cecil as if he were a piece of dung he had stepped in on the street. Which essentially, he was, Gwendolen thought.

Angel glanced towards her. "I was going to deck you, Cecil. It would be no less than you deserve. But I see you bear my wife's handprint already on your white cowardly face. Mark it well for you shall not get off so gently the next time, you wildebeest-faced vulture. Any man who preys on a woman deserves far worse."

Gwendolen was somewhat impressed by the interesting combination of animals. She would have to tell Angel she'd had similar ones in mind.

"What makes you think I wasn't giving her exactly what she'd been asking for?" Cecil sneered.

Gwendolen cringed a little for him. Unable to keep his mouth shut. But it was too late. She hardly saw the blow coming—Angel was that fast. His fist shot out smoothly, the other raised to block. And then Cecil was yelping and reeling backwards, clutching at his eye.

"You've blinded me, you fool," he was shrieking, dancing about.

Like a monkey, Gwendolen thought wildly, trying not to giggle aloud.

"What on earth is going on here?" A new female voice had joined the fray. "What is the meaning of this? Lord Leicester, what are you doing? Are you all right?" That last question was asked belatedly with less interest than the first.

"No, I'm bloody well..." Cecil looked towards the woman to whom the voice belonged and seemed to make an effort to pull himself together, in an almost manly fashion.

Lady Julia stepped forward, peering down at them all from her fine aristocratic nose. Her hands rested on her shapely hips, drawing Gwendolen's eye to her dark emerald satin gown which matched the catlike hue of her eyes, which were currently narrowed disapprovingly.

"No, I'm not all right," Cecil was saying. "This fool has..."

"Oh, pull yourself together, Cecil," Julia snapped, looking at him as if he were a toad. "Come back inside. You may tell me whatever you were about to say in there." She looked at Angel. "Our sincere apologies, Your Grace. My fiancé has drunk too much ratafia this evening."

"Ratafia!" Cecil exclaimed. "I loathe the stuff—" But whatever else he was about to say about the nature of ratafia was drowned out as Lady Julia took him by the arm and led him firmly back through the terrace doors.

Angel stared after them for a moment, then looked at Gwendolen.

"And I thought we were an odd couple," he said slowly. "I had no idea ratafia was such an unpopular beverage these days. I admit, I have not tried it in years."

"A wart-hog. Not a wildebeest."

"Hmm?"

"Cecil. You called him a wildebeest-faced vulture."

"Aren't they the same thing?"

"No. A wildebeest is more like a cow. Whereas a wart-hog is..."

"No, no," Angel raised a hand, a hint of a smile forming. "Let me guess. More of a pig-like creature? Yes, I see your point. My apologies. Shall I go after him and clarify things?"

"Maybe next time," Gwendolen murmured, turning away. She leaned back on the ledge. The feeling of temporary serenity had vanished.

But Angel's presence had at least brought back some vestige of a sense of safety.

Oh, to be a man and not have to be reliant on another's strength so constantly. Though she had slapped Cecil quite hard. She was proud of that.

"You left a beautiful imprint," Angel observed, coming to stand next to her. He looked out into the night. "You know, this is becoming quite familiar. You, alone in the night. Me, stepping out of the shadows."

"This was the first time I got to hit anyone," she reminded him.

"True. More's the pity. Perhaps I should give you boxing lessons. Would you like that? I bet your sister would."

"Would you?" Her eyes widened. "Are you serious?"

"I wasn't, but if you are, if you'd truly like that..." He looked at the intense expression on her face and his own darkened. He shook his head. "I can understand if you feel like you must rely upon yourself. I... failed you tonight."

She considered letting him go on thinking that way. He had neglected her, certainly. It had not been the evening she had hoped for. But he had not failed her.

"Not at all," she said quietly. "You are my most stalwart protector."

He seemed to perk up a little, so she went on. "My faithful knight."

He met her eye. "At your service, my lady."

He bowed so beautifully that she could not help but be impressed and charmed. Once again, she was so quickly in his thrall.

"Pass the flask," she commanded abruptly.

Angel raised his eyebrows but did as she asked.

She took a long swig, then wiped her lips with a sigh of pleasure.

"I see the stuff is quite growing on you," Angel observed, looking entertained. "Be careful that it does not go straight to your head."

"Oh, I want it to," she explained. "I have had quite enough of this night. Forgetfulness, I welcome thee."

"Ah, embracing the dramatic. But... You mean it was not a pleasant evening, even before that worm appeared?"

She shook her head, unwilling to deceive him on this point.

"My poor duchess," he said softly, looking at her carefully. "I have quite neglected you, haven't I? I was so caught up in making sure I played my part. I forgot that this is all quite new to you. Whereas for myself—" He shrugged eloquently. "—'tis my birthright, but one I usually manage to avoid."

"Now I understand why," Gwendolen said. "I have had enough of balls to last a decade."

"We did not even waltz," she added a little mournfully, before she could help herself. She looked away.

A warm hand gripped her chin, gently but firmly turning her head back.

"My poor lovely duchess," Angel said again. "Well, it is not too late for that." He gestured towards the house. The low strains of a waltz could faintly be heard. He held out his hand.

"Out here?" she asked incredulously. "Someone might..."

"...see? I think we're beyond that, don't you?" He smiled. "Please?"

It was the please that did her in.

She slipped into his arms.

He led them expertly through the steps. She hardly had to exert herself at all.

She closed her eyes and let herself fall into a dreamy state. The cherry brandy was flowing nicely. She felt warm and tranquil. Cecil was but a bad memory from long ago. She was here now. With an angel, dancing on a terrace, wearing a lovely dress.

She rested her head against his chest and heard him draw in his breath a little.

"I'm sorry," she apologized, opening her eyes and looking up. "Did I tread on your toes?"

"No," he said haltingly, "it's not that..." He hesitated.

His lips were parted slightly. He was close and tall and firm. He was masculine and strong and beautiful. He belonged to her. He had kissed her. He was dancing with her.

Perhaps she was not so very repulsive to him after all. Perhaps he would not mind...

Before she could second guess, she reached up both hands and gently clasping them behind his neck, pulled him down towards her.

In his relatively young life, Angel had kissed his fair share of women. Actresses, courtesans, widows. A tavern wench here and there. He had even fancied himself in love on more than one occasion —albeit briefly.

But he had never kissed like this.

Been kissed like this.

She touched him so gently, as if he were the weaker sex. Her hands tugged his face to hers, almost pleadingly.

Their lips found one another. At first the kiss was tentative, slow, even shy.

Very different from the quick, jesting kiss he had given her at the wedding breakfast—which had become more heated than he had planned.

This time, he gave her free rein. Followed her lead.

Her hands were running through his hair, lightly over the back of his neck, running over his shoulders.

He closed his eyes and let her explore. With his eyes closed, the sensation of her lips on his own was heightened. They were soft and sweet, pressing firmly yet oh so tenderly.

There was something hesitant, almost cautious, about both her kiss and her touch. She kissed him lightly, a brush of lips that might have been swift and fleeting.

As if she had never kissed before. Touched a man before. Or if not never, rarely.

He may have been imagining it, seeing inexperience and innocence merely because it suited him to think of her this way—more girl than widow. Or he may have been correct. And because he did not know which was true, he opted for restraint.

The kiss was hers and he was at her bidding.

When she nestled her body closer against him, it took all his restraint not to pull her tighter. But he kept his hands loose on her waist, caressing her through the dress. More soothingly than passionately—for now.

Of course, there was restraint and then there was desire—and for now, his desires were second to hers.

Then she deepened the kiss.

His whole body warmed.

Her lips pressed against his harder, then parted them, and he was lost. Her tongue stroked his lower lip, then nibbled—so quickly and gently that he might have imagined it.

It was the kiss of an innocent—he had not been wrong.

But an innocent awakened.

She began to drink him in, as if he were water. As if she had a thirst only he could quench.

Angel was only too happy to oblige. He met her kiss for kiss, enjoying the wave of pleasure passing through him.

The fire he had attempted to bank was now being painfully stoked.

She pressed against him again and he felt the softness of her breasts against his chest, the heat of her body flush against his own.

In another place, with another girl, things would have already progressed much farther. His hands would have roamed more freely. His mouth would have taken many more liberties with her own.

He longed to do those things.

But he cared about this woman. This woman who was so strong, yet so wounded, too. He knew there was much more to her story than she had shared.

So, he held back, tasting her passion sweet as wine, giving her only a glimpse of his own in return.

When she finally pulled back, she was breathing quickly—her face beautifully flushed with color. Her lips the lovely natural red that only came one way.

He resisted the urge to pull her back, to take her mouth hard, push his body against her own and let her feel...everything.

Instead, he merely lowered his head to hers, and nuzzled her gently —as if more mare than man.

It felt right though.

He kissed her hair gently, then brushed his lips over an ear. He lowered his head a little more and let his mouth trail feather-soft over her neck. She gave a little gasp and her fingers dug into his skin.

Angel recalled where they were.

A few short steps away were throngs of people, dancing, laughing, imbibing. It was only a matter of time before a few of them decided to take a breath of air or decided on a cool stroll through the gardens below.

Perhaps some were watching them through the tall sash windows right now.

Let them look, he thought. This was his wife. Could a man not kiss his wife with... tenderness? He would not even think the other word.

Suffice it to say there was nothing improper about the kiss.

Though this was as far as it could go if they remained here.

"How do you feel?" he whispered, his mouth at her ear. He felt her quiver again at the touch of his warm breath.

"Lovely," she murmured back.

She was. He longed to tell her so—again, and again, and again. In many different ways, some quite wordless.

She was the prettiest thing he had ever held in his arms, and what was more...

He swallowed.

What was more was that he enjoyed being with her. He loved speaking to her, teasing her, hearing her voice, waiting on every word she said. He longed to learn her mind, not merely her body—her history, her memories. He wanted her to trust him, to lean on him like this—not merely for the span of a carriage ride or a ball, but always, her safe place to turn.

And if she were as innocent as she seemed... Well, then he must admit to himself at least that he wanted to show her with his body all that she had missed out on. He wanted to pay her homage in every possible way, delighting in the sounds of her pleasure with each new act of his worship.

But not here.

"Perhaps it is time for us to depart, milady?" He meant the words as a playful question. Even an invitation.

But he felt her stiffen, then nod.

"Of course," she said, and stepped back.

He quickly clasped her hand before she could slip away entirely, in body and mind, and tucking it over his arm led the way.

Through the sash windows, which opened noiselessly, letting them step back in as if they had never been gone.

The nastiness with Cecil had been forgotten. Recalling it now, he emphatically pushed it away, looking down at his duchess and keeping his hand over hers as he led her through the crowd and back towards the wide marble stairs.

"It feels as if everyone is looking at us," she whispered, so quietly he would surely have missed it if he had not kept her so close.

"Let them look." He couldn't help but grin down at her, a wave of happiness spreading through him head to toe and replacing the heat he had felt on the terrace. He had not felt this excited since... Well, not since he crashed into that grocer's cart a few weeks back. It seemed like ages ago. Had he truly been such an idiotic boy so recently?

He felt as if he were returning to himself, after years playing the young blade. The maturity he had gained in the army had dropped away so quickly when he had returned. Even a dukedom could not replace the sense of purpose he had found there, nor the camaraderie, the brotherhood—that feeling of being part of something much larger and more important than himself. He had mellowed there, from boy to man. Only to return and become the little lost orphan.

Rather than stew in his grief, he had taken up hedonism. Far better to play than to cry. Far better to surround himself with strangers, than to ever consider... Well, to consider starting something greater than himself on his own.

A family.

Yet then this woman had appeared, with one ready-made.

Bold and brave and beautiful. Yet also lost and in need.

She needed him.

Henry needed him.

They made him feel like a man again.

They were coming up the stairs. He passed people he knew, but allowed only the briefest of glances, murmured the polite greetings quickly as he swept her past.

He wanted to get her away from here. Before the moment on the terrace was gone forever. Before she could remember Cecil or the rest of her evening—lonely as he now realized it must have been. He kicked himself for not staying by her side. Not only might she have enjoyed herself more, but the unpleasant encounter with Cecil would never have happened.

But he would not dwell on that now.

To the carriage.

From the carriage, to their home.

And once at home. To bed?

Separately? Or together?

He knew he was wishing for something that might not be. Something she might not even want.

He squeezed her hand and felt her squeeze back after a moment's pause.

But perhaps she did.

Perhaps she wanted him, more than she realized, more than he had expected.

Perhaps he could hope.

Her arm went slack in his. Her hand slid from his grasp.

She stopped.

He looked at her inquiringly, uncertainly.

After what felt an interminably long time, she met his eye.

"I... It's nothing." She shook her head. "It's nothing. I'm sorry." She smiled, but it was a forced one—any fool could see that.

She continued towards the door.

He did not reach for her hand this time.

Something was wrong.

What had he done?

They reached the carriage. He helped her in.

Was it his imagination or did her hand leave his as quickly as possible?

Inside, she sat, huddled, to one side. The carriage top had been raised to keep out some of the cool night air. It was nearly pitch-black inside. He could hardly make out her face, let alone her expression.

They drove in silence.

At first he tried to think of something to say, something to lighten her mood.

Then he began to worry and to go over everything he had done and not done that night.

He must have done something, or she would not have turned away.

He leaned back against his seat, trying not to simply gawk at her the whole way home.

The only way to avoid doing so was to close his eyes again. He did so.

He felt numb.

And alone again.

Gwendolen knew she was being cruel. Or if not cruel, then confusingly obtuse.

She felt Angel's eyes on her for the first half of the drive. Finally the pressure lifted and when she turned her head slightly, she thought his eyes were closed.

Perhaps he had fallen asleep.

Perhaps he had not even noticed her change.

If she had been able to help it, she would have.

But once she had seen Redmond on the flight of stairs, all she had wanted to do was run to the carriage. She had managed not to, merely walking quickly.

They had passed him just as they reached the top.

He had brushed by her, his coat touching her bare shoulder as he went past.

She had only seen his face for a moment. She was not even sure he had noticed her.

But a moment was long enough for her heart to pound and the bile to rise in her throat.

Henry was at home. Henry was safe. She repeated the words to herself as they drove.

Angel had reassured her, said they were good, honest men he had found. She had to trust him.

She was not sure why she had not told him. What would he have done if he knew?

She could picture any number of scenarios. Most of them involved the three of them at the center of a spectacle viewed by the entire ballroom full of ton.

Angel was a large, imposing young man.

But he did not know Redmond like she did. He was a serpent. Capable of anything. He was a solid man and had been in the military. Gwendolen had no doubt he was capable of bloodshed. Nor would he refrain from stooping to the underhanded or the devious.

Angel knew Redmond only through Gwendolen. She would not have him embarrassed before his peers because of her. Or worse, hurt.

She could not bear it.

She followed Angel's example and closed her eyes.

Soon they would be home and when they were, she would take Henry in her arms—sleeping or not—and hold him tight.

Letter 13

MISS CLAIRE GARDNER TO the Right Hon. Countess of Leicester

January 21, 1811

Orchard Hill

Dearest Gwen,

You are a mother! I can hardly believe it as I write the words. My sister, a mother!

I cannot wait to meet my nephew and kiss his sweet cheeks. Are they as round and plump as Gracie's were? Does he look like you? Like a Gardner? Or like a Gibson?

I cannot believe you went through your confinement alone, Gwen. If it had not been for Gracie's illness, we should all have liked to have been there.

I told Mother she could trust us with Gracie and go to you herself, but apparently twelve and thirteen are too young to manage even such a small household for a few days.

If Gracie had not been sick, I suppose she might have risked it. But when the doctor thought Gracie might have scarlet fever, I think Mother decided it was too great a chance to take with your health as well as your baby's.

But to think, you did not even have your own husband there by your side! To think he went away so soon after you were wed and will not return yet for *months*!

Oh, Gwen, how can you be happy this way?

Why, oh why, did you marry such an old man, Gwen? I cannot fathom it. How much happier you might have been if you had waited to find another. Someone... well, younger. You might have waited for someone who truly suited you. Someone you felt a genuine affection for.

I know you say you are fond of Lord Leicester, that you respect him. I am sorry, but to me those do not seem adequate qualities to base a lifetime upon.

It was only your first season. You married with such haste.

Ah, well, Rosalind has just poked me and said to stop making you feel bad. It was quite a hard poke, so I shall end here that I may go and find her to return it.

Love,

Claire

P.S. At least you now have a beautiful son to share your life with. He is beautiful, is he not? He must be a pretty baby with such a pretty mama.

P.P.S. As soon as Gracie is fully well, Mother says we will all come to visit. I cannot wait to hold darling Henry. We all love him already, Gwen. Rosalind cannot stop telling everyone she meets in the village that she is an aunt. She is so proud!

P.P.P.S. This is Rosalind. Claire has left me with a mark on my face that I am sure shall become a scar. I look as if I have had the pox. I shall box her ears after I write this. I miss you, dearest sister, dearest Gwen! All my love, Rosalind.

Chapter 12

SHE COULD NOT SLEEP.

It was nearing daybreak and she had been trying for hours.

Henry had been asleep in his bed when they arrived. As Rosalind lay beside him on top of the coverlet, Gwendolen had contented herself with a quick caress, not wanting to rouse them.

They made a pretty picture. Rosalind looked no more than a child herself, her cheeks rosy and her dark blonde hair strewn over the pillow, one arm tossed over her nephew protectively.

Had her sister noticed the appearance of strange men patrolling the halls? If so, Gwendolen would have some explaining to do in the morning.

There were not many plausible reasons for the presence of the extra men besides the truth. Not ones which Rosalind would believe, at least. She would receive a truncated version of the story then, and Gwendolen would have to hope she did not immediately rush off to demand boxing or fencing lessons from Angel so that she could defend her nephew herself.

Why did women not receive any such lessons in self-defense? They were physically weaker than men, not to mention much more likely to be prey than predator. Nine times out of ten the predator was male. Yet women were entirely at men's mercy in a nonsensical loop, strictly instructed to depend on their menfolk for protection.

She should be grateful to have found an honorable man.

She should learn how to use the knife, was what she should do, she thought grumpily, and expand her repertoire of essential skills. Perhaps Aunt Eliza could teach her. It was easy to picture Eliza holding a knife. Or a sword. Or a pistol. Any weapon really. With her mastiff growling by her side.

Herc was a softie really. He was gentle with Henry. But Eliza had quietly assured her that Hercules would not hesitate to rip out an intruder's throat.

At least, Gwendolen thought it was supposed to be reassuring.

She pressed her eyes tightly shut and tried once more to sleep.

No, it was impossible.

Impossible not to think of Angel lying in the adjoining room a few steps away.

Impossible not to think of kissing him on the terrace.

Impossible not to think of kissing him, full stop.

She owed him an apology for how unfairly she had treated him. From the moment she had seen Redmond, all she had thought of was flight. Flight and Henry.

Now, at home, in the Englefield fortress, having seen the men patrolling and Henry safe in his bed, she felt rather a fool—for panicking a second time with no explanation.

She had destroyed the brief moment of intimacy they had shared.

Angel had been incredibly patient. But he must be wondering when she was going to let him in.

The trouble was that she was not entirely sure of that herself.

Apparently, her body was more eager than her mind for before she knew it she was slipping out of bed and moving towards the connecting door, without even snatching up a dressing gown.

She paused with her hand on the door.

This was ridiculous. He was almost certainly asleep. What was she going to do? Stand over him staring longingly? Kiss him in his sleep again?

That would not be pathetic at all.

Poke him until he woke up, a stubborn part of her said. Poke him until he woke up and paid attention to her. Until she knew what he was going to be to her and she to him. For the terrace had muddled matters and now she could not sleep and so he should not be either.

Her hand pulled the latch. She opened the door slowly, planning to simply peek in. If he was asleep, she would go back to her bed, she decided righteously. She would demonstrate maturity. Wisdom.

Cowardice.

The traitorous door creaked loudly, opening wider than she had planned.

She froze, moved to pull the door closed.

"I am not asleep." A deep voice spoke from the dark, tinged with amusement.

In the dim, she saw Angel sit up.

He was bare-chested, she could see that much.

He had a very pleasing shape, even in the shadows.

"Is there something I may assist you with?" He sounded so matter-of-fact, as if she had come into the library and not his bedchamber in the middle of the night.

"I couldn't sleep." Her voice sounded small and mouse-like.

She stepped into the room. Then closer towards the bed.

Before she knew it, she was beside the bed.

"By all means, make yourself comfortable." He gestured to the open space beside him.

When she hesitated, he turned the coverlet down on that side.

"Shall I light a candle?"

Now that she was inside, the room was not pitch black after all. The curtains had not been fully drawn and moonlight was streaming onto the bed.

Angel was lit up as if beneath a street lamp. Her eyes traveled over his form, taking in the golden skin, the muscular curvature of his shoulders, his broad chest. His face was beautiful, with almost delicate features. But his body was bulky and strong. The build of a boxer rather than an indolent nobleman.

Looking more closely, she noticed his chest had a long, wicked-looking scar running from a few inches below his collarbone. It ran all the way down, disappearing beneath the coverlet.

She had seen scars before. It was not an uncommon sight with so many English soldiers returning from overseas, many of them wounded. A scar was a lesser injury. Some men returned with far greater marks—burns from cannon-fire, missing limbs.

"The scar?" Angel was looking back at her. "Shall I put a shirt on?" He moved as if to rise and find one.

"No, please—not on my account. Unless you are cold. Please. I am not..." She was flustered.

"Disgusted?"

"Yes. I mean, no. I am not disgusted. It is merely that..." She took a breath. "I had not thought of you as a soldier."

"Merely a spoiled rich boy?"

"A spoiled rich duke," she corrected.

"Ah, so that is a yes then."

Standing in the dark, she shivered—not from the conversation but because the room was chilled. She wrapped her arms around herself.

"Oh, climb in already, won't you?" He patted the spot beside him. "I don't bite."

In fact, she would not mind if he did.

Blushing a little, she picked up the skirt of her night rail and climbed in.

Angel was leaned back against his pillows.

Oh, he was fine-looking. In the light or in the dark.

"Now where were we?" he asked blithely. "Oh, yes, you were admiring my scar and considering how surprising it was that I have spent at least a small part of my wastrel life doing something worthwhile for crown and country."

"You make it sound as if I quite disdain you!" She smiled. "Nothing could be further from the truth."

She saw his eyebrows go up.

"Truly! I was merely disturbed when I saw it... because..." She stopped.

"Because?" he prompted.

"Because you might have died," she finished, meeting his eyes. "It is long and the wound must have been a deep one. How did it happen?"

Was he ashamed of the wound? Had someone commented on it before? Unflatteringly? Had he repulsed another woman with the sight of it?

Gwendolen did not like to think of her predecessors.

But it was a fact that there must have been many.

She was the one with him now though.

She reached out a hand and traced the scar lightly with her fingers. The skin still rose in a puckered ridge.

She went to move her hand away, but he surprised her by grasping it and keeping it in its place. Palm open, flat against his chest.

"It was in Portugal. The Battle of Salamanca."

"A Portuguese soldier then? No, what am I saying... They were our allies." The summer of 1812. The middle of her first year as a mother. Her first year of marriage. A lonely year. "A French soldier," she corrected herself.

Angel laughed humorlessly. "Not a French one."

"What do you mean?" She thought a moment. "It could not have been cannon fire. It would not leave such a clean cut."

"The mind of a surgeon! You are right. It was a saber blade. Wielded by one of my own countrymen, in fact."

"An Englishman!" She was shocked. "How did that come about?"

"Suffice it to say we had a disagreement." He leaned back a little, still holding her hand. He lifted it from his chest and looked at her palm. "But this cannot be what you came here for. To discuss my military service?"

"My chest, on the other hand..." He grinned charmingly. Provocatively even.

Gwendolen's face grew hot.

"It is a lovely chest," she ventured.

"Thank you," he said, formally. His eyes danced with mischief. "I am sure yours is as well, milady."

If it were possible for her face to grow even warmer, it did. She glanced down at her night rail. The fabric was thin and did nothing to hide the shape of her breasts. Her nipples were already hardened from the chill in the room and poked out boldly.

"Fair is fair, I think?" Angel said gently, and reached a hand towards her, running the tip of one finger ever so lightly over one hardened tip, then the other.

She shivered. Not from the cold.

He withdrew his hand quickly and suddenly looked uncertain. "I'm sorry. Is this what you wa—" he began to ask.

She stopped his mouth with a kiss. Leaning forward on her knees, she slid closer to him, her hands reaching out to hold onto his shoulders for support. Her lips moved over his, exploring, tasting. With every kiss her breasts brushed against his chest, her nipples puckering into even harder buds, more sensitive with every movement.

When she broke the kiss, Angel's mouth was damp from hers and his breathing heavy.

"Gwendolen," he said hoarsely.

She pulled the night rail over her head. There was nothing beneath it but her.

"Do you want me?" she whispered, hoping for reassurance, but also hoping not to sound pitiful. Dear God, did she want him. So frighteningly much. She felt a deep ache inside of her like nothing she had known before.

She wanted Angel. His mouth. His body. She wanted him, heart and soul.

One thing at a time.

He laughed and for one awful moment, her heart sunk.

"Oh, God, Gwendolen," he said, looking at her with naked hunger, letting his eyes roam over her form. "How can you ask that?"

And then his hands were on her, lifting her onto his lap.

His hands were everywhere, cupping her bottom and squeezing her more closely against him, running up and down her back, her shoulders. There was something provocative but also soothing about the gentle way he touched her. As if she were fragile in his hands.

Their lips had met again, but the tone of the kiss had shifted from soft and tentative to searing and thirsty. He caught her bottom lip between his teeth, licking and nibbling. His tongue teased her, parting her lips, then brushing and swirling against her own, making her head swim with pleasure.

He kissed her passionately, with a heat stronger than anything she had felt before. Not that her experience had been precisely broad. Yet he was patient, too. There was nothing rough or hurried about the way he was touching her. That, too, was different.

There was something wonderfully erotic about the way he was taking his time, as if they had all the time in the world. Which she supposed they did. Her heart beat a little faster thinking of all the time in the world with Angel. Had she any inkling of what she was getting into when she first met this man? If she had, would she have run towards him or in the opposite direction?

It was too late now; she was here and there was no turning back.

She stroked her own tongue against his, wanting to assure him of her equal ardency. Perhaps she did too good a job as she heard a groan escape him and he broke the kiss, leaning back from her a little.

His eyes went to her breasts. She wondered what he saw when he looked there.

They were not quite the breasts of a maiden. She had nursed Henry herself for over a year, unfashionable though it was, just as her mother had done with her and all her sisters. Yet neither were they unpleasing to the eye. High and curving, swollen with desire. They had not lost their firmness. Her shape was a little changed, her hips a little wider. Her curves more full, more womanly.

She looked back up.

"Perfect," she heard him whisper and she felt a warm glow run through her.

He lifted his hands and moved his palms to lightly brush over the tips of her breasts, eliciting a small moan from her at the sensation, before filling his hand with the soft globes, kneading, then letting his thumbs make small circles over the tips of her nipples.

She let out a gasp and saw his pleased expression.

"Well, if you like that," he murmured, then lowered his head, catching one nipple in his warm mouth and stroking it hard with his tongue one moment, flicking delicately the next.

It was the sweetest torment. She wanted more.

As he clutched her tighter against him, taking more of her breast into his mouth, sucking and licking, she could feel his hardness, and impulsively rubbed herself against him, feeling ripples of pleasure as she did.

She felt rather than heard him groan, and though the coverlet still separated them, he lifted himself a little to meet her. She buried her hands in his hair, moaning as she did.

The coverlet still separated them rather chastely and crossly, she wished it gone.

As if reading her mind, he shifted his hands to her thighs, trailing his fingers lightly along them, first on the outside, then moved her slightly so he could reach the softer skin on the inside higher up.

He was so close to where she wanted him, though what she wanted she would not have been able to say.

She shifted a little, moaning in frustration.

"So soft," he breathed, before slipping a hand between her parted thighs, and cupping her mound with his palm.

Gwendolen gasped. Her back arched instinctively, leaning back a little to give him greater access, and he took it enthusiastically, putting one hand behind her back to keep her positioned while stroking the soft seam of her sex with the other.

His fingers were practiced, moving deftly, stroking back and forth, exploring upwards. When his thumb met her swollen nub, she let out a gasp, her grip on his shoulders tightening.

His mouth moved to her ear. "Shall I continue?" His lips passed over the delicate skin of her neck and she shuddered, nodding slightly.

"Don't stop," she whispered. Don't ever stop, she wanted to say.

His thumb was making careful circles over her sex while his fingers stroked below, parting the soft folds of her center, before pushing one inside, then two, through the slick wetness, and thrusting, first slowly, then more insistently.

Her legs spread wider as she moved to take more of him in. Her head fell against his almost dreamily as he moved within her, his delicate fingers dancing expertly over her most sensitive parts.

Something was building inside her, more intense than anything she had ever felt when touching herself. Angel was... well, he was experienced. She supposed his years of practice were working to her benefit and rather than allowing any hint of envy, she relished the work he was doing.

As the feeling grew, she twisted her head back and forth before pressing her mouth to his shoulder, sucking and biting, gently at first, then a little harder. She had the satisfaction of hearing him groan, then her mind went blank as his fingers gave another swift thrust and something in her was rising, rising, rising, a wave of bliss passing over, leaving her warm and weak in its wake.

There was silence for a few moments. Angel's hand slipped away and clasped her back instead, holding her against him.

"That was..." she said, shakily.

"Divine? Incredible? Ecstasy inducing?"

"I was going to say... utterly new," she said, shyly.

He looked surprised, then another emotion passed over his face.

"Do you mean to say..."

She interrupted before he could ask the wrong question. Or the right one.

"The earl and I..." She paused to take a breath. "We were... not intimate."

"Not ever?" he asked, incredulous.

She shook her head, biting her lip. Should she say more? Did he deserve to know?

"I have only ever..." She bit her lip again, this time because she could feel a swelling of unwanted tears. She looked up at the ceiling of the room. The beautiful craftsmanship of the elaborate molding. "There was only the one time. And it was...not like this."

"Only the one time?" He sounded even more incredulous. His eyes narrowed. "What do you mean not like this?"

She closed her eyes. "I mean... It was... Well, not so nice. Rougher. Painful. I did not want... But he would not..." She rested her head on his shoulder again.

"You mean you did not want him," he said fiercely. "Yet he would not stop. Is that it?"

She nodded against his shoulder.

"Oh, Gwendolen." Angel sounded tired. "I did not know. I had no idea. I am so very sorry that it should have been like that for you, the first time. How awful it must have been."

She raised her head to look him in the eye. "It was," she said, a little surprised by his sincerity. "I had thought I loved him, you see. But then... he would not listen. He would not stop." The last words were whispered. She closed her eyes again to keep the tears in, but felt one trickle down her cheek.

Angel touched it, brushed it away.

"That bloody brute," he muttered. "Bloody, bloody blackguard. Brainless beast. That blasted..." He paused.

"Barbarian? Bully?" she supplied helpfully, a little smile playing on her lips.

"Bully. Decidedly a bully. Any man who forces a woman deserves to be shot," Angel declared decisively.

She kissed him firmly on the mouth.

"Thank you," she said.

"For what?" He leaned his forehead gently against hers. He had done it before and she liked it. It was a tender gesture and she would take all of those that he wished to give.

"I like it when you..."

"Threaten violence against the evildoer who wronged you?" He tried to grin, but she could see what she had told him had disturbed him.

"Should I..." She stopped. "Should I not have told you?"

"No! Of course not." He buried his face in her hair and pulled her closer. "I'm glad you did. Ever so glad. Gwendolen, I..."

Whatever he was going to say or do was abruptly interrupted by a commotion in the corridor. Raised voices. Running footsteps.

"What on earth..." He leaped out of bed, pulling trousers hastily over his drawers, allowing a brief but lovely view of a well-muscled backside.

In a few seconds he was at the door, about to pull it open.

"Angel!" Gwendolen gasped, hastily clutching the coverlet to her chest and looking at the floor for her night rail.

"Oh. Right." He grinned looking back at her. "I'll be quick. No one will see."

And then he was gone, and she was left sitting on the bed, nearly naked, hoping he was right and that she had not just given one of their footmen an eyeful of duchess.

Letter 14

HIS GRACE THE DUKE of Englefield to Mrs. Archibald Coley

August 13, 1812

Almedo, Portugal

Dearest Aunt Eliza,

By the time this missive reaches you, I am sure you will already be familiar with the events of the battle at Salamanca on the 22 of July.

Firstly, rest assured I am safe and well. I took a slight saber cut which the surgeon stitched up. It is healing up nicely. A few bruises on my legs from the stones from which they saluted us in the breach, but a short time will bring me completely round. Hugh fares a little worse, having taken a musket shot just above the knee, but the surgeon hopes he will make a good recovery in a few weeks. (He is writing to his mother now, so do not scold me for not telling him to do so.)

You will already know the enemy was beaten before the day was ended and at great loss of life, to both sides. The early injuries sustained by their commander cost the French the battle.

My comrades have spent the last days rejoicing at our good fortune —and it is true, I should be thanking God for making it through alive when many did not.

But I find it hard to be grateful after some of the atrocities I have witnessed these past months. Particularly when the source of the worst of these was a British soldier in my own regiment—and a so-called gentleman. I have already mentioned the name Robert Wyndham to you in an earlier letter, complaining of his slovenly habits. But from mere drunkenness, brawling, and stirring up the men, he has now escalated into actions more vicious.

Back in Lisbon, he took up with a woman—a girl, really, she could not have been more than fifteen or sixteen. Following him, she left her family and home and has traveled with us these last seven months. Many times, Hugh and I observed Wyndham's neglect and mistreatment her—from failure to provide her with the basic necessities to applying his fists in anger.

More than once, we intervened. After a few months, it became apparent she was with child—yet Wyndham's treatment of her did not improve. If anything, it deteriorated.

When we reached Estremoz on the Badajoz-Lisbon road, Hugh and I noticed she was no longer with us. Speaking to the men, we learned Wyndham had forced her to remain behind, instructing her to return to her family.

Receiving permission to return to Estremoz, we found her huddled in a filthy alley along one of the streets. The girl had no money, no means of provision. She claimed she was unable to return to her family for fear of their reprisal.

To be blunt, she believed they would kill her, Aunt, especially as she was increasing and unwed. As a matter of family honor.

The bastard had left her there, knowing this, Aunt—caring nothing for her or his child. As if she was a stray dog to be discarded when he chose and not a girl who had given him all that was most precious and was left utterly vulnerable for having done so.

Upon returning to the camp, Hugh and I endeavored to speak to Wyndham's sense of honor. We spoke with our mouths. Then I spoke to him more loudly with my fists. In both cases, we failed to stir any feeling of compassion or responsibility for the girl he had treated so vilely. We left him battered but unrepentant, merely angrier than before and spewing threats of revenge.

Taking up a contribution from the men, we made plans to return to the girl the next day—without Wyndham. We had enough to set her up in decent lodgings, with enough left over to sustain her through her confinement. We planned to instruct her to write to us when the babe was born so that we could send more for their welfare.

We reached the town a second time, only to find the worst had already occurred.

Believing herself betrayed and abandoned, she had done away with herself. Her body had been found hanging from an arch that morning.

Her name was Teresa Da Rosa. She was hardly more than a child.

We had her buried as best we could, no church being willing to take her due to the manner of death. We sent word to Lisbon.

God pity her poor parents. Little did they know they would not see their daughter again in this life when she foolishly left them.

Although I cannot help but despise them a little, knowing that she feared them so much that taking her own life was preferable to risking their judgement.

Back at camp we sought out Wyndham again, but like a snake he slipped our grasp and eluded us constantly. I did not see him again until the battle began a few days later.

A few hours into the fight, I caught sight of him—regrettably too late. A young French soldier knelt before him, his musket thrown down and his hands in the air. The boy was clearly capitulating. Had Wyndham possessed any honor whatsoever, he would have returned him to camp as a captive of war.

But I am sure you already know what occurred instead.

As our eyes met Wyndham raised his bayonet and slashed the boy's throat. In the next instant, a shot rang out and, in my efforts to remain astride, I confess I lost sight of him in the fray.

He has not been seen since.

An officer has reported seeing him take a musket ball to the shoulder, but claimed he did not appear to fall.

Perhaps he perished of the wound. Yet if so, why has his body not been recovered? I believe it far more likely he has deserted. He knows that if he reappears, he has much to account for. Indeed, he will be lucky if he is not hung.

A man with no honor does not wait for judgement to be passed when he well knows his guilt.

Soon he will be reported killed or missing, his family notified, and no one will remember the girl or the boy who lost their lives to his villainy. It is beyond infuriating to know he may yet live and roam the continent a free man, merely repeating similar crimes.

Hugh says I must put the matter from my mind, calm myself if I am to move past these troubling events.

But I will not forget them.

I see you reading this now, feeling the same anger I do. I am sorry for putting the burden of knowledge upon you. But it has helped a little to get the words out onto the page, to know Wyndham's dark deeds have been recorded—at least to this extent.

The country we are in now is rich and green with rolling hills. I might fancy myself near Englefield Abbey were it not for the language. Such beauty amidst such horror.

Please believe me,

Your affectionate nephew,

Angel

P.S. I still cannot believe they are gone. At night, I see them so vividly. Mother smiling over the pianoforte. Father standing by her shoulder to turn the pages. But they will not be there when I return. They will never be there again. Perhaps that is why I am so reluctant to come back. I know I must take up my responsibilities. I shall do so, in time, I promise you. Just... not yet. I trust all to be well left in your capable hands.

Chapter 13

ELIZA WAS JUST OUTSIDE. She put a hand to her throat as he came out.

"Oh, good. We were just about to wake you."

"What is it?" he asked, tersely.

"One of the men you have patrolling thought he heard an intruder in the morning room. When he went to see, one of the windows was slightly ajar." Seeing his face, she added, "Now that does not mean anything, Angel. Anyone might have left it open by accident. It was a warm day."

"Yes, of course." He was already distracted, starting down the passage. "Have they searched the house? Have they checked the nursery?"

"The nursery?" Gwendolen was there, modestly dressed once more, a soft blue wrapper over her night dress. "What has happened in the nursery?"

"Probably nothing," he assured her. Aunt Eliza nodded. "But we are taking every precaution."

"One of the men thought they heard an intruder," Eliza explained.

"Oh, my God." Gwendolen covered her mouth with her hand.

A door opened a little further down. "What's going on out here? Does no one sleep in this house?"

Angel saw Gwendolen's eyes widen as she looked at the source of the cross voice. A young woman, perhaps Rosalind's age, peeped out with a suspicious expression.

"Claire?"

"Gwendolen?"

"What on earth are you doing here!"

"What do you mean what am I doing here? You sent for me. Rosalind wrote telling me you wished me to come. So here I am. Sleepless, no thanks to all of you. Are there frequently parties in the hallway in the middle of the night in this house? Or is this the first?"

"It is not a party," Gwendolen replied slowly. "There may be an intruder in the house."

With a loud squeak Claire fled back into her room, emerging a minute later wearing a heavy dressing gown. She marched up to them.

"You must be the duke." She held out a hand. Angel took it with amusement.

Gwendolen rolled her eyes. Claire was the second eldest sister and at eighteen was not lacking in assertiveness. She was dark-haired where Gwendolen and Rosalind were fair. Her hair hung in plaits around her shoulders. She was taller than both of her sisters, with a slender willowy figure.

Right now, she was clutching her dressing gown to her neck as if she were an elderly matron.

"Whoever it is, they are not after *you*," Gwendolen said, irritably.

"Well, who are they after then?"

Gwendolen exchanged a glance with Angel. He touched her shoulder. "I cannot stand this. I'm going to find some of the men. They are probably making rounds of the house now. I'll help them. Find Henry."

Gwendolen looked to Eliza who nodded grimly. Putting her fingers to her lips, she gave a sharp whistle.

Claire, who was standing beside her, cringed. "Was that really necessary—" she began, rubbing her ears.

There were thunderous footsteps.

Paw-steps.

A deep bark.

The paw-steps grew louder. Gwendolen saw Claire step back as a galloping mastiff higher than her waist and as wide as a horse—or at least a small pony—reached their group.

Hercules halted, panting, beside his mistress. She rubbed his head. "Good, Herc. Come."

She turned and strode down the hall in the direction of the nursery, Gwendolen quickly following.

Claire took up the rear, muttering under her breath about all that was not being said and all of the sleep that was not being had.

As they reached the other wing where the nursery and additional bed chambers were located, a figure was already coming down the hall towards them.

The oil lamps dotting the walls had been turned down so for a moment they continued towards one another, Gwendolen hoping that the figure would not turn out to be the intruder.

But if it was, she had every confidence in Hercules.

Not to mention Eliza.

Claire could also kill with her crankiness.

The figure was too slight to be male. It was shorter than Claire

"Gwendolen!" Rosalind came towards them, a sleepy Henry in her arms. "We heard raised voices. Albert came to see if we were all right, then practically ran out of the room. Henry was awake by then and he wanted you, so here we are. Whatever is happening?"

"We are under siege," Claire muttered. "Or one would think so."

"Did you invite Claire?" Gwendolen asked Rosalind wryly, rubbing a hand over Henry's back before lifting him into her own arms.

His arms went around her neck immediately. "Mummy..." His voice was sleepy. "Auntie Claire is here?"

"So, it would seem. Go to sleep, sweetheart," Gwendolen murmured, smoothing his hair and kissing his cheek. He was safe. Everything would be all right.

Angel would see to it. It was difficult to feel properly fearful with Henry safe and after what had just happened between them.

"I thought it would be lovely for us all to be together," Rosalind said happily. "A wonderful surprise for you both!" She looked between them thoughtfully. "Although the surprise was supposed to wait until morning."

Claire grimaced. "That would have been nice." She yawned widely. "Well? Can we go back to bed now?"

They all began walking back in the direction from which they had come.

As they were reaching the end of the hall, they heard footsteps and Angel came around the corner, Albert the footman close behind.

"There you are," he said with relief. "And there is Henry. I was just coming to check on him again, but of course, you got there first. Albert told me he was all right." He looked towards his aunt. "We have searched the house. No sign of anyone here who should not be. I am having the men search again." He shrugged his shoulders.

"An overzealous watchman, perhaps?" Eliza suggested.

"I would rather they be overzealous than lax. Although this has rather upset the whole household for what does seem like nothing now. The poor fellow who raised the alarm probably feels awful."

"He's not the only one," Gwendolen heard Claire mutter to herself. "Nearly twelve hours by coach. Twelve! Then, finally, a bed..."

"Yes, yes, Claire," Gwendolen shushed her. "Come along and let us get you to your room."

"Perhaps we can all sleep with you, Gwendolen?" Rosalind said brightly. "An impromptu slumber party?"

"Oh yes, Mummy." Henry perked up. "I would like that. I want to sleep with you."

Gwendolen kissed him. "Of course, you may. And Auntie Rosy and Auntie Claire, too, if they like." She hoped Claire would go back to her own room though. She tended to be a kicker.

"Can Herc come, too?" Henry asked.

Gwendolen opened her mouth to answer but thankfully Aunt Eliza rescued her.

"No, he may not. Hercules will be sleeping with me tonight. Otherwise, I shall be very lonely."

Henry nodded sagely. "You may have one of my aunties if you are too lonely, Aunt Eliza."

"That is very kind, Henry." Eliza looked truly touched.

Angel walked them to their rooms and left them at the door.

He looked as if he were about to lean in to kiss Gwendolen as she turned to say goodnight, then thought better of it and merely smiled instead.

Blushing, she carried Henry into her room.

Angel did not return to his bedchamber. Instead, he and Albert made their way through the house once more, checking in with each pair of men.

All was quiet. All was well, they were assured, each time.

"Go to sleep, Albert," Angel said, clasping the young man's shoulder. "And thank you. I appreciated having you by my side. Tell Westcott you must sleep late tomorrow."

"Oh, I couldn't do that, Your Grace!" Albert looked horrified. "I have my duties. I couldn't possibly..."

"Then have the Cook make your favorite dishes at breakfast. But something, Albert. Let a duke thank you, for Heaven's sake." And then with a grin, he turned away.

He made one last pass by the nursery.

The door was still open. Rosalind must have left it ajar when she came out with the lad.

He leaned in to shut it. Something caught his eye.

The curtains were blowing in the breeze. The sash widows were open wide.

He stepped forward, looking more closely. The fabric of the curtains had been cut to pieces, as if by a sharp blade.

He strode over, looking outside. There was no one there. Or, at least no one he could see. The garden was quiet and dark.

He turned back to check the room and stepped upon something soft. Bending down, he felt a familiar shape. Henry's toy rabbit. In two separate pieces where it had been one. The rabbit's head had been ripped off.

"What is it?" Aunt Eliza asked quietly from the door, Hercules steadfast beside her.

Angel held up the torn toy.

"Henry would not have done that."

"I agree," he said.

"Nor would Hercules, if that is what you are thinking. He is very gentle with children. This is something he might have done as a puppy, but he has seen Henry with the toy…"

"You speak as if Herc could tell it meant something to the boy," Angel interrupted. "He is only a dog, after all, Aunt."

"He is an intelligent creature who has spent a great deal of time with Henry of late and knows his preferences. In any case, chewing household items is not one of his pastimes. He prefers his beef bones." She crossed her arms. "Those curtains behind you are slashed to ribbons, Angel. There is more to this than a broken toy. What are you not telling me?"

Angel passed a hand over his face. For a while, he had expected the night to go in quite another direction. Could this truly be the same evening he had attended a ball? Punched an earl? Kissed his wife?

Well, not just kissed. Done considerably more than that, and had hoped to do still more.

Now he was crouched fearfully on a nursery floor, racking his brain of a way to protect his new family from a man who was trying to kidnap his own child. A brutal man, by all accounts.

He looked down at the little ripped rabbit. Whoever had done this was not a man who should be the father of a sweet boy like Henry.

He let himself imagine, just for a moment, the consequences of losing Henry.

Not only would the boy's life be horribly altered, Gwendolen would be destroyed.

And Angel would never forgive himself.

He had offered his protection. That was how this had all begun.

Now he stood on the precipice of failure.

Only sheer luck had resulted in Rosalind sleeping in Henry's room tonight, missing the intruder when he came to search for the sleeping boy only to find him already gone.

If Rosalind had not brought him out as quickly as she had, they may have reached the nursery too late.

He would have to commend the night watchman. The man had not been an alarmist after all, merely admirably observant.

His aunt stood waiting.

"I think it is time we left London," Angel said, standing up and meeting her eyes. "The Abbey is beautiful this time of year. Now that Gwendolen's sisters are both here, perhaps they would enjoy a visit."

Eliza nodded slowly. "I will have a message sent immediately to let the housekeeper know we are coming. When would you like to leave?"

"Tomorrow."

She raised her eyebrows. "So soon."

She stood in the doorway a moment, looking at him in silence.

"You've changed, Angel."

"Have I?" He was distracted, his mind racing in different directions. Was this the first attempt the earl had made to take Henry? Or merely the first they had noticed?

He had thought marriage would be enough to protect Gwendolen and deter the man harassing her. That had been an incredibly naïve assumption, apparently.

Would the courts uphold the right of a father who had abandoned his child? A child who was then born within wedlock and claimed as another man's legitimate son? Unlikely.

But if the man was ruthless enough, heartless enough, to take a small child from his mother, then surely that man would also not hesitate to take the child far from where the laws of England could follow. How easy it would be to take a ship to the continent, raise the boy as his own. Or have someone else raise him.

Gwendolen had said the earl could not sire children. Hypothetically, then, someday he would bring the boy back as his heir.

After what would likely be a warped upbringing, would Henry remember his mother or have any feeling towards her?

"Have I?" Angel murmured again. "How so?" He looked up, trying to focus his attention.

She was smiling a little. "Yes. Decidedly so, and swiftly." She shook her head. "Your life has had a strange trajectory, Angel. You went from a rather coddled youth of ease and privilege to one of hardship and battle. You did so by choice, and in the process became a man. But then..." She shrugged. "You lost your parents. Went through unspeakable things. You returned and lapsed into boyhood somewhat. Perhaps a way of escaping?"

"I suppose I would not argue with that assessment," Angel said wryly.

"But now," she went on, "You've encountered evil once more—" Angel's brows went up. "Well? It is evil, is it not? To harass and terrify a woman, to attempt to steal a little boy in the dead of night? What else would you call it?"

"Entitlement. Callousness. Selfishness. A complete lack of empathy."

"Well, you call it what you will, but it is certainly the opposite of good. Yet you chose to take it on."

"I think you give me too much credit. To be honest, I think I underestimated quite what Gwendolen was up against when I first encountered her."

"Regardless, the prospect of protecting her from unknown troubles did not dissuade you from marriage."

"It did not. However, I would have expected you to say this was a sure sign of my immaturity and not the opposite. Rushing headlong, blindly one might even say, into a permanent union with a woman with a child—both of whom I hardly knew."

She smiled. "But that is where the pure goodness of it comes in. Balancing the evil. Unbeknownst to either of you."

"What do you mean?"

"You are a perfect fit. The three of you. Your love balances out the evil."

Angel shifted uncomfortably.

"Oh, please, Angel. I have known you your entire life. You care for this woman, more than you will say, perhaps more than you even know yourself. And her child?"

"Henry. He is my responsibility. I care for the lad, of course." His heart tugged at him fiercely, suggesting that might be an understatement.

"Yes. You'll grow to love each other, too. I have become remarkably fond of the little fellow even in this short time. Haven't I, Hercules?" She scratched the mastiff's head.

"All of this talk of good and evil," Angel grumbled. "I had not thought you a religious sort of woman."

"I am not," his aunt replied, looking thoughtful. "But I do believe there must be a balance to the world of some kind. It cannot all be chaos, can it? The ancient Greeks believed there could be nothing bad without something good. And didn't Aquinas say 'Good can exist without evil, whereas evil cannot exist without good'?"

"I don't know," Angel replied blithely. "Did he? I fear I have forgotten my theology. It was scant to begin with."

"Jest all you like, Angel, but you know there is truth to what I say. Now, come, my foolish brother's son." The expression she gave him was both frustrated and affectionate. "Let us discuss how you will protect your family."

"Ah! Plots and machinations—now that is much more your terrain," he said, trying for cheerfulness, slinging an arm around her shoulder as they left the nursery behind. "Speaking of which, did you know Rosalind had plans to invite her sister?"

He saw his aunt smile.

"She mentioned something about it, yes, and I saw no harm. I believe she invited her whole family to descend upon us, but her mother sent a kind note saying she and her youngest are still occupied. She sends her regards to you. And her love."

"I look forward to having the opportunity to someday meet the lady who produced such a wide-range of young women," he said, thinking of how different Gwendolen was from Rosalind. Not to mention the cantankerous-seeming Claire.

"Let us hope the rest of Miss Gardner's night is satisfactory or we shall not hear the end of it at breakfast," Eliza said, her lips twitching.

"You are not fooling me, Gwendolen!" Rosalind whispered loudly.

Gwendolen cracked one eye open.

They were in bed. Claire had, blessedly, returned to her own room, while Rosalind and Henry had joined Gwendolen.

Henry lay between the two sisters, breathing softly, his face relaxed and beautiful in sleep.

"Isn't he lovely?" Gwendolen said softly, touching his cheek. "I made him, you know." She would not credit the other party. She never would.

"Yes, I know you did. You have mentioned it before. That is not what we are talking about. We are not discussing Henry. Stop changing the subject. We are talking about you and Angel. Your husband!"

"Shush!" Gwendolen hissed. "He's in the other room. Besides, I would have thought you'd be more interested in talking about the excitement with the intruder this evening…"

"But there was no intruder, was there?" Rosalind interrupted. "Angel said they found nothing. One of their servants has an overactive imagination. Besides Claire being absolutely horrid in the morning from not getting enough sleep, nothing frightful has or will have occurred."

Gwendolen bit her lip. She had shared enough for one night, she decided. She had gone all of this time without telling Rosalind and Claire this part of her history. Perhaps they would never need to know.

"I know you're in love with him!"

"With whom?" Gwendolen asked innocently, feigning a wide yawn. "May we please go to sleep now?"

"No, we may not. With Angel of course!"

"My husband? But I already told you I was. That was why we got married."

"Can you see my eyes rolling in the dark?" Rosalind asked, sardonically. "Because I would like to assure you, they are rolling as far as they can roll. Yes, you told me. But I did not believe half of what you said for a second. Especially after that kiss at your wedding breakfast. Why, you looked as if it was your very first one!"

Rosalind waited, then lifted herself up on her arms a little. "I'll take your total silence as confirmation. I knew it!"

Her tone changed to one of confused amusement. "But why? Why had you never kissed him before? And why did you lie and say you were in love with him when you were merely about to be *truly* in love with him—which is quite different altogether. And why..."

Gwendolen groaned. "Why all of these whys, Rosalind?"

Rosalind was quiet for a moment. Which was a remarkable thing.

"You have always been the reticent one, Gwendolen. You seemed much older than us both growing up. I suppose now Claire and I seem that way to Gracie as she is only seven. You must seem positively ancient to her. But that's not the point. The point is... You. You are the point. You are in love." She tried to sound triumphant.

"No, I'm not," Gwendolen said crossly. "I'm cranky and I'm sleepy and I'm finished with this interrogation."

"If you think this is an interrogation, I should let Claire have a go at you!"

Gwendolen shuddered. "Please, no." She considered. "I am very... fond. Of my husband."

"Fond. Yes. I am fond of cheesecake. Henry is fond of biscuits. No, you are not fond."

"What am I then? If you are such a know-it-all about my innermost thoughts and feelings? I am the one rolling my eyes now, Rosalind, in case you cannot tell."

"Oh, I can tell," Rosalind replied cheerfully. "You are smitten. You are enamored. You are not fond of Angel, you are in love with Angel. If I had any doubt before now, it is gone. I could see it as soon as you came towards us in the hallway tonight. You were positively glowing."

Gwendolen shifted a little, thinking of just how glowing she must have been.

"Does he know? Or are you torturing the poor man?"

"Torturing him?" Gwendolen said with genuine surprise.

"Torturing him into thinking he is the only one in love!"

"Oh." Gwendolen sighed. "He is not in love with me." She was not sure what he was. "At least, he has not said so."

"You sound quite sorry about that. Almost as if you cared."

Gwendolen sat up and grabbed a pillow. "I am going to sleep now, Rosalind. I am either going to fluff this pillow or smother you with it, no matter Henry's presence. Which will it be?"

"Fine, fine. We can discuss it more in the—" Rosalind yawned. "—in the morning. Goodnight, sweet sister."

"Goodnight, sweet harpy."

Gwendolen lay there in the dark a while, her heart racing. It would soon be morning. She had hardly slept.

In love.

The phrase was ringing in her ears.

She had thought herself in love once before. And ever since, she had decided she would never let herself believe something so ridiculous again.

But now... Something had come alive inside of her.

Even in the midst of fear, she felt happier than she could remember.

Letter 15

MR. HUGH CAVENDISH TO Mrs. Archibald Coley

August 15, 1812

Almedo, Portugal

My Dear Eliza,

Tally-ho from the trenches!

Now, I wonder which letter you will receive first—my own, or the one written by that fibber of a nephew of yours.

He covered the page as he wrote last night, which is why I knew he would not share anything resembling the truth—at least not where his own welfare was concerned. I managed to peek enough to see he made mention of the tragedy concerning the young lady.

But did he speak true of what had befallen him? I doubt it greatly.

I bet the knave even claimed I had fared worse than he had.

I will be concise, but I feel you have the right to know. Particularly as we two are all that are left of those closest to him, now that... Well.

I can hear you rushing me on. Stop dawdling, Hugh Cavendish.

Very well.

We almost lost Angel in the Battle of Salamanca.

Until a fortnight ago, we were not sure he would pull through.

The blackguard, Wyndham, whom I know Angel has mentioned to you—though given a less than full-report—stooped to utter cowardness and callousness in battle.

I regret, I was not by Angel's side to see it, but from what I am told, Wyndham brutally slaughtered a young lad in front of Angel's eyes— a French soldier who had been trying to surrender.

Angel charged him, Eliza—not to slay, but to apprehend, as he tells it. But his saber was raised for he had already been in the fray.

He was also already wounded—a slash to the chest. Minor, but enough to be a distraction.

Perhaps Wyndham did not understand that Angel's intent was not to execute but to escort him back to the camp. Though I shall not say that excuses his conduct which was utterly shameless.

He raised his saber to your nephew and cut him down. Angel managed to parry the first thrust, and even got in a jab with his own blade. But Wyndham's cut went deep.

We found him hours later, lying on the ground, amidst many others.

I confess, I thought he was dead at first. There was so much blood. His chest was carved open. It must have been a brutal blow.

Wyndham had, of course, vanished like a thief in the night.

Why tell you any of this when you might be spared the terrible knowledge?

He bears quite the scar, for one. It is healing well. The surgeon hopes it will fade to nothing in time. Or if not quite nothing, at least nothing that will be noticeable with proper cover.

The scar on his soul is another matter.

His parents' deaths had already done much to crush his ordinarily indomitable spirit.

To be betrayed on the battlefield by a fellow Englishman—a supposed gentleman. To have been unable to prevent the young woman's death. Nor the young Frenchman's.

Well, it weighs on him. I see it.

When he returns, I pray you will make allowances. As will I.

Your humble servant,

Hugh Cavendish

Chapter 14

"YOUR GRACE?"

Gwendolen peered out the window. It was raining steadily. One might even call it stormy. Yet Angel was insisting they depart for the Englefields' country seat. Immediately. He was driving the household on with the persistence of a bloodhound.

She had a good idea as to why.

Last night's upheaval had scared him more than he would say. If the man who had offered his protection believed they would be safer outside of London, she had no objection. She had grown up in the country. The city held no great allure for her. Besides bookshops and dress shops. And milliners.

But those would be there, waiting. Books could be ordered.

Besides, Redmond was in London. She had not heard from him since her marriage, but seeing him at the ball yesterday had been a frightening reminder of how easy it would be to encounter him again.

She was sure he had not seen her last night, but the next time she might not be so fortunate as to escape his notice.

"Your Grace?"

The voice was speaking to her, she belatedly realized, turning away from the window. Would she ever get used to the title? From being a mere Miss Gardner to Lady Leicester to a duchess. All this for a girl who had never wanted anything more than a simple life with a loving husband and a bevy of children. The simple but happy life her parents had chosen.

"Your Grace, I found this in the pelisse you were wearing last night."

The maid held out a piece of paper. Not Nancy, but one of the duke's own staff. A young Irish girl, with pretty red cheeks.

"Thank you...?"

"Molly, Your Grace."

"Thank you, Molly." She gave the girl a warm smile, then sat down at her desk, holding the paper.

What could it be? Could Redmond have...? No, he had not been close enough.

There was no name on the outside. Just a paper folded into quarters, unsealed.

She opened it up.

Gwendolen,

I do apologize for Lord Leicester's behavior this evening.

Men can be beasts, can they not? Especially when they have imbibed.

Of course, your own is no exception to this, despite what you may think.

I believe my cousin's name rang familiar to you the other day on the street. The Earl of Redmond, Robert Wyndham.

He fought alongside the duke, in Portugal. Did you know that?

Wyndham tells me the strangest things, Gwendolen. For one, he says you have a grudge against him. He knows not what for.

—Here Gwendolen choked out a laugh—

But no matter, it is your husband he tells the strangest tale about of all.

It seems there was a girl—there always is, isn't there? This was in Portugal, just before the Battle of Salamanca. The duke was younger then and quite in love. Head over heels, my cousin says. When she spurned him for another, the duke—well, he was not yet known as the duke then, for his parents' deaths were not yet common knowledge. In any case, the duke became incensed. He could not be held back by anyone. He drank to excess. He brawled in the streets with any man who would fight him.

Then he went after the girl. Wyndham tried to stop him. They fought. But the duke could not be held back. He shot her, Gwendolen. Wyndham says it was the greatest tragedy, for she was with child, you see. Angel's child. He only found out afterwards. Can you imagine?

There was no penalty. The battle took place soon after and in the aftermath the girl was forgotten, I suppose.

Well, not entirely forgotten. I am sure the duke remembers, though he may not speak of it.

To think he harbored such a passion for a woman! I wonder if anything has ever come close to it again.

Well, you and I are women of the world. Such things cannot shock us. I am yet unmarried, I know, but Cecil and I shall soon be wed. You must know something of his true character. He will not be an ideal husband. But I believe I shall know how to manage such a man.

As for you, I wonder if you can say the same. Or will your Angel soon fly away again?

Perhaps it would be for the best. One would not really wish for that sort of man to be around a small child. He might fly into another senseless rage and then who knows what might occur.

I speak of this only as a friend. From one woman to another.

Julia

Oh, Julia.

Gwendolen folded the letter neatly again and looked down at it.

Such a poison-filled message on such a small piece of paper.

Julia had known the late Lord Leicester her entire life. He had been a close friend of her father's. When the widowed earl had unexpectedly married Gwendolen, after nearly a decade unmarried, Julia could not have been more than sixteen.

John had once said something about the Pembrokes having hopes he would wed again. Had he left out that those hopes were that he would wed their eldest daughter? Gwendolen knew that John had lent the family money before. Julia's father was a gambling man. She did not think the money had ever been paid back. It would have tied things up neatly for Julia to marry John.

Of course, Julia was tying things up neatly now—by marrying John's son, who had inherited everything.

That stung a little.

Though if Julia realized the nature of Cecil's overtures towards his stepmother—assaults, would be more accurate—then that could not possibly be helping matters.

Nor could Gwendolen's unexpected and swift marriage to a rich and handsome duke.

All things considered, there were rather a lot of reasons for Julia to harbor spite. And reading between the lines, she sounded desperately unhappy.

The letter was meant to drive a wedge between Gwendolen and Angel, clearly. To fill her mind with uncertainty and jealousy.

Of course, most of it was lies. Wyndham's word could not be trusted.

Whether Julia was aware of her cousin's expertise at deception was another matter. Gwendolen suspected artifice ran in the family.

It could not all be false though. There was a seed of truth there, no matter how warped a retelling Wyndham had given.

But which was seed and which was chaff?

Had Angel really loved this girl?

She closed her eyes and leaned her head against the foggy cool pane.

That would explain a great deal.

Why he had so hastily proposed marriage. Why he had claimed not to care if he sired his own heir. A chaste marriage had not seemed to discourage him. Nor had the idea of marrying for a reason so far from love.

Because he was still in love with someone else? A girl who had died years ago.

She could not compete with the memory of a dead love. One who had died with Angel's child in her belly. One who was perhaps accidentally killed. By Angel?

Angel could not, would not, have ever done something like that, she told herself fiercely. It was simply not in his nature. He would never mistreat a woman.

Or he would not... now.

Had he been different then? Had he changed after returning to England?

Was this his attempt at redemption? Saving Gwendolen and her son? Sacrificing his own chance at happiness in the process?

She thought of the night before. Their bodies pressed against one another. His hand in her most secret of places. The pleasure he had given her.

Given, being the keyword. He gave, he did not receive.

Perhaps he had felt sorry for her. The lonely widow, sneaking in from her cold bed, desperate for male warmth.

Perhaps he had simply pleasured her out of pity.

She shuddered and turned away, crumpling the letter in her hand, and tucking it deep into a drawer.

There was a tap at the door.

"Gwendolen? Are you ready? The carriage is outside. The duke says you're to ride with Henry, Rosalind, and myself." Claire's strident voice rang clear through the heavy wood panel. "Gwendolen? Do you hear me?"

Gwendolen stepped away from the window, opened her eyes.

"Yes, I hear you. I am coming," she called, drearily. Picking her bonnet off the bed, she turned towards the door.

Angel felt like a mother hen trying to gather a brood of chicks. He suddenly had the utmost empathy for mothers with large families.

The household was in a state of upheaval. Maids and footmen dashed to and fro, carrying out the many tasks required for removal from Sweetbriar Hall. Angel had been waiting for half an hour and in that time, the mass of trunks and other necessities that lay at the foot of the grand staircase had grown from a modest heap to something more approaching a mountain.

Even Hercules was complicit. Two footmen had arrived bearing a trunk monogrammed with the dog's initial, swaying under its weight.

It was larger than Angel's own.

Stealing a peek inside, he could see brown paper wrapped packages of what he assumed were beef bones, as well as blankets, canine toys, and even what appeared to be a set of dog slippers made of red plaid.

When he had asked his aunt whether the carriage horses would also be bringing their own luggage, she had merely looked at him coolly as if packing for a dog was not unusual in the least.

Now he stood in the foyer by the mountainous pile of belongings, tapping his foot as the minutes turned to hours and the day slipped away.

To top it all off, the woman he was going to all this trouble to safeguard had been avoiding him all day. Or at least, that was how it felt. She had scarcely said two words to him since he had informed her they would be leaving London.

Perhaps she was irritated that he had not consulted her first.

It was deucedly awkward trying to recall what one was supposed to do with one's wife. He certainly did not wish to be one of those men who ran their household like a despot and never consulted their wives. At the same time, the truth was that he had not asked her because he did not want to give her any opportunity to say no. Not after what he had discovered last night.

He also found he had no desire to tell her about what he had found and add to her fears and worries.

Or to cause her to doubt he was capable of protecting her and her son, a small part of him suggested.

A pattering of footsteps drew his attention and he looked away from the pile of trunks to see Rosalind coming down the stairs.

"Rosalind! Thank goodness. You're ready to depart then?"

"Depart? Oh, no, I was looking for my..." Her eyes darted to a small table in the foyer. "There!" She snatched up a book from which dangled a red hair ribbon.

"They make excellent bookmarks, you know," she explained.

Angel closed his eyes. "Rosalind. Are you and your sisters anywhere near to being ready to leave this house? Today, preferably?"

"Well, Claire certainly is. She is not in the best of moods about it, however. When I last saw her, she was lying on her bed grumbling about having to leave as soon as she had arrived. Which I suppose was fair. And after last night..."

"Yes, yes, so Claire is ready. What about you? And Gwendolen and Henry?" Angel interrupted. "I would like to arrive tonight." The truth was he was prepared to drive until dawn if it meant arriving at the Abbey sooner.

Rosalind gave him an appraising look. "I see. It seems very important to you to leave London as soon as possible."

"It is," Angel agreed.

"Almost as if you were running away from something."

Angel opened his mouth but she continued.

"Something you don't want my sister to know about perhaps? Something to do with her?" She raised her eyebrows and Angel feared she had seen through him. "With Henry?"

Her eyes narrowed. "Would you care to share any of your knowledge, Your Grace?"

Confound these Gardner women. Fortunately, he was rescued from further speech by Gwendolen coming down the stairs with Henry.

She was wearing a dusky rose velvet dress with a ribbon sash tied neatly beneath her breasts. It drew his eye to the region and he swallowed hard, remembering the perfect mysterious softness that lay below that privileged fabric.

God, she was lovely. Even in the shadowy hall.

Even in the dim moonlit room last night. Especially in the dim moonlit room last night.

Holding Henry by the hand, she was the picture of pretty motherhood. Soft and warm and... And definitely avoiding meeting his eye.

His heart sank. Was this to do with last night? She had finally opened up to him, shared painful secrets, then eagerly embraced him. She had seemed to take pleasure from his touch and when they were interrupted, he had gone out feeling buoyant with happiness and excited to return to her.

That had not been possible. Her bed had been full, while his had been... well, rather lonely without her. Her presence in his bed had felt so natural. Both comforting and exhilarating. And oh, so very right.

He sighed, then moved his way towards her, and was about to ask if something was wrong when her sister came clomping down the stairs, carrying a large leather valise.

"Oh, Claire! A footman could have helped with that," Gwendolen exclaimed.

"I. Am. Perfectly. Capable," Claire grunted as she reached the bottom, panting a little.

"I can help Auntie Claire!" Henry scurried over to help drag the bag to sit with the rest of the luggage.

Aunt Eliza appeared, gliding majestically out of a hallway with her hound behind her. "Are we ready to depart?"

Angel nodded. He supposed a conversation with his wife would have to wait.

Letter 16

LADY JULIA PEMBROKE TO the Right Hon. Earl of Redmond

February 1817

London

My Dear Cousin,

It is like a miracle to have you returned to us—and with such a rise in your fortunes besides!

I am sure you could never have imagined coming into an earldom in such an unexpected way. We must thank the cholera for decimating all who lay in the path between it and you.

I jest, of course. But you and I both know it is far better off in your hands than going to a sniveling boy of fourteen or his cousin of ten. They would not have known what to make of such a thing!

Far better to go to a man of our family, a capable man, a man of honor and valor. For, after all, though I know you do not speak of them, you have the battle scars to prove it, do you not?

I pray you will not shy away from sharing more regarding your Lost Years on the continent. I am simply dying to know what took place while you were considered vanished from the face of the earth.

It is strange that only once the earldom had fallen to you, did you resurface so suddenly. But as I have said, it is a miracle—and the Pembrokes never look a gift horse in the mouth. You arrived just in time to bail Papa out yet again from the debts he had incurred. For that alone, you have my undying devotion and gratitude.

Visit us soon, when you next return to London.

Your loving cousin,

Julia

Letter 17

THE RIGHT HON. EARL of Redmond to the Right Hon. Earl of Leicester

April 5, 1817

London

Leicester,

It seems we have both come into titles recently and unexpectedly. I will not waste words wishing you sympathies. I doubt you mourn greatly for the loss of your *pater*, while I will freely admit I rejoice over the departure of my distant cousin from this earthly realm.

Before you begin to fully enjoy your birthright, however, I wish to recall something to your mind:

The summer of 1810.

Seven long years ago. Yet I have no doubt you will recall the period vividly. We were in Bath together. What a merry summer it was.

A few words more:

Lizzy Brown

Ah, that will have jogged your memory, I think.

God rest her poor soul. The mystery of her death must weigh on her poor parents' mind even to this day.

That mystery is one which may stay unsolved and the memory kept between us if you do what I require of you.

Your stepmother and I share a past acquaintance. She has something which belongs to me and which I plan to recover.

To do so, I wish for her to understand the precariousness of her situation in life.

You have inherited all of your father's property. I assume this means the London house where she resides with her son as well.

You will have her leave that home without delay and without any further provisions.

I do not think I need say more, but if a second letter is required you will regret the writing of it more than I.

Redmond

Chapter 15

ENGLEFIELD ABBEY WAS AN estate like nothing Gwendolen had ever seen. Her marriage to the Earl of Leicester had made her accustomed to the trappings of grandeur—or so she had believed until now. The Leicester estate was large and lovely, though John preferred to primarily reside in the London townhouse.

The Abbey was on a different scale entirely. Magnificent, beautiful, and immense.

It was just past sunset as the carriage entered the grounds, driving through vast forest of wild brush and ancient trees.

As they grew closer to the house, the landscape became more cultivated. Everything about it gave the impression of natural beauty and yet everything about it had also been clearly created to appear just so. Walkways and avenues led over endless lawns and through groves of perfectly cropped trees and shrubs.

They passed through two areas which had been distinctly themed. One with chinoiserie bridges and pagoda-inspired follies, the other taking a Greek influence with columned rotundas and faux-antique temples dotting the landscape around a manmade lake.

Near the house, they caught a glimpse of a walled garden with a miniature medieval tower looming out from the center.

"There is a maze within, you know," Angel offered, helping the three sisters down from the carriage as it pulled up before the main house. "I would not suggest Henry entering alone, however. I spent an entire afternoon inside one summer, unable to find my way out, until my mother finally found me napping inside the tower."

Gwendolen could not help but stare upwards as she stepped out.

While it may have been called an Abbey, the mansion had been constructed to look more like an ancient Greek temple with classical facades and a resplendent Corinthian portico with elaborately carved columns.

"My parents loved Greek architecture," her husband said, coming to stand beside her. "They traveled through Italy and Greece together before I was born and were inspired. All this was constructed in their lifetime. The other side of the house is pure Baroque as you'll see when you walk around it."

"That would take an entire day, I should imagine," she said, smiling a little. For a moment she had forgotten her discomfort around him.

"Perhaps I might show you the grounds tomorrow, once you have rested. There is an exquisite folly, designed as a replica of a temple to Athena, you might enjoy..." His voice faded as he looked at her.

"Yes, well, we shall see." This time her smile was forced. "Henry!" she called, turning back.

She was being very unfair to him. She knew this.

But when she looked at Angel, his beautiful face, his tall imposing masculine frame, and thought of how she had sat naked in his arms and made cries of pleasure as he touched her, she now could not also help imagining another woman. A dark-haired Portuguese beauty. A girl with a body lithe and flawless, untouched by childbirth. In her mind, Angel looked at the girl with a flame in his eyes and kissed her with a passionate intensity.

He must have loved her very much, if he had been willing to fight for her.

If that part of the story was even true, she reminded herself.

She would never believe he could be responsible for her death. Never.

But what had happened?

She could ask him.

But how? She had left the letter back in her room in London. Now she regretted this. Perhaps it might have been as easy as putting it into Angel's hand, letting him read for himself, and then listening as he disclosed the truth.

But now she would have to describe how the letter came to be found, summarize its contents, reveal the sender, and above all walk a fine line between questioning and accusing. Without revealing the pain and, yes, the envy she was feeling at the idea of him caring so deeply for another woman whom he had wanted with no compulsion, no sense of obligation or duty.

A woman he had merely desired for herself. Rather than having been compelled into marriage by a misguided sense of honor.

Was she, Gwendolen, a stand-in even now for the girl? The woman Angel could not keep alive?

She went through the rest of the motions of the evening in a kind of daze, unable to bring herself to go to him. Greeting the staff. Attending to Henry. Viewing parts of the house. Then she had a light meal brought to her room rather than going downstairs and felt quite cowardly. For once her sisters left her alone—perhaps both tired out from the journey themselves.

When she climbed into bed and closed her eyes, she realized she had not thought of Wyndham and his threats in hours, which was unusual for her. Her mind had been too full of the pain of fearing Angel lost to her before she could truly win him.

"Finally decided to bring me into your confidence, have you? Well, what's it all about then? What is your bride's deep, dark secret? Is she a bigamist? A retired pirate? Pirate-ess? No, that doesn't sound right..." Hugh tapped a finger to his chin.

"Oh, would you hush," Angel said, looking at his friend with a mix of amusement, irritation, and concern. "It's a matter of great delicacy. Furthermore, these are not my secrets to tell."

"Secrets, eh? More than one?" Hugh walked beside him across the lawn.

They were drawing near to the little temple Angel had wished to show Gwendolen. Instead of walking with her by his side, he had mouthy Hugh.

Why had he invited him? It had seemed like a good idea at the time. Hugh might be a jester, but he had also fought alongside Angel before. There was safety in numbers.

"I will tell you only what I think you need to know in order to help matters," Angel said abruptly. "If the need even arises. It probably will not. But if it does..."

"Yes, yes," Hugh waved his hand impatiently. "Get on with it, will you. We don't have all day. Well, we do in fact. But I cannot take anymore suspense." He rubbed his hands together. "It's like a gothic novel. I'm on the edge of my seat. If one can be on the edge of one's seat while standing. Perhaps I should sit down." He looked around, as if for a bench.

Angel rolled his eyes.

"Listen, then, you great idiot. It concerns Henry more than Gwendolen in fact."

Hugh's eyebrows raised.

"How can I say this, without it seeming a ridiculous fancy?" Angel ran a hand through his hair in frustration. "It is not a novel. It is all too real and all too dangerous for my liking with a small child involved."

He looked at Hugh directly. "There is a person who wishes to abduct Henry."

He held up a hand, seeing his friend's eyes widen. "Before you question me, know that there has already been at least one attempt— at Sweetbriar. Perhaps there have been more and I was too deucedly oblivious to notice. I really don't know."

They had reached the folly. Angel sat down on the stone steps, his hands folded together.

"I told her I would protect her. And Henry," he said softly, looking down at the grass. "I am not doing a very good job of it."

Hugh sat down on a lower step. He was silent a minute.

"What do you mean there was an attempt at Sweetbriar?"

"I mean that an intruder came in the dark of night and actually entered the nursery. It was only by the grace of God that Rosalind had taken Henry out of the room already. If he had been there, asleep in his bed..." He shook his head. "Well, Gwendolen would be... I don't know what she would be. I abhor even imagining it."

"Devastated," Hugh said quietly. "We lost my younger brother to a fever when he was seven. My mother was never the same. Having a child stolen... it cannot be much better."

"Do you think fathers feel it the same way?" Angel was curious. His own feelings toward Henry had been deepening daily, the more he spent time with him. Reading stories to him in the nursery, playing ball with him on the lawn at Sweetbriar. Watching Henry chase and be chased by Herc, up and down the stairs and around the house.

The feelings surprised him.

Now, the prospect of having his stepson abducted made his heart clench with fear and rage.

"I do not know. Not yet, at least. I know my father felt Ben's loss terribly. He did not show it, but his hair grew quite gray that year. We do not nurture them in the same way women do though. Perhaps that is why that closeness to a child seems to develop later for many men."

"My father cared for me, even when I was a babe," Angel said thoughtfully. "Oh, I had a nurse, of course. But my parents were there every day. Involved in the minutia of my life, not merely visiting the nursery as some do."

"You were lucky then. As is Henry, from all I can see." Hugh frowned. "Do you truly believe whoever is trying to take him will follow you all this way? Will they even know where you have gone?"

Angel set his lips in a hard line. "It would be all too simple to learn where the Duke of Englefield's other residences were or to question a neighbour or a chattering maid. I should like to think we are secure here. But now that we have arrived, I wonder if I have not made things worse by leaving the city. The house here is so much larger, more difficult to protect, to fortify."

"You make it sound as if we are to go to war," Hugh said mildly. "This mysterious stranger who wants the boy. He has his own private army, does he?"

"No, but he is privileged. Wealthy. Titled."

"Have you ever met him?"

Angel shook his head. "I wished to. I wanted to go to him, call him out. Gwendolen asked me not to. She said she had no idea where he resided or even if he was in the city. When I made a few inquiries, all I could learn was that he had only inherited his title recently. He is some sort of relation to the Pembrokes. The Earl of Redmond."

"Redmond," Hugh repeated. "Haven't heard the name. There are a great many earls in England, however. Many more than dukes." He grinned. "You're a rare breed, Angel. In more ways than one."

"And speaking of breeding," Hugh began again.

"No, we are not speaking of it."

"But the noble line must continue, must it not? I still cannot fathom how you promised a loveless and—" Hugh coughed. "—well, a marriage free from the marital dues."

"Dues?" Angel quirked his mouth. "Is that what you shall call it when you marry? You will ask your wife for what you are due, will you?"

Hugh had the grace to blush. "Of course not. She will simply acquiesce to my charm and rush to my bed eager to be ravished."

Angel grinned.

"Now stop changing the subject," Hugh complained. "What did you tell her? How could she agree to marry you and... not also commit to siring at least one heir?"

Angel shifted a little on the cold stone. "I told her there were plenty of heirs already."

"You what?"

"I told her I had four or five... I cannot remember the number now. A handful of relatives, all eager to inherit with sons of their own."

"She has not yet realized that Eliza is your only aunt? And that she is childless?" Hugh smirked.

"The subject has not come up."

"Yet." Hugh rolled his eyes. "Oh, Angel. Very well. You may extricate yourself from that one when the time comes. Enough of this. Why am I here? What would you like me to do?"

It was a good question.

"Just... be here, I suppose. Help me keep watch. Keep an eye out for anything odd or unusual. Have an extra eye on Henry."

"Surely Gwendolen will be with him most of the time, now that she has come so close to losing him... Ah, I see. You have not told her."

"I did not wish to frighten her even more. As far as she knows, they have finally enjoyed a reprieve from the harassment she faced."

"So, she does not know that an intruder nearly snatched her son from his bed a few nights ago? Last night?"

"Last night." Angel groaned.

"You must tell her, Angel," Hugh said gently. "At the very least so she may stay near him, keep watch. Not to mention the fact that she'll kill you when she finds out."

"Her sisters are here and they are more than capable young women, as you shall see. Together the three of them stick to Henry like glue. Even sleep in his bed some nights when they tuck him in."

"Yes, funny how a small child can so easily wear out even the most energetic of adults." Hugh sighed and stood up. "Come on then. Introduce me."

"To your wife's sisters," he added, when Angel looked at him blankly. "I take it they are trained fighters? Armed with pistols? Dueling sabers? Pocket knives?"

"They have their wits and their words, which may be quite enough to scare off an invader, as you will see," Angel said, rising.

Gwendolen walked towards the part of the house where her husband's study lay. Or at least, where she hoped it lay. She had taken directions from a young maid who assured her she had seen Angel there only a short while ago.

The house was so large, however, that she was now in this corridor only for the first time, peeking into doorways, looking for a likely room.

She poked her head into another room and spotted bookshelves, a large rolltop desk, and a man seated in an armchair, smoking.

This must be the study. But it was not Angel.

"Hugh!" she exclaimed. "When did you get here?"

"This morning, bright and early," Hugh responded cheerfully.

She was disappointed he was not Angel, yet there was something encouraging about Hugh's presence. Perhaps because he was so entirely committed to merriment and the uplifting of others' spirits so that they might join him in it. Of course, Angel was much the same way. Only now more burdened, thanks to her.

Hugh Cavendish was a rather dapper man, too, she reflected. Chestnut hair, a slender figure, always well-dressed. One might even call him a dandy.

"What a beautifully-tied cravat," Gwendolen noticed.

Hugh looked down, then up again with a grin. "Why, thank you. I will be sure to tell my valet. The man is an artist with knots."

He stubbed out his cheroot. "Were you looking for Angel? He was here a moment ago but an excited little boy came and dragged him away to play pall mall outside on the lawn. I'm supposed to join them.

I expect it'll take all afternoon considering the players. Care to come along?"

"Perhaps," she said, distractedly. Angel was occupied and with Henry. Not the right time for the discussion she was hoping for.

"Not who you were hoping for?" Hugh said quietly, watching her expression.

She tried to smile.

Hugh looked as if he were about to say something, but stopped himself.

"What is it?" she asked.

He scratched his chin. "Well. I suppose I was about to say I am sorry for all the trouble you have been facing recently. Then I thought better of it as perhaps that is not something you wish to be reminded of. Or to have shared," he said, apologetically.

"Angel told you."

"The very barest bones, I promise you," Hugh assured. "Only so that I might be an extra stalwart male around the place. I know this will shock you—" Hugh took a deep breath. "—but Hugh Cavendish has been known to engage in fisticuffs once in a while."

"A pugilist?"

"Taught Angel everything he knows," he boasted. Then he grinned. "All right, that's not quite true. It was another man in our regiment, in fact. Incredibly skillful. He could have started his own club. Perhaps he has."

"You were in service with Angel? That is a part of his life I know almost nothing about," she said, somewhat shyly.

"You mean he has never boasted of his heroism on the battlefield? Of single-handedly rescuing a Portuguese family from a group of French soldiers? Of carrying a wounded man off the battlefield over his shoulder?" Hugh's tone was light, but clearly these were real events. Gwendolen wondered how long the list was. "What would you like to know? Ask me anything."

"Anything?" She paused. "How did he get his scar?"

Hugh raised his eyebrows. "You've seen it have you?"

She blushed. "Only briefly."

"Ah. Well..." He coughed. "That's not a pleasant tale."

"What do you mean?"

He gazed at her soberly a second. "For a while, I thought I would be writing to Eliza telling her she'd not only be in mourning for her brother and sister-in-law but her only nephew as well. Thank God it did not come to that."

Gwendolen sank into the other armchair. "How did it happen?"

Hugh seemed ill at ease. "Well, that's the part I'm not sure Angel would wish me to discuss. The man who dealt that wound... Well, he was a very brutal man. There was a history there, too, between them."

"A history..." Gwendolen said slowly. "Angel said the scar had been dealt by an Englishman."

"Yes, that's right. Unbelievable, isn't it?" Hugh shook his head in disgust. "What a blackguard. Turned on his own country in the end. He ought to have been shot."

"Wasn't he?"

"Oh, no, he disappeared when Angel fell. Angel has always been confident he must have died, however. If not on the battlefield, then soon after. Angel held his own. If he says the wounds he gave were deep enough to kill he is probably right. Myself, I have never been so sure. If that was the case, why was his body never found? The man was a snake in the grass. Crafty and malicious. I have no idea what he was doing in the army. He certainly had loyalty to nothing and no one other than himself. I have no trouble at all imagining him deserting after what happened."

"What kind of a history?" When Hugh looked blank, she reminded, "You said they had a history. Did he seek Angel out? Was it revenge?"

"You might call it that. It could have been. Things were bound to come to a head, but I did not expect it to happen the way it did. Angel caught him committing a heinous act, you see. Something no honorable soldier would ever do. The Battle of Salamanca—Angel has probably told you he fought there. Angel was in the thick of it when he saw a young French soldier, already wounded. He'd put down his weapons and was trying to surrender. Just a boy, perhaps no more than sixteen or seventeen. But Wyndham ran him through mercilessly, for no reason other than pure bloodlust. That, plus the bad situation with the girl, put together and I'm sure things would have boiled over between them eventually..."

Gwendolen had gone pale. "Wyndham? Was that the other soldier's name?"

"Yes, Robert Wyndham. Son of a tradesman, I believe. A constant troublemaker within his regiment. He would never have moved up the ranks based on his conduct, and he had no money so could never have afforded a commission. An opportunist. Killing for sport. What a disgrace to the English army."

"Yes, yes, indeed." Gwendolen had a hand to her mouth. She stood and began backing slowly out of the room.

"Why, you look white as a sheet! Are you quite all right? Shall I ring for a maid?" Hugh was rising to his feet.

"No, no, please, sit down," Gwendolen said quickly. "I am quite all right. Just a little dizzy. I must have stood up too quickly."

Hugh looked anxious. "If Angel finds out I've told you all of this, he'll have my head. It wasn't a topic suitable for a lady. I do apologize if I went into too great of detail."

"No, Hugh, it's fine. It's all right," she assured him. She had reached the doorway. Could she get to her room? She would have to. She stood up straighter and clasped her hands in front of her.

"There. You look a little better. Some color to your face," Hugh said, with relief. "Shall I walk you somewhere? To the morning room perhaps? We can ring for tea. Or outside for some air? We could meet Henry and Angel on the lawn..."

"No, thank you," she interrupted. "I believe I shall go upstairs and lie down for a little while. The journey yesterday," she added, by way of explanation. "It was a long day."

"Oh, yes, of course. Well, if you are sure." Hugh was sitting back down reluctantly.

"Yes, I'm sure. I will see you at dinner." She tried to smile.

Walking the hall, she looked for the path back to her room.

How could this be possible? How could it be the same man?

She racked her brain, trying to recall what she had told Angel about Wyndham.

She had told him the man who troubled her was an earl.

She had refused to give a name.

When they had met Cecil and Julia in the street, Julia had mentioned the Earl of Redmond. Angel had put two and two together then, but he had not asked for the earl's given name. And perhaps he had not made inquiries.

Hugh was right. Wyndham was of modest birth. But he had bragged to her of his connections to a noble family. Now it seemed he had unexpectedly inherited by way of that distant connection.

For all of Gwendolen's first marriage, there had been no sign of Wyndham. No reply had ever come to her initially beseeching letters. Now she counted herself fortunate for that.

The last word they had received was that he had entered the army and gone abroad, but she had assumed he must have returned long before now.

But perhaps he had not.

She had assumed his lack of contact before this was for all sorts of other reasons.

Perhaps Wyndham had not even known of Henry's existence until he returned to England.

Perhaps John's influence and position had intimidated him and kept him away, particularly if Wyndham was still untitled and unrecognized.

Perhaps Wyndham previously had no need for an heir or had received the injury which left him unable to sire children only lately.

Or perhaps he had not been in England at all these past years.

Perhaps he had deserted the English army just as Hugh suspected and had been living on the continent, only drawn back to English soil by the news he had inherited a title.

He must be quite confident that title would protect him from any repercussions—not only for murdering a surrendering soldier, but for attacking a fellow countryman, especially a duke.

Of course, years had passed. Had Angel even reported the crimes he had witnessed or had he not bothered, falsely believing his foe to be dead and gone?

Wyndham had nearly murdered Angel. She struggled to wrap her head about it.

Now she had brought him into her husband's life again. What would he do if he encountered him? Perhaps Angel would not be so lucky the second time.

She stood to lose not only Henry but the man who had offered her his protection.

Numbly, she thought through her options. She could leave. Go back to her mother, to Orchard Hill. Surely Wyndham would not bother Angel if Henry was not with him.

And from there? She could take Henry abroad. She had sufficient funds of her own for that at least. They could live modestly, somewhere Wyndham could never find them.

Would hopefully never find them.

Was it ridiculous to contemplate fleeing her life, her husband, her family? To protect Henry, nothing was ridiculous. And if this would mean also protecting Angel, she would do it in a heartbeat.

Far better for Angel to live a long life without them then to lose it fighting a battle against a ruthless foe so lacking in honor.

Hugh had mentioned a woman. A girl.

That part of the letter had been true then.

But there had been no ignoble fight in a tavern.

Very likely, whatever had happened to this girl had been Wyndham's doing, not Angel's.

Her heart swelled and sank at the same time.

Angel must harbor rancour against Wyndham even now, if the man had been responsible for the death of the woman he loved.

She could not risk their coming together again. She could not.

She shuddered to think what might have happened if they had recognized one another on the bridge that first night.

How fortunate they had not noticed one another at the ball!

No, there had already been far too many near misses.

She would pack carefully tonight and leave in the morning. Perhaps if she brought Rosalind and Claire into her confidence, they would cover her departure for at least part of the day.

She would think of something.

She had to.

Letter 18

THE RIGHT HON. EARL of Leicester to the Right Hon. Earl of Redmond

April 9, 1817

London

Redmond,

I shall do as you ask. Threats were not necessary. I assume you mean the child. I am not so dense as you seem to think. I was with you in London that summer, do you not recall?

Just as I fully recall your fleeing after ruining the girl. It was rather comical at the time how you made her care for you so easily and had her so quickly. You have always been an excellent actor. Look at you now, acting the part of the fine nobleman—to the manor born and bred.

Why you are so set on claiming your bastard now, however, I do not know. He cannot inherit your title. If you claim him, he will be a nothing and a nobody. I had not thought you a man of sentiment.

Yet this seems like the very greatest sentimental idiocy. Have you finally found some sense of familial affection? I shall believe that when I see it.

Why not find another girl, get her with child in wedlock? Then you will have a true heir.

But persist in this nonsense if you wish. It suits my plans in a way so I shall not balk at doing as you ask.

Let us hope luck is with us and we may both come away from this with what we desire.

Leicester

Chapter 16

THE HUNTERS CAME IN the night.

Rosalind had fallen asleep in a chair in the dayroom of the nursery suite. Someone had covered her with a blanket. The book she had been reading was still on her lap, without a hair ribbon marking the place. Instead, her finger was tucked inside and had lost all its feeling.

Something had woken her. What was it?

She looked around the room. The curtains had not been closed. It was a full moon and the light streamed in, almost bright as day.

What time was it?

She started to yawn, stretching her arms out over her head. She would make her way back to her own room. Spend a night without Henry kicking her for once. (Although he was also lovely to snuggle. That soft little almost-baby body, so sweetly curled up to her. Someday she would have babies of her own and cuddle them in their beds. It was nice to look forward to.)

Someone screamed.

It was Claire. No one else had such a blood-curdling scream. Rosalind would recognize it anywhere. Usually, Claire reserved it for things that did not actually warrant it—such as the time she found red current jam stained all over her prettiest white frock after Rosalind had stuffed it into a closet corner.

She did not usually scream for no reason in the middle of the night.

In a flash, Rosalind was on her feet and running to the door that connected the dayroom to the nursery sleeping-room.

She had known something strange was afoot. Ever since that night with the house in an uproar over a possible intruder. Angel urging them out of London so swiftly was only more evidence.

Henry's voice joined Claire's.

Henry crying loudly. Claire shrieking.

Rosalind turned the handle slowly and pulled open the door, only an inch at first so she could see what she was heading into. She had read enough novels to think ahead. She was no dimwitted, helpless heroine traipsing through a castle in the middle of the night and getting herself kidnapped. No, thank you.

Nevertheless, what she saw was more startling than any novel.

Two men were in the room. One had Claire by the arms. He was trying to restrain her, to pull her arms behind her back, but Claire was stubbornly holding fast to Henry. She had their nephew by the waist while the second man was pulling the boy, trying to get him away.

It was like a horrid re-enactment of the story with King Solomon.

Henry was crying and whacking the man with his little arms, screeching for his mother.

The man's lips were curled back in an unpleasant snarl and he was spitting with rage.

Claire had that effect on people.

But clearly this man deserved it.

"Let him go, you little bitch. Davies, hold her, goddammit!"

The other man tightened his grip on Claire, only to step back suddenly howling.

"Bloody hell, she's just a girl. Hold her fast!" the other bellowed.

"The bitch bit me! I'm bleeding!"

"Get a hold of yourself, you stupid fool. What kind of a man are you, you can't even subdue a little bitch of a girl? Hit her, goddammit. Knock her as many times as you need to. I don't give a bloody damn what you do with her, just get her off the boy."

Rosalind gasped with outrage, and was about to open the door—though to do what she still did not know—when she saw two things.

The first was that Henry had brought up a pall mall mallet and left it leaning against the wall.

The second was that there was a third man present. He was hovering over the large, open sash window. Truly hovering—or least that was how it looked. He must have been perched on a ladder.

He did not look happy to be there. His eyes were wide, his mouth agape—he was missing quite a few teeth, Rosalind noticed. He was rubbing his hands nervously.

"You didn't say nuffin' about hurting no lass, guv," he burst out.

The man trying to take Henry whirled about, his teeth bared like a dog. Which was an insult to Hercules and all dogs in general, really.

Rosalind shuddered. He was not an unattractive man. Many women might call him handsome. Yet he was awful to look at. There was something about his face that made him appear crueler than any dog ever could. Something harsh and pitiless. His face was a contortion of a normal man's face. A furious mask, spit flying from his rage-swollen lips.

What on earth would a man like this want with Henry?

"I'll do what I have to do, and you'll keep your bloody mouth shut if you know what's good for you, Baggins," the cruel man roared.

Poor Baggins shrank so far back Rosalind worried he might tip off the ladder.

She let out a small sound, then covered her mouth.

The other man had already turned his back, but Baggins' looked about the room.

Before she could decide whether to pull the door shut, he had spotted her. His eyes widened. If it was possible, he looked in even more imminent danger of falling off the ladder.

She put a finger to her lips. The man was clearly uncomfortable with the violence taking place.

Perhaps he was even a decent man at heart.

One could hope.

A few seconds passed. Then he nodded ever so slightly.

Relief flooded through her. She shifted her eyes to the mallet, then back at the man. His eyes widened and he shook his head.

No help from that quarter then. But at least he would not interfere.

The mallet was close. Rosalind could swing the door wide and have it in hand almost instantly.

Then what? She would swing it, of course. At which one?

There was no question, really. At the man holding Henry. As hard as she could. Aiming for his head, of course.

For now, the man had Henry fully in his arms, while the other man called Davies had one strong arm wrapped tightly around her sister's neck. So tightly Claire could not even scream.

Rosalind glanced back at the window, but Baggins had disappeared.

In a moment the two men would follow and Henry would be gone.

She swallowed hard and flung open the door.

No one noticed her immediately. The monstrous man was dragging Henry towards the window, yelling foul-sounding words at Baggins, presumably.

She took up the mallet and ran towards his turned back. Distantly she heard Davies call out a warning and saw the man holding Henry begin to turn back towards her.

She brought down the mallet with a loud crack on his head and had the pleasure of seeing him fall back.

For a joyous moment she thought he might actually topple out of the window, but instead he gripped the sill to catch himself, letting go of Henry.

From somewhere nearby came the sound of smashing glass. Then raised voices and loud barking.

"Run to the door, Henry," Rosalind cried. "Find help."

Her nephew's lower lip trembled but he did as she instructed, pulling the nursery door open and running out into the hall.

"Claire," she cried again, seeing her sister's face turning a disturbing shade of purple, watching as Claire's fingers frantically pulled at the arm that choked her.

At least one of them would be saved, Rosalind thought despairingly, as she felt hands grasp her from behind.

Letter 19

THE RIGHT HON. EARL of Redmond to the Right Hon. Earl of Leicester

April 12, 1817

London

Leicester,

I want the boy. That is all you need to know. He is my flesh and blood. Call it sentiment if you like. In my dotage, I find that blood means more to me than I ever expected it to. Now I have the means to indulge myself in this and I shall do it.

He will not inherit the title, but he will inherit all else. I shall see to that.

Moreover, he will be brought up in my image—a stronger, better version. It is not too late to shape the boy, to condition him as I should have been conditioned from the start to the ruthlessness and brutality that is being a man. Let him learn it early on as I never did and he will have the world at his feet when he grows to manhood.

When I am finished with him, he will be a scorpion rather than a mere ant.

To the scorpions of the earth,

Redmond

Chapter 17

ANGEL WAS ROUSED BY a pounding on his door. Blearily he sat up, rubbing a hand over his face.

The door burst open without further warning and Hugh stood there with a pistol in hand.

"A rock just flew through my window," he announced.

Angel stared.

"Well? Are you coming? Haven't you heard the screaming?" Hugh demanded.

Never had a man scrambled out of his bedsheets so quickly.

"The nursery," he choked out. Oh, Henry.

"Do you have a weapon?" Hugh asked as they raced down the hall.

Angel had never felt more stupid in his life.

"I have my fists," he said, shortly.

"That will have to do."

They rounded the corner to the nursery and a small figure crashed into Angel's knees.

"They're hurting Auntie Claire," the little boy sobbed, as Angel scooped him up into his arms, holding him tightly.

"Henry!"

Angel turned and saw his wife running towards them, her arms outstretched. He passed Henry over and ran to catch up with Hugh who was moving ahead quickly towards the nursery bed chamber.

"Be careful, at least one of her sisters is in there," Angel said quietly, a hand to Hugh's shoulder.

His friend nodded.

The nursery door was open and the sound of angry voices could be heard.

Although Angel knew there were intruders, he was still in no way prepared for what he saw.

Two men each held one of Gwendolen's sisters.

One of them was Robert Wyndham.

It was like seeing a ghost.

Angel felt the blood drain from his face and briefly gripped the frame of the door to steady himself, as the connection came clear. Redmond and Robert Wyndham were one and the same. Gwendolen's tormentor was also his own.

Hugh was impatiently trying to push past him. With effort, Angel re-focused his attention on the struggle taking place.

Rosalind was not making it easy for Wyndham. Her hands were stretched towards his face as he gripped her tightly by the wrists, holding her off him.

The other man, a burly rugged fellow, had a beefy arm clenched around Claire Gardner's neck and was tugging her none too gently towards the window.

"Let's get out of here, guv," the man was saying, his voice filled with apprehension. "You heard the sounds. The house is up."

"Not without the boy," Wyndham replied angrily.

"Let them go!" Hugh's voice rang out, harsh and loud, with all of the authority of a former captain of the English army.

The man holding Claire let his arm fall away as he whirled towards them. Spotting the pistol, his eyes widened in fear.

"Against the wall. Now," Hugh commanded. He grabbed at Claire's hand and drew her to the door, pushing her gently out into the hall.

But instead of obeying the instruction, the burly man was frantically and rather incompetently clambering over the window ledge. When Hugh stepped towards him the man let out a yelp and teetered on the sill.

Then he was over.

Hugh rushed to the window and peered out.

Angel was already making his way towards Rosalind. "Is he dead?" he asked of Hugh, not particularly caring about the answer one way or another.

It was Wyndham he cared about. Only him.

From the moment he saw him, his eyes had not left Wyndham's.

Now they stared at each other in silence.

"Sadly, no. Though I do believe the poor man has broken his leg." Hugh clucked. "That's going to be an awful nuisance to run away on."

Angel ignored him.

"Let her go, Wyndham," he said, softly. "What are you going to do? Drag her out the window?"

"Do you really think I wouldn't? I want my son," the other man hissed. "Bring him to me and I'll let her go."

Angel shook his head. "You must be mad if you think you're taking Henry or the girl anywhere with you. There is nowhere you could go where I would not hunt you down."

Wyndham sneered. "Is that so? You did not do so good a job of it before now."

"You bloody bastard. I think I did well enough when it came to some parts of you. Isn't that right, Robert? Isn't that why you're here? To claim the only part of you that isn't diseased, that isn't befouled, like the rest of you—corrupt body and soul. Damaged beyond repair." Out of the corner of his eye, Angel could see Rosalind fixed upon him, her body tensed and ready. He talked on, stepping slowly closer and closer.

"You're not fit to be a father. To have a son," Angel went on. "How many chances have you had, Wyndham? How many children did you seed, only to discard them each time? Teresa carried your child. You abandoned her like some stray dog. But now—because you have inherited some ancient title, one you are utterly unworthy of— now you feel you are due... what? Entitled to what? An heir to your miserable name? Even if it means taking, plundering? Killing? How far would you go?"

"He is my son," Wyndham snarled. "He *belongs* to me."

"He belongs to himself. He belongs to his mother, who bore him, raised him, loved him as you never cared to, even when you had the opportunity. And if you think you have the faintest chance in hell of taking the boy, you must know you will have to kill me first," Angel snarled back.

Rosalind had let out a little gasp while he spoke. He was not sure if it was from surprise at the revelation regarding Henry's true parentage or merely from being held so roughly.

"Shall I finish him?" Hugh asked, from where he stood behind. "No one would blame us, regardless of his title. He has threatened a boy and these women. Broken into a duke's home. Shall we finish this once and for all?"

It was a bluff, Angel knew, for Hugh could not shoot while Wyndham still held Rosalind.

Then Rosalind saved him the trouble. Abruptly thrusting herself forward she broke from Wyndham's grasp, and whirling around, lifted a foot and kicked him hard in the face.

Her foot was bare, but he let out a cry of pain nonetheless.

Regretfully, he did not fall as his comrade had done. Merely touched the blood that streamed from his nose with a finger, shooting the girl a look of pure malice.

"That was for my sister," Rosalind announced.

"And this..." She darted forward to pick something up off the floor, then started towards Wyndham again. "...is for Henry." She swung a mallet towards the man but this time he was prepared. His hand shot out and grasped the wooden pole, wrenching it from her hands.

Angel caught her as she fell back.

In a second, Wyndham was scurrying down the ladder like a rat on a sinking ship.

Hugh rushed to the window, "Shall we follow? I'll shoot the bastard, shall I?" He had the pistol raised and pointed to the ground but Angel was already shaking his head.

"Let him go," he commanded.

Hugh turned back in disbelief. "Let him go?"

"Let him go," Angel said, giving his friend a meaningful look. Hugh's eyes narrowed but he stepped back.

"He won't get away with this," Angel said quietly, for Rosalind's sake but also for Hugh's. "I promise you that."

Already a plan had taken shape in his mind and he knew he would follow it through to the end. He did not wish to speak of it before Gwendolen's sister, however. Or to his wife.

But this would end. Once and for all. Soon.

As it should have ended five years ago, for all their sakes.

"Angel." A low voice spoke from behind.

Gwendolen stood in the frame, still holding Henry in her arms. A shaken-looking Claire stood a few feet behind them, her hand to her neck.

In two strides he was beside her and had enveloped them both in his arms, his mouth brushing against his wife's hair.

"You're squeezing me," Henry complained, not sounding altogether put out. "You're squeezing me too hard, Papa."

"I'm sorry, Henry," Angel replied after a moment's pause, feeling a wetness in the corner of his eyes. He closed them a moment to blink it away.

"I'm sorry," he repeated, lifting his head to look at Gwendolen. "I'm sorry this happened here. I failed you." He held her gaze steadily, ashamed but ready to be sentenced, a knight before his queen.

"You did not fail. Or I would not be holding my child in my arms." She leaned over Henry and let her lips touch his. Briefly but softly.

"I thought you were angry with me," he said so softly against her cheek he was not sure she would hear.

"Not angry," she whispered back. "Not that." She touched his face. "Are you hurt?"

"I wish that I was," Angel said, bitterly. "But I am unscathed. The same cannot be said for your sisters." He looked at Claire and was opening his mouth to ask after her when a loud growl drew their attention towards a kerfuffle down the hall.

Three figures were making their way towards them, one most reluctantly.

Hercules was dragging a man by the leg of his pants, while Eliza walked proud as a queen beside them.

"I was wondering when you were going to appear, Hercules. You have failed in your duties as a guard dog," Angel complained.

"He did not fail," Eliza retorted indignantly. "He was merely occupied elsewhere. And as you can see, he has caught one of the intruders." She peered into the nursery. "Can you say the same?"

"Touché," Angel replied. He looked down at Hercules and his catch. "Excellent work in apprehending one of the foul villains, Herc. I'm surprised you didn't make mince meat of him. He looks rather disappointingly whole."

"Not a villain," the man whose clothing remained firmly betwixt Hercules' teeth muttered.

"Oh, no?" Angel asked politely. His eyes widened. "Baggins? Is that you?"

"Baggins!" Gwendolen exclaimed, peering at the man. Then, more reproachfully, "Oh, Baggins. Whatever are you doing here?"

Baggins looked puzzled, so she added helpfully, "The lady from the bridge. How are your eight children, Baggins? Perhaps you could settle something between my husband and myself..."

"'e's yer husband now?" Baggins asked. "That were fast work it were."

"Thank you," Angel said. "When one finds a precious gem one does not leave it for another to pick up."

"Did you just compare me to a stone?" Gwendolen asked, sweetly.

"A precious stone...but yes," Angel groaned. "It was supposed to be a beautiful metaphor."

"The thought was there," Claire interrupted gruffly. "Well done."

"Thank you, sister," Angel said, smiling at her. "We men do try sometimes, you know."

A loud "Humph" was all the reply he received. He turned back to the bumbling burglar.

"Now, Baggins, what have you to say for yourself? I thought we had encouraged you to give up your life of crime. Now it seems you have merely escalated it and taken up even worse company."

"Didn't know 'e was worse, did I? Said he was a nobleman. Thought we was doin' a good deed." Baggins stared down at the carpet mournfully. "Did try to set matters 'aright. Ask 'er." He nodded towards Rosalind who was standing just inside the nursery door.

"It is becoming rather crowded," Angel murmured. "Perhaps we should remove ourselves to the drawing room? Some beverages and food might be in order?"

"Good idea, guv," Baggins said eagerly. "'aven't had nuffin to eat all day."

"You mean your noble employer did not see fit to feed you? Tsk tsk." Angel looked at the mastiff. "Perhaps you might allow Mr. Baggins to have his parole from here to the drawing room, Herc?"

A few minutes later had the crowd settled more comfortably in a hastily lit drawing room. Sustenance had been called for and everyone had found a seat. Henry had resumed his slumbers and Gwendolen had laid him out on a chaise nearby and covered him with a blanket.

She would not be letting him out of her sight anytime soon, Angel thought ruefully. It was a miracle the boy had fallen asleep at all. What would they say to him in the morning to explain the terror he had just experienced? Would Gwendolen ever tell her son who the man who had tried to take him truly was?

"All right, Baggins," he said, turning to the man. "Tell us why we should not bring you before the magistrate."

Hugh had seated himself beside the fellow and was now watching in amusement as Baggins endeavoured to stuff himself with every kind of biscuit and sandwich he could find on the tea tray.

"Mmmph," Baggins replied, trying to swallow.

"He did seem very put off by the violence," Rosalind contributed. Baggins nodded enthusiastically. "And he had no part in it. When he saw how rough the men were with Claire and Henry, he... well..." She blushed. "He scampered."

"But he was frightened, understandably," she added hastily.

"Yes, so frightened that he left two defenceless women to deal with things on their own," Hugh said, scowling at Baggins.

Baggins managed to gulp down his mouthful. "Sounded the alarm though, didn't I?" he gasped. "Quick as a wink, I was."

"Ah, so it was you who threw the boulder which nearly bludgeoned me in my bed?"

"Worked tho didn't it?" Baggins asked, looking around the room. "Meant no harm to the lad, I swear it. The swine said we was doing a good deed, restorin' the boy to his rightful home, takin' 'im back where 'e belonged."

Baggins looked down at his ripped trousers, shaking his head. "Won't get paid now. Wife'll have me hide."

"Not to mention your children," Gwendolen said gently. "What were their names again?"

"Their names?" Baggins looked blank. "Whyever do you want their names for?" He looked down at his hands, shaking his head in bafflement, and began to count on his fingers. "Less see now, there's Andy, Betsy, Charlie, Davy, Emmy, Fanny, Georgy, Hermione, and Hippolyta."

"Aha!" Gwendolen said, triumphantly, looking in Angel's direction. "I knew you would never tell a fib about something as sacred as family, Baggins." She looked back. "But Baggins, that's nine."

Baggins recounted on his fingers. "So 'tis." He scratched his chin. "'ermione and 'ippo—that's what we call 'er for short, see—are twins. Always mix 'em up and think of 'em together, I s'pose."

"A very orderly naming scheme," Eliza complimented.

"Very creative at the end with the Hermione and Hippolyta," Rosalind chimed in. "Was your wife reading Shakespeare perhaps? That is where mine came from."

"She's a reader, my Sally," Baggins said, with pride. "'an she did pick up a parcel of books from the parish right when the twins was born. Found 'em inspiring, she said."

"How lovely. We shall have to make up a package for you to take back to them," Rosalind said, clapping her hands. "I have a few books your wife might enjoy. If she has the opportunity to read now, with nine children..."

"Oh, the older 'uns watch the young 'uns to give her a break. 'An I take 'em all out walkin' on Sundays," Baggins explained. "Give her some quiet."

"You are a very thoughtful husband, Baggins," Gwendolen said, smiling. "It seems to me that you merely fell into the wrong company. In the hopes of providing for your family?"

Baggins nodded remorsefully.

Gwendolen looked meaningfully at Angel. "We must take that into account then. It would not do to have a father taken from his family. The blame does not lie with Baggins, after all, but with the instigator of all of this."

At that reminder she suddenly grew pale.

"I am quite in agreement," Angel said gently, putting his hand over hers. "Baggins, you are free to go." He looked at the man. "I hope your employer will not seek you out for some kind of retribution, however. You did scuttle off on him partway through the job. And he is not the forgiving sort."

Baggins sat up straighter. "'E'll get more'n he paid for if he comes round my 'ome. My boys are brave 'uns."

Angel stood up. "Well, it's been a very long night. I'm sure we all need some sleep." He looked down at his wife. Her face remained wan and her eyes were fixed on her sleeping son. "Gwendolen, I assume you'll want..."

"Gwendolen," Eliza interrupted, rising and coming over to her. "I would propose that Henry sleeps with me."

"With you?" Gwendolen echoed, looking up.

"Yes, with Hercules and I. Our room is in order. I do not expect Henry will appreciate being returned to the nursery tonight, nor do I expect you will wish him to sleep alone. Your sisters have had quite enough excitement---"

"Is that what we're going to call it?" Claire muttered from the corner in which she sat, sipping tea with the demeanor of a dowager.

Rosalind hushed her.

"—and you need some rest," Eliza finished. Her expression softened. "Hercules and I will guard him well, Gwendolen."

"I can sleep outside in the hall," Hugh offered. "Right outside your room, Eliza."

"Oh, that is very kind, Hugh," Gwendolen murmured. She still seemed hesitant.

"I would appreciate the opportunity of speaking with you, Gwendolen," Angel murmured softly.

She looked up at him, biting her lip. "Very well. Yes, you may take him, Eliza. Thank you." She reached out to squeeze Angel's aunt's hand. "We have brought so much trouble down upon you and your house. I am so very sorry."

"Not a bit of it," Eliza replied firmly. "I wouldn't trade you and Henry for anything now that you are here. You are both exactly what we needed." She looked at her nephew with a small smile. "Goodnight to you both."

The room began to empty out. Hugh picked up Henry and carried him out, with a nod to Angel, Herc at his heels. They would discuss matters in the morning.

Hugh was the only one Angel would be taking fully into his confidence.

Baggins could return with them to London the next day. In the meantime, a brawny young footman escorted him down to the kitchens for some rest before morning, after Hugh had sternly whispered in his ear not to let the man out of his sight. Repentant or not, Angel agreed, Baggins had been involved in something rather too nefarious this time and bore watching. Not that Angel truly believed the man was a hardened criminal. Merely foolish and willing to risk much for coin.

Gwendolen's sisters lingered and the three young women sat in the corner of the room speaking in low voices for a time. Angel could only imagine the conversation. They had not been aware of Henry's origin. Would learning of it change their opinion of their sister, knowing of her missteps? He doubted it. The Gardners were a strong family, linked together by love and loyalty. Much like his had been before his parents died.

Much like it might be again.

After all, all of Gwendolen's sisters were a part of it now, not just her and Henry. He decided to write a letter to Mrs. Gardner the next day, just a short note introducing himself further and making it clear that she and her youngest daughter were welcome at anytime they wished to visit.

Finally, Rosalind and Claire went out and Angel was left alone with his wife.

Letter 20

LADY JULIA PEMBROKE TO the Right Hon. Earl of Redmond

June 27, 1817

London

My Dear Cousin,

I hope you will pardon yet another request. You have already done so much for us since your return, and we are exceedingly grateful. The scandal that might have come from Papa's excessive debts would have certainly ruined us.

Now I wonder if you might see your way to intervening on my behalf in another way.

Papa is insistent that I accept a proposal from a man I feel certain I would not suit. As I believe that he is a friend of yours—the Earl of Leicester—I wondered if perhaps you might discuss the matter with Papa. I bear no ill will against the man, but feel certain I would not bring him happiness—nor he me. Perhaps you might even make him see this.

Otherwise, I fear his proposal will come shortly and Papa will force my hand in accepting. Please consider interceding for me, Cousin, as you have been so kind to us in the past.

Yours affectionately,

Julia

Chapter 18

FOR A MOMENT, THEY simply looked at one another and Angel wondered if this was how it would be. If they were to remain separate, if she would shut him out again—physically and otherwise.

She would be absolutely right to be angry with him after tonight, he told himself. It would only be fitting. Exactly what he deserved.

Then she flew across the room and melted into him, her arms around his neck, her face burrowed against his chest. His hands found her waist and pulled her closer.

They stood like that for a long moment, warm and together.

It was a blissful closeness.

Angel closed his eyes and let his chin rest on her head. She was his. He was hers.

More accurately, he was lost. He was hers. Whether she knew it or not. Whether she wanted him or not.

He wondered if his father had fallen this hard for his mother when they met. He would never have the opportunity to ask.

Well, he could ask Eliza. He would do so.

It must have been something like this. What his parents felt.

How wonderful to know they felt it for one another, knowing each was loved in return.

His throat constricted. "Gwendolen..."

She was saying something, muffled against his chest.

Gently, he pushed her back just a little. "What was that?"

"Angel, I am so sorry. So unspeakably sorry," she was saying. "I had no idea. No idea that you knew him."

"Knew Wyndham? You knew that I knew him? How?" He stopped. "Hugh?"

She nodded. "It wasn't Hugh's fault. He had no idea. He mentioned it quite in passing only yesterday. I had asked about your time in service together. I had no idea. If I had known." She shook her head. "I would never have married you. Never."

Angel swallowed. "Never?"

She shook her head again, looking miserable. "I was going to leave. Tonight."

"What?" He looked down at her incredulously, taking a step back and letting go of her waist. "And go where? Why?"

"I... Away... Away from you, away from here..." she stuttered. "To protect you."

"To protect *me*?" he choked out. "When I should be the one protecting you?"

She put her hands on her hips and suddenly was the determined girl from the bridge once more. "I have already been too reliant on you, Angel. And now look how things have worked out. I have brought the very man who tried to murder you right into your own home!"

"That is not your fault," he countered. "There was no way you could have known..."

"Couldn't I?" She shook her head. "I kept everything from you. Yet you made me that... absolutely ludicrous offer, anyway."

"Ludicrous?" He flinched.

"Not only ludicrous!" she cried, turning away so he could not see her face. He saw her take a deep breath. "Noble. Brave. Selfless. Romantic."

Romantic was better.

"Stupid? Impulsive? Foolish?" he offered.

She turned back, smiling a little. "All of those things."

"Romantic, you said?" he asked, hopefully.

She looked at him closely, then took a step back towards him.

"Very romantic," she said softly, tilting her head up.

Her hand reached behind his neck, tugging him down to her. Her lips parted.

Her lips were silky and soft, gently parting his lips, working her velvety tongue between them. Angel shivered, clasping her tighter against him with one hand, raising the other to play in her soft golden hair, then dancing his fingers lightly over her neck.

He raised both hands, cradling her face between them, intensifying the kiss she had begun. Did she know how much he wanted her? Let her feel it then.

He sucked her lips, gently, then with a greater urgency, nibbled, bit, kissed a trail from her lips across her cheek and down her neck, kissing the column of her slender neck, as his hand moved back to her waist, pulling her flush against him and letting her feel his need.

It was becoming rapidly apparent that this kiss was filled with a desperate desire.

Desire which could not be suitably consummated in a drawing room, Angel despaired. Or could it?

"Take me upstairs," she whispered, pushing her body even closer to his, her breasts warm and soft against his chest.

She leaned back in his arms, resting her hands on his shoulders. "Please, Angel."

He kissed her one more time, then did as she asked.

There was no Wyndham. There was no Henry.

There was only them.

As it had never been before.

Nothing crowded in. She would not let it.

This was to be theirs alone. Something beautiful after the horror of the night.

Something she had never experienced before.

She felt bold and brave and nervous all at the same time.

When they reached their suite, she slid from his arms and tugged him by the hand, leading him through the door into her room.

This man had seen her naked before. He had touched her most intimate places already.

Yet she was as shy as if it were the first time.

Because this time would be different, she told herself. This time she wanted everything from him. And to give everything in return.

Could she please him as much has he had already shown himself capable of pleasing her?

She untied her robe and let it slide from her shoulders, standing before him in a thin lace night rail which left little to the imagination. One of the many she had that she had little use for. Until now.

Angel stood looking down at her. Beautifully imposing all over again. Broad-shouldered and strong. So much larger than she.

It was a pleasant difference though, and she shivered a little imagining his strong body covering her own with no barriers between them.

"Are you cold?" he asked, thickly.

She shook her head. "No. Not cold. Only..."

"Yes?" he encouraged.

"Do you want me?" she asked, hesitantly. She knew she was echoing herself, and hated it, but she could not help feeling desperate for the reassurance.

"Do I want you?" Angel's voice was hoarse as if from lack of use. "Do I want you?"

Then he gave a deep slow chuckle. "I want you more than any woman I've ever met, Gwendolen."

He stepped towards her, a finger sliding carefully under one of the shoulder straps of the nightdress.

"I want you every way there is to want. I want you in any way you choose to share."

He slid the strap off her shoulder and let it fall along her arm.

"I want to touch you. Undress you. I want you bare."

His hand moved to the other side, shifting the lacy fabric off her shoulder.

She shifted her arms slightly so that the dress did not fall entirely off.

She stood there, her breasts naked before him, feeling wanton and sinful. Which was ridiculous, wasn't it? For was he not her husband? Nevertheless, it was true.

He looked at her breasts with a hungry expression and let out a small growl. "I want you sweet and slow. I want you hard and fast. I want to pleasure you in every way there is, every way I know."

He cupped her breasts in his hands and rubbed his fingers over her nipples, letting them harden into firm buds.

"Yes," she whispered. "Yes, please." She closed her eyes, relishing the feeling of his hands on her, already imagining them elsewhere, everywhere, all over.

"But what do you want?"

She opened her eyes. Angel was waiting, his hands paused.

"What do you want of me?" he repeated, smiling slightly as if he knew the answer, but wanted to hear it even so.

"Everything," she whispered, and let the gown fall to the floor.

She heard him let out a groan and it stirred her beyond doubt and shame. She lifted one of his hands off her breasts and placed it close to the center of her thighs, shifting a little closer against him.

"Ah, I see," he whispered huskily, leaning forward to breathe the words into her ear. "You've missed me?"

His hand gently parted her legs, worked between them, cupping her mound, then moving back and forth across her skin, slick and hot. He plunged a finger deep into the wetness and she gasped, clutched his arms, then moved her hands down to pull his shirt out of his trousers.

Her hands were shaking, desperate. She fumbled with the fabric. She could hear herself moaning under his hand while he continued his ministrations--the position awkward, the angle wrong, his fingers teasing her rather than satisfying.

He took his hand away and she let out a small cry.

"Let me help? It will be quicker." He gave her a smile that held a hint of pity. He was enjoying the power he had over her. Let him. She could no longer feel embarrassed of her want, only desperate to have her desire fulfilled.

He pulled the shirt over his head, revealing a well-muscled chest. The scar stood out to her but she ignored it, moving her hands over his skin, up to his nipples where she brushed her fingers lightly then reached her mouth up to lick and flick.

Angel pulled her against him, lifting her head up to his and kissing her deeply.

Her hands went back to his trousers, fumbling at the buttons. His hands came to help hers, working quicker than hers could.

He stepped back a moment, slowly pushing them down, then his drawers and stepping out, grinning.

"You're giving me a show!" she exclaimed, not sure if she was complaining or not.

"Am I?" He smirked. "Is it a good one?"

She let her eyes roam over his form from head to, well, she did not get to his toes. Instead, they lingered somewhere in the middle.

He was finely shaped in all ways, she concluded.

She blushed. "I have little basis for comparison."

"Oh, come now," he chided. "That's no way to talk to a gentleman. We need our compliments, too, you know."

"I doubt you've met with any complaints," Gwendolen countered. "And that is all I shall say on the matter." She gave him a saucy smile in turn, then backed away from him towards the bed.

"Where do you think you're going?" he demanded, and suddenly she was running to the bed with a shriek of laughter, hearing him behind her. She jumped up onto the bed, and turned back to face him, kneeling and breathless.

"Good God, you're lovely," Angel said admiringly, coming to stand before her. He was completely comfortable in his nakedness and she loved him for it. His body was beautiful. Perfect, really.

And it was hers, a little voice said. All hers. At least, she hoped it was.

He pushed her backwards gently with one hand, and she let herself fall, her hair tumbling out of its loosely-held coif around her.

She lay before him, naked on the coverlet, letting him look his fill. Trying to imitate him in his confidence with his body.

"So perfect," he whispered, trailing a finger over her thigh and climbing up beside her.

He lowered his lips to her breast, sucking and nibbling while he kneaded and caressed the other with his hand.

His head popped up over her, a mischievous expression on his face. "Close your eyes."

She obeyed, and stayed motionless as she felt his hands slide down either side of her body, not knowing what to expect. Not knowing what he was going to do.

If she had, perhaps she might have moved, tried to stop him.

Instead, when she felt his tongue between her legs she shot up on her elbows with a gasp. "What are you doing?"

"Something you'll like," he said, looking up and smiling. "Trust me."

She lay back reluctantly.

She supposed she should. God knew he had more knowledge of such things than she did.

She let out a little moan as his tongue flicked against her clitoris, then harder, repeating the motion until she was writhing, her hands reaching down to clutch his hair.

"Stop," she managed to gasp.

He looked up in surprise. "Does it not feel good?"

"Too good," she said, biting her lip. "I think I shall die."

"That's the hope," he said, playfully, and went back to his ministrations.

He opened his mouth wide over her, diving his tongue in between her lower lips, before moving back up, sucking and licking until she was writhing her hips and arching herself shamelessly into his face.

When he slid two fingers into her, thrusting them rhythmically, she fell apart, crying out loudly and wordlessly, her body feeling wave after wave of exquisite pleasure.

What had he done to her? Something wondrous, something diabolical. Something she immediately wanted again.

"What did you do to me?" she breathed, lying motionless a moment.

"Again?" he asked.

"No!" She sat up and pulled him up against her by the arms until he was hovering above her.

The tips of her breasts touched the skin of his chest and she saw him shudder, closing his eyes a moment. Looking down she saw he was as aroused as she. That much at least she knew from all of John's folios.

She rubbed her breasts against him more firmly, lifting herself a little, taking his mouth in hers and pulling him down tight against her.

She wrapped her legs around his hips, gasping with the feeling of him between her thighs, his member touching her where she was still so sensitive, the feeling heightened by the pleasure she had just received.

"Gwendolen," Angel was whispering, his hands all over her.

"What do you want?" she whispered back, before kissing him sweetly, slipping her tongue between his lips and tasting herself on him. It filled her with even more want, if such a thing was possible.

"I need you," he said hoarsely, and that was the most perfect thing he could have said. She felt filled with warmth, not just from the pleasure, but from him, all of him, and before she could stop herself, the words came out.

"I love you, Angel."

He froze, poised above her, body against her. Their skin against skin, nearly nothing to separate them besides their own minds.

Gwendolen felt her stomach sink. "I'm... sorry," she said. "I know you didn't... want this."

"Want this?"

"To be married. To have a wife. A real marriage. A real wife," she choked out. She could feel warm wetness at the corner of her eyes and closed them, trying to squeeze the tears away. "To be so constrained."

She felt his lips press against hers.

"Oh, my love," he whispered against them. "My lovely love."

She opened her eyes. His brown ones looked back at her intensely.

"I want you. I need you. I love you," he said. "Don't you know that already? I thought I was so obvious." He gave a rueful smile.

She shook her head back and forth against the coverlet.

"No? I suppose I should be glad I have not been wearing my heart on my sleeve as much as I thought I was," he said, kissing her lightly, then trailing a hand gently along her face.

He loved her. He loved her, too. He wanted her.

She was flooded with warmth and light again, her body buoyant. Desire returned tenfold.

She lifted her hips against him and felt his hardness between her legs. Still roused.

"Take me," she pleaded, moving against him. "I want all of you, Angel."

He looked down at her as if he would devour her entirely, the time for words passed, and then he moved himself carefully between her below.

She gasped a little at first, feeling him entering her and not knowing how to comprehend the touch. She had only had it once before, and that was a memory she did not care to recall.

This was utterly different.

Wanted, needed, and so wonderfully pleasing.

He moved his hand down her body to stroke between her legs and plunged into her fully, eliciting a cry.

"More," she breathed out, not wishing him to think it was a cry of pain. "More, Angel."

He moved his hand to grip her hips firmly and drove deep, again and again, his thrusts growing fiercer and then still more so as she began to meet them with a rhythm of her own, pushing back, her body arching.

She had craved this without knowing what this was or how it would feel, this masculine hardness inside her, against her, encompassing her where there was so much to feel.

She lifted and strained against him, arms wrapped around his neck, pulling him even closer into their embrace, her lips hungrily meeting his as his thrusts grew stronger, faster, and her head swam with pleasure and passion.

He moved a hand down again, fingers sliding to the sensitive cleft between her thighs, and it was all she needed. She arched her back hard against him, hearing him cry out, hearing herself begging him not to stop, to go harder, faster, deeper, not caring who heard, not caring for anything but the feeling of him against her, inside her, above her and then the tide swept over her again, and she felt Angel shudder in turn, until they both fell silent, wrapped against one another.

Angel's head rested on her breast, and she ran her hands slowly threw his hair. She felt languid, heavy with the aftermath of pleasure.

Yet she was also intensely curious.

"Was that...pleasing? For you?" she asked, tentatively.

His head snapped up, bumping her chin.

"Ouch!"

"I'm sorry. What did you say? Was that *pleasing*?" He was looking at her as if she were witless.

"I mean..." She tried to find the right words. "You must have had so many other..."

His face softened and he brushed his knuckles against her cheek. "Oh, Gwendolen."

"I'm not stupid," she said crossly, tugging his hair a little roughly.

"Ouch! I know you are not stupid," he said, grinning. "Far from it."

He sat up and leaned back against the headboard, pulling her up beside him and wrapping his arms around her.

"Well? Haven't you?" she asked, refusing to let the question slide.

"Had many other women? Am I an incredibly experienced lover? Oh, most definitely," he said, solemnly. "I expect there are broadsheets devoted solely to the topic. The Erotic Angel."

She slapped his chest, not very hard. "You idiot." She sighed. "Very well, leave me in the dark then."

She felt him kiss the top of her head softly and snuggled in closer against his chest. Broad and warm. Nothing could hurt her here, not with him. Despite the events of the night, she was still certain of that. She was here, wasn't she? And Henry. He had not failed them, no matter what he might think.

"This was very different," he said quietly.

"Bad different?"

"Not at all. Simply like nothing I've ever experienced before."

"What do you mean?" She leaned away from him to better see his face. "How is that possible? Did I do something wrong?"

"Absolutely not. It's just that..." He hesitated, giving her a look that seemed almost bashful. "Well, I've never been in love before. I've never done *this* with a woman I've loved before."

She stared at him, her mouth forming a silent O.

"Are you in shock?" He laughed, a little awkwardly. "Stop looking at me that way, you'll have me blushing."

"I should like to see that," she said softly, moving towards him, offering her mouth to be kissed.

After a few moments of that, Angel pulled back, and put his hands gently on her shoulders.

"Gwendolen..." He was blushing now. "This is deucedly awkward to ask but I must know. Though you may tell me to go to the devil and mind my own business."

"Yes?"

"How is it that you've never done this before? I mean, besides the time..."

"When I was raped?" She put her head against his shoulder. She took a deep breath. "I think it happens to many women, you know. Far more than we realize. We leave women in such ignorance and so unprotected. Not that my mother does not teach her daughters more than the average, I believe. But she had no experience with..."

"Men who turn out to be devils in disguise?" Angel rubbed her back gently.

"Yes. Just so. But... you meant with John. It is a fair question."

Gwendolen thought a moment. She was fairly certain of the answer but had never shared her belief with anyone before. "I loved John—" She felt Angel shift, and hurried on. "—but as a father. Or a wise friend. Not a husband. Nor did he ever love me that way. I do not think he ever loved a woman that way. Not even his first wife."

"What do you mean? He has a son, does he not?"

"Yes," she said, thoughtfully. "Though Cecil is nothing like John, in personality nor in looks. Which is sad to say, for John was a good man."

"Are you saying Cecil was...?"

"Another man's son? Perhaps. After my experience with him, I do not believe John would much care. He had an heir from his first wife, and he loved Cecil. Just as he truly loved Henry. It is sad, really, that Henry will not remember him at all. Even now he can hardly remember him. Children forget so quickly at this age and to be fair, John was not around much. Not in Henry's every day life."

"So, your husband had no one? You believe he lived as a monk?"

"Oh, I did not say that." She tapped Angel playfully on the chest. "Perhaps I am more worldly than you in this regard. But no, you must know, do you not, that some men prefer the company of other men to women?"

Angel stared down at her. "You believe John was one of these men?"

"I do," she said softly. "I say it with no judgement or malice of any kind. It simply explains a great deal. Oh, it took me a few years to arrive at this conclusion, but once I did—well, the pieces fit."

"How so?"

"Well, his closest companion throughout his life was not his first wife nor a mistress, but his secretary, Matthew Stevens, who shared his passion for antiquities and travel. They went on every expedition together, planned their trips together. Stevens was almost always at the house. He even had a suite of rooms. When we went to the country estate, he would join us. He was as much in Henry's life as John was, in fact."

"A male lover..." Angel said slowly.

"Please, do not think less of John for my having told you this."

"To be frank, I do not think of your John much at all. Except now, to wonder how on earth he could have married you and—" He coughed. "—not bedded you countless times."

He tickled her suddenly and she shrieked. "Nay, thousands, even."

When she had caught her breath, she said, "I wondered that at first, as well. But then I became, well, grateful. Grateful to not have to play that part. To do my duty. Especially after..."

"Yes, I can understand that." Angel ran his hands over her hair, gently, reassuringly. "You have such lovely hair."

"So do you," she said, looking up. "An angel's...."

"Don't say it," he groaned.

"...golden halo. What?" she asked, laughing. "Why should I not say it?"

Then she understood and was embarrassed. "You've heard it many times, I suppose. Did the women always compliment you?" she teased. "Or was it ever the other way around? Did you merely strip slowly and then lie down while they admired your beauty?"

"You make me sound like a courtesan!" Angel exclaimed.

"Oh? Were you not?" Gwendolen asked innocently. "Can a man not be a courtesan? I am so new at these things. Please, teach me, wise husband."

"Oh, I'll teach you all right," Angel said, pouncing and tickling her mercilessly.

Later, and after a slower second love-making, they lay beside each other in the bed.

"I should check on Henry," Gwendolen whispered. "It is almost morning." She yawned. "I'm so tired. We have not slept at all."

He kissed her cheek. "We have been preoccupied. Our time has been spent much more pleasantly. Though sleep would be welcome at this point," he agreed.

He got out of bed and looked around for his trousers.

"What are you doing?" she asked, sleepily.

"I will see to Henry," he said. "You rest. Would you like me to bring him back to you? I can probably carry him without waking him."

"Oh, would you?"

The relief on her face was so palpable that he felt heroic for having mentioned the idea.

"Of course," he said, stooping down to cup her face and kiss her. "Of course, I will bring him. You will sleep better with him beside you, will you not?"

She lay back down and he began pulling on his clothes.

"You know, I do believe this is exactly what my Aunt Eliza had in mind for us," he remarked.

"A wicked night of carnal pleasure?" Gwendolen said, smiling.

"Is it so very wicked? You are my wife, after all," Angel grumbled.

"I prefer to pretend we are being wicked," she said, lying on one side, turned towards him. "Utterly wanton."

She was still completely naked and her breasts were too beautiful to leave untouched. He leaned over and planted kisses on each nipple, enjoying the way they immediately hardened under his mouth.

"My beautiful wanton wife."

Gwendolen smiled up at him. "I may fall asleep before you get back."

"Good. Get some rest. I'll have Henry beside you soon." He kissed her forehead once more and left the room.

In the hall, his thoughts quickly changed to other matters. He could not in good conscience continue to enjoy his wife or profess his love for her while that blackguard still roamed free.

Wyndham—nay, Redmond—had proven himself totally devoid of restraint.

The proper thing to do would be to bring him up before the House of Lords.

But that would mean exposing all of the sordid details that Gwendolen had spent so long trying to keep secret. And which, to his credit, her late husband had as well. It would expose Henry, possibly to ridicule. At the very least it would set off a storm of scandal, with

Henry and Gwendolen at the very heart. Aunt Eliza would be stoic but silently horrified by it all. To say nothing of how Gwendolen's sisters' prospects would swiftly plummet as a result.

No, there was another route to justice. A much speedier one.

That was the one he planned to take.

He found Hugh still awake, lounging in an uncomfortable looking wooden chair in the hall, a book in hand.

"Oh, there you are," Hugh said, looking not the least bit surprised. "Have a pleasant evening?"

"Parts of it have been more pleasant than anticipated," Angel admitted.

"Aha." Hugh smirked. "So, you've told her then?"

"Told her what?"

"That you're in love with her, you dolt. Oh, how the mighty Angel is fallen."

"Oh, that. So, you knew?"

"I'm sure everyone knew except your wife," Hugh said cheerfully. "About time she found out for herself. I suppose she returns the sentiment?"

"I certainly hope so," Angel said. "She says she does."

"You're blushing," Hugh pointed out with delight. "So, love makes grown men blush, then? I shall have to avoid it. I have no wish to look like a dreamy schoolboy."

Angel gave him an appraising look. "To tell the truth, the sensation is so altogether pleasant overall that I don't give a damn how red my face is. I love her and it's heaven."

Hugh groaned. "All right, all right. Save it for your lady. That's not what you're here for anyhow, is it? Come to check up on your night watchman? I haven't fallen asleep, as you can see."

"No, but you should get some. I'll have need of you. I've come to taken Henry back to Gwendolen. I'll be there to keep an eye on them the rest of the night... or morning."

"Leaving for London, are we?" Hugh guessed.

"How did you know?"

"Considering your shocking willingness to let the man who had broken into your house and attempted to kidnap your wife's son and do God knows what to her sisters go, there is really only one thing that would explain it." His face was serious as he looked up from the chair. "I'll be your second, of course."

"Of course," Angel said quietly. "Thank you, Hugh. For... everything."

"Don't thank me yet. Are you sure you know what you're doing, Angel? There is a safer route. One which would guarantee your living a long, happy life with your wife and child. And future children."

"The House of Lords?" Angel shook his head. "Slow. Incompetent. The outcome almost certain not to be what I desire, what justice demands. Total exposure of Wyndham's deeds, yes, but also the destruction of his victim's privacy. No, I will not do that to her."

"Well, that's what I thought you'd say." Hugh sighed. "How are we going to find him?"

"Oh, I suspect Baggins can lead the way, no matter how he feigns ignorance. He's a clever fellow for all his bluffing. I'm sure he'd enjoy seeing Wyndham get his comeuppance after tonight, too. It would ensure his own safety and his family's."

Hugh nodded. "In that case, perhaps I'll toddle off for some rest."

"Yes, dandies need their beauty sleep, I'm told," Angel agreed, grinning.

He turned to knock on his aunt's bedroom door.

THE RIGHT HON. EARL of Redmond to Lady Julia Pembroke

June 29, 1817

London

Cousin Julia,

I will do no such thing. Rather, I strongly urge you to accept the proposal and do your duty as you should have done years before.

How long has it been since your debut? Three years? Four? Five? It is a wonder you have received such a promising proposal at all at your age and considering the state of your family's finances.

Yes, I intervened for your father once—to fulfill a debt I owed him from my youth. Please be aware I shall not do so again. The next time, his creditors may not be so patient.

Wedding a man like Leicester is the ideal solution to your situation. He gains a pretty girl to bed and sire for him. You gain a rich husband with the means to provide for you and your imprudent family. You would do well to take what you can get. Indeed, I am surprised his title alone does not draw you. But then I suppose you have heard of his reputation and are put off.

Believe me, Julia—no man is a saint and you will not find one who is. Men are brutes and that is simply a fact. Accept it and you will find greater contentment in life than you would if you persist in a stupid romantic notion of male gallantry. Be grateful that Leicester is drawn to you at all and not put off by your age or your lack of dowry. For what you bring to the table is pitiful otherwise. Your looks will not last forever. Indeed, they are fading fast.

I urge you to accept Leicester's proposal. Cease putting off your duty as a woman and daughter. After all, this is what women are for. Continue on as you are and you shall be of no use to anyone and desired by no one.

Redmond

Chapter 19

WHEN GWENDOLEN CAME DOWN to breakfast the next morning, Henry holding her hand, Angel was gone.

"Where has my husband gotten to?" she asked, seating herself across from Eliza who was sipping her coffee and reading the paper.

"Oh, he had some estate business to attend to," Eliza replied, vaguely. "He'll be back by tonight, I should expect."

"Tonight!" Gwendolen raised her eyebrows. "He did not even mention it to me."

Eliza looked up, her face softening. "Yes, he said to give his apologies for that." She paused and for a moment looked as if she were on the brink of saying more. Then it passed and she looked back down at her paper.

Gwendolen shrugged. It was odd, certainly.

But after last night, she had no doubts left about Angel.

"Where is Hugh?" She asked, looking around the table. "I would like to thank him for keeping watch. As well as you, Eliza. Thank you for keeping Henry so that we could have a... reprieve."

Eliza looked back up, smiling. "Of course, my dear. As for Hugh, I believe he ate earlier and went out. Perhaps he is with Angel, I'm not quite certain."

"Mama, I want some bacon," Henry demanded, tugging at her sleeve.

She had sat down before she had filled their plates—an amateur mistake when one was a mother. She quickly rose and went to the sideboard with him.

Rosalind and Claire swept in together, both looking impressively bright-eyed and pretty for two girls who had faced down invaders only hours ago.

"Where is Angel?" Rosalind asked in surprise, looking about. "And Hugh?"

Gwendolen caught the questions before Eliza had to repeat herself. "They have both gone out. Eliza believes they will be back before nightfall."

Rosalind was wide-eyed. "How very odd."

Claire was frowning. "Leaving all of us here after last night. It does seem rather strange."

"Hercules and I are here to protect you," Eliza said calmly from her place at the table. She took a sip from her cup. "Not to mention the fifty or more men who work on the estate and have all been put on the alert."

"That didn't stop them last night," Claire muttered under her breath.

Wisely, Eliza pretended not to hear.

"Well, shall we go out walking after this?" Rosalind said sunnily. "The grounds looked so lovely when we drove through. We have hardly explored any of them. I'm sure Henry would enjoy visiting that intriguing maze, wouldn't he?"

Gwendolen smiled, appreciating her younger sister's reliable good spirits.

All that they said was true, however. It was odd. It was strange.

There was something Eliza was not telling them.

Angel patted his coat, making certain he had not left the letter inside.

"She'll be furious, you know," Hugh said, looking exasperatingly smug. "Absolutely furious. I'm surprised Eliza went along with it, in fact."

"So am I," Angel murmured. He had left Eliza with strict instructions not to tell Gwendolen where they had gone. Later that afternoon, or better yet, that evening, she was to give Gwendolen a note.

Angel planned to stay with Hugh while he was in London. That way Eliza could tell Gwendolen with a clear conscience that he was not at Sweetbriar. He was sure his aunt could easily guess where he would be staying, but hopefully she would not share it.

Once things were settled, over with, he would send a message to them all.

Hopefully that would be by dawn tomorrow morning.

They were nearing London.

Hugh had slept a little.

Baggins was still dozing, toppled over in his seat, his mouth open. He looked rather sweet, Angel reflected. Funny how sleep made everyone look so childlike.

Baggins had been someone's child. Someone's beloved son. Perhaps still was. How odd to think of this strange man with nine children who led a misguided life of petty crime as an innocent babe.

Wyndham had been a child once. Did his mother still live?

If she did, tomorrow she might be mourning the loss of a son.

His heart hardened. Far better that, than Gwendolen mourn the loss of Henry.

And what of Teresa and her child?

No, Wyndham had much to pay for. Angel refused to feel guilt for wishing to take the life of a man who rightly should have died five years ago.

He shuddered to think of the havoc Wyndham had wreaked between the battlefield and now. How many other abandoned girls like Teresa had there been in the meantime?

Angel had been right about Baggins. He knew more about his erstwhile employer than he had declared.

Not only had he surreptitiously followed Wyndham to his London address, but Baggins had also met with him at a location very near to White's.

As the day passed, Gwendolen became more anxious.

The morning had been spent traipsing over the grounds with her two sisters and Henry, all three of whom had been delighted with what they found. The estate was full of charming spots to discover. Grottos for a small boy to explore, rock faces to climb, fish in ponds to feed.

Although she was pleased they were content, her own state of mind was deteriorating the more certain she became that Eliza had not disclosed all she knew and what she knew might be something endangering to her husband.

Now, late in the afternoon, Gwendolen had gone in search of her only to be told that Eliza had gone in the direction of the stables.

It was a lovely day for a ride. There was nothing peculiar about Eliza wishing to go out.

Yet as Gwendolen approached the stables, she saw a carriage being readied and Eliza holding a small valise. Hercules stood beside her, panting. Her constant companion.

Picking up her skirts, Gwendolen hurried forward, sharp words at the ready.

The words died on her lips as she saw Eliza's expression.

"I'm going with you," Gwendolen announced, instead, resolutely. "You look terrified. You are never terrified. Therefore, something dreadful is about to happen. You may tell me about it in the carriage."

Eliza's mouth opened, then closed again.

She regarded Gwendolen a moment, then nodded. "Will you need time to pack?" she asked, appearing extremely reluctant to be posing the question.

"Only a very few, and to leave a message for my sisters. I take it you did not?"

Eliza looked chagrined. "A message was left, but it was not to be delivered to you until this evening."

"From you?"

"From Angel."

Gwendolen closed her eyes. "Tell me in the carriage," she said a second time, and began striding towards the house.

"I will be only a few moments," she repeated, calling back to Eliza over her shoulder. She would not pack so much as throw a few necessities into a small bag with her reticule. She would also leave a message for her sisters.

She picked up her skirts and ran, heedless of who saw her.

Less than fifteen minutes later, they were seated in the carriage as it rolled down the drive.

If her sisters had not been there, Gwendolen thought, she would not have left Henry behind.

If Angel had not left them, she would not have left Henry behind.

But Angel would never have left them if he had not thought they would be safe.

Ergo, Henry would be safe.

But Angel, on the other hand?

He was going towards the danger.

And now she and Eliza were following.

At least there was one thing that could be cleared up as they traveled.

She looked across to where Angel's aunt sat. Eliza sat turned towards the window, but her gaze was unfocused. She was a handsome woman, her hair still lovely and dark, and her face as regal as a queen's.

Right now, that queenly face was drawn, almost morose. Eliza's lips were pursed tightly together.

"What is it, Eliza?" Gwendolen asked, gently. "We are in this together now. Will you not tell me?"

Eliza turned to her slowly. "Of course. You deserve to know. I told Angel that. I want you to know."

"Where has he gone?" It was taking everything Gwendolen had not to keep her tone controlled and her impatience hidden.

"To London—" Eliza hesitated. "—to seek out Wyndham."

"Yes?" That was not surprising. She had expected it.

"To challenge him."

Somehow, she had known those words were coming. Yet, even so, an uncomfortable feeling of nausea burgeoned in the pit of her stomach.

"I see," she said, quietly. And she did. She should have seen much sooner.

"Eliza..." It was her turn to hesitate now.

Would Angel's aunt think her a fool? A jealous woman? It did not matter. In the end, she had to know. But how to start? Admit she had received the letter? Had believed it?

Eliza was waiting expectantly.

"Angel and Wyndham... They have a history together..." Gwendolen stopped.

"You wish to know it?" Eliza did not seem surprised.

Gwendolen nodded. "I understand there was a... woman."

Eliza's eyes widened a little. "There was. Who told you that?"

"Hugh did." Well, that was partially true. "But only a very little of the story," she added. She closed her eyes a moment, opened them again. "Eliza, is Angel doing this all... for me?"

"Who else would it be for?" Eliza responded, her brow furrowing.

"The girl. From Portugal," Gwendolen said quietly. "I understand Angel loved her very much."

"Loved her?"

"Yes. And that Wyndham had something to do with her death. That must have been... awful for Angel."

Eliza was staring at her strangely.

"Mustn't it?" Gwendolen bit her lip.

"Oh, my dear," Eliza was saying softly. "I am not sure what Hugh told you..."

"Please, don't be sorry for my sake," Gwendolen said quickly. "I am only too grateful to your nephew, I assure you. For doing all that he has done for Henry and I. Of course, I know he had a life before us.

Other... women... he must have cared for. Of course. And to go through what he went through, to be so terribly injured, to lose a girl he cared about so deeply. Well, it is no wonder he has gone after Wyndham now at last." She drew a deep breath and rushed on. "I am only so deeply sorry for bringing this wretched man back into his life."

She met Eliza's eyes. "And for putting your nephew in danger," she finished, miserably.

"Oh, my dear," Eliza said again, shaking her head. "I do not think you understand. I am not sure what Hugh told you precisely. There was a girl, yes. But Angel did not love her. Oh, of course, he cared for her in a way—" She held up a hand, seeing Gwendolen about to interrupt. "—but so did Hugh."

Gwendolen's look of confusion brought a small smile to her face. "Because they are both honorable, good men, Gwendolen," she said gently. "Wyndham was the one who was involved with the girl. When he learned she was increasing, he abandoned her after having taken her away from her family. Essentially turning an innocent maid into little more than a camp follower. Angel and Hugh had seen Wyndham's mistreatment of her before. When she was finally abandoned, they tried to return for her to at least leave her with something to support herself and the babe when it came."

Eliza let out a heavy sigh. "They were too late. The poor girl had done away with herself by the time they arrived. All they could do was make arrangements for her burial."

She looked across at Gwendolen. "It affected Angel very much, of course. As it did Hugh. Not because they loved the girl, but because of the terrible waste of life and because they were tired of this dishonorable man's despicable deeds. Then, on the battlefield, when Angel saw Wyndham..."

"Yes, I believe Hugh relayed that part accurately," Gwendolen said.

Eliza was looking at her curiously. "Where did you get the idea that Angel had cared for the girl? I cannot see Hugh..."

Gwendolen blushed. "It does not matter. It was an unreliable source and I should have known it as such. I apologize. It was foolish of me to trust it."

"It is not foolish to care. When it comes to Angel, I believe you care very deeply."

The two women looked at one another. Eliza's gaze was steady.

"I do. Very much," Gwendolen said.

"Excellent." The word was brusquely said, yet there was a tender look in Eliza's eyes. "You are good for him, you know. You and Henry. In spite of his ridiculously cultivated reputation for rakishness, Angel is a family man at heart. When he returned home, he was very changed, Gwendolen. Not only had he lost his parents—who were very dear to him, especially with his being their only child—but he had been gravely wounded. Oh, he was all bravado, of course, but some part of him must have known how close he had come to joining them. Then, to not have been able to save that young girl, her child, or the young soldier... I believe he felt like he had truly failed. And Angel is not accustomed to failure."

"No, I can see that," Gwendolen said, quietly.

"In a way, I believe you are his redemption," Eliza went on. "He is becoming the man he always would have been."

She turned to look out the window again. "The man he would have been if my brother had lived."

The conversation seemed to be over for now. Gwendolen respected Eliza's silence and settled back in her seat, leaning her head against the jolting carriage side and peering out her own window at the passing fields and cottages.

There was no other woman.

Not one who had held Angel's heart, at least.

He was doing this for her and for Henry.

He was doing it for an innocent young girl he had hardly known and for a young French soldier cut down heartlessly.

She imagined Angel as a boy, loving and gentle and passionately committed to defending those weaker than himself. Much like Henry.

Now this white knight was setting out to issue a challenge to his most formidable foe, putting his own life on the line when he did so.

Angel was good. Angel was true. But Angel could die.

There was a tightness in her chest, and it remained, unbudging, for the rest of the journey.

Wyndham was at White's. More specifically, he was inside a dark and smoky gaming room playing whist.

The familiar tones of the Earl of Leicester could be heard emanating from within the room as Hugh and Angel stood just outside in the hall.

Apparently, Cecil was inside as well. Losing badly and swearing foully to make up for it.

Angel wondered briefly if the two men knew one another. It would not be surprising.

"Are you sure about this?" Hugh muttered one last time.

Angel nodded and turned to the door.

The room inside was dim, the dark curtains pulled closed, and a large chandelier hanging in the center of the room provided the only light.

Through the haze of cigar smoke, Angel could make out clusters of men seated at whist tables throughout the room—perhaps twenty or so.

A few heads turned in their direction, then went back to their games.

But one man looked up and did not look back down.

Angel met Wyndham's gaze, feeling the solidity of Hugh's presence behind him—constant and reassuring.

The Earl of Redmond was seated at a table with a glass by his elbow and a pile of notes beside the glass. Luck had been with him, as it had not been with his friend Cecil, Angel observed. Lord Leicester was at the same table, his back to the two men.

Cecil had been in the midst of saying something, from the look of it. But seeing his companion's attention shift to the door, he turned to see the source.

Perhaps it was merely Angel's imagination but it seemed as if the room was going quiet, gazes shifting from cards to the men who were looking at one another unspeaking.

Minutes passed. It was not his imagination. The room had become silent, except for a few furtive whispers.

Without speaking, Angel looked into Wyndham's face, conveying his message: I am here. I am not leaving. You will deal with this now.

It was a handsome face, Angel realized, belatedly. Straight teeth, a square jaw, and the same narrow aristocratic nose Julia had. As well as those cold grey eyes. The same as Henry's, though his had a warmth that Redmond was lacking.

Years before Angel had not noticed much about the details of Redmond's appearance, nor cared. Now, the knowledge that Gwendolen had once thought herself in love with this man, that he was Henry's true father—well, it changed things.

Yes, he was a handsome man. He made a fine earl. Well-dressed, yet a rugged complexion that spoke to years of soldiering.

Of course, no one in the room besides Angel and Hugh knew just what kind of a soldier Redmond had been.

Why did men like Redmond do what they did? Gwendolen might have been his wife, not merely a woman he had abandoned with child. A fine, lovely, intelligent woman with a sweet-temper and a brave spirit could have been his, but he had left her by the wayside and gone off to seek a better fortune. Only to repeat the same sin again. Who knew how many times in all.

What led a man like this to murder? For even on the battlefield, that was what it had been. And might have been two lives instead of one.

Angel had taken something from him that day, and he was glad.

Not his manhood, no. But something nearly as precious—this man's ability to replicate himself and grow another child in his image. This time, not a boy like Henry to be carefully molded by a gentle mother, but a child Redmond might have raised to be exactly like himself. Cold, cruel, and disdainful.

He was rising. Throwing his cards down on the table.

"What do you want?"

Angel let the moment stretch before answering, appreciating the arrogance of the question coming from the mouth of a man who had broken into his house not twenty-four hours before.

"Perhaps we should discuss this outside."

"Here."

"Very well," Angel said, coldly. He had been gracious enough to offer a choice. It would be the last time. "You know what I seek and why. But if you wish to make it public before these witnesses, so be it. I seek amends for your crimes. Crimes against my wife, my child, my household. Crimes against a woman named Teresa Da Rosa and the child she never had the chance to bear." He paused. To list the next would be to announce Wyndham's treason. His attack on a duke—before he had become an earl himself.

"Crimes." Wyndham was shaking his head, the hint of a smile on his lips.

With that one word, he threw into question everything Angel had said. The men in the room might continue playing on after this, able to dismiss what they had heard with uncertainty. The private quarrel between two individuals.

Yes, a duel had been all but announced. But between two peers of the realm, the quarrel might take place with near-impunity—a fact on which Angel was counting.

He maintained his composure. He would not argue with this man.

"Enough," Wyndham said, shortly. "You are right about one thing. We must finish this. Where shall we meet?"

Angel's breath quickened. More with fear or eagerness, he knew not.

He named a place he and Hugh had already discussed. Outside of the city, solitary, desolate. A time was established. Leicester would be Redmond's second.

It was very civil.

They all knew the rules for this special kind of violent justice, this ancient form of settling disputes between men.

Of course, the very idea of Redmond following rules of gentlemanly conduct, a code of honor, was laughable.

Angel could only hope and pray that he would show.

Pray, yes—for he was confident that if anyone had right on his side, it was he. This was not pride or conceit. Merely the facts of the matter.

Angel would fight to uphold a chivalric code—to do no harm to women, to children.

While Redmond would fight to tear it down.

Having right on his side did not mean a thing, however, Angel knew.

In a war, the good perished alongside the wicked just as easily.

Chapter 20

IT WAS A FINE morning.

Bright sunshine. A wide blue sky.

A park-like setting, with trees and singing birds.

Gwendolen supposed it made no difference. Even the most beautiful place could become the setting for death.

Many battlefields had been pastures and meadows at one time. Now they were sown with the blood and bones of men.

She shuddered thinking of Angel's blood.

The carriage rattled along the heavily-rutted road, slowly rolling to a stop.

A man came around the side and helped Eliza down.

His name was Lance Carlisle, and he had not wanted them to come here.

When she and Eliza had arrived in London, it was past nightfall and nearing dawn. The drove in silence, both aware that time was running out.

Eliza had dismissed returning to Sweetbriar. Angel would not be there. They visited Hugh's home, but the men were not in.

Their next stop had been White's. They had sat in the carriage, looking up at the stone façade in silence, before Gwendolen had finally gotten out.

A small group of men had just spilled through the door and onto the street in front of the club, and their raucous laughter jarred her awake. Standing straight, she marched over to them and as they silenced, noticing her, she asked if the Duke of Englefield was inside.

She might have known they would not tell her. Her desperate face meant nothing to them. For all they knew, she was merely a pathetic wife trying to corral a gambling spouse back home.

But one man looked at her with pity in his eyes and noting it, she cornered him.

"You have seen him, haven't you?"

The man backed against the wall, away from her, but she moved closer towards him until she stood only a foot away.

"Please..." It was all she could get out.

Rather pathetically, she thought she might actually cry. They were not going to tell her anything. They would not let her inside this bastion of men. Angel might be inside even now. Or he might be lying dead in a field already, Wyndham's bullet lodged in his heart. No one would tell her. Because she was a woman.

But the man was drunker than she had realized and his inhibitions lowered sufficiently enough to lose his sense of discretion.

The words were slurred as he told her. That Angel had been there. That a duel was to occur and where.

It must have added an extra sense of excitement to their evening, she thought. These rich, bored men all struck with the somberness of knowing one of their coterie might kill another shortly.

She was turning back to the carriage when a hand shot out and gripped her tightly by the arm.

One of the men was not so drunk after all.

"Who are you?" he had demanded curtly, and she had looked up into intense dark eyes set in a hard masculine face, lips firmly pressed together in a displeased expression.

She had yanked her arm away, and whirling around, snapping that she was the duke's wife, thinking to dismiss this uncivil man. But it was not so easy.

He followed her to the carriage. "You should leave this be. You cannot stop it. You will only make things worse."

"How do you know that?" she cried. "What business is it of yours, in any case, what I do or do not do?"

"It is my business because he is my friend," he had said tersely, bringing her to a halt. "I should not like to see him struck in the head by a bullet because his wife came bolting onto the field at an inopportune time."

She had looked at him more carefully then.

"We are going, whether you like it or not." She gestured to the carriage, letting him catch sight of Eliza who peered out. "You cannot stop us. And if you touch me again, I shall scream."

He had looked at her with obvious disapproval, but accepted her decree. "In that case, I will join you."

He was not an ideal companion, but he had said he was Angel's friend. She would not argue with him.

Eliza could do that, she decided firmly.

Yet instead, inside the carriage, Eliza had practically embraced this ill-mannered, stern man.

"Lance! You know where he is?"

"Another gentleman told me where they will meet," Gwendolen explained, looking at Lance Carlisle pointedly. "This man says he is a friend of Angel's."

"Indeed. A very old one. Are you joining us then, Lance? Shall we be a trio on this adventure?" Eliza laughed shakily—a brittle laugh that revealed to Gwendolen how truly anxious she was.

How terrifying this must be for Eliza. She leaned over and squeezed Angel's aunt's hand, receiving a tight clasp in return and a grateful look.

The carriage had rolled away, leaving the drunken men outside.

Now they were here, and she was weary, so weary.

She fingered the small, circular reticule on her lap. Satin with beaded flowers, it was an unimposing piece of baggage, and the only one she had brought. Now she pulled out its contents and stuffed them into one of the large linen pockets of her skirt.

Just in time.

Lance turned back towards the carriage and offered his hand. She took it, quickly stepping out.

"There they are," Eliza said suddenly, pointing across the field.

A part of him was truly surprised when Redmond showed up.

But he was only too glad to have been wrong in his doubts.

The waiting was what was excruciating. The same as before a battle. All too quiet and the air charged with excitement mixed with fear.

Hugh had offered himself in his stead, as a good friend would do. Angel would have done the same in his place.

He was roundly rejected, of course. This was not the task of a friend, no matter how dear.

The satisfaction would be his alone. If there was to be none, the responsibility and consequences should rest only on Angel and no one else.

Had it not been his own idiocy that had involved him in this beautiful mess in the first place? That night on the bridge when he had come across a man and a woman. A woman he had mistaken for a harlot. His lips twitched thinking of it even now. If he lived, it would be a never-ending joke between them. She would never let him forget it, he was sure. How he had insisted her client pay her what was due.

Well, this was his due. It was owed to her. To Teresa. To the boy.

They would be avenged, their wrongs finally settled. And he would be redeemed of his terrible failures from so long ago.

Hugh had been left with instructions in the event of his death. He did not wish to leave Gwendolen in the same precarious position her first husband hand. A will had been hastily but properly written out and signed. There was a letter to be given to Eliza, and in the event that there were any issues with the will, he had beseeched her to settle them and see his wishes fulfilled. He knew she would do so if required.

Hugh was to remain a faithful protector. Though what he could do if Angel were dead... For Henry, for Gwendolen. He could not think on it now. Hugh would manage. But it could not come to that.

His pistol was ready. He was as fine a shot as any man he knew. He had as good a chance as any, perhaps better.

His cloak and waistcoat lay on the ground.

Leicester had merely sneered and turned away when Hugh had attempted to make the token effort of reconciliation.

Finally, it was time.

He stood back-to-back with his foe. Close enough to feel the uncomfortable warmth of his body.

Then they were walking away from one another, twelve paces, pistols in hand.

One shot each.

Angel did not plan to miss this time.

At the signal, he halted and began to turn around, seeing Redmond doing the same. But Redmond had a different plan in mind, and before the cry to fire could come, he raised his pistol and fired.

It was a split second of waiting for the pain to come, enough to close his eyes.

He did not cry out.

And then, it did not come.

He opened them in time to see Hugh fall.

"That bloody, treacherous bastard," Gwendolen heard Lance hiss as they saw Hugh sink to the ground. He took off at a run towards the men, leaving the two women behind.

Gwendolen watched as if from behind a screen.

Angel running to his friend and, reaching his side, kneeling down. Stripping off his shirt and pressing it against Hugh's shoulder.

She saw all that.

Lance had nearly reached the two men. A surgeon had emerged from a small carriage across the opposite side of the field and was walking quickly towards the cluster.

Eliza had caught up her skirts and passing Gwendolen was hurrying towards her nephew.

She saw all that.

She also saw something else.

She saw Redmond whisper something to Cecil. She saw Cecil's troubled expression, even from the distance. She saw Redmond reach over and tug something away.

And then she saw him turn back towards where her husband knelt, a second pistol in his hand.

She was ever so calm. Calmer than she had any right to be or had expected to be.

And much faster than she had ever been in her life.

Her hand had already rested on the object in her pocket.

Now it flew out.

She leveled the pistol and fired.

It was a small one John had laughingly referred to as her "muff pistol," using the common expression for a lady's weapon. It was small to be sure, but no less deadly than a heavier firearm, he had explained, as he and Stevens had taught her how to aim and shoot. She had become quite good, had even enjoyed it after she realized she could excel at the task and even outmatch John and Stevens.

They had admired her skill and joked about taking her along on their next expedition as a bodyguard.

Of course, she had not fired one in months. Not since her last visit to John's country estate, after his death. She had been numb then, as she was numb now. Numb but not frozen. Perhaps that helped.

She looked at the body lying on the ground a little way off and then turned aside and vomited.

She was wiping her mouth when she felt a hand, gentle but strong, on her back.

"My darling, my darling," Angel's voice said. Then she was tugged carefully towards him and pulled against his chest.

They were safe. It was over.

Letter 22

MR. MATTHEW STEVENS TO Her Grace, the Duchess of Englefield

July 27, 1817

Liverpool

My dear Duchess of Englefield,

You will be shocked to hear from me, I am sure, after having been informed that I perished along with your husband over a year ago. In spite of reports to the contrary, I assure you, I am very much alive. Although I might not have been able to assure you so emphatically up until a month ago. The malaria which took John left me stricken as well. Tell the truth, for a while I had no wish to live. Not once I knew he was gone.

But life does not ask one what one wishes, does it? I find myself still an earthly resident and as time passes, my spirits slowly return. I have been well cared for by a kindly local woman and her family who had set us up in a little hut and nursed us as best they could. To have done so for over a year in my case was true kindness indeed.

Now that my strength has come back, I am applying myself to correcting the errors that have been perpetrated during my supposed demise.

One of these errors is so great it will only do to speak of it in person. Which is why I am on my way to you now. I do not know if this letter will reach you before I do, but send it out regardless in the hopes of preparing you for my arrival.

Gwendolen, my dear, I do truly congratulate you on your marriage and wish you every happiness. I know John would have wished you the same. I look forward to seeing you and Henry again soon and meeting your husband.

Your Faithful Friend,

Matthew Stevens

Chapter 21

"OH, MY POOR ACHING bones," Hugh lamented, loudly, from his place on the sofa where he lay propped with pillows. "Oh, my fevered brow."

"Do you need someone to wipe it for you?" Claire asked calmly, keeping her eyes on her knitting. "I can summon a footman."

"A footman?" Hugh narrowed his eyes. "A footman? Am I not entitled to having my brow wiped by a beautiful maiden?"

"I'll do it, Uncle Hugh," Henry said from the corner where he had been playing with Herc. He scrambled up and started towards the sofa. "I can wipe your feral brow!"

Hugh cringed and held up a protective hand. "No, thank you, Henry. The last time you upset the tea tray onto my lap and I was scalded for weeks."

"It is very sweet of you to try to minister to your poor old Uncle Hugh, dear boy," Hugh added, as a second thought. "Perhaps you might ring for some of those chocolate biscuits I saw you eating a little while ago and we can share another plate?"

"I'll ring for some, Hugh," Gwendolen said with a smile, snatching Henry as he tried to race past and plopping him onto her lap. "Would you like some, Rosalind?"

"Hmm?" Rosalind said absent-mindedly, looking up from the book she had been reading with a dreamy expression. "What was that, Gwendolen?"

"She asked if you would like to wipe Hugh's fevered brow," Claire said.

"Fevered?" Rosalind wrinkled her nose. "No, thank you, Hugh. Perhaps we should call the surgeon back if you're truly feeling all... well..."

"Clammy?" Claire offered.

"Yes, clammy. Thank you, Claire," Rosalind said, looking back down at her book and becoming absorbed once again.

"Take a bullet for a man and this is the thanks you get," Hugh complained. "No maidens. No chocolate. No wiping. Only exquisite pain and suffering. Well, that and the knowledge one has nobly done what was right no matter the cost."

"Not to mention the exquisite delight of playing the martyr for days on end," Claire muttered.

"I heard that, Claire!" Hugh gave her a mocking glare. "Downplaying my heroic deed as always."

"You make it sound as if you chose to be shot," Claire said. "Or as if you were the one who saved Angel's life. When in fact it was..."

"...Your sister," Hugh supplied, sighing heavily. "Yes, I know. The Glorious Gwendolen. Gwendolen the Gallant. Who knew she was such a sharp-shooter. Stealing the glory from we fellows."

"Saving your bloody hides from utter foolishness is more like it," Claire muttered.

"Why, Claire, that is not a ladylike expression," Hugh said primly. "And there are children present."

"Well, one child," he amended, looking at Henry.

"No, I'd say there are two," Claire agreed, a smile quirking on her lips.

A knock at the door saved Gwendolen from having to settle things down.

Angel poked his head in. "Gwendolen, my love? You have a visitor." He was smiling a secretive smile that immediately piqued her curiosity.

Gwendolen was rising to her feet when Angel opened the door wider and a distinguished-looking older gentleman appeared at his shoulder, a broad smile on his well-tanned face.

"Oh, my goodness! Stevens!" Gwendolen rushed towards him.

"My dear girl," Stevens murmured, embracing her gently. "It has been too long." He looked across the room. "And look at you, Henry," he said, fondly. "You've grown at least a foot since I saw you last."

Henry was looking on curiously. It had been over a year since he had seen his "Uncle" Stevens and his face was no longer familiar.

"How is this possible?" Gwendolen wondered, not taking her hands off his arms.

Beneath the tan, his face was gaunter than before and she could feel the bones of his arms. But he was alive.

"Well, my dear, I am only sorry it is I and not John who survived." His smile faltered. "Though I suppose then you would not have this strapping young man as your husband if he had," he went on, awkwardly.

"Oh, Stevens," Gwendolen said softly. "I am so sorry. I know how much he meant to you."

"Do you?" Stevens asked, looking at her closely. "Perhaps so."

"You knew him much longer than I did, Stevens," she persisted. "Traveled together. Lived your lives together much more closely than I ever did. You know it is true. You must miss him very much."

"I do, my dear. I truly do. It is so hard to believe he is gone. He cared for you, my dear, and Henry—very much."

"Yes, of course," she said, quietly, hoping that Stevens would not ask any questions relating to the earl's estate.

"There is something of a private matter I must discuss with you, my dear. But first, I suppose I must greet all of your friends," Stevens said, turning to the rest, and trying to muster a smile. "Why, Rosalind, Claire! You are young ladies now! Wonderful to see you both."

Rosalind beamed back at him, while Claire merely nodded with a small smile. She had never been fond of John or Stevens, Gwendolen recalled, interpreting John's absences as the sign of a negligent husband and seeing Stevens as the one who was constantly taking her sister's husband on arduous journeys. Her complaints were somewhat fair, but if she had known the whole story she might have come to think very differently. Perhaps someday.

"Now who is this gentleman over on the sick bed, my dear?"

"This is our good friend, Hugh Cavendish," Gwendolen explained. "He is recovering from an injury he sustained a few days ago."

"Gwendolen puts it too mildly, sir. The truth of the matter is—" Hugh paused for dramatic effect. "—I was shot."

"Good Lord! A hunting accident?"

"No, nothing so mundane," Hugh replied. "It was attempted murder."

"Murder!" Stevens looked truly shocked. He turned to Gwendolen. "What is this all about, my dear? What has been happening? Are you quite all right? You and Henry? Your mother?"

"We are all fine," Gwendolen assured him, patting his arm and drawing him over to a comfortable chair. Stevens had always been a robust man. It was so odd to see him weakened. But his former health could still return. He was not much older than her mother, who was still a rosy-cheeked, pretty woman though her hair had greyed. "Hugh is being dramatic, that's all."

"Am I?" Hugh interjected. "Et tu, Gwendolen?"

Gwendolen ignored him. "Our family is fine. Henry is fine. Hugh is recovering very well. Though we did have some excitement a few days ago," she admitted.

Angel had taken a seat near her and had a hand resting protectively on her shoulder. Now he squeezed it.

"Oh, Gwendolen," Rosalind sighed, looking at her sister with a mix of affection and frustration. "Why not simply tell him? He will find out anyhow, I am sure."

"The long and short of the matter," Claire announced, "is that a mad man known to Gwendolen's husband from his soldiering days took it into his head to break into his house in order to try to kidnap Henry, and when he did not succeed in anything but terrifying us all, Angel followed him to London—"

"With his steadfast and gallant companion," Hugh added.

"With his friend, Mr. Cavendish, of the delicate disposition, who you see lying prostrate here on the sofa—" Claire went on, ignoring Hugh's exclamation of protest. "—and challenged the blackguard to a duel."

Claire glanced over at Gwendolen, as if for approval.

She and Rosalind had been fully informed as to Wyndham's true motives and Henry's parentage. Significantly, Claire had not included these details in her abbreviated recounting of events. For the sake of delicacy, Gwendolen supposed, and she was grateful. Even though Stevens must know or suspect the truth, it was a topic better left unmentioned in front of her son, even amongst friends.

Though she had given her sisters only the briefest recounting of her relationship with Wyndham as a girl, they had quickly grasped the essential facts and understood that her loss of virtue had not been by choice.

It would not change how they felt about Henry. She knew this beyond a shadow of doubt.

As Henry grew, he would remain John's son, though it was evident Angel would be the only father he would ever remember.

"A duel!" Stevens looked towards Angel with interest. "My goodness. Well, I must say, a man must do what he must to protect his family."

Angel nodded and smiled appreciatively.

Gwendolen squeezed his hand and leaned back against him a little, enjoying the comfort of his warm body. Angel and Stevens would get along well, she could see. Which was gratifying, for watching Stevens, seeing his changed state and his sadness, had already made her conclude they must make a real effort to involve him in their lives now that he had returned to England.

Stevens was not close to his extended family. Henry had been very dear to him before. He could be again. Stevens must know he would always have a place with them as the years went on, she determined. It was what John would have wanted. It was the least she could do for them both now.

"Yes, but in the end, it was Gwendolen who saved the day," Rosalind was explaining, excitedly. "We did not even know she knew how to shoot!"

Stevens turned to Gwendolen. "What is this? You shot the man?" He sounded more impressed than anything. Seeing her nod, he continued, "I always told John it was worth teaching you to shoot. An important life skill. One never knows when one might need to defend oneself—even a woman. Even in England! Though I did have it more in mind as a hobby for you. But excellent, excellent." His smile was warm and genuine. "Proud of you, my dear, very proud."

"Yes, she is a bastion of courage," Hugh agreed, only sounding slightly sardonic. "If only she had shot him before he shot me."

"Oh, Hugh," Gwendolen said, laughing. "I would have if I could have." She crossed the room and kneeling beside their wounded friend kissed him carefully on the cheek, before putting the back of her hand to his forehead. "Yes, it does feel rather fevered." Maintaining a serious expression, she took up a nearby linen and patted his brow gently before rising again and returning to her place by Angel's side.

"That's much better," Hugh said, looking cheerful. "A beautiful lady is just as good as a beautiful maiden, I do believe."

"Yes, well, don't get used to it. Find your own lovely girl to spoil and wait on you, Hugh. This one is taken," Angel said with a grin, wrapping his arms around Gwendolen's waist and pulling her close.

"Oh, no, they're going to kiss again." Claire groaned loudly.

"Claire!" Gwendolen exclaimed, blushing with embarrassment. "We will do no such thing. We do not... do that... in public."

"No, but you'd like to," Rosalind said, brightly, winking at Stevens who winked right back. "Why don't we all go for a stroll? It is such a beautiful day. The grounds are lovely, Stevens, and there are the most charming follies scattered throughout. I suppose they are nothing compared to the real things," she added, thoughtfully.

"No, my dear, I should enjoy a walk nevertheless. Some of these designs are really quite clever. I once saw a miniature Parthenon that was the splitting image of the real thing. Wonderful little creations." Stevens was already starting towards the door and Henry ran towards him and took his hand.

"I'll come with you, Mr. Stevens," Henry said, smiling up. "I think I remember you now. Did you bring me any presents?"

"Aha! The memory of presents!" Stevens chuckled. "I should have known that would be what would jog his memory. Sadly, no, Henry." He paused. "Though I have quite forgotten. I do have something for your mother. Perhaps you all might go ahead without us? So that I may speak with her for a moment? And your husband, if His Grace wishes, my dear."

The others went out and Gwendolen and Angel arranged themselves on a settee.

Stevens had put his hands in his pockets and was pacing. "I am not quite sure how to say this, my dear. It is a little awkward, you see."

"Yes?" Gwendolen could not imagine what it could be about.

"Well, it is like this, my dear," Stevens said. He stopped and rubbed his forehead. "Before John passed, he was quite lucid for a time. He was not sure he would pull through—he hoped he would, as did I. We both had no idea how bad things were to get, really. But he was uncertain, and in his uncertainty, he decided to do something he should have done long before and revise his will. He dictated to me— I was not as ill as he was then. It was witnessed by myself and some locals but it should be quite binding. I have brought it here with me today." He paused to look at her. "It is quite different from the one which was read, my dear, as you might imagine. He wanted to provide for you and Henry in every way imaginable and was very generous in what he laid out. Of course, Cecil—"

Gwendolen winced at the name.

"Yes, I've never been very fond of the boy either." Stevens sounded genuinely sorry. "He did not take after John in the least in temperament, which is a pity. Not that it was to be expected..." He trailed off with a sigh. "In any case, this would change things rather drastically for poor Cecil."

Angel looked at Gwendolen and rolled his eyes covertly. "Not much of a loss," he whispered. "Poor, poor Cecil."

Gwendolen shushed him as Stevens continued.

"Now my dear, we had best decide how we shall tell him and bring the document to John's barristers, of course..."

"Stevens," Gwendolen interrupted. "Stevens, that will not be necessary."

Stevens looked at her with surprise. "What do you mean, my dear? This is what John wished for you..."

"Stevens." She paused and took a breath, trying to decide how to explain. "Stevens, you have no idea how happy you have made me. Simply by telling me this." She looked up at the ceiling, feeling her throat constrict. "You see, I thought..."

Stevens was crossing the room and coming over to her quickly. He knelt by her and took her hands in his. "I know, my dear. I know. You must have thought he had forgotten you both entirely. How awful. No, you must know that he truly cared for you and Henry. He never regretted—" He stopped.

"Regretted marrying me?" She squeezed his hand. "I understand, Stevens. And Angel... Well, he knows," she said, looking at her husband. "John was so kind. He could have remained a widower and been quite happy that way, I know. For he had you." She met his eyes carefully. "You were his true companion, Stevens."

"Well, that is very kind of you to say, my dear." Stevens eyes were misty. "Very kind to have it put that way."

"In any case, simply knowing I had not done anything wrong to cause him to... Well, leave Henry and I out. That means everything. You have put my mind quite at rest now. That means more than anything John has left me."

She swallowed. "I would prefer to leave things as they are, Stevens. Henry and I want for nothing. We are very happy now and well-provided for. There is no need to stir things up." Or to have to see Cecil ever again, preferably.

Was he married to Julia now? In spite of the letter, she could almost feel sorry for the girl. She deserved better than Cecil at least. Julia's letter had revealed a bitter and envious heart, but Gwendolen understood. She had much to envy.

Now she had lost her cousin, as well, Gwendolen remembered. Would the full story ever reach Julia or would Cecil tell some version of the truth? Would Julia mourn the loss of such a man?

Gwendolen suddenly remembered something. "That is, unless the new will changes things for you, Stevens. If you were better provided for in this one, then by all means..."

"No, no." Stevens was waving a hand. "I am quite self-sufficient. John wrote me into his will quite early on in our lives, in fact. If you are not interested in having your affairs altered, I will put this away and say no more about it. I quite understand."

He got to his feet again. "Now, shall we join the others outdoors? Fresh air is exactly what we need after such a gloomy discussion."

Outside, after catching up to the rest of the group, Gwendolen caught hold of Angel's arm and held him back. As they lingered behind, slowly the distance between them and the rest of the party increased until they were well out of earshot.

"Stevens seems like a fine man," Angel said, covering her hand with his own where it clasped his forearm. His touch never failed to send a warm glow through her. Every time he touched her, she could hear him silently saying he needed her, wanted her, loved her. Would she ever get used to such a joy? "I believe we shall get along splendidly. Perhaps he will visit us again?"

"I should like that," Gwendolen smiled gratefully. "He is so very alone now, Angel. John and Henry and I were his family. It must be devastating to have things so changed. Even his home is gone, for he spent more time at Leicester House than anywhere else. Henry has forgotten him but in time he may remember. And even if he does not,

I should like him to be in Henry's life again. He is a good man. Not to mention a fascinating scholar."

"For John's sake. Of course, we will," Angel said, lifting her hand to his mouth. "It is agreed then. We will consider him as dear as family."

They walked in silence a few moments. Then Angel turned them in a different direction from the others.

"You know, I still have not shown you the little Grecian temple. May we walk there now? Unless you'd rather catch up with the others?"

"Some time alone with you is exactly what I would wish for," Gwendolen said, meeting his eye. She resisted the urge to reach up and pull his lips down to her, remembering Claire's remark. But once they were truly out of sight...

It was all very well and good to have such a gracious, generous-hearted, and affectionate wife. But when she had bent over Hugh to wipe his forehead, her lovely hips swaying slightly and her pretty violet dress tightening tantalizingly over her beautiful backside, Angel had wanted to swat his friend off the couch and pull his wife down onto it instead.

Preferably without the presence of others.

He stole a glance at his wife as she walked. "Wife"—even thinking the word was enough to send a pleasant shiver down his spine. It was not a fearful word. Rather, it had taken on a connotation so agreeable that it had gone from ordinary to beautiful.

She was his wife.

His. Wife. Until death, they had said. In sickness and in health.

There was nothing in the marriage vows about promising to save your husband's life by shooting his would-be murderer. But Angel's wife had done so. And he was incredibly proud of her.

She had taken a life, and that was a grave thing. It would stay with her—he knew that better than most. But she would have the comfort of knowing she had saved one as well.

Gwendolen appeared to be lost in her own thoughts, her eyes fixed on the path ahead. Her fair hair was loosely bundled at the nape of her neck. The warm summer breeze had caused soft tendrils to escape, framing her pretty face. The lilac gown she wore was made in a Grecian style, with an empire waist and gold and white embroidery on the sheer cap sleeves. Also adorning her were small pearl earrings and, of course, her wedding ring.

Overall, the effect was of feminine softness, delicacy, and grace.

She took Angel's breath away.

Yet this was also a woman who had faced down a killer and delivered his death knell.

The place they were walking towards was a fitting backdrop for such a woman.

"You know, I don't believe I'll ever get over the idea of your being a better shot than me," Angel said, conversationally.

Gwendolen looked up at him from her reverie, smiling. "Is it so surprising that a woman might be an excellent shot?"

"Not at all. Eliza excels at all sorts of typically male skills. Smoking, for one. No, it's simply that you were so utterly terrible with that knife that it left me convinced you had no means of self-defense whatsoever. Speaking of which, why on earth did you not bring that little muff pistol of yours with you on the bridge that night? Or even the second? It would have been a much more effective choice of weapon."

Gwendolen seemed surprised. "You know, I did not even think of it. Perhaps it would have been too effective. I had no wish to murder anyone. At least, not at that time. Merely to try to frighten him away. Which I made a bad job of," she admitted.

"If Redmond had known how brilliant you were with a pistol, we might have saved ourselves a lot of trouble," Angel quipped.

Gwendolen eyed him thoughtfully. "Would you truly have wanted that?"

"What?"

"To have been saved all the trouble?"

Angel coughed. "Well... Admittedly, no." He grinned suddenly and taking her hand, spun her towards him. Once her hands were resting on his chest, her face upturned to his, he continued.

"I suppose I should be eternally grateful you brought only a knife that evening, or you would have had no need of me whatsoever."

He kissed her, gently, quickly. Enjoying the feel of her lips against his but taking only a slight taste. Merely a hint of what he hoped was to come.

Then he tucked her arm back into his and drew her onwards.

"None whatsoever," she murmured.

"Now, you must tell me what other weapons you have failed to admit proficiency with. A saber? A musket? A Puckle gun?"

"A Puckle gun?" She wrinkled her brow and laughed. "Sadly, I have not learned to fence. Yet. Perhaps you will teach me. I know Rosalind would love to learn."

Angel grimaced at the thought of being stabbed by his wife's most enthusiastic younger sister.

"I suppose I should mention archery," Gwendolen went on. "It would have been rather cumbersome to bring a bow and quiver along though."

"Archery? Not javelin throwing?" Angel teased. "Never mind, you have other things in common with the goddess."

"The goddess? Which goddess?" Gwendolen gave him a puzzled look.

"Look ahead and you'll see what I mean." He lifted his hand to point.

They had been walking along a treed path and now had come out along the edge of a lake. Ahead of them, on a large verdant hill, stood a little Grecian temple of white marble.

"How lovely! What is it?" Gwendolen exclaimed, plainly enchanted.

"A miniature of the temple of Athena Nike," Angel explained. "At the Acropolis of Athens. Nearly a full-sized replica. It must have cost a fortune when my parents had it constructed. They had it made when I was no older than Henry. I can remember running around the worksite and getting in the way of the builders. I felt like I had stepped into the ancient past each time I played there as a boy."

The temple was of the Ionic order, with four large columns at the front and back of the *cella* chamber. As with the original, along each side were carved friezes, including a copy of the most famous one of all —Nike adjusting her sandal.

As they drew closer, Gwendolen walked around the building, looking at the details closely and murmuring her appreciation. When she came to the frieze of the goddess engaged in the simple task of fixing her footwear, she stopped and traced her fingers lightly over the stone drapery of Athena's clinging gown.

"She looks like a real woman. Beautiful, but..." Gwendolen looked at her husband, blushing slightly. "But imperfect, too."

"Beautifully imperfect," Angel emphasized. "Her body is curving and womanly, as it should be. Strong and capable, as a goddess of victory."

He stepped toward her to cup her face with one hand. "Just like you."

Gwendolen blushed more deeply. "Believe me, I am no goddess. Simply an average mother." She bit her lip. "If you only knew how imperfect, I really am... And how foolish at times."

Angel laughed aloud. "You are the least average woman I have ever met, Gwendolen. I have only known you a few short months, but I have yet to reach the deepest depths of your mysteries."

He watched her closely. "But what did you mean?"

She sighed. "Only that I was foolish enough to believe something about you that was quite untrue and which I allowed to cloud my judgement longer than it should have."

"And what was that?" he asked, thoroughly curious.

She looked back, unsmilingly. "That you had been in love with and had... well, accidentally killed... the girl in Portugal."

"Accidentally killed her?" Angel felt a pulse of rage. "Who said this? Did this come from Wyndham?"

"No," Gwendolen said, hurriedly. "Not from him." She looked upwards and sighed. "Julia Pembroke. She wrote me a letter. I found it the night after the ball."

"Julia!" Angel laughed drily. "That poor, unhappy girl. I believe she would say anything to you to make you as miserable as she seems to be."

"She does seem unhappy, doesn't she?" Gwendolen agreed. "Even though she is marrying an earl. Perhaps status was not all she was after in the end. Oh, I truly hope Cecil is not cruel to her."

It was probably a futile hope.

"You were acting very curiously that evening, when we left," Angel recalled, feeling satisfied that the little mystery was being finally cleared up.

"Yes, but that was not why," Gwendolen said, rather guiltily.

"Oh, no?"

"No. Wyndham was at the ball. We passed him on the steps. I was terrified he had seen me. And then later that evening…"

"He was there! That night?" Angel burst out. He calmed himself. "I might have saved myself the trouble and challenged him then and there."

"That was exactly what I was afraid you would do," Gwendolen said, shaking her head. "And so I did not tell you."

"No, you merely switched off—like a candle going out," Angel said, quietly.

Gwendolen looked miserable. "I am sorry, Angel. It was stupid of me. I should have confided in you then and there. As well as when I received that letter."

"I understand. You merely wished to retain your aura of mystery, I suppose," Angel teased.

"Mystery!" Gwendolen laughed. "I assure you I am quite ordinary. I hope you will not be disappointed. You make me sound quite captivating."

"Oh, I disagree strongly. Let's see." Angel tapped a finger to his chin. "A mysterious beautiful lady cloaked in the shadows, holding a blade, in the dark of night. A lady full of secrets too terrible to tell. A lady so brave and invincible she rescued her one true love and his closest friend from imminent peril, dealing the deathblow to her greatest foe. That's the story I'll be telling our children. My version." Angel grinned.

"Her one true love?" Gwendolen mused. "Who would that be, I wonder?"

Angel groaned. "Hugh, of course. Shall I go and find him for you? Perhaps you can wipe his fevered brow again."

The sound of Gwendolen's mirth echoed off the marble walls. "Don't you dare!"

It was her turn to draw him close and kiss him eagerly.

"Let's go inside," he suggested, breaking away finally. "The goddess awaits our supplications."

Gwendolen raised her eyebrows with a smile, but followed his lead.

"Shall we take a bridal tour through Greece?" he asked, as they approached the porch and walked up the shallow marble steps. "I gather Stevens and your husband did not include you in any of their expeditions?"

"Greece!" She sounded breathless. "I should love that. I've dreamed of visiting. Perhaps we might tour the places your parents loved, the ones which inspired this place."

"I should like that," he said softly, eyes aglow as he looked at her radiant face.

They stepped into the temple interior—a single room with columns along two sides. A stone ledge reaching nearly as high as Angel's thigh ran around the edge of the room and served as a makeshift seating area for visitors.

In the center stood Athena Nike herself, high on a carved stone pedestal. She had been sculpted of pure white marble, with gilding on her accoutrements. The goddess was garbed in battledress. Her helmet was carved with griffins. In one hand she held a spear, while at her feet lay a shield. Her face was beautiful but solemn. There was something fierce to the set of her mouth and the look in her eyes.

"Nike was supposed to have wings, but in this temple, Athena Nike was carved without them," Angel noted.

"Why?" Gwendolen asked, curious.

"So that she could never leave Athens. She had to stay and protect the city forever. Just like you with me," he said with a grin.

"That said, I should prefer to have it mostly the other way around," Angel amended. "If it is not too much trouble."

"Do I threaten your manliness?" Gwendolen murmured, stepping closer to him. She pressed herself against his chest and slowly moved her hands up it, before linking them around his neck.

"Oh, absolutely," Angel agreed. "I'm absolutely emasculated by you. Can't you tell?" He shifted, pressing himself against her, and heard her give a little gasp.

"Is this why you brought me here?" she whispered, seductively. "To defile me in a temple?"

"I did have something of the sort in mind," he admitted, sheepishly.

"Well, then do proceed, good sir," she said. "Although I do hope Athena won't smite us for it. She is a virgin goddess you know, and I am neither a vestal virgin nor a priestess. I'm not sure she will be pleased with our offering."

"You are as lovely as an ancient priestess might be," Angel said softly, already untying the ribbon at the back of her dress to loosen her bodice a little.

Then his hands were cupping her soft breasts, eliciting little moans of need and pleasure. His thumbs rubbed her nipples to hardened points.

"I want you. Now." Her voice was low and throaty. "Please."

He lifted her up and carried her over to the stone ledge, then pushed her skirts up slowly, until her thighs were bare. Her legs were spread wide, as he placed himself between them.

The ledge was the ideal height. As perfect as he had imagined. And yes, he had imagined this precise scenario quite a few times recently. Making love in a bed was well and good, but taking her, naked and hard on a stone ledge in a pagan temple had an added thrill to it.

He pulled her dress down around her shoulders, running a trail of kisses over her neck, the hollow of her throat, her shoulders, before lowering his mouth to one of the buds of her breasts. His hand cupped the other, gently squeezing the perfect softness. Her hands were tangled in his hair, her head leaned back against the marble wall.

When he had taken his fill of her breasts, he lifted his mouth to hers, hungrily, plundering her lips like a soldier returning from battle, desperately yearning for his cravings to be satisfied. She met the kiss with equal ardency, playfully nipping and biting before thrusting her sweet tongue into his mouth.

When his hand moved to the wet slick space between her legs, she froze mid-kiss, spreading her legs apart even wider to give him better access, and whispering a desperate "Please" against his lips. Her own hand snaked down to his trousers, finding his hardness pressing firmly against the taut fabric, and running her fingers over it in a way that was almost painfully pleasurable and drove him mad with want.

His fingers left her wetness to fumble with his trouser buttons. He savored the sight of her as he did so—her full bare breasts, nipples rosy pink and rigid, skirt hiked over her thighs, legs spread apart. Waiting for him.

With the sunlight streaming through the temple doorway, she was bathed in a golden light, her hair loosened from its confines and tousled around her shoulders. No goddess could ever have looked so desirable or been more perfect in his eyes.

As his cock sprang free, he moved his hands down her body, pushing her dress down farther still until he clasped her naked waist.

Gwendolen's lips found his again as her hand moved towards his hips, brushing gently along his skin, then lower still, until she had his cock in her hand and was stroking it so gently, so wonderfully that Angel had to exercise all the control he had not to let go right then and there.

When she gave a gentle tug, he let out a gasp and his hands constricted more tightly around her waist, dragging her closer towards him, letting her body come flush against his, as his cock brushed against her wet opening. Her lips were sweet and warm, but even sweeter was the moan that escaped from them as she felt him press against the soft flesh between her thighs as he entered, settling between her and spreading her wide, moving his hands down her body and grasping her bottom with both palms, cradling her against him as he thrust strong and deep, each jolt pushing her up against the wall until he feared he was hurting her.

"Should we move somewhere more comfortable?" he asked hoarsely, forcing himself to pause, praying her answer would be no.

"No," she panted. "Harder, please. More."

So, he complied, thrusting more powerfully and more deeply than before, controlling each thrust to the edge of his limits, waiting for her to reach her crescendo, reveling in each sound that slipped from her lips as she gradually lost all remnants of control.

When he could take it no longer, he slipped a hand between them, rubbing his thumb between her legs until she was clutching him, biting his shoulder, trying to keep her cries contained.

When her body seized, arching backwards suddenly, a loud cry escaped her, which he might have mistaken for pain if he hadn't known better. The sound of her pleasure echoed through the stone chamber, as he plunged into her deeply again and again until reaching his own release.

She fell forward against him, her head coming to rest on his shoulder, breathing deeply. He closed his eyes. Treasuring the moment. The feel of her in his arms, her body pressed tightly against his.

He felt satiated, not only physically, but in his heart. He loved her, yes—so incredibly much.

But knowing she loved him in return was equally powerful and intoxicating.

She loved him, she cherished him, and she would value him through both their lifetimes.

She was his mate, his partner.

Their adventure was only beginning.

Epilogue

NOVEMBER, 1817

Englefield Abbey

Henry ran shrieking across the lawn as a handsome blond giant raced after.

"It's no good, Henry," the tall man called. "I'm going to catch you! And when I do, I'm going to tickle you!"

Henry's shrieking grew even more shrill as he ran as fast as his short little legs would take him.

Gwendolen smiled as she watched. She reclined on the grass, a soft wool blanket beneath her and a shawl tucked around her shoulders. It was an unusually fine day despite the nearness of winter, and they were enjoying it to the fullest.

With the sun's warmth upon her and the sounds of a delighted Henry nearby, she felt as if she would brim over with contentment.

Happiness was there, yes. Joy, yes. But contentment—that was the ultimate state. This feeling of peace and calm. The sense that all was right in her world. Not only between Angel and herself, but with her whole sphere of friends and family.

She rested a hand on her swelling stomach as a sharp kick demanded her attention. The little one within was feisty. They kicked much more frequently than she could remember Henry doing. They also had the hiccups more often. Angel loved to put his head against her belly and wait for each tiny vibration.

Angel was sure it was a girl. He hoped it was. He said the world needed more Gardner girls in it.

He had said it again when a young woman showed up on their doorstep in the rain one day, a few weeks after Gwendolen had sent her a letter.

Lady Julia Pembroke's arrival was unannounced and completely unexpected.

It was preceded by only one communication: A letter from Gwendolen to Julia, responding to the one she had received the night of the ball.

In her letter, Gwendolen gently corrected Julia's erroneous accusations, voiced her regret over the loss of their former friendship (even though an acquaintanceship might have been a more accurate description, she decided to be optimistic), and—this was the most delicate bit—offered her condolences on the death of Julia's cousin, the late Earl of Redmond.

She made no mention of the part she had played in Redmond's demise. Perhaps Cecil had already done so. Perhaps he had not. Perhaps Julia knew of Redmond's actions leading up to the duel and what kind of a man he truly was. But perhaps she did not. Perhaps she would toss the letter into a bin as soon as she received it. Perhaps it would go unread altogether.

Gwendolen had written it anyway.

Because some part of her—the part of her that had been deeply wounded as a young girl in bloom—saw similar hurt in Julia, under that lovely but brittle exterior. A hurt so deep it spilled out as bitterness and threatened to contaminate everything it touched.

Who knew what lay beneath that bitterness? Possibly someone quite different from who she appeared to be.

No news had reached them of Julia and Cecil's marriage, but Gwendolen assumed it had taken place.

However, when Julia appeared on their doorstep, looking pale and drawn, with deep shadows under her eyes, it became clear there had been no wedding. Nor had she wished for there to be, as she eventually explained to them all.

She had come to apologize, she said to Gwendolen, as they sat in the drawing room together with Angel and Eliza. But after doing so, it was evident she had no intention of returning to her father's house in London, nor had she anywhere else she might go.

After four seasons amongst the crème de la crème of ton society, Julia confessed frankly that she was sated and cared very little whether she ever returned to that life again.

She claimed she had no wish to ever marry, but Eliza had eyed her shrewdly and then told her to never say never. Life was long. She had many years to go before she might claim eternal spinsterhood.

In the meantime, Eliza declared, Julia had shown pluck and grit by not allowing her wretch of a father to push her into a mercenary marriage and she was welcome to stay on at the Abbey as a kind of female companion. Eliza had known George Pembroke since they were children, and if he came looking for his daughter, she avowed she would show him what was what.

Hearing his mistress's proclamation, Hercules had barked his approval and settled at Julia's feet, shocking everyone in the room.

Gwendolen had rather expected Julia to kick the dog aside and complain of hair on her gown, but instead the dark-haired beauty had reached down to scratch between Herc's ears.

That had been almost two months ago.

Now Julia and Eliza walked through a grove a little way off, probably discussing a trip Eliza wished to take to visit some cousins in Scotland. Julia had expressed interest in accompanying her, and they were planning to go the following summer, after Gwendolen's confinement.

A sharp kick made her wince.

"Are you all right, my love?" a concerned voice said from above. She looked up with a hand over her eyes, squinting at the handsome face.

"Only a kick," she explained. "They're exceedingly anxious to escape their prison, it would seem."

She rubbed her stomach, as if to soothe the little being who dwelled inside.

Not that it ever worked. When she was resting, the baby was sure to be kicking and when she was active, the baby was sure to be asleep. Still, in spite of the discomforts, she would not trade it for anything.

She could not wait to meet Angel's child. Her child.

Henry would never be any less precious to her, but it gave her a thrill to know this child had been made from real love.

A love that was still so hard to believe she truly had.

"You look a thousand miles away," Angel remarked, sitting down beside her and pulling her gently towards him so her head could rest on his lap. "What are you daydreaming about?"

She looked up at him, his fine-looking face framed by the wide expanse of clear blue sky. "I'm dreaming of you. I'm dreaming of this. I'm dreaming of today."

Then she closed her eyes and waited for his kiss.

Thank You

DEAR READERS,

Thanks for joining me on this romantic voyage! I hope you've enjoyed your latest encounter with the Gardner family. If you'd like to learn more about how the girls' parents found true love together, you can sign up for my newsletter at www.fennaedgewood.com to receive their prequel story.

If your time spent in the pages of this book was pleasant, I hope you'll consider leaving a quick rating or even a review—as an indie author, your feedback is extremely valuable to me and will help other readers decide whether to read my books as well.

I wish you continued happy reading! May your TBR list be never ending!

A Sneak Peek at Mistakes Not to Make When Avoiding a Rake

AVAILABLE ON AMAZON

Chapter 1

To begin, Dear Reader, we know that the kind of reading which young people are naturally most fond—those fictitious stories, novels, that so enchant the mind—may also inflame the youthful mind with unseemly passion, and rather than educate in moderation and restraint encourage the opposite. For in these stories, youths enter a world full of deceit and falsehood, where few persons or things appear

according to their true nature and where vice hides its deformity
beneath the garb of borrowed virtue. We therefore urge our youth to
guard against such reading.

The Beauford Chronicle, June 1818

"Dash it all!" Claire swore under her breath, gritting her teeth and removing the sharp needle from her finger.

She was sewing while trying to read simultaneously. Something she had believed she had finally mastered.

However, having reached a particularly engrossing passage, she had lost concentration. She was on the third volume of The Romance of the Forest and Theodore had just been wrongfully imprisoned. Although the book was nearly in tatters for she had read it more times than she could count, she had nevertheless been wrapped up in the story once again.

Where did Mrs. Radcliffe come up with her wonderfully horrid ideas? Why was it so much more enjoyable to read about terrible events than to live them? Claire would not wish to live within a novel—she had already come closer than she had liked the previous year while helping to extricate her sister Gwendolen from her own series of misadventures.

While Gwendolen had recovered and moved on with her life, Claire felt irrevocably altered. It was one thing to read about evil villains in a book, and another thing altogether to encounter one in real life. Her impression of the male sex, not particularly favorable to begin with, had not been improved by the experience.

There was a firm rap at the door.

Claire jumped. Had she imagined the sound?

She waited in silence.

She had an imagination, but it was not generally overactive to such a degree.

The knock came again.

"For Heaven's sakes!" The exclamation came out before she could think properly. Whoever it was, she was not interested in a visit.

Had she really said it out loud? Possibly she had only thought it. If she stayed quiet, perhaps they would simply go away.

In annoyance Claire envisioned her quiet afternoon being eaten up with tea and small talk. It was just her luck to have unexpected visitors on the day her mother had gone into town, and she was alone at Orchard Hill with only Gracie for company.

There were a few seconds of silence.

"Pardon me, Madam?" A muffled male voice came from behind the door. It was not a familiar one. "We were wondering if we might impose upon you for some assistance."

She sighed. When one wished to live within polite society, one must play by the rules no matter how tedious they may at times be. Or so her family kept telling her.

She rose and entered the hall to yank the door open—rather more forcefully than she had intended.

"Good afternoon," she said smoothly, hoping she appeared more gracious and unruffled than she felt.

Two men stood on the step. She had never seen either before.

The man closest to the door had his arm up as if he had been about to rap again. Claire was tall for a woman, but he was taller. He had a friendly smiling face. The sunlight shone on his light brown hair. He appeared to be no more than ten years older than herself, perhaps around thirty.

His companion looked younger and was more striking. Taller, darker, with thick black hair curled in natural ringlets around his face, making him look quite Byronic. Claire would have found him handsome were it not for the scowl on his face.

Both men were dressed in fashionable riding habits, not quite suitable for muddy country roads. Londoners then.

"Good day, Madam." The fair-haired man inclined his head. "My name is William Campbell, and this is my brother, Thomas. I am sorry to impose upon you, but we have been out riding nearby and one of our horses has gone lame. We are new to Beauford. We recently purchased a house nearby, on the other side of the village. As we are to be neighbours, we wonder if we might impose on you already for some neighbourly assistance? I do apologize for the intrusion, but it is some miles back to the house…"

"Yes, of course." Claire answered automatically. Then she remembered. "I mean, no."

The men looked confused.

"My mother is out with our carriage," she explained. "And our servants have the afternoon off."

"Oh." William glanced at his brother as if wondering where to go from here.

Realizing they might be put off on her account, she exclaimed, "But I am not here alone. My younger sister is with me. Gracie."

Although she was not sure how reassuring that would be. Gracie was not much of a chaperone when it came down to it, being only eight-years old. Also, Claire had no idea where she might be.

"You are bleeding." The darker man spoke abruptly, staring at her hand.

Claire glanced down. There was quite a bit of blood dripping onto the stone step. She hoped none had gotten onto the baby bonnet she had been trying to finish for Gwendolen. It felt as if she had been working on it forever.

"I am sorry, Madam, but I do not think you have mentioned your name. Miss...?" The fair man smiled expectantly.

"Oh, yes, my apologies. I am Claire. Miss Gardner, Miss Claire Gardner." Could she not get out a complete sentence today?

"My mother should return with our groom quite soon. I am sure Arthur would be happy to help when he comes back. If you would like to come in and sit while you wait." She gestured to the room behind her.

"An excellent notion. We appreciate your hospitality," said William, stepping inside.

His younger brother made no comment but followed. He had not greeted her either.

Claire rolled her eyes as he passed. So that was how it was to be. She had no patience for rude men, no matter how handsome. She hoped Thomas Campbell would at least be civil to her mother when she returned or she might have to poke him with her needle.

She followed the two men into the room and looked about for a piece of linen with which to wrap her hand.

Before she could sort through her work basket to find a scrap, the younger Mr. Campbell turned to her with his handkerchief pulled out.

"Allow me," he said, stiffly, reaching for her hand.

"I am quite capable..." she started to snap, then closed her mouth. Likeable or not, these men were guests in her home. "What I mean is that... although I am capable, I would not wish to stain your handkerchief. Thank you for the kind off—"

But Thomas had already reached for her hand was pressing the cloth against her bleeding appendage. She resisted the urge to snatch it back. He had removed his own gloves and his skin was warm against hers. Standing so closely she could smell the masculine scents of leather and sweat. Not a completely repulsive combination. Rather an agreeable scent.

"Thank you very much, Mr. Campbell," she said briskly, finally pulling her hand away. "Please, make yourselves comfortable." She turned to her place on the sofa where her book and sewing still lay. There were spots of blood on the white muslin. "Hang it all..." she began. William began to cough loudly behind her. She tucked the bonnet into her work basket with a sigh and pushed the book aside.

"Keep the pressure on it until the bleeding has stopped," Thomas commanded shortly as he sat down.

"Yes, thank you. I would never have considered that." She fluttered her eyelashes, hoping she looked sufficiently stupid. Clearly that was what he expected. She wondered if it was Thomas's horse that had been lamed. If this was how he spoke to animals as well as women, she had the utmost sympathy for the horse.

Nevertheless, there was something about him which suddenly made her self-conscious of the fact that she had not glanced at a mirror since that morning. She looked down at her rumpled dress, quite wrinkled after being curled up on the sofa for hours. Hopeless, utterly hopeless. She put a hand to her hair, smoothing back the auburn strands as best she could in what she hoped was a subtle way.

"What a pretty little room." William seated himself in an armchair near the hearth and looked about. "You must receive excellent light here in the mornings. Look at the picturesque view this bay window provides, Thomas. Your apple orchard must be lovely in the springtime, Miss Gardner."

Thomas did not appear in the least bit interested in the view or the orchard. Instead, he was scrutinising his surroundings as if he expected the old house to collapse at any second.

"Yes, we think so." Claire turned a smile on William.

"Have you and your family lived here long, Miss Gardner?" William inquired politely. At least one of the brothers could make civil conversation. Claire appreciated the effort. It must be difficult to have to constantly compensate for the rudeness of one's sibling.

"Since my father passed away eight years ago. We moved houses a little after. Gracie was only a babe then." She remembered how peculiar it had felt to have to welcome a new life into the world while they were all still passionately grieving the loss of another.

"I am very sorry," said William quietly.

"Oh, please don't be. It was a long time ago. We have been very happy in this house. It is a beautiful part of the country."

"Indeed! I could not agree with you more. Charming neighbours and lovely country. I hope we shall see one another often." Claire smiled at his enthusiasm. What a contrast these brothers were.

"Is Gracie your only sibling, Miss Gardner?"

"There are four of us girls in all."

"Four girls?" Thomas appeared quite shocked.

"Yes, that is what I said, Mr. Campbell. Four. Girls. There are four of us." She emphasized the words slowly, raising her voice a little, choosing to pretend he was simply deaf instead of misogynistic.

Thomas glared at her from behind his dark brows.

"My younger sister, Rosalind, is in London right now visiting our eldest sister, Gwendolen and her family," she explained, turning her attention back to William.

"It must have been enjoyable growing up with so many sisters. Thomas and I have but one. Elizabeth is only fifteen. She has remained behind with our aunt in London for now."

"How nice," Claire said mechanically.

William was an acceptable albeit unexciting conversationalist, but she could still feel Thomas glowering at her from across the room, and if he did not stop soon, she was not sure what she would do. Nothing good.

She glanced at the clock on the mantle and wondered when her mother would be home. Or a servant. Or Gracie! Where on earth had she gone off to? Claire hoped she was not stuck up in a tree like last week. By the time they found her, it had been almost pitch black.

Gracie chose that precise moment to storm through the front door.

"Claire! I found some baby frogs. May I put them in a jar? Oh, and there are two strange horses outside!" Her apron was wadded up in her hands... and it was wriggling.

"Gracie! Did you bring frogs into the house?" Eying the apron with amusement, Claire tried to stifle a smile. "You are soggy. And muddy. Go upstairs and change and then come and greet our guests." Gracie curtsied quickly, glancing curiously at the two men, before dashing upstairs.

Thomas looked after her with a furrowed brow.

"Are you fond of frogs, Mr. Campbell? Perhaps Gracie can spare a small one for you," Claire asked him sweetly.

He turned his head towards her. She swallowed. He was fine looking; she would give him that. A powerful blend of dashing and dangerous. His gaze was so intense she felt herself begin to blush.

She quickly shifted her gaze to the older Mr. Campbell, who, of course, was smiling. Did he ever stop smiling? At least he would make some woman a very pleasant husband.

"May I offer you tea?" Claire asked, endeavouring to do her duties.

"You said your servants had gone out." Thomas's stare was accusatory.

"I did," Claire said slowly, turning unwillingly to look at him again. "I am quite capable of making us tea, however, Mr. Campbell. Do you mean to say that you think a lady to be incapable of boiling water? You will not find ones quite that high and mighty here in Beauford."

A cold stare was the only response she received.

"I shall go and see about the tea." She rose, feeling only slightly regretful about her rudeness.

Returning shortly with the tea tray, Claire paused in the hall as she heard the two brothers speaking.

"...a charming pair of sisters, do you not agree?"

"The girl is ill-bred and her older sister mulish, if that is what you mean by 'delightful,'" came the reply.

"Yes, well, you are not being exactly gentlemanly yourself. Kindly remember that these are our neighbours now, Thomas, and act accordingly."

Well, this was what she got for eavesdropping. Her mouth twitched a little. Mulish was not an altogether inaccurate description, although coming from Mr. Thomas Campbell's mouth, it was obviously meant as an insult. At least he had received the scolding he deserved.

"Tea?" She smiled brightly as she entered, placing the tray on the low table in the middle of the room and sitting down to serve.

"What has brought you to our area, Mr. Campbell? You mentioned you have recently moved to Beauford." Claire made sure to look only at William as she spoke. She sat back to sip her tea.

"Yes, we have family interests in the vicinity. Thomas and I agreed that being closer would be more convenient than London." Mr. Campbell glanced quickly at his brother at he spoke, before switching subjects. "I look forward to showing you the house, Miss Gardner. I think it is charming. Lovely grounds. Formerly owned by a Sir Arthur Darby. I am sure you will have heard of it, living so close—Northwood Abbey."

"Oh, yes, that is a grand old house. The Darby family was well-known in these parts. My sisters and I used to walk the grounds when we visited Sir Darby's two daughters. They are older now. One is married and one is in London for her second season. A good-natured family and well-liked in the area. We were sorry to see them give up the estate."

"Not," she added hastily, "to say that you will be any less agreeable as neighbours." At least not the elder.

"Why are you not in London for the season, Miss Gardner? Unless I am mistaken you are, what, nineteen? Twenty years? Do not all girls long for gowns, balls, and husbands at your age?" Thomas made no attempt to keep the disdain from his voice.

William looked embarrassed.

"It may surprise you, Mr. Campbell," Claire answered sweetly. "But not all women are, in fact, the same. Some enjoy reptiles and climbing trees, for instance, while others do not put finding a husband above all other interests." She was not about to tell him that she would be sent to London for a season the following year when her mother could better afford it. Or that marriage was one of the least appealing things to her right now.

"Oh, pardon me." He did not sound the slightest bit sorry. He gestured to the book beside her. "I merely assumed that as you enjoy reading such fanciful stories your head was as full of romantic nonsense concerning love and marriage as most girls your age. And—"

Thomas looked about the room before continuing. She followed his gaze. It was a cozy little sitting room but would probably be considered small by the Campbells' standards if their expensive riding habits were any indication of the size of their fortune. While there were no wide cracks on the ceiling, there were a few smaller ones. The carpets were faded with age and use, as was much of the furniture. Four young girls could be quite as rough on a house as four young boys. The walls alongside the fireplace were covered in shelves which were filled to the brim with books. Fresh flowers Gracie had picked the day before were in a vase on the mantle. The fireboard had been painted by Rosalind with a lovely trompe l'oeil scene of Paris—well, what Rosalind imagined Paris to look like. None of them had ever been further than London.

Overall, Orchard Hill was more cottage than manor. It was a pretty estate, if one could call such a small piece of land an estate. But it had plenty of space for their needs. With only a cook, one maid, and a groom it was not as if they required expansive accommodations. Nor did their situation allow for it. Her older sister, Gwendolen, had married well and wished to be generous to her family, but Claire's mother would not accept more than a modest contribution. She was a practical, modest woman who believed in living within her means. She had no grander ambitions of a larger or more ostentatious home. Particularly when they were all so settled, and the house held so many fond memories.

"—I would have thought the conditions in which your family live would make the finding of a husband a priority for..."

"Yes, Thomas," William interjected.

Claire's mouth had dropped open. She stared at Thomas, astounded by his rudeness and presumption. How could these two be brothers?

He looked back at her indifferently, as if he had not given cause for offence. In fact, she believed his lips were twitching.

William was rushing on. "I for one am glad to be away from London this season. So many people all gathered, gossiping and gawking. I prefer the quiet of the country. I think we shall be very happy here. Thomas enjoys the outdoors a great deal, Miss Gardner, as do I. Walking, riding, hunting, and the like. Not that we do not enjoy the company of good neighbours as well. In fact, I have been considering holding a dance quite soon at Northwood. You and your family will have to attend."

Claire still simmered with rage but managed to return her attention to Mr. Campbell. Unfortunately, she had missed most of what he had been saying.

"A dance, Miss Gardner? Would such a thing be to your liking? And to your mother's, of course." He looked at her a little anxiously.

Claire tried to smile. "I do enjoy dancing, yes, Mr. Campbell. That is a very kind thought, to hold such an event for your new neighbours."

"It is a plan then. You shall receive a card very soon, Miss Gardner."

He was so charmingly sincere that Claire could not help but return his warm smile.

"Does your mother permit you to waltz, Miss Gardner?"

Claire was a little surprised. "The waltz is not often danced here, Mr. Campbell, though I know it is quite the thing in London. I do enjoy the quadrille, however. It is very popular in these parts, especially with the young people." Although confused by the interest he was taking in her dancing preferences, she was glad to see her response pleased him.

"You are not in London anymore, William," Thomas spoke up. "But I'm sure you'll find your fair share of fortune hunters wherever you go in England."

It was an odd remark to make at that junction. Thomas certainly had his back up against the female sex. She was opening her mouth to issue a harsh rebuttal when, providentially, the front door opened once more.

"Claire!" Her mother's voice rang out. "Oh! Good afternoon." She stared at the two men with surprise as she stood in the entryway, beginning to unfasten her bonnet. Caroline Gardner was a warm, maternal-looking woman. Petite and plump, she shared the same dark auburn hair as her second eldest daughter.

Claire and the Campbells rose.

"Gentlemen, may I introduce my mother, Mrs. Caroline Gardner. Mother, this is Mr. William Campbell and his younger brother, Thomas. They have acquired Northwood from Sir Darby."

"What a lovely place!" Her mother beamed.

Claire knew she was simply glad to have the Darby house occupied again but looking over at Thomas she worried her mother's enthusiasm might be misinterpreted by such a cynical young man.

Gracie ran downstairs to join them. Soon it became apparent that she had merely transferred her frog offspring to a new apron. Claire was grateful to be spared any further arrogant comments from Thomas for the remainder of the visit. A little while later the Gardner's groom had made arrangements to transport the men and their horses back to Northwood and she and her mother saw the two brothers on their way.

Once they were gone, Claire determined not to spare them another thought.

Mistakes Not to Make When Avoiding a Rake

The Gardner Girls Series

Available on Amazon.

Read FREE in Kindle Unlimited.

In the sleepy country village of Beauford, the promise of love can transform the most world-weary rake, and the power of passion can move a proud young woman to repent of even her most stubborn prejudices.

A cynical rake...

The arrival of Thomas Campbell and his elder brother has the village of Beauford abuzz with excitement. Not only is Thomas tall, dark, and handsome, he is also rumored to be a most notorious rake.

Claire Gardner is young, innocent, and completely infuriating. Yet given an opportunity, Thomas can't help teaching the headstrong beauty a lesson in desire.

A quiet life for a lady...

Content with a simple rural life, Claire Gardner has no wish for a season in London nor is she eager to wed. But after a catastrophic mistake compromises her honor, Claire finds herself ensnared in scandal.

Claire is quite certain reformed rakes do not make the best husbands. She would rather face shame than lose her freedom to a man she is convinced does not love her. But as rumors swirl regarding her ruined reputation, the condemnation of her neighbors becomes more than she can bear.

Tormented by a bitter betrayal, Thomas has steeled himself against ever loving again—but he harbors a secret which leaves him in need of a wife. Will the truth about the other woman in Thomas's life destroy their marriage before it has even begun?

Masks of Desire: A Prequel to the Gardner Girls

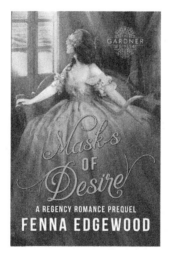

Meet the Parents of the Gardner Girls...

Childhood sweethearts become forbidden lovers in this Shakespearean-esque second chance romance where secrets and lies throw two opposing families into turmoil.

Romeo and Juliet, meet Henry and Caroline...

Caroline Gardner has always had her very own white knight. Her childhood sweetheart, Henry Gardner, is handsome, kind, and passionately in love with her. Or so she believes, until one day she is told everything she knows about Henry is a lie. In an instant, their long-time engagement is broken and Caroline's world is shattered.

Henry Gardner has been told that the girl he's loved all his life has cruelly betrayed him. But no matter what she may have done, his love for her will not dim. The only problem? She's about to marry someone else.

Less than twenty-four hours until he'll lose her for good...

Stealing an earl's bride on the eve of her wedding might be an insurmountable challenge for some men, but Henry is determined to make sure Caroline knows that forever is a promise he means to keep. Even if doing so comes at a perilous price.

One boy. One girl. One future they must fight for together.

Her one true love may have returned, but after all he's put her through, Caroline has no intention of falling back into his arms. But when she stumbles onto a terrible family secret, Caroline must make a leap of faith and put her heart in the hands of the one man she swore she'd never trust again.

About Fenna

Fenna is an award-winning retired academic who has studied English literature for most of her life. After a twenty-five-year hiatus from writing romance as a twelve-year-old, she has returned to the genre with a bang. Fenna has lived and traveled across North America, most notably above the Arctic Circle. She resides in Canada with her husband and two tiny tots (who are adorable but generally terrible research assistants).

Fenna loves to connect with other readers and writers. If you'd like to get in touch, receive the latest news on her releases, and get access to free bonus material, please sign up for her newsletter at www.fennaedgewood.com or simply shoot her an email at "info@fennaedgewood.com"

Website: www.fennaedgewood.com
Facebook: facebook.com/fennaedgewoodbooks
Instagram: instagram.com/fennaedgewood
Newsletter Sign-up: fennaedgewood.com/newsletter/

Printed in Great Britain
by Amazon

19414290R00215